The Barriers Between
Vol 1:
Hammer and Heart
By Erica P. Christie

ISBN eBook: 979-8-9913936-0-7
ISBN paperback: 979-8-9913936-1-4
ISBN hardcover: 979-8-9913936-6-9

Editor: Brady Chester
Editor: Mandy George
Developmental Editor: Gawain Van der Bijl
Cover Art: David McAllister
Formatting: Huckleberry Rahr

Acknowledgements

This book was made possible by an entire IT department, higher powers, and a community of supportive, hilarious friends. I'm grateful to you all.

Luke, my life partner: Thank you for supporting my artistic adventures, reading every draft, helping with research, and always believing in me.

Rowan, my child: Let this book prove that dreams are worth fighting for. Find your life's purpose and be passionate.

Izabelle, my chosen sister: Thank you for your unconditional love and support during difficult times. I'm here to support your dreams, as you have done the same for me.

Maggie: You are always there when I need a shoulder to cry on, a sister to talk to, or when I need a partner in crime. Your belief in my potential has been invaluable. Thank you for helping me see that where there's a will, there's a way.

Brady: This process has deepened our friendship. Thank you for your logic, humor, and constant presence in my life.

Dave: Your kindness and empathy have enriched my life. Thank you for contributing to the book, including the amazing cover art.

Mandy: You helped me find my voice and discover hidden parts of myself. I'm grateful for our journey together.

Special thanks to:

Huckleberry, for being willing to take me under your wing and help my dream come true.
Justin, for research assistance.
Mike, for honest friendship.
Gen for help untangling puzzles.
Molly and Tyler, for the insightful beta reading.

I appreciate the love and patience from everyone who endured my intense emotions during this process. Your support made this book possible.

Love to you all. I owe you an eternity of thankfulness.

N
WESTERN MOUNTAINS
FAR NORTH
EASTERN ISLANDS
BAULHTUUAG OCEAN
LUNA SEA
Belleview
Morirraen
Snake River
Kyrauhl
Ironhaven
Rose Lily
Ostarie
Riverside
The Realm Of
CROSSFIRE

I

KNOMUCCA

The cold stone beneath my boots chilled through to my feet. My thick, wavy hair swept gently across my upper back, brushing over my exposed arms and loose grey tunic. Daggers, throwing darts, a set of gardener's gloves, and a heavy iron axe hung from a thickly braided belt around my waist, the added weight a familiar comfort against my tightly knit stockings. My sword was grasped firmly against my palms, my hands thrumming excitedly as I strategized my movements.

Everett met my eyes with a fierce intensity, his face firm and calculating as he studied my sword. Everett stepped outwards, widening his stance, the fabric of his cotton leggings shifting to reveal the tattoo across his right calf. His iron war hammer rested upon his shoulder, the hammer's head eclipsing the sun from behind him.

He swung. I ducked. The flat of my carnelian longsword met his hammer with a clang so loud the echo thrummed throughout the realms. My hands reverberated against the pommel, my fingers instinctively tightening as I watched how Everett moved. His broad shoulders stretched in the sunset, his muscles sculpted and strong as he shifted his hammer across them.

"Perhaps I shall best you this time 'round," Everett teased. My exhale was quick and sharp as I thrust my sword towards him.

"You know I dislike it when you strike a gamble," I said playfully, my brief annoyance fueling the downward momentum of my sword.

He dodged flawlessly, swiveling on the toe of his boot and dropping his body to the right.

"Reckon it could be a harmless wager..." Everett said as he adjusted his hammer. "I shall raise you a smoke...whomever is defeated shall have the pleasure to provide."

"I shall accept your challenge, despite my better judgement," I said with a grin, deciding I was to claim his offer, for I enjoyed the prospect of sharing with him.

"Excellent," he said, the neatly kept scruff across his jawline threatening to disrupt my focus. "Aim... mark... strike."

Pointing my sword to the sky, I stepped into my fighting stance, planting my boots firmly against the stone. Everett shoved his hammer towards me with a grunt, following the momentum of a powerful, arching swing. Rushing to the left, I spun gracefully out of his reach, gaining my footing in preparation for a rebuttal. As I guided my sword upright, I fluidly regained my footing.

"Is that all you have," Everett thrashed his hammer with a wink. "I wish to feel the fire you possess."

His hammer dipped low, veering sharply towards my legs. I reacted on instinct, parrying his advances with three low kicks. My movements were blocked by the enchanted mahogany handle of his hammer, the contact of bone against the handle vibrating sharply through me.

"Bloody Hells," I breathed heavily, fighting to keep my balance. Pain rang up my shins as I stumbled backwards, the hot sting across my skin motivating my lighthearted annoyance. "The promise of smoke rolled by my hand must really invigorate you; the strength behind your swings almost feels genuine this session."

"It is my intention not to be lenient," Everett teased with a smile, covering the space between us with a large, solid step.

Breathing loudly, he jabbed his hammer upward in a forceful strike, thrashing it squarely in proximity to my left shoulder. Swerving to the right, I dodged his attack, dipping low as his hammer returned its momentum across my body. I righted myself with the flick of my hips, planting my boots solidly before throwing my elbow towards his jaw. He smirked, blocking my jab easily with his calloused, muscular hand.

"You shall have to do better than that," Everett mused, his eyes sparkling playfully.

"I intend to," I said coyly, following the movements of my body and swirling my sword across my center.

We fell in a fluid rhythm, moving across the battlements with a flurry of swings, blocks, and kicks. On this day, we found ourselves sparring atop the enchanted wall surrounding the castle, Morriraen, the fortress we had called home for the entirety of our lives. The wall was carved from cut Tanzanite, reflecting cobalt blue in the fading sunlight. It was six strides wide and laced with hidden traps; one false step and a life could be forfeited. Only our dedicated hours of training help us to avoid the deadlier ones.

The castle Morriraen was nestled several leagues up the Snake River amidst the rolling hills in the astral plane of Crossfire. Created from the chaos and darkness of the cosmos, Crossfire was a prosperous yet unstable realm, as its pantheon had not yet been solidified. Parallel to The Realms of Life, Death, the Heavens, Hells, and the Divine, Crossfire was sculpted from the magic that flows in and out of all things. The Realm's innately magical essence attracted the masses, coaxing many folk from far and wide to live here amongst the forests, caves, and mountains.

Everett thrashed his hammer towards my head, slamming his body sideways as he spun with the momentum.

"Oi! Everett! Cuttin' it close," I panted, lurching suddenly to the right to avoid being struck.

Using the gap in his form, I slashed at his legs, noticing his retreat leftward to evade my attack.

"You replied with quick thinking," Everett complimented breathlessly, recovering after stumbling out of range of my sword. "My apologies for the closeness of my swinging... reckon if I desire victory, I shall have to be more precise."

"You shall indeed..." I agreed, raising my blade to block the blunt force of his hammer. "For I have thus far failed to knock you from your boots."

Everett lunged again, laughing as he careened the spike of his hammer in a flawless arc towards my face. I twisted rightwards and dropped my body, slamming my sword and hands against the ground as I bore my weight upon them. Shifting my torso, I flipped backwards onto my feet, countering with a spinning kick from my right foot. My heel slammed against Everett's sternum, sending him backwards to tumble through the air. He landed near the Southern Watchtower with a thud, sliding to a stop and swearing loudly.

Sheathing my sword, I strutted towards him, smiling proudly as I moved. My thigh-high black leather boots pounded across the stone, my golden blonde hair bouncing freely against my shoulders as I closed the gap between us.

"I would fancy some mugwort, if you would be so kind," I said playfully, extending him a hand as I watched him struggle to stand. His muscles rippled with the effort, sending a jolt of delight through my body.

"Do not be modest," Everett began, retrieving his hammer from beside his boots and wiping it against his tunic. His voice was level and steady, his full, irresistible lips forming the words as he spoke. "Mugwort is frequent and common enough to carry on my person, nothing worthy of a duel well fought and a wager fairly won."

"It is perfect," I said, retracting my hand and speaking quickly. "Anything you have is perfect, really..."

"Paired with sweet grass and lavender, it does make quite a pleasant smoke," Everett said, brushing off his jerkin.

Noticing my hand, he bowed, attempting to hide the blush that crept across his cheeks. "My apologies, Your Worship, though I reckon I can manage."

I waved away the formality, speaking to cover the awkwardness.

"You are quite formidable. Fortune smiles upon the troops who are blessed to serve beneath you." I said with a nod, then thought to myself, And I reckon I'd experience such fortune in serving beneath you as well...

Everett blushed again as if he had heard my thoughts. Taking a pull on the water skin that hung from his belt, he attempted to hide his smile with a long drink.

"Thank you kindly, Your Worship," Everett released a controlled breath, mirth rippling across his cheeks as he straightened his lips from a smile. "Though, I believe it is you the people are blessed to serve... myself included."

"Everett... you know I prefer when you call me by name," I said, stepping around him on his left and approaching the Southern Watchtower. Despite my station as ruler of Crossfire, I disliked the formality forced between us.

"Aye, indeed... I shall work on it," Everett said, giving me a subtle wink as he composed his smile once more. "Though I make no guarantees."

My heart pounded and fluttered as I watched Everett sling his hammer across his back, delighted by the sight of him as he stretched outwardly to crack his broad, sculpted shoulders. His forest green tunic complemented his steel blue eyes and tanned skin, the soft hemp fabric wrinkling as it tucked into the belt of weapons and tools hanging around his waist.

"Excellent," I said satisfactorily. "Your efforts are appreciated."

Everett combed his fingers through his dark, auburn hair, swiping the mid-length waves from his steel blue eyes to form a semblance of style. His face grew slack as he released a breath; the relaxed bliss spreading across his cheeks tightened my body excitedly.

"Pardon me," Everett said as he noticed my watching him. "I simply needed a moment to collect myself..."

"Please, take all the time you need," I said, fighting to keep my composure steady, yearning to caress his hair with my hands. "Appearances are important."

"I believe I have finished," Everett said with a sudden salute, reminding me forcefully to remain professional. "The wind ruffled it more than my liking is all..."

"If you are certain," I said with a nod.

"The gusts are stronger with our added height from the wall..." Everett continued as if he hadn't heard my interjection, "though despite the gales your hair appears nicely windswept."

"You are kind in saying so," I said, cutting the rising tension between us with a playfully crude gesture with my hand, "though... I reckon yours could still use some tending across the top!"

"You slight me," Everett teased with a hardy laugh. "Perhaps I need not have bothered..."

"I only meant to tease. Your appearance is perfect, really... I speak only the truth," I said, pulling open the Southern Watchtower door to end the silence that had formed between us. "Come along then. If we are no longer sparring, we had best set off towards Valvang for supper."

"Aye, supper would be appreciated," he said, smiling courteously as he passed me on the right.

Everett walked through the door, my steps following momentarily behind him as we descended the stairs. The tower stairwell was awash in the light of torches casting flickering shadows over the many ancient murals and inscriptions that covered the walls. Deliberately, I ran my hand along the wall, over many symbols of the divine gods and etchings of fierce dragons, until I found a particularly familiar crest. It was a fire-red shield with a slender black tree, the long gnarly roots swirling into perfect fingerholds.

I pressed my fingers into the crest, watching the wall split to reveal a shortcut. It was dark and cold, with long, smooth walls just wide enough for one. Water dripped far off in the darkness, its steady, maddening rhythm echoing off the stone. The smell of distant mushrooms and rosemary clung to the walls, twitching my nose from the fragrant and fresh odor.

"Should we not go around?" Everett paused, noticing I was no longer behind him.

"I must admit I lost track of the hour whilst sparring," I said with a shrug. "I have some business to tend to after supper, and taking the passage spares me several moments."

"If you are certain," Everett said.

"I am indeed," I said with a nod. "And once across, we could partake in the herb before we part ways for the evening if you wish to..."

"That would be excellent," Everett said as he stepped before me. "Please allow me to escort you, Your Worship... I would prefer to take the lead if that suits you."

"That would be appreciated," I said with a smile.

"Please take a hold of my shoulder if you wish to," Everett said with a salute as he stepped into the narrow passageway.

"I would be delighted," I said, in no way needing his guidance or protection yet seizing the moment to touch him.

Placing my hand on his shoulder, I followed closely behind him through the gap in the wall, hearing the stone scrape closed behind us with the triggering of a pressured stone slab. I became intensely aware of Everett's warmth beneath my fingers, my heart racing as I tingled with the temptation of his body in the darkness.

"Are you ready then?" My breath caught in my throat as Everett whispered.

"Aye, proceed onward," I said, feeling as Everett stepped forward with his left foot.

Walking straight, we continued through the passage, passing hundreds of alternate tunnels that twisted through the rock. Much of my younger years had been spent playing in the winding, shadowy mazes of Morriraen, and I preferred traveling through the tunnels whenever I could instead of taking the castle's main routes. The tunnels were secluded, gifting me quiet moments whenever I wished to be alone and free from responsibility. The dark, stagnant air had become a comfort. The interwoven, sharp, sweet scent of rosemary cut through the darkness, bringing a feeling of peace as I walked with Everett through the passage.

"Is all well and good, Your Worship?" Everett asked suddenly, keeping his voice low as a reflex from the darkness.

"Aye, all is well," I said, smiling broadly from his concern.

My footsteps quickened with my excited pulse, subtly encouraging Everett to walk faster. Fighting to calm my breathing and slow my steps to prolong this moment, I felt Everett guide us leftwards as we twisted through the tunnels. Despite my efforts, my footfalls quickened once more, urging us to the end of the passageway along a gradual slope to the right.

"We have crossed the passageway, my lady," Everett said, stopping firmly as he shifted his weight.

"I appreciate your escort," I said with another smile, resisting the urge to squeeze his shoulder as I removed my fingers from his tunic.

"It was my pleasure," Everett said, grasping a heavy iron bar that jutted from the wall.

"I'm glad it was not any trouble."

Everett pulled on the iron bar. Light pooled in as the doorway opened, the sudden glow harsh in the thick black of the tunnels. The torches beyond the threshold illuminated the tunnel behind us, revealing the crest of the gnarled tree carved along the walls.

"After you, my lady," Everett said, gesturing me forward with a sweep of his hand.

I gifted him a smile and stepped around him, moving through the threshold as he held the door open. The weapons at my waist clanged loudly in the receding darkness, my footsteps echoing from the smooth stone as I ventured from my sanctuary.

"Thank you kindly," I said, listening as the heavy iron door slammed closed behind us.

Crossing into the bypass, we emerged into the South Hall, the corridor surprisingly void of castle folk as supper was now being served. This hallway, connecting Valvang with the castle's southernmost sanctuary, had become fairly trafficked with the upcoming Sabbat. The castle residents and visitors would dine late into the night and then stumble drunkenly into the ornate temple for prayer and meditation. They would thank the gods for life and the harvest, paying homage to them as they smashed ceramic goblets or cut their palms to give blood in sacrifice.

Smoke from incense always filled the South Hallway, and this night was no different. I was thankful to smell lemon balm in my honor, an offering of immortality and happiness that made the air smell fresh and citrusy. Thanking the soul responsible, I pushed positive blessings towards them, focusing on my breathing as I relaxed and centered my energy.

"The aromas of supper are quite enticing," Everett said after allowing silence between us as he noticed my meditations.

"That they are," I agreed, wishing I could disclose just how enticing his aroma had become after sparring. "This night with you has left me quite famished."

"I enjoyed our kinesthetics," Everett said, retrieving a spliff from his smoking sack as we turned rightwards from the hallway. "Are you certain you wish me to provide mugwort? Certainly, we could partake in a smoke once we meet for a feast in the morrow, and I could take the time to arrange something special..."

"You are kind to offer," I said sincerely, "Though the frequency or abundance of an herb in your pipes doth not lessen the value of it."

"Wise words indeed," Everett said, pausing beside a torch to light his smoke.

His eyes widened contemplatively, though he remained silent, focusing on gently igniting the tightly wrapped herbs in the flames. Inhaling deeply, he blew out a spiraling ring of smoke, smiling as the scent of mugwort filled the air. The bitter herb was paired with sweet grass and lavender, subtly flavored with honey and the juice of sour green apples. Pinching the spliff between his thumb and forefinger, he took a second pull, stepping away from the torch and handing me the smoke with the burning end pointed upwards.

"Thank you kindly," I said, my fingers brushing slowly across his skin as I accepted the aperitif.

The herbs blended sweet and smoothly, tasting fresh across my tongue. They had been bound tightly in the dried skin of an onion, the usual pungent taste masked in the honey and sour apples Everett had expertly added for flavoring. Taking several dense drags, I puffed long, wispy clouds, smiling as I tasted subtle hints of skullcap and coltsfoot. The herbs were gentle and allowed me to relax, my energy beginning to rejuvenate after our vigorous time sparring.

Walking down the hall, we smoked in comfortable silence, passing the spliff between us as we moved towards the castle's center. Approaching a grand, spiraling staircase, I began to hear the noise of Valvang; the familiar chaos of laughter, chatter, and clattering dinner dishes filled my ears pleasantly. Handing the partially finished smoke back to Everett, we began to climb the stairs, the glossy black marble shining from the golden sconces above us.

"I have always admired this staircase," I said, wishing to break the silence as I began to prepare my courage. "The stone is quite gorgeous and pleasant to walk upon."

"'It is quite beautiful," Everett said as he met my eyes. "Though...I reckon it is a bit long for my liking."

"I will admit it takes a season to climb," I exaggerated playfully, delighting as Everett gave me a hearty laugh. "I fear that when we crest the peak, all of supper shall be consumed."

"Perhaps we ought to expedite our venture and climb faster whilst adding a pinch of spice to our endeavor..."

"You are striking gambles again," I observed, accepting the smoke from his hand before returning it swiftly.

"Merely another harmless one," he said, his eyes flashing with a brief moment's shame.

I sighed, disliking my tendency to flatter his vices, though appreciating when they meant him no harm. "What did you have in mind?" I asked.

"Would you care to race?" Everett asked suddenly, pulling deeply on his smoke as he met my eyes challengingly.

"The notion intrigues me," I mused with a smile, "If you believe you possess the stamina after our time together, then I reckon I can muster the strength to defeat you."

"Excellent," Everett said, taking a final pull from his smoke before we readied to run. "Aim, mark, strike."

In the briefest of moments, Everett hesitated, shifting his smoke into the hand opposite me before darting forward. I cast my eyes down his body as I watched the patterns of his feet, noticing how his boots met the stone before I was to run alongside him. Bounding upwards, I conquered the stairs in several stretched strides, reaching the top at the same moment as him and pausing at his right.

"Not as quick with smoke in hand," I teased, following the smell of roast and garlicky potatoes to the left and down the hallway.

"Perhaps I am lacking in my full strength as I was recently knocked from my boots," Everett retorted in jest. "When one travels tail over teapot, they are like to feel a bit fatigued."

"I suppose that's excusable," I said with a soft laugh, moving down the hall as a set of heavy doors came into focus.

Pausing beyond the doorway, we rested in our familiar haunt against the western wall, Everett exhaling a final gust of smoke before beginning to speak.

"Here is this for you to finish," Everett said, gingerly returning the smoke to my hand. "Since you managed to uproot me, I reckon it's only fair you take the rest."

"Aye, thank you kindly," I smiled, taking a long, crisp pull where his lips had touched.

"It is my pleasure," Everett said, his eyes raising to meet my face as I searched for the right words.

"Are you dining with the troops this evening?" I asked, unable to think of a better way to begin.

His eyebrows raised suspiciously. "Perhaps we partook in too much sweet grass... for you know I must dine with them..."

"You could always break tradition and sit with me," I said with my exhale. Mustering my courage, I finally readied to tell Everett, rendering silent as I suddenly swallowed my words.

"You know it is customary that the captain breaks bread with his men the night before an upcoming voyage," Everett said with a smile. "Though, I appreciate your invitation, Your Worship."

"Aye, you would be correct, of course," I said, holding in a mouthful of smoke. "Though it was my pleasure to offer, anyhow." Turning away briefly, I snuffed out the remainder of the spliff in a long silver ashtray that hung outside Valvang, speaking quickly to cover any awkwardness. "The smoke was appreciated... though we best make our way into supper now I reckon..."

"Aye, glad you enjoyed it," Everett said, smiling broadly and beginning to step forward.

Crossing through an embellished bronze doorway, we entered Valvang Hall. High, vaulted ceilings echoed with the chatter of the castle folk, their waves of laughter bouncing from the carved stone bricks. Hundreds of candelabras flickered light and shadows across the looming walls, the candles scented with lavender. Large stained-glass windows covered most of the western wall, allowing views of the pink and fading sunset that overlooked the castle grounds' grasslands.

The castle folk dug into fruits, meats, potatoes, and greens, piling high on silver trays atop wooden circular tables. Beef juice dripped from the gaping mouths of the men deep in conversation, wiping the grease with the backs of their hands and smearing it onto their tunics. Some gentlemen had long beards, with bushy eyebrows and hair to match, while some wore cloaks with their hoods pulled tight, drinking their mead in solitude. The women munched on buttery, fluffy bread, gossiping about the day and adjusting each other's luxurious gowns. Other women were soldiers adorned in leather leggings and knee-high boots, their swords slung across their backs as they chugged wine and laughed.

Everett paused courteously beside me, watching as I slid into my chair. Immediately, I retightened the black titanium gauntlets I wore upon my hands, twisting the chains, clips, and clasps firmly into place once more in conclusion to our sparring. I disliked the maintenance of these metallic accessories. The fetters had become required to contain the imbalance of my magical power. They constantly required readjustments due to the shifting of my moods or energies.

"Thank you immensely for the sparring session, Everett," I said, suddenly self-conscious as I glanced upwards to find him watching me.

"Aye, it was my pleasure," Everett said with a salute. "We could spar again once we return... if you wanted..."

"I would like that very much," I said with a nod, tugging upon the gauntlet securely fastened across my palm. Shaking my hands, I was satisfied when the gauntlets failed to shift, allowing them to rest at my center before Everett spoke again.

"How excellent," he said, saluting once more. "I am happy to see you have made yourself comfortable... If you do not mind, I will be setting off towards my table."

"Faire thee well... Enjoy your supper, Everett."

"Stay wise," Everett said with a smile.

"Love and light," I replied, nodding in return to Everett's final salute and following his path leftwards with my eyes.

Exhaling a blissful sigh, I enjoyed watching Everett walk past, admiring how his muscles flexed into toned perfection. My eyes scanned up and down his sculpted back, drifting lower to gaze upon his firm, curved backside. His calves were muscular and strong from the hours he'd spent on horseback, his inner thighs bulging tightly into hard ridges within his thin cotton leggings. Moaning softly, I returned my gaze upwards, taking in every inch of the deep green tunic stretching over his shoulder blades when my view was suddenly obstructed.

A tall, well-built lass with curly blonde hair wove through the chairs and tables on Everett's right, placing a hand temporarily on his shoulder as she scurried around him. Inaudible words were shared between them, prompting her laughter. Everett saluted crisply as he continued towards his seat. Moving rightwards, she followed Everett's previously traversed path, approaching the table where I sat and taking the chair to my right.

"Oi, Sister. Observing Everett, I see..." my twin mused as she sat beside me. The light, breezy smell of chamomile billowed around her as she plopped into her chair. Her lacey purple dress accentuated her bright green eyes, her painted and polished hands matching the violet perfectly as she reached for the nearest flagon of wine.

"Aye Syler... reckon I was," I confessed playfully, regretting the invitation for the relentless mockery that was certain to come.

"He does look quite handsome in green..." Syler said gently, her calm and caring voice trailing silently as she began to focus and think. "Though imagine him in a jerkin that was a blue to match his eyes... his hammer sheathed in a shining black leather sling with fresh pressed leggings and a crisp pair of boots -"

I blushed despite my attempts to guard my face, my twin smiling triumphantly as she patted a gentle hand across my shoulders.

"I like seeing you happy," Syler said, her hand gliding across my shoulder blades in the comforting gesture learned from our mother. "Loosening the reigns even if only a little."

"I loosen the reigns plenty," I said, glaring at her playfully from over my right shoulder.

"Aye, we shall outwardly agree, though inwardly it shall not be the case," Syler said with a satisfied smirk, signaling a passing servant to tend to our plates. Roice did so with a smile before quickly moving on to attend to matters in the kitchens.

"Pardon me, My Ladies," a thick, smokey voice came suddenly from over my right shoulder. "I apologize for the interruption, though I possess an update on the kitchens and tidings of the Festess..."

The head chef, Chatza, approached with a hot cup of tea. Her long yellow skirt was embroidered with strawberries and their leaves, the red fruits matching the lace upon her blouse with shortened hemmed sleeves. Her blonde poufy hair was pulled in a frizzed ball atop her head, the curly locks laced with a crown of daisies and woven Linden Tree branches. Her dark blue pinafore was tied with black string, the cords braiding through the heavy fabric of the apron to keep it in place atop her dress.

Chatza had served our castle, Morriraen, for thirty years in addition to the twenty she possessed before we were born. She was a dear friend to my mother; the pair often spent many lengthy hours in the castle's library pooling over books with my sister and me. A wise spakona, Chatza infused her magic, healing herbs, and generous flavors into every delectable course she prepared, her pastries surrounding the Sabbats being her most exquisite creations. She could heal almost any ailment with a hot cup of soup, having extensive knowledge of ancient herbs and long-forgotten medicinal practices. Chatza had lived for over half a century, though she looked a quarter of her age due to the lavish herbal masks she would apply to her face on a weekly basis. The mug of tea she carried in her hand steeped and steamed with honey and peppermint. The consumption of herbal infusions before, during and after supper was a regular occurrence for Chatza and her kitchen staff.

"Excellent, Chatza," I said, readjusting my gauntlets as I continued to speak. "How did the kitchen fair this day?"

"Well, Your Grace." Chatza took a deep drink of her tea before she spoke. "Scores of scones, a dozen pigs, sheep and lamb, several soups, breads, cakes, greens, and an endless catalogue of other delicacies are ready to be baked in the morrow for the start of the Sabbat and arriving castle guests... 'It is quite kind of you to be contented with scones, squash soup and Harvest Bread to celebrate your Name Day upon your return. I wish to prepare you something more elaborate -"

"My feelings on the matter are genuine," I said, watching Chatza shift her mug between her fingers and glance quickly beneath the rim. "The spoils of the Festess are well worth my enjoyment upon our Name Day."

"It is certainly appreciated," Chatza said. "Though, in preparing the meals for the coming days I must report that I dwindled the supply of grains, cheese, fruits, and wine."

"Aye," I said with a breath, "Samarin of Poets Cove shall be depositing goods to the castle this evening, I would expect the kitchens shall be replenished in the morrow, provided there are no delays with the upcoming Sabbat."

"There are always the emergency provisions if the need for supplies becomes absolute," Chatza said, adding a taste of wine to the remaining tea in her mug.

"As for the wine," I continued. "You know you always have access to the cellars and my personal supply in the brewery."

"And I thank you for your blessing, Your Worship," Chatza said, puckering her lips slightly from the sourness of her wine and tea. "And though it has been gifted, the right shall rarely be used..."

"I can understand," I said, feeling Syler shift in her seat and nudge my leg beneath the table.

"And whilst we are on the subject of wine..." Chatza's voice lowered as she suddenly became serious. "I was hoping to persuade you into brewing something new for this upcoming winter season... With all the snow foreseen, I reckon we are like to be spending much of our time in the castle and I would fancy being gifted a tart wine to indulge in..."

"Is this for you personally, or for the castle?" Syler asked suddenly. "There are still raspberries that need harvesting in the orchards, I could have my apprentices keep them aside for you if that is something you would fancy."

"That could be lovely," Chatza said with a smile. "I have no preference, and I rather quite enjoy a wide range of tastes... the wine would be for me personally, and I pray it is acceptable that I sought you for your talents as a winemaker."

"With all you tend to in the castle," I said gently, "you most certainly deserve something both sweet and tart to indulge in these future winter months..."

"Aye, thank you kindly," Chatza said with a smile.

"I shall not be able to tend to it until after the events of the next few days," I confessed with a sigh. "Between the Equinox, my Name Day obligations, The Ascension, and finalizing the Merchants Banquet preparations... I find myself unable to oversee anything else at present."

"Understandably so," Chatza said, "this season always proves to be the busiest for you, and for this I shall apologize. I meant not to suggest urgency or priority... I simply know you require foresight in order to plan your time and energy and I wished to communicate such for once you were settled after The Ascension."

"I appreciate that," I said. "I would satisfy your cravings with sour wine at this exact moment had I had the supplies to do so. And I would continue brewing wine for you well into your Name Day... you are quite pivotal to myself and the castle's well-being, and I am honored you should come to me asking for my wine."

"You have quite a talent," Chatza said, her cup now drained.

"I appreciate the complement," I said, resisting the urge to adjust my gauntlets as my hands suddenly throbbed with discomfort.

Nodding courteously, she thanked me with a charming smile, twirling her empty mug in her hands politely. "I noticed you have not begun your meals yet... May I watch you test your plates?"

"Aye, please." I encouraged, filling my platter with a baked potato and a pile of boiled greens.

Syler followed suit, plucking bread and cheese from a passing servant to place beside her dish. Reaching around my neck, I untied a small leather pouch, peering in at the brittle green-blue herb and grasping a pinch of the papsal between my fingers. Offering the pouch to Syler, I was honored by her acceptance, smiling as she fished the herbs from my bag instead of using her own. Crushing the plant in our hands, we sprinkled the seasoning neatly over the food, using the plant to detect poison. If the herbs crackled, the food had been tampered with. Though if the seasoning failed to sizzle, it added a barely detectable salted flavor.

"Thank you kindly for allowing me to observe," Chatza said once the food proved to be safe. "May I offer you ladies anything else? Do either of you wish to discuss the finalizations for the Merchants Banquet?"

"We shall discuss them once Frek graces us with his presence," I said with a smile. "There is nothing further on the matter that's needed to be discussed presently. Unless you possess anything that you wish to convey."

Chatza reached forward, seizing a flagon of wine from the table.

"Nothing regarding the Merchants Banquet..." Chatza said as she poured the deep red wine into her mug. "I trust Frek can handle the matter with the pair of you sufficiently enough without the need for my supervision... Though... There was a separate matter I wish to bring to light..."

"What is it that plagues your mind?" I said, wishing for a goblet of wine, though knowing it was wise to wait until our conversation had concluded.

"I would hate to be a nuisance of any kind, though I must trouble you again to finalize your decision for the main course at The Ascension Feast..."

Lowering my eyes shamefully, I released a sad sigh, adjusting my gauntlets as they seemed to tighten with my sorrow.

"Nay... I hath not yet decided..."

"You have had more than enough time to make a decision, Knomucca." Chatza released a patient breath, maintaining her composure though annoyance flashed subtly behind her eyes.

"I realize this is so," I said, keeping my tone steady as my hands burned beneath my gauntlets. "It has been a weight against my conscience... I understand and appreciate all you are undertaking in preparing the Festess, The Ascension Feast and everything else, and I am aware my fickleness is inhibiting your progress-"

"Share your confusions with me, Knomucca," Chatza said, taking a small sip of her wine. "What is withholding you from making the decision?"

"I wish to serve a simmered or roasted duck," I said, my voice threatening to quiver as Chatza's eyes widened.

"Still determined to serve meat then?" Syler asked, her voice light and nonchalant.

"Aye."

"It is quite the risk, Knomucca," Chatza said seriously, her cocoa brown eyes flashing in brief alarm. "To serve meat to the dead... It'll leave quite the impression -"

"I understand," I said, my gauntlets thrumming as I released a breath. "The consumption is a delicacy they shall soon be without, and I wish to provide it whilst I can. Ducks were sacred in our land, believed to represent prosperity, clarity, protection, love, and harmony. My actions shall be seen as a proclamation that I am striving to make them comfortable... the afterlife can be long for those who have nothing with them to bring joy."

"You are quite thoughtful for wanting to convey such a message," Chatza began with a sigh. "Though I worry it shall not communicate what you wish it to... I worry your actions shall offend, and that is not advisable given you shall be newly united with the pantheon-"

"I have a good feeling about my decision," I said firmly.

"You must not entirely if it took you this long to decide if it was wise," Chatza furrowed her brows, her lips smoothing to a thin line. "Knomucca... I have a very unsettled feeling when I think upon this culinary decision, and I must seriously advise against it."

"I appreciate your wisdom," I said, though I knew the matter was more complicated.

"Please, reconsider, Knomucca," Chatza's eyes pleaded silently as she began to form her words. "It could wind up causing more harm than health-"

"Certainly, it could," I said with a reassuring nod, "so goes the same with all the other decisions that I am forced to make at present-"

"Oi, you are grinding stones," Chatza chided, concealing her voice from its full frustration. "I shall admit I admire your audacity... though you might wish to broaden your perceptions as I have a sense that those events may not evolve as you plan-"

"I understand," I said again, my tone softening with appreciation. "I realize you mean well... though I have contemplated the matter quite at length, and this is what I wish to do."

"I noticed," Chatza said, glancing longingly towards the flagon of wine yet refusing to refill her cup. "And you are certain I cannot persuade you?"

"I have spoken enough on the matter," I said, feeling Syler step painfully atop my foot from beneath the table to demand I guard my temper.

"Very good," Chatza said with a respectful nod.

"Shall that be everything?" I asked, hoping to dismiss her as I wished to consume my supper in silence.

"Aye, that is all."

"Excellent. We must thank you," I said, "for our trust in you has not been led astray."

"You have truly blessed us and the castle," Syler said in gentle agreement. "We are forever indebted to you and your kindness."

"It is a pleasure to serve you both and honor your mother," Chatza said with a sad smile. "Awfully proud of you she would be if she could see you now... Even despite these recently questionable proclamations."

Our words fell silent, interrupted by the surrounding clattering of dishes, friendly conversation and waves of billowing laughter.

"I ought to be returning to the kitchens," Chatza said.

"Aye, I appreciate your time," I said with a grateful smile. "Stay wise."

"Love and light," she replied, whisking herself away.

Chatza swirled towards the kitchen on the path she had come, the fragrant scent of daisies lingering in the air in her absence. Through a throng of surrounding servers, she moved away on the right, weaving past their loud and excited voices as they discussed upcoming plans for leisurely time once the cooking chores were finished. The Festess spirit was bright and abundant in the servers and castle folk, their merriment obvious from the small games of Shepard's Claw that had begun on the far end of the soldiers' tables.

I ought to have a final goblet of wine whilst I can enjoy my time in the castle, I thought, pulling a flagon of wine from across the table and swiftly refilling my cup.

Centering my breathing, I released a blessing of gratitude, taking a moment to thank the elements and livestock for their sacrifice before I set to eating. Preferring to use my own blade, I unsheathed a simple golden dagger from my boot. I began to slice into the bloody beef, carving it from against the bone so as not to be wasteful. Heaping a fatty piece into my mouth, I sighed with happiness, the flavors melting blissfully. Apple and smoky tones filled my mouth, complementing the salted potatoes and crispy greens. Chatza had once again outdone herself. I silently consumed my supper, glancing over my right shoulder as I felt my sister watching me.

"Are you well, Knomucca?" Syler asked, finishing the rice and vegetable dish she had exchanged for the cut of pork. "You've been quiet since Chatza left..."

"Angry with myself I suppose," I said, taking a sip of wine before I continued speaking. "Had I chosen to deliberate upon the matter outwardly and openly with Chatza from the beginning, perhaps I could have persuaded her towards my passions instead of recruiting her anxieties..."

"It is an immense decision," Syler began gently, "try not to dwell on an unobtainable course of past hypotheticals. What is done is done... and it might interest you to know that if anyone could manage to serve meat to the dead and convey it to be meant as an act of love, I believe it to be you."

"Aye, thank you kindly, Sye," I said with a sincere smile.

"For future knowledge, however," Syler said, her tone reaching a firmness that had reminded me of our mother, "you should do all you can to give Chatza as much time as possible to prepare a feast for such an important occasion."

"Aye... it is in part why I am carrying annoyance and anger at myself," I said with a heavy breath. "Chatza shall need to be preparing the Feast during the frivolity of the Festess and tending to the Merchant's Banquet."

Chatza would be catering for hundreds of living, dead, and divine at The Ascension Ceremony, and I felt ashamed it had taken such a length to affirm my decision for the course. I was determined to serve duck at The Ascension Banquet, wishing to create an afterlife that allowed the dead to feel honored, safe, and secure. As I had been trained from birth to fulfill my upcoming station as Goddess of Death and the keeper of the Underworld, I yearned to use my magical gifts and knowledge to keep the spirits of Crossfire contented, comfortable and catered to.

"Worry not," Syler said as if she knew what I was thinking, "she is forgiving and mightily talented... so long as we express our gratitude, she shall have not a slight to bare towards you."

"I hope this is so," I said, suddenly worrying that I would do something to disappoint Mother.

"It is so, dear twin," Syler beamed over the top of her wine. "We will roast her some cacao and say a blessing for her at the Feast... we shall gift her flowers and Everett's finest smoking blends... she shall feel pampered and appreciated once we have finished treating her."

"I hope it is so," I said with a sigh, thinking of the upcoming camaraderie of the Festess and wishing I could partake. "What I would not give for some of Mother's harvest cinnamon cake..."

"Aye, or her lemon logs," Syler said with a mischievous smile. "Our lemon trees were quite abundant this harvest season, perhaps Chatza shall surprise the castle guests with a fresh batch of lemon pastry..."

"That would please Everett," I said, watching him as he ate his bread, now sitting alone at the soldier's table. "Provided any of the delicacies remain once we return to the castle."

"I shall inquire about the matter and spare him one, if possible," Syler said, noticing my wandering glances and masking her smile behind her goblet.

"I appreciate the gesture, though there is no need to do so," I said heavily, taking a silent moment to indulge in my supper. "The upcoming nights could prove to be terrible, and we could fail to Ascend, fall prey to death, or worse, be betrayed..."

Syler's face fell, her eyes narrowing darkly as she firmly studied her cup.

"Oi... your words, though rather sudden – strike an iron truth," Syler said, taking a long sip from her goblet. "I could never forget Rejj and his cowardice... the thought of him trying to end you with a crossbow at our Blood Solstice still makes me livid."

Absently, I reached behind my right ear, feeling the gnarled scar that stuck out against my skin.

"Aye," I said, rubbing the scar with my fingers. "Maintaining vigilance is best for the events of the upcoming days... best not to attract any unwanted attention or surprise."

Syler sat silently, her shoulders tightening in sorrow as a memory flashed across her eyes.

"Share what plagues your mind," I said, contentedly consuming my supper as I waited for my twin to speak.

"Thank the gods. His weakness with angles and measurements spared your life," Syler said heavily, her energy softening as the vision left her mind. "Had his arrow not ricocheted from the candelabra before it pierced you, the damage would have been far more severe."

"All is as it should be," I reassured her seriously. "Though I believe his life should have been spared as mine had been."

"You know the penalty for an attempt on the life of a Prospect is death," Syler said with a note of finality. "And personally, I believe he got what he deserved... Put to death and hanged on the gallows. Thank the good gods for that, if you bloody well ask me. "

"Aye," I said, thinking of Rejj now tending to the scrolls in the Underworld's library. "Thank the gods, indeed."

"The Power has a way of possessing people," Syler continued, her voice strained as she absently moved the remnants of her supper around her plate. "I concede with you entirely darling, that we best not do anything rash until after we Ascend."

"Best not indeed," I said, "or I might be forced to retaliate against you in a way that would displease the memory of our mother..."

"Careful Sister," Syler warned with a surprisingly serious gesture. "If you anger her too severely you might incur an unsolicited visit from beyond her grave."

I laughed, feigning delight at our banter. My hands itched and tingled painfully through my gauntlets, the discomfort growing, and I prayed Syler wouldn't notice. Guiding my fingers upward, I combed them through my hair, trying to distract myself from the pain. Spotting Everett between the strokes of my hand, I watched as he sat alone, his supper mostly finished on a platter in front of him. A wine goblet was pressed to his lips, and I couldn't help but wish I were that cup, immensely desiring to be pressed against him and held tightly in his hands.

Our eyes locked, and we held each other's gaze for a long moment, my heart pounding nervously as it fluttered and skipped a beat. Involuntarily, I smiled playfully, winking from the rush of my mirth before fully realizing I had done so. My breathing slowed though never relaxed, my breath catching slightly as Everett held my gaze intensely. I dared not blink nor look away, craving only to relish in his gentle face and steel blue eyes, his dark auburn hair glowing a soft red in the gentle candlelight around him.

Vaguely, in the distance, I heard my name being spoken by a firm voice threatening to disrupt my longing. My body was paralyzed with anticipation, and I had no desire to break away from Everett's gaze. Ignoring the voice momentarily, I continued marveling at Everett's beauty, feeling a sudden hard tap upon my right shoulder. My concentration wavered, and I soon turned away from him, regretfully shifting in my seat to see who had disturbed me.

"Good evening, Your Worship," Frek, our childhood friend and recently promoted advisor, stood at attention beside our table. "My pardons for the interruption... I would inquire if I may take a seat?"

"That would be delightful," Syler said, delicately sipping her wine before she continued. "Would you not agree, dearest twin?"

My gauntlets pulsed once more. "Most certainly," I said, gesturing with a hand for Frek to sit and join us.

Frek pulled the chair to Syler's right with a whispering glide, dropping down into the creaking wooden frame. Folding his lean arms over his chest, he looked much too big for the seat he occupied. His shadow-black hair fell over his caramel smooth face, his soft, loyal eyes hardening with deeply churning anger as a nearing full moon drew closer.

"I appreciate the invitation," Frek said with a smile, hiding his irritation well behind his eyes.

"My pardons it was not so swift," Syler teased, meeting my eyes boldly as I stomped her foot from beneath the table.

Turning towards Syler, Frek raised a hand, brushing the shaggy long hair from his face before he began speaking.

"I wanted to convey, Your Loveliness, that we are finalizing preparations for your journey northwards, and gods given, they shall be finished by morning.

"Excellent," Syler said, refilling her wine. "Would you mind, too terribly, in verbalizing the status of the preparations at present?"

"Indeed, Your Loveliness," Frek began with a reassuring nod. "The supply wagons hath been ladened, the horses have been groomed and bathed with scented soaps, the soldiers tending us have gathered and procured the supplies needed for the voyage, and there should be plenty of luxuries for you to be comfortable whilst away from the castle."

"Truly kind of you indeed," Syler said with a soft smile. "And what came of your conversation with Chatza regarding the Merchants Dinner preparations?"

"Nothing unexpected," Frek said, running a hand in a comforting rhythm across Syler's shoulder. "Chatza shall prepare multiple batches of the Festess favorites that will honor the elegance of both the Festess and the Merchants Dinner."

"That is an excellent idea," Syler said, her wine wetting her lips as she continued speaking. "Our castle guests are expecting culinary confections worthy of the Equinox... I see no reason as to deprive them of Chatza's house squash soup, cinnamon topped bread pie, and lamb stew."

"Nor do I," Frek said, his hand lingering in the crook of Syler's arm. "I shall admit I had selfish intentions for suggesting such... for once the Merchants Dinner concludes the chance for Festess frivolity and delicacies shall be far again from your enjoyment."

"Must you be so dispirited?" I asked, shaking my head as I adjusted the clasps and chains of my gauntlets. "Our Name Day and Ascension fall upon the Equinox, we shall have the three days post to celebrate and enjoy our time, assuming all unfurrows as planned."

"I am inclined to agree," Frek said, never fully meeting Syler's or mine eye. "I simply wanted to ensure plenty of merriment, best I could."

"Thank you kindly... it is very much appreciated," Syler said, leaning across the table towards Frek and kissing his cheek affectionately.

"Anything for you, Syler." Frek said gently, brushing a lock of hair behind her ear. "Are there any other matters you wish to discuss?"

"As of now I have nothing new for you to accomplish and implore you to relax whilst you can."

"Aye, excellent... that would be divine," Frek said, indulging in the leftover meat on a tray nearby. He slid the tray across the table and placed it at his front, finding a platter of roasted greens, which he quickly set to eating. After consuming a hearty meal, he released a sigh, consuming a hefty flagon of water before he spoke again. "Pity... I forgot to offer you ladies a Festess whiskey."

"I will take some if you care to offer," I said, eagerly anticipating the still.

"I brought a second flask, simply for you, Knomucca," Frek said with a smile, "I can always rely on your indulgence whenever Festess whiskey flows."

"It is rather enjoyable indeed," I said with a smile.

"Syler, Sweetness, are you caring for any Festess whiskey this evening?"

"I would prefer my wine," Syler said, taking another large sip from her cup. "Thank you immensely for the offer, however."

"Anytime, Your Loveliness," Frek said with a nod towards Syler. "Wine is always an excellent choice."

Frek retrieved a clean goblet from the servant's carts, blowing tersely through its center before he placed it at his front. Lifting the flask, he began pouring the warm spirits, the honey-gold hue glossing in the torchlight. Sliding the goblet across the table, Frek followed its path with his eyes. I clasped my fingers around the rim, breathing in the subtle notes of cinnamon and almonds as Frek continued to speak.

"I would like to revisit the agenda regarding the upcoming days," Frek began slowly as he drank a large swig of his whiskey. "For as the time draws nearer, I find myself growing increasingly nervous."

"You are not alone in those feelings," I admitted, taking a large pull of whiskey. The spirit was smooth yet burned pleasantly, the sweet and spicy notes of warmed coconut a refreshing surprise against my taste buds.

"I suppose it is wise to be nervous," Frek spoke whilst I continued to drink. "In being nervous one is prudent, and prudence shall guard your life."

"Indeed... indeed," I said with a nod. "Anyhow, what may I do to ease your mind?"

"Please listen whilst I relay the plan as I understand it and correct me if I misspeak."

"Understood, proceed," I encouraged.

"Aye, very well," Frek began with a breath. "Your Name Day is four days' hence, falling squarely upon the Autumnal Equinox. You shall leave on the morrow and begin your trek towards Riverside, for far in the south is where your Ascension Ritual shall occur."

"Correct," I said, taking another large gulp of the fire.

"Simultaneously to your departure is the night of the Merchants Dinner," Frek continued as he absently rested his hand against Syler's arm. "Proceeded by our Midnight chariot ride from the castle as we begin the trek to the Far North to fulfill Syler's Ascension Ceremony."

"Correct again," I said with a sip of whiskey. "And I must remind you of Samarin's request to house himself and his guests in the secluded cottages of the Orchards... best see to it there are logs in the fireplaces and freshened blankets and linens."

"It is already been settled," Frek said gently. "Worry not - all shall progress smoothly, and I shall do my best to ensure nothing is forgotten."

"Mark in your records that I shall be requesting a reading of flames from my sister once she has Ascended into her Goddesshood," Syler said with a sly smile. "Consider it reimbursement for my having to host the Merchants Dinner by my lonesome."

"A shortage in time forced my hand," I said as my palms began to itch. "That these annual events occur so close together is unfortunate. The harvest is now upon us, and the farmers can secure our goods and trade -"

"I recall, Sister," Syler retorted, glaring through her hair as she snatched the flagon of wine from the center of the table.

"You are acting as though this can simply be overlooked," I said firmly. "Though you know it must not be... Stable realms are prosperous realms, the fruit of plenty paint the vines of bounty."

"Aye, so saith Mother," Syler glared and rolled her eyes, playfulness lingering beneath her sea-green irises. "You could delay your departure a night and host the dinner alongside me... Riverside is a mere three-day ride from here, and with your riding through the night, you could arrive there with a breeze..."

I took a long drink, using the whiskey to hide my annoyance. Though Syler's words struck truth, I knew the matter was more complicated, preparing myself for her criticisms and judgements before I continued speaking.

"Everett shall be urging the soldiers onwards without myself," I said, wishing I could gift myself a smoke as Syler rolled her eyes.

"You are traveling east against my advisement," Syler accused, her earlier annoyance now boiling into righteous anger.

"It is against your advisement, though, in honor of my favor," I said as my hands thrummed against my gauntlets.

"Mother would boast of your logic and wisdom," Syler snapped, "yet if she should hear you from her grave, I fear she shall know you've been nothing but foolish-"

"Oi, Syler, retract your claws," Frek said, his grin faltering once he noticed I had not found her comment amusing. "You think it wise to travel to the sea alone?"

"I shall have Thornin," I said, resisting the urge to sigh in outward annoyance.

"That may be so..." he said slowly, "though would you consider taking another companion?"

"All the personnel whom Thornin enjoys and tolerates are occupied with either the soldiers, Festess, or Syler and her pursuits northwards," I said.

"Could you not ask Everett?" Frek said, meeting my eyes boldly as Syler's body tensed. "The General could oversee the soldiers until the lot of you returned, could he not?"

"He is more than capable of such," I agreed with a nod. "However, I would rather not separate the pair of them if I can avoid it... not with the instability that is like to come with the Equinox."

A silence fell between us, for though neither Syler nor Frek wished to vocalize their agreement, it flashed briefly across their faces.

"I have given much thought to the matter," I said gently, patting Syler's arm. "I wished to request Everett's company on my voyage Eastward, though it is not what is best for The General..."

"It is daft for you to only think of his needs and none of your own," Syler chided, her eyes blinking quickly as she composed her face. "Traveling alone cannot be what you truly want or need."

"Regardless of if it should be my desire or necessity, it shall prove to be well," I began as my hands burned painfully in my gauntlets. "I shall be swimming the reefs in order to obtain an angelfish eye... and I shall be faster if I simply take only Thornin and return swiftly-"

"It is not prudent to travel east," interjected Syler. "Especially without reinforcement of some type to protect you-"

"All will be well, Syler," I said firmly. "I will be departing on the morrow for the Luna Sea, and I've made my mind up on the matter."

A silence fell amongst us at the table, filling with the clattering of cutlery, clanking cups, and laughing of the camaraderie in the castle. Syler's face was stoic and flat, her eyes glancing sneakily towards Frek in a way she hoped I would not notice. Clearing her throat, she placed the now emptied flagon onto a passing server's cart, spinning her chalice in her hands before she began to speak.

"Your ambition is admirable," Syler said with a sigh. "Despite Mother's readings of the legends of Ozwal the Great you are determined to pursue such avenues... He too sought the sea in obtaining worthy sacrifice for The Creator and was murdered for his endeavors."

"Legends and gossip depict that he was murdered," I said, "nobody knows what truly happened to him. There is no written record, merely unconfirmed rumors and slurs from sailors. His ship could have sunk, or his crew could have starved or gotten scurvy."

"Be cautious whilst stepping in another's shadow," Syler said seriously. "Though the sea may possess many worthy gifts for The Creator, it doesn't mean you have to obtain them by yourself."

"Wash it down the river," I said, meeting Syler's gaze. "We shall be grinding stones if we are left to discuss this for the duration of the evening."

"Knomucca is correct," Frek said despite Syler's glares. "Regardless, if we wish for you to travel alone or with a companion, this is the decision you have made, and you are quite rooted... You shall not change each other's opinions no matter how valid they might be once you have set them in stone."

"Wise indeed," I said, indicating with a gesture I did not wish to continue the conversation any further.

"We seemed to have digressed anyhow," said Frek, finishing the last of his Festess whiskey. "May I continue explaining the events of the upcoming days?"

"Please," I said, swallowing my whiskey as I regained my composure.

"Excellent," said Frek. Taking a piece of cheese from a tray across the table, he tore it into large chunks. Popping several bites in his mouth, he allowed a moment to pass. "When The Ascension is complete, we will use The Ascension Temple in The Far North to join you in the Underworld for the Banquet."

"Aye," I said with a nod. "Rejj will escort you once Syler opens the portal and he will make certain you arrive in Heimaaila safely."

Frek furrowed his brow in disgust at the mention of Rejj's name. "Bloody swine."

"Oi! Mind your manners," I said with a shake of my head.

"My pardons, Knomucca." Frek said seriously. "I do not mean to ignite the kindling... though I shall admit I dislike the thought of you allowing such a person to perform such valuable tasks when they once tried to end your life."

"I dislike the notion as well," Syler began with a soft sigh. "Though it is as you said... My sister is stubborn and rooted."

"Those are all the proceedings as I understand them," I said to Frek, ignoring my sister with a playful glare.

"Excellent," Frek said with a smile. "I am glad to know I have understood everything."

"As am I," I said genuinely. "Feel free to carry on in your Festess frivolity... though I must admit I shall not have much more past this whiskey..."

"I will have another on your behalf," Syler said, smiling broadly and pouring herself more wine from a new tankard. After taking a large sip, she indicated she was about to change the subject with the gesture of her free hand. Leaning in close, she spoke low, burning up the inside of my nose with the smell of fermented grapes.

"I had one other matter to discuss, Dearest Twin," Syler said mischievously. "Did you summon the courage to tell Everett whilst sparring?"

"I decided against it," I said heavily. "Such fraternization is unwise, as it is forbidden by the Creator to seek such indulgences. It could risk our focus wavering from the realms."

"I was sincerely hoping to hear you had changed your mind on the matter," Syler said with a sad smile. "Though... nevertheless... I reckon you will tell him when you are meant to."

"Perhaps I shall never confide in him my feelings," I said. "It is an immense risk. I already possess feelings of worry when I see the pair of you openly exchange your affections for one another... Additionally, my confession could complicate our relationship, and I wish not to jeopardize our dynamics once he knows how I feel about him."

"He already knows how you feel about him," Syler said much too loudly, signaling Roice to take her empty plates as he walked past.

"Perhaps," I gestured for Roice to take mine as well, deciding to have green jasmine tea for dessert. "Though I cannot assume that he does."

"I believe it is safe to assume everybody knows," Frek said, returning my newly replenished goblet into my hands.

My eyes narrowed, and I glared into his face, angrily downing my tea in three gulps in an attempt to distract myself from the pain growing through my fingers.

"It is one thing to assume and another to voice it aloud," I said seriously.

Frek raised his shoulders innocently, the urge to smirk curling his lips as he managed to continue calmly, "I honestly believe he would be receptive, and could be trusted to remain professional until all was said and done."

"Cease your howling, Wolf..." Syler hushed, her face turning a deep shade of tomato red in embarrassment.

Despite the unfair treatment Frek received throughout his life as a werewolf, he had always felt at ease here, especially around Syler. Ever since our mother offered him a home and a chance to leave his life on the road behind him, he had become one of our closest and most loyal friends.

"My pardons," Frek said, allowing the chuckle to escape him. "Your affection towards each other is as clear as the waters of the orchard ponds... all I had simply meant was that I wished for you to confess and be happy."

"As my quartermaster, you are forgiven," I said with a playful smile. "As my friend, however, you can shove off."

"I reckon I deserve such farewell," Frek laughed, stealing a large drink from Syler's chalice. "Though if you send me away, who shall bring you whiskey as frequently as I?"

"You provide stable arguments," I said through our laughter. "And I shall admit, the spirit was quite delightful."

"Came from the southern village," Frek said, fondly reminding me of the Ironsides Inn. "The General gifted me the brew a few days prior after his day's work at the tavern, and I have not had a spare moment to drink it until this eve."

"Understandable," I said.

"It is quite sad we shall not be able to partake in our usual Festess frivolity," Syler sighed. "How I wish we could summon our gentlemen from the soldier's table and begin a game of Shepard's Claw..."

"As do I," I admitted with a sad sigh.

"Promise me you shall tell Everett of your feelings, Knomucca," Syler pleaded. "Allow yourself the fantasy for every Festess that would be to come, and how all the more magnificent they would be."

Roice returned suddenly from the kitchen, sparing me an answer with his offer to clear the table.

"We have not yet seen all our advisors," Syler said, "though you can feel inclined to take what no longer serves purpose."

"Excellent... reckon there'll be games of cups and cards as the meal progresses," Roice said after filling a cart with dirty dishes.

I made certain my dishes had been cleared, glancing towards Everett once more whilst I imagined throwing knives with him in the orchards during the Festess.

"Your Worship," Roice said, interrupting my thoughts. "May I offer you anything else for your supper?"

"Nay, Roice, that shall be all," I said, giving him an empty tankard and the rest of the night free.

"Very good," Roice said, accepting the tankard from my hand.

Roice bowed and swished away, his fluffy brown hair bouncing with the gusts of his movements.

Syler and Frek laughed and whispered beside me, the pair of them kissing sweetly before each retrieved their goblets to propose a blessing.

"To The Creator and His gifts," Syler said, sipping her wine. "May our Ascension be successful and our futures abundant."

"Abundance indeed," I said, nodding in approval with her sudden proclamation. "I really must be going now."

"I think not," Syler teased, stepping playfully on my foot, demanding my presence linger at the table. "Your lack of confession to Everett is acceptable. Though, I admit, it shall not satisfy me..."

"Is there anything that would?" I asked, dreading the answer as her eyes glinted mischievously in the torchlight.

"Could we fantasize about you in Mother's finest gown for yours and Everett's wedding?"

II

EVERETT

Valvang Hall was noisy as I joined the troops at the table. A partially eaten roast sat in the center on a large silver platter, surrounded by plump potatoes and topped with leafy greens. Empty cups and full pitchers of wine punctuated the table, inviting me immediately to pour myself a large drink.

"It is a wise idea to indulge in the wine," a firm and charming voice across from my seat caught my attention suddenly. "It is quite bitter... I reckon it could become one of your favorites."

"I have already noticed a very pleasant aroma," I said, lifting my gaze from the table as I emptied the flagon into my cup.

Kiyoko sat across the table, his eyes steady and sparkling as I regarded him with a smile.

"Aye, it possesses a delightful bouquet," Kiyoko said as he shifted in his seat. His words made me stir as the embroidered cherry blossoms woven across the sleeves of his favorite plum-purple kimono had often made me think the same of him.

"I shall take pleasure in drinking it," I said, struggling to keep my voice level as I kept the thoughts to myself.

"You look warm," Kiyoko mused with a wink, polishing off the wine he had been drinking. "Where have you been hiding this evening?"

"I was sparring with Her Worship," I said, enjoying the way the pomegranate wine tasted on my lips.

"Are you certain that was all?" Kiyoko teased and shifted in his seat once more. "Your energy feels... flustered."

Meeting his eyes, my attention wavered, noticing a tall, voluptuous brunette tangled around him. Lorraine Charlotte, an apprentice to the Head Gardener, was enjoying Kiyoko's company as she teased her tongue along his ear. Her hands vanished beneath the table, her skirts cleverly concealing them as she perched on Kiyoko's left. I fought not to betray my envy, taking a long swig of wine to allow myself a brief moment. Seeing Kiyoko behave so sociably was rare, and I knew with no uncertainty he was doing so to hassle me.

"As certain as the sun rising on the morrow," I admitted, slamming my cup of wine and pouring another.

Kiyoko smirked upon my noticing his companion, his spirits visibly brightening in doing so. His copper-brown eyes glistened like soft morning sunlight, a view we shared most frequently when restless nights were upon us. He searched my face with a curious expression, his pupils flicking softly upwards as he playfully pretended to read my energy.

"Your loss I reckon," Kiyoko said innocently, meeting my eyes with a mixture of jest and temptation. "Though, I shall confess, the glow of your sparring suits you quite nicely."

"I would offer you a round after supper," I said with the boldness to match his own. "Though... I can see you'll be otherwise... occupied."

"Aye..." he paused briefly, "though come the morrow, I shall hardly leave your side." Kiyoko's eyes lulled backwards blissfully, his maiden sitting upright in her seat before taking a glass of wine from beside his plate.

"Aye, come the morrow," I agreed, exhaling in anticipation of the days to come, my heart thrumming.

Kiyoko's rare psychic gifts were useful in his role as my right hand, second in command of the Gods' Guard, and being my closest friend.

Though his title of Sneak was known to only a small, trusted circle, I had come to rely on his abilities as often as they came 'round to bite me in the arse when he chose to wield them against me. At that moment, he noticed the pulsing change in my energy and winked – sending my heart into my throat.

Kiyoko sipped more wine whilst Lorraine sipped his skin. She kissed his neck, running her fingers over his chest and drinking him in with her hands. She kissed her way up to his ear, nibbling and biting as he finished his wine. Dropping his goblet on the table, he turned in his chair to better please his maiden, wrapping his arms around her and kissing her with an open mouth. She moaned, parting her lips wider as they mixed their wine with their tongues.

I blushed, using the remainder of the wine in my cup as an excuse to overtly glance away. Snatching the pitcher from across the table, I shifted in my seat, pouring the wine and turning away from Kiyoko. Leaning my body forward, I peered over the roasts and piles of food, letting my eyes drift towards the head table. Her Worship, Knomucca, sat in her high-backed chair, engrossed in a conversation with Chatza. Her eyes were fixed in concentration on the witch, her brow creased slightly as she focused on Chatza's words.

I loved it when Knomucca made that face, and it was one she made quite often. Her focused, emerald eyes were nearly always consumed in some book or parchment, her thirst for knowledge her most attractive quality. It was far from unordinary to stumble upon Knomucca curled blissfully with a book in hand, tucked in secret alcoves hidden throughout the castle. The earliest memory I possess takes place during my fourth year, on a cold night during the Winter Solstice upon my readying to sleep. Her Worship is five years my elder, and during her ninth year, she gifted my family with a reading of The Winter Mitten, which remains one of my favorites.

Sipping my wine, I watched as her full lips moved, her confident, premeditated words lost in the noise of Valvang. Knomucca held her composure well as she was exceptionally poised; the pauses in her speaking were deliberate as she valued tact and subtlety. She was shrewd and thorough, clever as a fox, and an exceptionally quick study, allowing her to learn what she needed and understand how to use it. Knomucca was stern, though she knew when to be gentle. Knomucca lent her strength and support to the bereaved and broken-hearted, soothing the dead as they transitioned and grieving with those they had left behind.

However, her dealings with the dead, gods, and the Underworld have caused complications. In years previous, rumors had formed after the disappearance of a smattering of castle servants, claiming Knomucca could reach through one's chest and rip out their still-beating heart. Just this night past, I had overheard servants drunk on pre-Festess wine whispering that she would consume those hearts, absorbing the powers of her victims to then use as her own. Such a notion was appalling, though I should admit the idea of her possessing such strength and power sent shivers down my spine. I loved that one so strong could be so kind. I hadn't yet told her this, wishing to protect her from any threats, both physical and social, grateful my position had gifted me the privilege of doing so.

My station as commander of The Gods' Guard, inherited from my father and his father before him, was as important to my family as it was to me. I, too, was born here, in the castle Morriraen, in the Warrior's Nursery overlooking the river, born and bred to fight and defend the realms of Crossfire from its enemies.

As soon as my family was able, they dawned me with a warhammer, bestowing its honor upon me. Nobody had wielded one in generations, adjudging it to only have been worthy of my seventh-great-grandfather. Absently, I grasped the shaft of my hammer, recalling that night on my fifth Winter Solstice.

I remembered how the door to the hallway spilled open, casting torch light across my bed. Hushed whispers fluttered like snow from the corridor, their murmurings interrupting my dreams. I fought to remain still and maintain my soft breathing, wishing not to betray to the familiar voices of my parents that they had woken me prematurely.

"Otis, please," my mother pleaded in a soft panic. "'Tis late; leave him to sleep."

"I must wake him," my father said. "Midnight has fallen upon us and the solstice has arrived."

"It's far too cold to take such a young boy to the cemetery," my mother's voice softly beckoned. "Can this not wait until the sun has risen? A boy with only 5 years to his name shall certainly catch his death from the wind and cold."

"You know it ought to be now," Father said, his voice growing stern. "With the solstice, light returns to our realms... we must use the vulnerability to consecrate Everett's hammer and magic."

"Otis, a boy his age, needs not fret for the fate of the realms," Mother spoke in a firm whisper.

"I shall speak to him not of the prophecy," Father promised, "only of our loyalties to the First Warrior and our pursuit for love over power."

"You endanger him by speaking of Anteyus... and of Knomucca's fated Ascension to Goddess of Death."

"He became endangered the moment of his conception." Father kissed my mother softly. "Fear not, dearest. Our son shall grow of mighty strength, love deeper than the vast oceans, and bring honor to us all. Worry not, for at the end all shall be well."

"But I insist, then, that I shall come with you," Mother huffed.

"Nay," father said urgently. "You and Angelara ought to stay where it is warm and rest... I shall have all seven of our strapping sons alongside me."

"Otis, if you are determined this evening to begin forging Everett's destiny, then I should wish to be with you..." my mother's voice softened once more. "Do what you must and wake them. I should prepare for our departure."

The words of my father from that night still echoed in my head. "Heed my warnings, dear son, for you must worship Anteyus in secret. You must never show you value love over that who created power." Putting the thoughts out of my mind, I took a bite of meat.

I refilled my wine as I watched Knomucca, thinking of how we grew and learned together, our friendship strengthening over the years. Though the times we spent together were often with Rejj, Kiyoko, Syler, and Frek, I still reveled in her willingness to be in my company. The frivolity of our days in the orchards, pulling berries off bushes or sinking chest-deep into gooey mud, solidified our friendship. As the years passed and our time together changed from hours of fun to long days of tedious chores, my feelings for Knomucca only strengthened. And after the approaching Ascension, gods willing, she survived; I would still hope to spend every day by her side.

Knomucca had been chosen at birth by The Creator to endure His Trials and become the Goddess of Death. The power and knowledge needed for her echelon were far beyond the maturity and abilities of a child, requiring her to be constantly in the shadow of her mother as the pair of them were always studying. Knomucca worked tirelessly to achieve excellence in her academics, using what knowledge she gained to protect and heal the realms. At that time, the realms were in chaos, the imbalance between the forces of nature, morality, and magical power endangering us all. On Knomucca's Blood Solstice, her mother lost her life, forgoing the guidance and protection she offered Knomucca as she continued the Trials alone.

Angrily, I slammed my cup of wine to the table, disgruntled by the thought of the pain and suffering Knomucca had been forced to overcome.

The sudden smell of bread dragged me back to the present.

"Oi... Everett... Finish this for me?" Kiyoko was shoving the browned end of a bread loaf in my face.

Reaching forward, I snatched his wrist, holding the bread against his fingers as I sternly stared into his face.

"Did you eat enough?" I asked, noticing the remains of potatoes, boiled pork and chard greens atop his smooth silver plate.

"I did indeed," he said with a nod.

"You appear to have consumed more of your companion than you have of your plate," I said, squeezing his fingers tightly in an attempt to gain the truth from him.

"I have been here many a moment," Kiyoko said, his pulse quickening beneath my fingers as he enjoyed my touching him.

"I reckon so," I said, brushing my fingers against his silken skin as I slid the bread from his hand. "I simply needed to make certain... hold you accountable..."

"Your concern is appreciated," Kiyoko said, the sincerity in his eyes bringing a smile across my lips.

Staggering to his feet, Kiyoko turned towards his company, hanging from the maiden's arm as his eyes glinted mischievously.

"Have a swell evening, Commander..." Kiyoko said as he gifted me a salute. "I will see you at first light...

"Enjoy yourself," I said with a glare, stuffing the hunk of bread in my mouth to hide my annoyance.

"Oi..." Kiyoko continued unexpectedly, his voice jarring as I had expected him to turn away. "Whilst we are making certain all is well... I noticed you've been drinking a fair lot of wine this evening..."

"It is simply to help me relax... do not be tempted to think you can take advantage of my stupor..." I retorted.

Kiyoko's eyes hardened. "Certainly not. I had considered the cause to be rooted in a fear you would not sleep on this night."

"It is as you suggested... I wish to be certain of a night well rested, as I have not had one in many days."

"I truly hope it finds you," Kiyoko said, his maiden gifting me with a flirtatious smile as the pair turned away. "Stay wise, Everett."

"Love and light."

I whistled crudely, my frustration lost in the branches of the cherry blossom tree embroidered across the back of his kimono. I wondered which kimono he would don for our venture south, though I reckoned it would be that which he wore at present. I enjoyed such a notion, for the way the plum purple fabric stretched across him, quickened my pulse excitedly. His muscular legs and bare feet poked teasingly into the torchlight as he strode away, making me wish I was being held in his sculpted arms.

Talking and laughter filled the air as mead was poured and meat was cut. Big juicy roasts were smothered with onions and garlic and served with red starchy vegetables and leafy greens. The wine had been made from blue-spiraled Tora berries, which were said to preserve life and good spirits. For dessert, a giant eighteen-layered cake sat in the middle of the hall atop a circular wooden platform. Everyone ate from the same pastry, the chocolate and Tora berry flavors uniting the castle in preparation for the Festess.

Between bites of food and cups of wine, I caught myself once more staring towards the head table. Knomucca's wavy golden hair was covering parts of her face, though I read from her body that she was in good spirits. Her hands were hidden beneath the table, her eyes alight with happiness as she spoke playfully with her sister. Syler sat beside her in a laced purple dress, her cheeks flushed with mischief and redness from wine.

As the twins leaned together, their hair fell as one, mixing Knomucca's subtle waves into Syler's noticeable curls. Had their hair been the same, distinguishing between them would have been difficult, though I could never mistake their identities. I'd always know Knomucca by her eyes, for they were emeralds sparkling with electric energy. Fair cheekbones accentuated her heart-shaped face, full lips, and tanned olive skin. Syler's almond-shaped eyes flowered like sea grass, and her skin was marginally paler. Syler was slim and slender, unlike her sister, who was muscular and athletic. Knomucca was seldom seen without wearing a pair of fancy, bejeweled gauntlets on her hands, whilst Syler enjoyed adorning her gowns with sparkling gemstones.

There is another way they can be identified, however. Both twins had symbols etched by ink, knife, and point across their bodies, each having vastly different designs between the pair of them. I had drawn the tattoos on their skin myself, learning to carve art into flesh from my father's father. Knomucca had a large, exceedingly intricate black spider between her shoulder blades, its legs weaving up the back of her neck to tangle beneath her hair. The moon's phases decorated her left forearm, and an owl spread its wings to soar across the right side of her rib cage.

Syler had an elegant, purple lily etched upon her right wrist and a bouquet of sunflowers, tulips and peonies trailing down her left leg. She had chosen those flowers to be in the bouquet as they are believed to promote happiness, prosperity and romance. Soon, the twins would have their Ascension, after which Syler was expected to become the Goddess of Love in our realms. Thus, she selected this symbolism to reflect her upcoming status. It was said in whispered tones she often favored those who sought her erudition; those same rumors acknowledging her advice and wisdom were sound of mind and deserving of praise. I had never sought Syler's advice on any personal matters, for I did not wish her to know the desires of my heart. I had, however, bore witness to her reading runes and dice in the herb garden, the words in her divinations flowing through me as I liked to enjoy my rare naps amongst the flowers.

On an interesting occasion, Syler had spread tarot cards through the grass in the orchard, becoming very intimate as she discussed a fear and inability to conceive. However, I didn't know to whom she had been speaking, for I slunk away unnoticed before my presence had been discovered. That evening, I had elected to fulfill the post of night watch as I was suffering a miserable bout of insomnia. The night had proven uneventful, the halls of the Western Tower silent as the sun had not yet risen. Near the western corridor, I rested atop a small wooden stool, smoking spliffs and meditating to pass the time until morning. Suddenly hearing shuffling footsteps, I lurched to my feet, drawing my hammer and standing at attention as a passerby rounded the corner. Captain Southwell of the Snake River Trading Port had left from the direction of Syler's chambers, shuffling into his rumpled cloak and tunic as his body gleamed in the overhead sconces. Nodding as he passed, I exhaled a breath and relaxed, remembering that this had happened sometimes. Other patrons sought Syler's wisdom and would leave before sunrise, with the exception of Frek, who eventually never left at all.

Returning to the present, I sighed loudly, finishing another glass of wine. Lowering my cup, I found myself looking deeply into Knomucca's eyes, my sudden awareness of my staring made apparent as the wine pulsed through my system. We held each other's stare for a long moment, my heart pounding like the hammer I possessed. Feeling as though I should find an excuse for my behavior, I moved to stand, placing my cup on the table and sliding back on my chair when Knomucca finally broke away.

Frek had suddenly materialized beside Knomucca, his face betraying his momentary annoyance. Anger flashed through me, and I returned his glare with one of my own, pouring another glass of wine as I fixed him with a piercing stare. Normally, Frek and I got on well enough, though in a few nights' time, the moon would be full once more, and thus, Frek's moods were rather unpredictable. Frek had been encouraged to practice managing his behavior as of late, for he was recently promoted from a soldier to Diplomat alongside Kiyoko this past season. He would need to maintain his composure whilst searching far-off realms for treasure, negotiating peace, and assisting in forming trade alliances. His acute animal sense of smell made him perfect for sniffing out hard-to-find paragons. However, his loyalty was his greatest treasure of all.

Knomucca shifted in her chair, smiling as Syler spoke over her wine goblet. With a gesture of Knomucca's hand, Frek was invited to sit, the three beginning to speak immediately. Turning away, I decided to finish the leftover food abandoned on Kiyoko's plate, taking the chunks of potatoes and popping them into my mouth satisfactorily. Slowly, my breathing calmed, and my pulse slowed as I settled from such intensity.

Perhaps I ought to turn in for the night, I thought with a shake of my head.

On the morrow, we would depart on our journey to The Heart, where Knomucca would accept full power as Goddess of Death. The Heart was an ornate Ascension Temple in the South at Riverside, a grand trading port three days' ride from the castle. The Heart contained the keys to travel to other realms, which would allow Knomucca to bring The Creator into the Underworld for her Ascension. In the temple, she would perform an elaborate ritual, creating a complicated potion as an offering to Him. If the Creator deemed her worthy, he would appear to her and finish The Ascension, elevating her into the divine. While all this took place, a small, trusted guard would stand outside the temple to keep Knomucca and The Creator safe.

After stuffing my supper and thoughts to fulfillment, I rose to leave. My subordinate, Kyreese, noticed me stand and she scurried over, weaving artfully between chairs and servants. Standing in front of me, she saluted, gently thumping her fist over her heart in quick succession, then leaving it to rest there while waiting for my permission before she spoke.

"At ease, Sergeant," I said.

"Good evening, Commander," Kyreese said, her voice gentle and warm as she lowered her hand.

"What can I do for you?"

"I counted the rations before dinner this evening. You'll find the parchment hanging in the stables, if you desire to glance it over."

"I shall consult you if I am in need of reference," I said, disliking reading in large amounts except when it was required of me. "How were all of our supplies fairing?"

"Everything that has been previously loaded, is present and accounted for."

"Excellent, I shall reward you with my pride."

I gifted Kyreese a salute. She smiled, returning my salute with one of her own. Her mahogany skin shimmered and shined in the surrounding candlelight, the glow sparkling down her arms as her sleeves were short and made of lace. Her wine-purple hair was in its usual braid down the length of her body, thrumming with an energy that made it feel alive. Her legs were muscular and toned, adding disproportionate curves to her gaunt and petite upper body.

"Do feel inclined to reward yourself and celebrate this evening, though be certain you get lots of rest," I continued. "As you know, we leave early in the morrow."

"Aye, Commander, be certain you do as well," Kyreese said with a serious expression.

"Aye... Kyreese..." I grumbled at the young Sergeant.

"With all due respect, sir, you are aware I do not appreciate being referred to by my given name," she said flatly, trying to conceal her scowl.

"My apologies..." I said dismissively. "My exhaustion appears to have the better of me."

Kyreese – Kye – I had to remind myself of her chosen name – smiled, her earlier annoyance quickly fading. "I overheard some of the lads at supper claiming the Chief was going to let us play Slayer tonight... would you be interested in having a go?" She asked, obviously excited about the game. "A hearty bout of Slayer could gift you a good night's rest."

I released a tense breath, wishing I could find myself passing the time winning coin from the rookies and celebrating the coming Festess with a rousing game of Slayer.

"Thank you kindly, though I must decline," I said, understanding it was best not to allow myself to be threatened by such temptation.

"Frek ought to be there," Kye teased, gifting me a subtle laugh as she gestured crudely. "You could attempt to settle the score from your last bout with him..."

"I shall admit the notion is tempting," I said, shaking my head, the motion loosening my hair. "Though I simply shall have to hope I will be gifted another time to face him."

"Knomucca knows we are to play this evening," Kye said in her final attempt to persuade me.

"I find this irrelevant," I spat a little too angrily. Taking a deep breath, I softened my tone as I continued. "Her Worship is hoping to find everyone alert and ready to commence in the morrow... and that best be remembered."

"It shall be," Kye said, exasperated. She rolled her eyes dramatically, her youth plain and sparkling mischievously through her aura. "'Twas said only to entice your company, 'twasn't meant to cause you harm or annoyance."

"I simply do not wish to ask her favor or pardon," I said seriously, ignoring her rowdiness as it was normal for a girl with seventeen years to her name. "If the game escalates and becomes too dangerous, please do not hesitate to find an alternative pastime to occupy your evening."

"Aye, Commander... I beseech thee, keep your faith."

"I shall do so indeed," I said with a nod, "though I still felt it wise to remind you of such cautions with The Ascension approaching."

"Aye Commander. We will not disappoint you."

"That would be preferable," I said, meeting her eyes with a serious expression I had received many times from my father. "Will that be everything then?"

"Aye, 'tis all I had," Kye said with a salute.

"Excellent," I said with a nod, saluting in return before edging towards Valvang's side entrance. "I'll be on my way then... See you at first light."

"Stay wise, Commander," Kye called after me, then disappeared in the throng of castle folk heading towards the Southern Sanctuary.

Pushing through the heavy iron doors, I wandered into the cold twilight. A loud bang came from behind me, cutting me off from the castle's warmth and noise. The path to my tower was long and cold with the coming autumn, tempting me with a smoke while I began walking. I placed the spliff between my lips and lit it on a torch nearby, leaning in closely to touch the spliff to the flames. The herbs ignited with a gentle sizzle, coaxing my lips to curl in a smile.

Having imbibed too much wine, my steps felt heavy, and once or twice, I nearly lost my footing. I ambled past the library, stomping onto the bridge that crossed over a small creek. The keep's towers were bright, filling the night sky with glowing, colorful flames that would lead me to my chambers.

I spotted the barracks tower, turned left and walked through a small, tranquil courtyard. Vast evergreens, arching cherry blossoms, and mighty maples punctuated the clearing, surrounding a ceramic fountain of a Naiads spitting water from her mouth. Due to the imbalance in the realm, winter threatened to come early, sprinkling a light sparkly frost over the rocks that made up the fountain. I was uncertain whether it was the wine or my lack of sleep, though even the Naiads herself appeared affected by the chill. Knowing the snow would be gone by morning forced me to stop and admire the statue and enjoy the way the crystals in the thin ice glistened on the water's surface.

As I contemplated the fountain, I recalled that the twins built this water feature on the grounds after their studies of Crossfire's previous Prospects. During that time, the dead were ruled by Ozwal the Great. He was one of the closest death god Prospects to ascend aside from Knomucca. However, his reign abruptly ended with his mysterious disappearance. He had met his demise when his ship unexpectedly sank, though the myths theorize Naiads seduced him and captured his craft. Nobody can confirm the stories, though; on a harvest moon's night, some swore they saw the silhouette of large sails gliding across the horizon.

Crossing the courtyard, I brushed against fluffy pine branches as I ducked between the trees. Slipping through a slatted wooden door, I climbed the creaking, spiraling stairs into the barracks.

I yawned deeply and rounded the corner, wishing I had had the energy to tour the orchards instead of returning inside for the evening. As I approached, the torches illuminated a narrow hallway scented with rosemary. Veering sharply, I followed it to the left. I began to whistle a jaunty tune as I walked, enjoying the echo of my melody through the darkened passageways until I found a ladder off to the righthand side. The rungs were cold against my skin, the chill of the iron sobering against my palms as I grasped my fingers around them.

I placed my heavy boots against the ladder, climbing the rungs two at a time as my footing had become second nature. I pulled my body through a slim bamboo hatch, reaching my bunk on an open platform amongst the soldiers' barracks. My loft rested at a height advantageous to observe the remainder of the troops from my quarters, allowing me to peer through an immense glass window framed in the center of the floor.

Turning rightwards, I spotted my bunk on the far wall, moving across the floor with quiet footing as an act of respect for those resting. Glancing to my left, I noticed my neighboring loft had been occupied, the overhead lamp ablaze with soft light as Ajax lay resting.

"Good evening, Commander," she said, recognizing my presence from the pattern of my footfalls.

"Fair evening, Colonel," I said in greeting.

Colonel Ajax, third in command of the Gods' Guard after Kiyoko, lay sprawled naked across the top of her loft. Her left arm was draped over her chest, tastefully covering her breasts from view. Her wavy, currant-red hair was knotted around her legs and waist, keeping her warm like a thick blanket. Her legs were long like the halberd she oft carried into battle, her aim precise and wicked as her tongue.

"Off to sleep?" Ajax began as she rolled slightly, her muddied-brown eyes meeting mine. "Or are you simply here to freshen up before indulging in the evening's frivolity?"

Ajax spoke, adjusting her body as she shifted against her sheets. A soft leather cover of a neatly bound book peaked from beneath her hair, the feather of a hawk pressed between the parchment as it held her place within the tome. Ajax moved her hair subtly with a sweep of her hand, concealing the book beneath the cover of her curls with a motion so swift a blink could have missed it.

"Reckon I am in for the evening..." I said, hanging my hammer on its hook beneath my loft. "Much wine was to be had at supper, and there is an early start to the morrow..."

"Where is the General?" Ajax inquired, the relief I had not asked about her book plain.

"Kiyoko is off galavanting," I said, climbing up the ladder and collapsing facedown onto my bed.

"I suppose he is entitled to some mischief every now and again," Ajax said with a wink. "Although... the pair of you have been separated quite frequently as of late..."

"We have had much to do," I agreed warily.

"May I inquire as to with whom he passes his evening?" Ajax asked, raising an eyebrow suspiciously. "Is he playing cups in Valvang with the server lads again?"

"He is playing the role of guest elsewhere this evening," I said, shrugging a shoulder. "He'll probably make his way to the Orchards once the night progresses."

"He certainly enjoys the Orchards," Ajax said with a nod. "During my post on the night watch this season past I noticed him and Her Worship spending a fair lot of time together in the Orchards... their sparring sessions seemed very intimate -"

"I'm certain they were following protocol," I confirmed, failing to pry my reddened face from my pillow. A green wave of envy flashed through my energy, the notion that the pair of them should be spending time together in the orchards without my presence aggravating me.

"Oi, drank the entire tankard at supper, have you?" Ajax asked as I glanced towards her.

I blinked my eyes rapidly, shaking my head hard to clear it as abstract shapes and blurs began overlapping Ajax in her bed.

"Worried you wouldn't sleep I reckon..." Ajax continued when I failed to speak, rolling lazily onto her side once more.

"Aye... the morrow shall require me to be at my finest, and I reckon I could use a hefty night's rest."

A silence swept through the Officers' Quarters, filled with my heavy breathing as I began to speak again.

"Have you finished all your work for the evening?" I asked, wishing I could drift away to sleep.

"Aye. Everything is as prepared as it can be," Ajax said with a heavy sigh.

Forcing my eyes closed, I took a deep breath, regaining my center before I spoke.

"Very good," I said, releasing the breath I was holding. "Some of the troops are playing Slayer before they turn in. You could join them and have a little fun if you wanted."

"I could say the same to you, Commander." I heard the rustle of her blankets as she shifted to a seat. "Though... perhaps you would prefer if I were to join you over there instead and we had a little fun of our own?"

I released a breath, slightly annoyed at myself for wanting to indulge in her body on nights when I was lonely.

"I'm washed too far downstream I reckon," I said as a way to deny her advances.

"I am a fairly decent swimmer," Ajax purred.

I waved a hand nonchalantly, having ended my occasional nights with her several months prior as I discovered she was developing feelings for me. I did not wish to confuse her further. My body and manhood may have needs, though my heart did not belong to her, and it was not befitting of my station to spend nights with a subordinate in such a manner. "Nevertheless... I am contented where I am."

"If you're certain," Ajax said, settling back in the sheets again. "Should you find your way back upstream, I reckon you know where to find me."

"I suppose I do," I said.

"Will you be well in the morrow, Commander?"

"I will be fine," I said, rubbing my face hard with my hand. "Though, I could use a smoke if you had any to spare."

"Definitely," Ajax said, ruffling the sheets as she rose from her loft. Her wardrobe doors creaked and squeaked, following the soft thud of her feet hitting the floor. I then felt the shaking of my loft as she climbed up the ladder. My mattress sank with her weight as she crawled towards my head, brushing the soft fur of a robe she now wore across my arm.

Ajax looped her long hair around her legs and sat beside me. I heard the familiar strike of a match and immediately smelled the deliciously sweet smoke. Her inhale was deep and long, making the herbs whistle as the moisture burned away from them. After two long drags, Ajax reached down, placing the tightly rolled smoke between my fingers.

"Aye, much gratitude for this Ajax," I said, enjoying how the sweet grass tasted fruity across my tongue. The smoke had been rolled in the skin of an onion, gifting a pungent kick I immensely enjoyed.

"It's my pleasure," Ajax said, watching my lips as I placed the spliff between them. "Could I ask you something, Everett? Consider it payment for the smoke."

A sinking feeling fluttered through my stomach, my face growing serious as I met Ajax's eyes. "Certainly... what is it you wish to know?"

"Your current mood... You're very drunk and a bit hostile..." Ajax laughed as she saw the annoyance flash through my face. "This isn't just in response to your fear of not sleeping... you decided not to confess to Knomucca your feelings whilst sparring, and now you're in a rage..."

I inhaled deeply, spilling burning smoke from my nostrils.

"You'd be correct of course," I said, deciding not to lie, though omitting my fleeting annoyance towards Kiyoko for his hassling me at supper.

Ajax and I had become close during the last several years. Until this season passed, her bunk was on the opposite wall of the barracks, her sleeping quarters transitioning to their current post after Frek's promotion to Quartermaster. We enjoyed each other and our company, talking intensely until the hour of the blue jay to fully disclose the haunts of our hearts. When my insomnia overtook me, it was nice to have her company. However, I always sought the chance to pass the nights with Kiyoko or Knomucca when the opportunity presented itself.

The most recent season had led to more tense conversations, her emotions strung high and fierce as I secretly challenged her and her character. Per Knomucca's request, I was to dissect the minds of the specially selected guards chosen to take Syler to The Far North. Ajax, along with Frek, would be leading the ranks. With the help of Kiyoko, we probed the soldiers with truth serums, spells, and situations to learn their truest intentions and darkest confessions, all whilst concealing our true actions with a clever word or whit.

Ajax was a natural conversationalist, our time always spilling over into the late hours of the night, even after her interrogations had finished. I respected her honest input and audacious attitude. We spoke thoroughly, and over time, Ajax learned as much of me as I had of her. Eventually, she learned of my feelings for Knomucca and my desire to express my devotion despite my fears.

"And why not?" she asked.

"It wasn't the right time," I said assertively.

"Come now Everett," Ajax said, taking the smoke from my hand. "We spoke at length about this."

"Aye, you know the situation is more complicated than that," I said, blowing out a tight ring of smoke. "I will not be the one offering distraction and risking the ruin of the realms. I shall wait until a later time to disclose my feelings... If I ever do at all."

"You're being daft," Ajax said. "She will be immortal then, and you will age into an old man. How are you expecting to spend your life with her then?"

"I can not tell her now," I said with a note of finality. "She has the realms to protect, and her duty lies with them."

"Everett, if you tell her later, you risk her falling from Grace for you. Could you live with yourself if she betrayed the gods?"

A long silence fell between us. Eternal damnation awaits those who have accepted the blood of The Creator and rid their bodies of mortal impurities only to betray Him or be corrupted by the weaknesses of man. Legends of The First Warrior disclose that his Fall from Grace occurred from his desire to give up The Power to remain mortal and spend his life with his lover. The Creator was furious Anteyus would rather have chosen a mortal man over supreme power and eternal reign, so He punished him. The First Warrior was strong and fought for his life well, dealing The Creator a blow that has scarred Him to this day. Though in the end, The Creator trapped his soul to spend forever alone and miserable, those who value love and war will always worship Anteyus as our true god.

"I know her better than that," I said after a moment's contemplation, "she fought hard to get this far. She will not put the realms through any more hell, and she will not waste all the work she has done."

"You are willing to wager a life of regret and your happiness on this?"

"I must. It is worth loving her from afar and watching her succeed than risking everything for a love that is not meant to be."

"Your logic is moronic," Ajax said, producing another smoke from the pocket of her robes, "though it is you who shall have to live with the choice."

"Ajax?"

"Aye, Commander?"

"Thank you kindly."

"For what exactly?"

"For your support. And for defending Knomucca, Syler, and the realms. I am trusting you all with their lives, and I am pleased in knowing you will not disappoint them."

"We are honored to serve the Prospects," Ajax said. "And do us all a favor; try not to get yourself killed out there."

"I will do my best," I said, chuckling as I polished off the smoke and discarded the ashes.

When my tiredness was too much to bear, I dismissed Ajax back to her bunk. Pulling up the thick blue blankets, I exhaled at length, feeling my muscles slacken as the weight of the day left my shoulders. Slowly, my pulse relaxed, my breathing deepening as I began to meditate. My eyes drifted closed, and my thoughts began to wander as I wondered how Knomucca faired. Her golden blonde hair floated through my mind's eye, her luxurious skin draped in an iced blue silk dress.

May your night be well, I implored, speculating upon the last-minute preparations she had to attend to. May you find rejuvenation when all your tasks are completed.

Vivid, swirling images of Knomucca brightened suddenly, the smells of leather and coltsfoot dancing across my aura. I relished in Knomucca's silken hair, reveling in the way her eyes glowed in the firelight. I caressed her curvaceous waist, inhaling her deeply as we kissed with fierce, open mouths.

"Everett," her voice whispered through my dreaming, "I love you, Everett."

Intense pleasure and warmth flooded through me as I finally drifted to sleep, relishing in my fantasies of making love with her amongst her sheets beside the fireplace.

III

KNOMUCCA

Chatza cleared the remaining dishes from Valvang, clanking the cutlery loudly with the other servants. Though passionate drunken storytelling had filled the air with noise, voices were beginning to die down. The light from the overhead candles extinguished, the smell of lavender wafting into the hall deliciously.

Inhaling the fragrance, I rose from my seat, sliding my chair backwards in what felt like a squeaking screech in the growing quiet. My table was still fairly crowded, gifted as my sister and I had become with the company of our advisors. Everyone grew still when they noticed my movements, though I indicated I had no final words to say to them with a wave of my hand. Laughter and wine flowed once more like water, causing me to linger momentarily to relish in its simplicities.

"...It was enormous," Frek said in the middle of a story on his latest expedition in Diah. "This cave must have had twenty passages leading underground, most of which were covered in a brown sticky goo. After a good day's digging, I found the most peculiar orange rocks incubating in the mud. I discovered them to be Trasper eggs, so hot their golden speckled shells burned my fingers upon their harvest."

"Trasper eggs are excellent in potions of fertility," Syler said over her glass of wine.

"Aye, so they say," Frek said. "I wanted to bring them home to you, however, they did not survive the journey. Their shells are rather fragile, and they tragically cracked in my saddle bags. After The Ascension I am hoping to return to the caves to retrieve more and continue with my studies, as I will be without you."

"Frek, how sweet," Syler said, setting down her glass to stare into his face. Their eyes met with a fierce intensity. Grateful for the lull in conversation, I turned to disappear in the throng of scattering servants pushing empty iron carts shuffled down the Western corridor, and I turned to follow them. The glossy granite walls veered in all directions, echoing with voices and rattling wheels as the servants sought the leftmost passageway. Their chaos and noise faded as I continued onward, causing my ears to buzz and thrum in the emptiness they had left behind.

Sconces overhead lit the oncoming night, casting large silhouettes across the reflective stone. A fluffed red carpet covered the gradually expanding floor, muffling my oncoming footsteps into a vestibule with large windows. Dark shadows stretched long in the torchlight, encroaching upon the canvassed granite walls of the surprisingly cozy room. The hallway grew and split again, branching off where blue-hot flames licked an elevated granite fireplace.

Firelight illuminated the outline of an iron statue in the far-left corner. The Moon Goddess, Senaya, rode atop a rearing unicorn, aiming her bow east towards the sky. The silver of her hair sticks shone brightly, sparkling defiantly through the braided metal. Her aim was steady, and her eyes were calculated, the smell of sandalwood a familiar comfort through the small alcove. Casually feeling past the face of Senaya's unicorn, I slipped into a narrow opening in the wall behind it. Her moonstone eyes burrowed down my spine, eliciting a shudder as I turned a sharp corner to the right.

The thin passageway ran north, twisting harshly past iron piping and lanterns. Mossy brick walls were visible through the cracks of old abandoned windows, lending an element of eeriness that made me walk faster. A slender stone-carved staircase came into view, the righthand side curving into the darkness. Only my practiced senses from years of taking this path could have recognized the steep, slippery steps unfriendly to anyone who traversed them too quickly.

I proceeded up the stairs. Five steps passed, ten, then twenty, carrying me up smoothly like water. After one hundred stairs, the stone walls squeezed together, leading me beneath a sharply cracked ledge, causing me to kneel and crawl forward. Curling my hand, I made a fist, rapping my knuckles repeatedly across jagged rocks in the damp darkness. The stone lurched quickly with a click, forcing a square panel of light to open at eye level.

Wriggling forward, I squirmed through the opening, pulling my body up to rest on a wooden ledge. Kicking my feet out, I dropped down, skimming my shoulder on the bookshelf standing tall behind me. A book jutted outwards next to my right knee, waiting patiently for me to push it back neatly on the shelf. The panel above me closed as the book fell into place, sealing the passage from my chambers to hide it beyond the walls.

My chambers were quite ostentatious, and I enjoyed them immensely. A large stone-carved altar took up most of the back-west corner, overlooking a small window into the sky. The altar allowed me to center my blessings and energies towards other gods, spirits, or mortals. Each of my altars were connected spiritually, enabling me to receive messages or energies from any shrine I made. The space was covered in gems, herbs, candles, and oils surrounding a five-headed chiseled wooden hydra. After The Ascension, I planned on redecorating my altar to reflect my new station, lining it with carnelian and changing the stone to obsidian. I planned to light candles upon the stone to scent the room delightfully, perfuming the air in cinnamon, vanilla, crisping apples, and pine whenever I should desire it.

I walked further into the chambers, smiling as I routinely admired the softly sparkling sapphire walls. Large bookcases took up the east wall, surrounding a large walk-in closet lined with red silken carpet. The brewing station rested in the south-west corner, temporarily obscured by a sumptuous orange velvet curtain. A mountainous, feathery bed was nestled between the altar and a bookcase, stretching to cover most of the north wall. A massive square window cast light across the bed every morning, warming the sheets with the rising of the sun.

A pair of stained-glass doors opened to an expansive balcony between my altar and brewing station. The smooth, white marble spread out wide against the outer walls. My dragon, Thornin, used the balcony to take off and land whenever we flew from the castle. Thornin was a fibrous, deep jasper dragon gilded in gold with a head crowned with spikes. The leather of his dark purple wings was malleable like the scales on his underbelly, his toned and chiseled muscles forming tight ridges across his abdomen. Trenchant claws were regularly sharpened against the golden-tipped spikes of his tail. His demeanor was unfriendly at best, disguising the gentle soul and good-natured heart dwelling beneath scales sharp as broken glass. His eyes alluded to his gentleness, their ice-blue irises invoking fear should his mood be unaffectionate. Even curled up and sleeping, Thornin was enormous, measuring eighteen meters from his snout to the tip of his tail. The setting sun was painted pleasantly across him as he basked in the remaining glow.

In the southeast corner of my chambers, a heavy wicker rocking chair was covered in blankets. The chair rested beside an immense brick-lined fireplace adorned with an elaborate mantel. Horseshoes punctuated the mantelpiece, intertwined with metal roses and statues of the moon. Flames licked across a charred pine log, adding an earthy aroma to the air, which I eagerly inhaled.

Entering the closet on my right, I slid out of my boots and leggings. After doffing my shirt, I decided on my evening gown, beginning to dress beside the floor-length mirror. The ice-blue gown was lace around the neck, forming into sheer grey silk across my back. Ribbon-lined and exceptionally low cut, the soft fabric tapered around my torso, exposing the owl inked along my rib cage.

Checking my reflection, I made one final adjustment. My current pair of gauntlets were much too dark for my appearance. Approaching the rack where they hung, I scanned the options, weighing through the selections as I decided which I fancied. The Healer enchanted every pair to house spirits and stabilize my soul. In undertaking The Gods Trials, pieces of myself had been lost in the Underworld. The Creator put forward several challenges to educate me and examine my worth. I fought demons, willingly sacrificed blood and flesh, and learned of the terrors held within the Seven Rings of Hell without my mother knowing I had been doing so. I watched as insanity decayed the unstable and underwent a myriad of traumas to attempt to prove I could embody the power.

Offering a guiding hand to the spirits travelling to the Underworld, my soul began to decay, slowly rotting the flesh of my hands. As my essence continues to decompose and I familiarize myself with the dead, I learn to take and manipulate souls. In my goddess form, I will be able to recycle spirits, carrying them from one life to live anew in the next. I could cast souls asunder into torturous realms, banishing them to a life of eternal misery and pain. My Ascension would allow me to create paradises or hells unique to each spirit according to the life they had lived. The gauntlets help soften the pain of my condition and allow me to interact with the physical plane and bodies of the living. Our bodies were to be cherished as vessels that carry life. Upon my Ascension, I would no longer need the gauntlets. The Creator will infuse me with His blood, binding me to His essence and the Realms between the living and the dead.

On the third shelf from the top, I found a pair of gauntlets that satisfied me. Forged fingerless, they protected only the back of the hand and wrist. White leather padded the metal beneath them, softening the sharp edges of the hooks and clasps. Small chains braided across the knuckles, widening to light grey emerald-encrusted iron plates covering the back of my hands.

The gauntlets clinked and chimed softly as I removed them from the shelf, placing them on a nearby hook whilst I undid the buckles on my current pair. Unfastening my left gauntlet, I prepared for the agony of the transformation. A sharp burst of pain shot up to my elbow as the air caressed the back of my hand. I cringed as my skin turned cold; the phantom black flesh withered with a sudden searing stab that made my fingers convulse.

I winced in misery as white-hot energy surged from my fingertips, releasing a small wave of heat from my skin. Blue blood throbbed heavily through bulging white veins, swirling into an etched, runic symbol of the life cycle on my palms. The skin cracked and flaked, shedding dried blood the way a snake sheds its skin.

Unclasping the new gauntlet, I crammed my hand quickly inside. Taking a deep breath, I relaxed, allowing my hand to temporarily heal. I inwardly flinched as the bones shifted, returning my hand to its original state and color. Violently, I shook out my fingers, feeling my knuckles tingle as blood returned to them. Tightening the straps, I ensured the gauntlet was secure, containing the spreading decay to my hands for the time being. I swore softly as I freed my fingers from the opposite gauntlet, glaring in disgust as I witnessed the transformation once more. Quickly, I donned the second gauntlet, pulling it on and clipping it closed before finally taking a relaxing breath.

After glancing at my renewed reflection, I turned to leave the closet. Pausing by a rack of knives hanging on my left, I selected one with a golden handle. I turned to the right and stepped over the closet's threshold, hearing the whispers of my dress across the ground behind me.

My attention turned to my potion, which had been started at midday before my sparring session with Everett. It sat cooling in a chilled stone mortar. This Dragon Scale Armor potion was a recipe that had been given to me by my mother before she died, to consume before my ascension. It would offer temporary physical and psychic protection as I ascended and accepted the Creator's Blood.

My cauldron, enchanted to turn any element into a liquid, rested in waiting atop a bundle of cherry logs. It roared to life when lit with a nearby match, sizzling slightly as the metal began to heat. Grabbing a wooden scraper from beside the mortar, I lifted the stone bowl, brushing my chopped ingredients into the cast iron with a light pattering. Returning the mortar to its place, I fetched a scroll from the lectern on my left, flattening out the parchment before I could begin.

Add large chunks of cinnamon, sage, and obsidian to form a base.

Having followed the instructions, I proceeded to the second step with pride and satisfaction.

Add a dark red wine of your choice to the mixture, bringing the solution to a boil.

Returning quickly to my altar, I perused through the selection of wines I had crafted in the castle's brewery as one of my favorite pastimes. Much of my schooling took place with Hazel in the brewery, for studying the elements and their connections was best done actively and with my hands. The Priestess was responsible for much of the castle's education, including teaching alchemy, enchantments, and explaining magical theory.

Deep, bitter wine was one of The Creator's many gifts. I enjoyed wasting an afternoon of luxury transforming a myriad of fruits and other elements into such divine nectar. I had become quite talented in the art. I enjoyed my experimentations. Crushing the fruit through the barrels was incredibly cathartic, whilst watching them ferment and bubble was always a calming influence.

A stained-glass bottle with a deep red brew stood out amongst the sea of scarlets and sangrias, the slim bottle resting snugly on the bottom shelf of my collection. Sliding it from the rack, I read the label; the words "Dragon's Blood," written in dark black ink, were stark against the pale parchment.

"Quite applicable," I said, smirking as I ran my fingers over the glass.

I yearned for the pitaya wine, the longing to have the night free of responsibility weighing on my spirits with the upcoming Sabbat. My smile turned to a sigh as I crossed back to my brewing station and uncorked the bottle. I decanted the wine with a satisfying sizzle, smelling a delicious cloud of sweet rouge floating in the air. Grabbing a wooden spoon, I stirred in the ingredients, abrading melting sage from the bottom of the cauldron with vicious scrapes.

Stirring occasionally, I waited for the wine to boil. Fruity, earthy aromas drifted up in the hot steam, warming my cheeks and making me sweat. A quarter-hour passed before the cauldron began to bubble, bursting in large red glops that popped and crackled. When the mixture was ready, I lifted the scroll once more, moving to the third step in my sequence of directions.

Combine sweet grass, sugarcane, and thirteen Tora berries in a stone mortar until creamy.

Stooping down, I searched through the plethora of drawers, doors, and shelves beneath my brewing stand, obtaining the ingredients from my baskets of botanicals. I placed them in a smooth stone mortar and began to crush them.

Lifting the mortar towards the cauldron, I scooped the mixture into the swirling potion, avoiding the scorching liquid that threatened to splash my arms and burn my fingers. I stirred in the elements and waited for a short moment, watching as the liquid lightened from red to skylight blue. The chunks within the mixture began to dissolve, turning the brew periwinkle with a spicy scent.

"Excellent," I said in satisfaction, smiling as I returned the mortar to its place.

Picking up the scroll, I continued to read, swiping my fingers down the parchment to follow the path of my eyes.

Collect blood from your right hand using a dagger, binding the wine and elements.

Raising my palm, I prepared for the familiar sting of the blade as I drew the golden knife across my skin. Blood dripped down into the potion below as I offered not only the sanguine liquid but my vital life energies as well, sending a hot puff of orange smoke harshly towards my face. Leaning backwards, I avoided the heat, clenching my fist to drizzle more blood into the potion. My hand throbbed, and my head felt warm, signaling to my brain that I had offered enough of my essences.

"Accept my blood, which has been willingly given."

Inhaling deeply, I released a cleansing breath, adjusting my gauntlets once more. Squatting down, I examined the drawers and doors beneath the brewing stand, locating a swatch of sturdy cloth to wrap my wound. Opening a chilled drawer on my left, I obtained a tankard of water, drinking it dry as I attempted to replenish my spirits.

"Water isn't enough," I whispered, squatting once more and rifling through my botanicals.

Opening the clasp on a hempen woven basket, I found my reserves of cacao, a delicacy I cherished for its magical value and delicious bliss. Consuming the bean after a major energy expense helps one find balance and rejuvenate one's spirits. I would require the assistance of this botanical after sacrificing my energies and blood, for offering such a vital part of myself was overwhelming and exhausting. Seizing a handful of the cacao, I rose to a stand, placing a large piece into my mouth to enjoy its rich bitterness.

A stroke of insight floated through me, my eyes flitting suddenly to the remainder of the cacao I held loosely in my fist. Extending my hand, I brought it over the roaring cauldron, dropping the chunks into the potion without hesitation, knowing it would help protect against corruption. The mixture turned a deep forest green instead of its intended sanded yellow, releasing black-tinted smoke into the air in a billowing swirl.

"How magnificent," I said once my cacao had been finished. "Such a glorious shade... reminds me of the lusciousness of the trees and surrounding woods..."

I drank three goblets of water, consuming an additional three of the cacao fruits before feeling hydrated and refreshed. Checking my progress another time, I reread my scroll, stirring my potion liberally before feeling comfortable enough to continue.

Next, add three ground dragon scales to the mixture.

Setting down the scroll, I left the brewing station, returning across the room and retrieving dragon scale gloves from the closet. The gloves were intricately crafted by my own hand using Thornin's fallen scales. Following my path traveled, I moved through the center of my chambers, making my way through the balcony doors into the crisp evening air. Thornin inhaled sharply, his eyes shot open; his sleeping jarred without warning as my footsteps approached him.

"Greetings, my sweet." I stared into his sleepy face and smiled broadly, slipping on the gloves before tracing over the bones and muscles in his cheeks.

Gingerly, I moved my hand over his roughened snout, pinching it gently between my fingers. Thornin snorted out a puff of hot steam from his nostrils, reaching his bristly tongue to kiss my arm. I dragged my thumb deeply across his jawline, massaging him in a favorite spot between his eye and mouth. His eyes closed into slits as he blissfully sighed, ready to fall contentedly back to sleep with my pats and scratches.

"That is a good lad," I soothed gently. My eyes scanned up and down his front, flittering to the first loose scale I noticed on his right leg. "Would you mind too terribly if I were to take some of your loose scales?"

Thornin sputtered out a grunt, blowing hot air across my cheeks.

"Oi, you are dramatic."

Thornin licked my hand forcefully, nibbling happily on my gloved fingers with his coarse and grating lips.

"Aye, that's a good lad," I said again, rubbing my thumb roughly against his inner ear.

I dropped my hand down to the scale slowly, all the while petting with the grain of his body. Passing over his warm, bumpy shoulder, I moved down him to find the loose scale near the top of his foot. I rubbed the scale with my thumb and forefinger, wiggling and tugging to pry it out of place. Thornin growled, angrily jerking his leg away.

"I'm sorry, Sweetness," I soothed, "I'm not trying to hurt you." Thornin hissed, blowing a gust of thick smoke into my face and making me cough. When the cloud cleared, I kissed the side of his head, growling playfully in return as I moved my hands down his body. "I just need a few more, and I'll leave you be."

On the bottom of his foot, I found two more scales hanging by thick skin strips near the pads of his paws. A quick tug had the scales sliding free, a dot of crimson dripping to the floor. Thornin flattened his ears, growling low and baring his teeth in a sneer. His tail shot forward in an arc towards my face, forcing me to swerve sharply left to avoid it. Despite my reflexes, his tail painfully skimmed my torso, causing my shoulder to burn with the pain of a biting fire.

"Forgive me, my sweet," I said, grabbing hold of his face and meeting his eyes. "Those scales were not as loose as they appeared, else I wouldn't have taken them."

Thornin glared into my face, taking long, deep breaths before settling again.

"Are we well?" I asked him, relieved when he gently nibbled my fingers, having decided not to tear off my hand. Roughly scratching and patting his enormous body, I discovered two more chipped and broken scales down by his belly. Tentatively, I prodded them with a finger, then gently collected them into my hand. My recipe only called for three scales, though I intuitively knew that adding an abundance would improve the potion's strength.

The dragon released a deep breath, exhaling a steady stream of steam. "Aye, we're happy again, are we?"

Grabbing his paws, I massaged and rubbed them vigorously. I moved my hands up his left front leg, finding another pair of loosened scales behind his knee. Twisting and tugging, I pulled them free, hearing another growl rumble through Thornin.

"You're unharmed, Thornin," I said, catching his tail as it neared my face. Acting on instinct, I pulled it playfully, giving it a forceful squeeze. Thornin's eyes sparkled mischievously as he swiped at me with his claws and rolled onto his back. Quickly, I took three more scales that dangled from his belly, ducking as he snapped at my hair with his massive jaws.

"Oi, enough," I said, coughing through the immense cloud of smoke Thornin huffed through his nose. I rose to my feet and held his face again, staring sternly into his eyes to indicate I was done playing. He met my gaze with a challenging expression, daring me to deny him a reason to choose affection over violence. I held my composure though my heart was pounding, aware of every breath and subtle movement he made. Finally, after a long and tense moment, he lowered his eyes, continuing to clench his jaws but allowing me to release him.

"I love you," I said, planting a firm kiss in a soft spot between his eyes.

Blowing out hot air, he dropped his head to the floor, expressing no wish to interact with me further. Taking my leave, I shuffled the scales through my fingers, grateful for my luck in acquiring such an abundance. Checking my shoulder, I was relieved to see Thornin's tail left only a wide and shallow scratch through the cut in my dress, a wound easily tended with echinacea paste and a good night's sleep. I doffed my gloves in the closet and returned to the cauldron, holding the scales over the rim for a brief moment.

After thanking the gods for my good fortune, I dropped the scales into the smoking potion. The deep green liquid immediately began to change color, darkening, then lightening to a vibrant cherry red. Grabbing my wooden spoon, I started stirring, heavily grinding and folding the scales into the liquid before they fully dissolved. The mixture changed color again, filling the cauldron with a brilliant raspberry hue. As the liquid transformed, an intoxicating smell of treacle filled the air.

Nearly finished, I thought, having picked up the scroll and checked over the work I had completed thus far. Skimming down the page, my eyes fluttered to a stop, coming to rest on the final section of directions.

Lastly, add the myocardium to protect against what you crave most.

Squatting down, I opened a concealed drawer at knee height, sliding it smoothly forward in a flawless motion. Rummaging through jars and sacks, I found a decorative square glass container in the back, the lid sealed closed with patchouli-scented wax. As I pulled the container free, the glass clinked and chimed, noticing the fleshy brown mass that floated in a dark red goo. My mother's heart had changed in color since I saw it last. However, upon its appearance, the nightwort solution seemed to have preserved it otherwise. Using my dagger, I removed the wax seal, peeling back the lid and taking in the earthy scent of herbs.

Gingerly, I fished the dark, stringy muscle out of the jar. Holding it delicately in my hands, I cautiously lowered it into the cauldron, hearing a gentle sizzle as the heart submerged. Sadness stirred from deep within me, and I couldn't stop myself from thinking of my mother. Syler and I had been chosen at birth to endure The Gods Trials, as we were twins born of the equinox during the thinning of the veil. Our mother was born into a traveling coven of witches, her sisters blessing us in the elements with our birth upon the Autumnal Equinox. This combination of celestial events was most pleasing to The Creator, Him summoning my mother soon after our birth to move us here to Morriraen as we would endure the Trials.

My mother was furious, believing that death, darkness, madness, and the Realms of Hell were no place for a child. Pleading with The Creator, she demanded to take my place until I came of age, eventually exchanging her soul for my own and becoming the Death Goddess Prospect. She infused herself with the Essence of The Creator, assuming the power I would one day possess for myself. This decision had consequences, for my mother became terribly ill, resulting in her thinning hair and deathly pallor. She hid her disease well, pushing Syler and me to advance our studies, never hiding from us that one day, we would be forced to partake in the Trials. It was best to be armed with the most knowledge possible. While we studied, my mother fought against her illness, using long dresses and hoods to hide how her skin began to tighten around her skeleton. She cloaked her appearance from my twin, for they were incredibly close and had shared a bond I often envied. Mother did not wish for Syler to see her grow so weak, in fear Syler would hold blame against me for her death and decay.

Though my mother did her best to protect me from the Trials, The Creator never truly left me, visiting in dreams and bringing me into terrifying reaches of the Underworld. Through Him, I saw the realms for the damned, the places where I would send the most deserving evil of men if I only allowed myself to want to punish them. Through His hands, I dunked souls into torturous Rings of Hell, sealing the fate of the wretched who deserved to suffer for eternity. Through Him, I knew true oblivion and understood the twisted demons that lurked in the shadows and the spirits that could never be laid to rest.

Stirring the potion, I sighed softly, grateful for my mother's inheritance. Thinking of her in the Underworld, I sent her warmth and happiness, doing anything I could to bring light to her eternally dark days. I prayed and hoped this potion was a good enough way to honor her spirit, thanking her for the sacrifices she made to preserve my childhood and help me rise to power.

"Missing you, Mum..."

A sudden pounding on my chamber door broke my concentration. Peering to my left, I checked the time on the sundial, gasping when I realized how much time had passed. Eight hours since midday had come and gone, now making it the hour of the wolf. After hiding the scroll for the potion beneath a towering stack of books, I placed the hot and wet spoon on a flattened riverstone for safekeeping.

"You may enter," I declared over the bubbling cauldron, then drew the curtain to conceal the brewing potion.

Samarin sauntered through the chamber doors, confidently swaying his large shoulders as he moved. Floor-length black and crimson robes trailed smoothly after him, sweeping in silent gusts and swirls at his heels. Glittering blue eyes twinkled with an overbearing, unsettling charm, slyly sparkling over an alluringly beautiful smile. A head of sheer black hair accentuated a perfectly firm jawline and a row of straight, white teeth. His flawless skin and good looks made me feel unsettled around him, and his persuasive voice could be very distracting from his unfriendly and aggressive demeanor.

"Greetings," Samarin said, glancing toward my brewing station with just the flick of his eyes. "I hope I'm not interrupting anything important."

"Nonsense," I said. From the corner of my eye, I noticed Thornin lift his head, questioning with curious eyes who had disturbed his slumber. I whistled a command for him to relax, listening as he lowered his head back to the floor. Grabbing a small wooden stool from nearby, I sat in front of the drawn curtain, meeting Samarin's eyes. "Would you care to have a seat?"

"I'd prefer to stand," Samarin said, turning up his nose as he purposefully fingered the goat's head crescent pinned to his chest.

Taking a deep breath, I reminded myself to stay calm. Conversations with Samarin always caused me stress, though conversing with him was a necessity. Samarin was the realm's wealthiest noble, often residing in his largest estate in Poets' Cove, high in the Western mountains. His vast collection of land and resources further supported his many endeavors. Access to rare gems and metals drove Samarin to corruption and greed, fueled by his anger from the tragedies he had endured.

A plague had befallen the realms five years after I had begun The Gods Trials. It was a horrible disease, infecting nearly two thousand people and killing half as many. The Creator had forced me to release the plague, convincing me that spreading the sickness would be a way to cleanse the realms. I had told no one I had done this, intending to take this secret to my grave. However, I had managed to unburden myself of this secret, for I had a Grimoire in which I sometimes wrote of my most troubled thoughts, detailing them in ancient runes as I did not wish them easily decoded.

During the height of the plague, Samarin and his wife had befallen tragedy. They finally became blessed with a daughter after struggling for years to conceive. At five years to her name, his daughter, Daphnelle, had contracted the virus. Samarin had pleaded with the High Priestess, Head Alchemist Hazel, for wisdom and treatments, failing to accept that despite all of his wealth and connections, there was nothing that he could do to save the youngling. He fruitlessly begged me to spare her, knowing the illness would claim her life.

Samarin cleared his throat, dragging me back to the present.

"My pardons Samarin," I began, rising from my stool and approaching my altar. "It would appear I am a little more distracted than I thought. Perhaps some wine would settle my senses. Could I interest you?"

"I am very particular about my wines; I doubt you would have anything I fancy."

"I have a freshly crafted bottle of honeysuckle wine," I offered, knowing it was his preferred vintage.

"You can dispense with the pleasantries," Samarin said, his ocean-blue eyes turning as dark as the stormy seas. "We both know I am only here out of obligation."

I poured myself a serving of the honeysuckle wine, smiling secretly with spiteful satisfaction. Often, I felt the urge to slap Samarin senseless but refrained by constantly reminding myself that the realms depended on the food his farms and fiefs provided. However, my patience would not last forever, for I had spent many years trying to placate him. Three wagons of gold, fine furs, and books had been delivered to his estate every year during our Festival of the Dead. I expanded the castle's library and named it for his daughter, hoping Samarin would understand the true depths of my sorrow. My books are my most prized possession, as Daphnelle was his. Elaborate treasures and decorations always adorn Daphnelle's grave, along with a small yearly feast in remembrance of her in the palace's finest dining rooms.

None of it soothed him, however. Many of his food rations had arrived at the castle spoiled. On several occasions, he did not provide the proper amounts of grain and rice he had promised. Samarin's pockets ran as deep as the mines he possessed. Despite my best efforts, he thwarted any investigations and trials set against him. His anger and pain towards me were becoming frustrating to endure, yet I saw him every month in my chambers as I knew it was best to keep a close eye on him.

Finishing my wine, I poured myself another.

"Shall we begin our business?" asked Samarin.

"I suppose we must," I said, returning to my stool with my goblet and bottle in hand. "Let us begin with the agricultural report."

"Very well," he purred in a melodic voice, making my stomach churn. "A load of grain has been deposited at the castle gate, along with three carts of apricots. As you know, the harvest thus far was very plentiful, and we should have scores of foods saved for the winter to come."

"Excellent, for the Autumnal Equinox will soon be upon us."

"Aye, and won't that be your quarter-century Name Day?"

"I am actually beginning my third decade," I said.

"Oi, starting your third decade you say? That's another year come and gone under your reign. It has felt like an eternity thus far."

Not wishing to respond, I sipped my wine, feeling a raging fire burn in my palms, worrying it would heat my wine.

Samarin broke the silence. "Do you have any concerns with the agricultural report?"

"None that I can think," I said.

"Very well." Samarin said gruffly, "let us move onwards then."

"Aye, let us indeed." I released a breath before continuing. "Were you able to execute the task I had asked of you for this encounter?"

Samarin sighed to express his annoyance. Reaching a hand deep into the pockets of his robes, he produced a small canvas pouch. He walked across the room, boldly meeting my eyes as he placed the bag on the nearby table. Forcing a smile, I rose to retrieve the small sachet, exhaling a controlled breath as I returned to my stool. Dried, white, circular petals crinkled in my fingers, releasing a strong, sweet scent to billow into the air.

"Pitiful flowers, those moon buds. Why would anybody want such puny, disgusting things?" Samarin scrunched his nose as he gave a dismissive wave of his hand.

Truthfully, I didn't want the flowers, but I needed them. For years now, I have been researching, experimenting, and studying in an attempt to pass The Creator's final test. I had proven to be gifted in the art of alchemy, and it was due to this fact I was to prepare The Elixir of Life as my final challenge. It is rumored The Elixir of Life is named as such, for when it is complete the Creator shall be able to use it to create gods.

After many years of deliberate calculation, I had finally discovered the recipe for the potion. I understood how crucial the alignment of the elements was for the success of the potion; everything from my timing, ingredients, and energy could not falter. I had already obtained a majority of the ingredients, storing them in the Alchemist's cart to be brought on our journey to Riverside.

I smelled the petals once more and crinkled them in my fingers. Moon buds are dried mushroom flowers that grow in mountainous caves. They inspired in me the belief that life can thrive even in the darkest of places when one only has the strength to adapt. Like all forms of life, it too followed a cycle, shedding and splitting into silver circular disks brewed for fertility, growth, and strength.

I set the pouch upon the bedside table and returned to my stool before speaking.

"There are many reasons to value them," I said, knowing if I revealed to Samarin the flowers' true purpose, I ran the risk of him confiscating them. "They smell delightful and are hard to grow. I fancy making them into a tea."

"You wish to drink fungus?"

"Aye, reckon so."

Samarin rolled his eyes, "I can't say I'm horribly surprised..."

I took a deep breath, my hands burning inside of my gauntlets as I withheld my violent urges. Thornin growled low from the balcony, sensing my annoyance and discomfort. With a sharp, harsh whistle, I quieted him, smiling inwardly as he puffed a large cloud of smoke towards Samarin's face.

"Wretched beast," the nobleman muttered, fanning the smoke from his eyes.

"Samarin... Perhaps it is time for you to take your leave," I said to him in a measured tone as I fought to maintain my composure. The burning through my fingers changed to a prickling tingle, a feeling I knew all too well as the desire to submerge his spirit into the Seven Rings of Hell. Taking a deep breath, I continued, hiding my dislike of him with a misleading smile. "We have nothing further to discuss."

"My pardons," he kowtowed, his eyes sparkling once more with feigned innocence. "I was being quite rude, wasn't I?"

"It is not as though I can blame you," I said, rising from my stool and ushering him towards the door. "I thank you for your visit. The hour is late, and you will want to be well rested for the Merchants Dinner on the morrow.... You will find the eastern cottages in the orchards have been prepared for you and your trusted cohorts."

Samarin pulled open the chamber door, lingering before turning over his shoulder.

"Much luck," he said, bowing low and avoiding my eyes. "Pray to the gods you are not in need of it."

I let the door slam behind him, feeling my hands pulse uncomfortably beneath my gauntlets. I enjoyed the lingering silence, deciding suddenly I desired another glass of wine. Uncorking another fresh wine at my altar, I drank from the bottle, pausing abruptly as the sound of frantic, muffled whispering came from beyond the door. Inaudible words were exchanged in rapid tones, followed by the fading tread of heavy boots and another pleasant silence.

How peculiar, I mused, deciding my curiosity to confront the whispering was not worth the risk of jeopardizing my potion or its progress. I best continue my work.

With bottle in hand, I returned to my brewing stand. The curtain swished to the side with a gentle pull, releasing a wave of heat that warmed my cheeks. Retrieving my wooden spoon, I gave the cauldron a stir, my concentration interrupted suddenly as another knock fell upon the door. I heaved a sigh of annoyance.

"You may enter," I called around my shoulder, adjusting my scrolls and spoon before again drawing the curtain closed.

The chamber doors flew open, admitting High Priestess Hazel into my quarters. Her bright green Priestess robes, accented with a darker trim, breezed and billowed around her despite the immense wicker basket she carried in her hands. Her short brown hair was tied back in a loose grey scarf, clearing her wall of thick bangs from her dark brown eyes. She wore a charm around her neck that I rarely saw her without, the talisman resembling that of ancient runes forged from iron and gemstones. She kept her appearance simple and sparse, for her frequent work with patients and potions was like to coat her clothes and skin with grime.

"Fair evening, Your Grace," Hazel beamed brightly as she nodded her greetings.

"Fair evening, Madame," I said pleasantly, resisting the urge to adjust my gauntlets as my hands thrummed painfully.

"Do you not look ravishing," She ran her eyes down the length of my body with a delighted expression. "Your appearance would certainly be most pleasing to The Creator..."

"Your complement is quite kind, Priestess," I said, hiding the discomfort I felt from her words. Shifting my gaze, I searched a lectern to the right of my brewery, consulting the day's itinerary and my remembrance of its events, "I do not recall scheduling a visit with you... has my memory failed me?"

"I shall admit I am here rather spontaneously," Hazel said, shifting the basket in her arms as she stood beside the fireplace. "I wished to replenish your supplies before our journey, so I will have one less thing to see to upon our return."

"How insightful," I said with a forced smile, turning on my heel and drawing back the curtain.

"I noticed your brewing stand is in use. Are you practicing for the ascension?"

"Aye, one cannot be overly prepared," I said, purposefully withholding the true identity of the Dragon Scale Potion.

"May I see what you have crafted?" She asked curiously.

"Certainly," I said stiffly.

Peering inside the cauldron, I stared through a cloud of steam, feeling the heat burn through my eyes. My mother's heart had fully dissolved in the liquid, turning the mixture a deep plum purple with cosmic flecks of glistening gold.

"Excellent!" Hazel asked, lowering the basket she held in her arms to the floor beside the brewery. She stepped forwards, moving around me on the left to look inside at the swirling liquid. The Priestess noted sarcastically, "Delightful shade."

"You would be correct, of course," I said, shrugging innocently and resisting the urge to scratch my palms. "The color is quite handsome, I reckon... I quite like the way the palate turned out."

"The hue is purple," her voice was stern yet oddly quizzical. "Handsome or no, it was to be red."

Clearing her throat, Hazel wafted the smoke away from her face, coughing from the overwhelming smells of cinnamon and sage. "Did you include a heart as the Creator requested?"

"I was able to find all I needed," I said, deciding it was best to keep her ignorant of the knowledge I had used my mother's.

"I shall admit your vagueness frustrates me," she said with a stern stare. "None of the castle folk appear to be missing... whom did you use, if you do not mind my asking?"

"The myocardium belonged to Lord Weever," I said with quick thinking. "He crossed over this summer past, if you recall."

"I recall authorities finding nothing suspicious about his death," Hazel said, never failing to lower her eyes from my own. "Your Courts ruled it a case of petty theft that escalated into blood and steel..."

"Aye, restless youthful townsfolk displeased with his leadership," I said, repeating the words of the official ruling yet knowing they held little truth.

"Perhaps," the Priestess said, "though the autopsy conducted by my hand revealed no secrets or identity to whom owned the sword that slayed him...."

"It is rather suspicious," I said, understanding from her words she had seen through my ruse.

"You mean to tell me you've been holding onto his heart all this while... when I know it to have been buried with his body?"

"Well of course," I said gently. "After his trial proved to be inconclusive, I simply liberated it from him... waste not want not, I was always taught..."

"You know, for best results, you ought to procure a fresh specimen," Hazel said, my blood boiling at the criticism in her tone. "If your words are true, and you used a noble heart, I doth not understand why your shade should resemble plums... unless you strayed from the scroll again..."

Her disdain for my willingness to experiment was a constant source of contention between us. "I am uncertain as to how you mean... I followed your instructions as you wrote them."

"Come now, Knomucca," she said, shaking her head in mild annoyance. "If that were true, your potion would not possess tones of plums and mugwort."

"Mayhaps I merely mismeasured my ingredients," I said, feigning ignorance and bashfully avoiding her eyes.

"Had that been truth," she tutted, "you would simply have brewed a smaller lot."

"I most certainly have had a portion fall victim to the steam..."

"Knomucca," Hazel crossed her arms, scowling coldly as she hardened her expression. "Did you stray from the scroll?"

"You already know the answer to that," I said, fighting to keep my composure as my hands burned hot.

"Oi lassie," the Priestess sighed heavily, turning over her shoulder and beginning to stir the cauldron. "Pray tell... what did you add without my knowledge?"

"It is as you suspect," I said, using her earlier words as sudden inspiration, "I thought the addition of mugwort along with the sweet grass would improve the elements nicely."

"Knomucca," Hazel's voice became crisp and clear, reminding me of the moments we had spent studying in the castle's brewery. "You know I enjoy your curious nature... though we discussed how dangerous such impulses could prove to you whilst creating potions for The Ascension..."

"I am a captive of my own intuition," I said, unashamed of myself or my actions. "You know this to be true of me."

"You must fight such impulses," she scolded, placing my wooden spoon onto the riverstone and turning to face me. "When you find yourself fortunate enough to receive another's wisdom, you should not be so quick to tarnish the words."

"I merely implemented my own creative energies. I hardly see how that would amplify such toxicity..." My hands clenched into fists, fingers digging into my palms, my anger threatening to show as I suppressed a sigh. "My apologies in veering from the scroll, Priestess. I shall attempt to linger in the ink next time around."

"That would be wise," Hazel said firmly. "You have been given approval on your scrollwork for The Elixir of Life... I best not hear of any divergences or the pair of us may find ourselves exchanging unpleasantries once more."

"Understood," I said, disliking the annoyance The Creator flashed through her eyes.

"Very good," she said, stooping downwards towards the basket I had forgotten she had been holding.

Hazel's hands were sure and steady as she rummaged through the wicker and unloaded the basket. Turning her back reluctantly towards me, she set to her work, replenishing my potion supplies. The bubbling of the cauldron brought me comfort and stability, my breathing lengthening as I relished in the moment's reprieve.

"Your potion needs a stir," her voice was suddenly bitter, jarring me sharply from my meditations.

"I am aware of the needs of my potion. However, I was not aware that I would be receiving a plethora of interruptions this evening," I said with a hint of irritation in my voice as I stepped to the Priestess' right and approached the brewing stand.

Retrieving my spoon, I set to stirring the potion, enjoying the wafting scent of mugwort as it floated from the cauldron. A flash of familiar glistening eyes echoed momentarily through my awareness, carrying the gentle sounds of Kiyoko's laughter as delicately as a distant wind.

"Did you hear something?" Hazel asked, rising to a stand when her basket stood empty.

"I do not believe so," I said, tapping my spoon upon the rim of my cauldron and returning it to the riverstone.

"I could have sworn I heard something," she said, stepping towards the brewing stand. "Let me stir your potion."

Hazel snatched the spoon from my hand and began to stir. A pair of bright emerald eyes reflected in the liquid, rippling with the motion of the spoon.

"Amoris Et Lucis." I could have sworn my mother's voice bubbled the words from my cauldron.

The scent of apples floated from the steam and filled the air, turning into thick smoke which wafted into her face. The Priestess began to choak, her eyes brimming with tears as she fought to breath.

"Hazel," I asked confused.

The Priestess coughed and fought for breath, her face turning a deep plum purple. The potion popped in a fierce bubble scorching the hot liquid across Hazel's hand. A silent screamed escaped her, her aura darkening in a heavy shadow as she attempted to shield herself.

"Hazel!" I reached out a hand and quickly pulled her away from the cauldron, smelling the scent of blood and iron through her energy.

She coughed viciously as her breath returned to her, her chest heaving like heavy waves. Hazel whirled towards me, razing an outstretched hand as though she were to slap me. The shadow tightened around her fingers, giving the illusion talons of a heron in the air waiting to strike.

"Is all well?" I asked watching as the dark shadow filled her eyes.

"Nay!" She spat with venom. "Whatever your bloody straying has done nearly stole my breath and burned my hand!"

"My apologies," I said, forcing my voice to sound sympathetic. "Though you did take my spoon without waiting for my reply."

"It is my right to do so as your elder." she angrily returned my spoon to the river stone. "You must stop this foolishness of straying from the scroll before someone else gets hurt."

"I shall do my best to linger in the ink," I said, forcing a smile.

"The Creator does not find your antics pleasing," the Priestess said, heaving the empty basking into her arms. "And He will take action if necessary."

"Will that be everything then, Priestess?" I asked, ignoring her threat in hopes that she would be leaving soon.

"I reckon it is," she said, meeting my eyes with a serious expression, her hand hesitating before she opened the door. "You best remember all we have discussed, I would certainly hate to have to repeat myself."

"Such actions are a waste of energy," I said, lowering my head in a curt nod as I bid her farewell.

"Stay wise, Knomucca," she said.

"Love and light," I replied, watching as Hazel pushed through the door and disappeared beyond it.

Returning across my chambers, I approached my brewing station, taking several long moments to stir the cauldron and meditate. I peered into the bubbling liquid, noticing the emerald eyes had faded from the potion's surface. *What in the seven rings was all that about,* I thought, growing angry as I recalled Hazel snatching the spoon from me. My rage boiled through me, my hands radiating enough heat to ignite my wooden spoon in flames.

"Shite," I swore, dunking the spoon in a flagon of water to extinguish its fire.

The distraction had dried the tears in my eyes, preventing them from spilling down my cheeks in fury.

"Gods have mercy," I prayed, extinguishing the cauldron's flames to begin the cooling process. "Mother, gift me strength... certainly I am to be in need of it."

The cauldron cooled in the lingering moments, its progress a relaxing muse as I fought not to dwell upon my sadness. My spirits brightened with wine and smoke, and the blend of peppermint, sweet grass, lavender, and nettles eagerly consumed to calm my mood. The sweet grass would prepare me for any ill effects from the Dragon Armor, for I did not yet know how my mother's heart would disturb my energies or equilibrium.

As I watched the bubbling brew before me, the pulsating liquid reminded me of the beating of my mother's heart. The power within me stirred, igniting my desire to consume her heart in the potion. Shortly after mother's death, I had found an immense, yet unwanted, pleasure in consuming hearts after I had accidentally killed the first servant. Much to my disgust, my craving for hearts only continued to grow, and soon after, many more servants fell by my hand. Consuming the mitochondrion had unexpected benefits due to my upcoming station. You can tell much about the dead from what their hearts tasted like, whether it was bitter, earthy, sweet, or strong. Each heart had the potential to make me madly sick or gift me a power that complemented my own.

Recently, I discovered the key to creating The Elixir of Life would be to add a human heart into the recipe. I did not wish to do this, however, for I would not offer The Creator any human sacrifice unless it became necessary. All life was sacred, and I hated myself for the moments when I forced its premature ending onto others when the power seized control of me. I still had time before I needed to brew the Elixir of Life, and I hoped I would find a feasible replacement for the myocardium worth the gamble of straying from the scroll. The Creator had already required me to sacrifice my mother and my close, personal friend Rejj. I had given enough, and I grew unsettled whenever I dwelled on those who would die in service defending the realms.

When the cauldron was cooled, I removed it from my brewing station and poured the potion into a peach quartz goblet. I lit a black fig candle atop my altar. I placed the potion beside it, allowing my energy to manifest whilst I cleaned up the cauldron. After my brewing station was wiped down and the utensils were cleansed, I drew the curtain once more. Three tightly rolled smokes rested beside the brewing station, and I retrieved them in my fist before returning to my altar.

Delicately, I lifted the goblet and brought it to my nose. Hot wisps of steam swirled into the air, smelling of cinnamon-spiced fruit. I exhaled a blessing of thanks and hope, forcing my might, will, and intentions towards a successful outcome. Parting my lips, I brought the goblet to my mouth, sipping the blistering hot liquid. Though the potion had cooled for nearly an hour, the mixture continued to boil, burning my tongue as I forced it down my throat. The potion was smooth but not particularly flavorsome, having had a far better aroma than taste.

I finished drinking the potion after seven scorching swallows. I returned the empty goblet to my altar, deciding I would leave it in a corner in hopes it would bring me luck. My search for fair fortune ended abruptly, however, when the burning sensation left behind by the potion caused me to fetch some water. I kept chilled flagons and other colder ingredients in an ice drawer beneath my brewing station, and I drank them empty.

The cold water crashed into my raging stomach, forcing large clouds of steam to painfully escape from my nose. Remembering my smokes, I shakily rose to a stand, recovering them from my altar before stumbling into my bed. The room had begun spinning, forcing bile to rise from my stomach into the back of my mouth. Gingerly, I grabbed matches from the bedside table, avoiding touching what I could against my warm and tender skin. My muscles ached, and my head throbbed, my body feeling as if I had spent a week in the direct desert sun. My vision blurred, and my stomach churned, pushing forth an immense wall of steam from my eyes and ears.

"Gods..." I hissed through the pain.

Gritting my teeth, I stretched out my fingers, striking a match quickly across my wooden headboard. It snapped beneath my shaking fingers, falling frustratingly onto the floor. Swearing, I struck another match, focusing through the pain as the smell of sulfur filled the air. The tiny flame flickered as I pressed it against the spliff, igniting the bundle of fresh herbs wrapped in the skin of an onion. The calm, cooling effects of the peppermint helped me relax, tempering the intense nausea flooding through my stomach. Lavender and sweet grass dulled my headache, allowing me to slowly open my eyes.

Suddenly, there was another knock at my chamber doors. I took in the hour on the sundial, bewildered by how quickly the night had been passing.

Unsure of who was knocking, I pulled a light sheet over my body, covering the ice-blue dress that now looked awkward against the redness of my skin.

"You may enter," I said, trying to maintain a stable tone to my voice.

The door swung open with a gentle creak, filling the threshold with torchlight. My servant, Roice, appeared in the doorway, pulling a laundry cart in his opposite hand. After setting the torch in a sconce on the cart, he entered the room, humming softly to himself as he closed the door behind him.

"Good evening, Your Worship," he said with a nod.

"Roice," I said with relief. "Charmed as I am to see you, I admit I am confused. I thought you left after supper with mead in hand."

"I fell behind in some work and had a few tasks to finish," he said, moving further into my chambers.

"Please explain how you mean," I said, pulling deeply on my spliff.

"The washing took longer than expected as the warmer weather is fleeting." Roice squatted downwards and began to rifle through the cart. "The linens require longer time drying and The Festess energy has everyone roaming aimlessly."

"I am envious of their frivolity," I said through a forced smile.

"Additionally, I was assisting Chatza in the kitchens," Roice said as he donned a pair of dragon scale gloves, then returned to a stand with piles of dinner scraps in his arms. "Poor lass is all in a frenzy with preparations for The Ascension, The Equinox, and your Name Day..."

"I thought I already disclosed I desired nothing for my Name Day," I said.

"Aye," Roice said with a nod, "though it is well known you strongly fancy cinnamon."

Roice crossed the floor with practiced ease, coming to rest at the threshold connecting my chambers to the balcony. Thornin lifted his head and met Roice's eyes, his nose sniffing wildly with the warm food in Roice's arms.

"Enjoy yourself now, handsome," Roice smiled, tossing Thornin the meat scraps from dinner.

Thornin huffed, a happy puff of wispy smoke twirling from his nose. Zealousness flashed through his eyes, and his jaws shot forward, snatching the scraps of food that flew through the air towards him. Inhaling the entirety in a single swallow, he leapt towards Roice excitedly, searching him for further indulgences.

"Thornin, that's all I had," Roice said firmly, my heart beginning to pound as I wondered if Thornin would strike him.

Thornin shoved his nose into Roice's ribs, sniffing wildly as Roice seized him by the ears.

"That's enough," Roice said sternly, meeting Thornin's eyes as the dragon's nose neared his face.

Thornin gifted Roice with a brief kiss, moving his tongue across Roice's cheek as the man glared into the dragon's eyes.

"Take a breath," Roice said, releasing the dragon as Thornin nuzzled him. "Aye... Aye... that's a good lad."

"Thornin, return to resting," I called, whistling a command to him as his ears perked to attention.

"You heard our Lady," Roice scolded, "go on back to sleep."

Thornin sighed, moving backwards gracefully and curling into a ball once more.

"Very good," Roice said, waving in farewell before returning through the threshold. Glancing towards the open doors, he signaled to them with the flick of his hand. "Would you like for me to close these? I reckon it shall be cold this evening."

"That will not be necessary," I said through my exhale of smoke. "Though I appreciate the offer."

"It's my pleasure to serve you," Roice said, returning swiftly towards the servant's cart before speaking. "My apologies for disturbing the dragon... I hope you are not displeased with such behavior, or disappointed that I briefly fell behind in my work."

"I am in no way displeased," I said with a smile, "merely impressed you stood your ground... he seems to enjoy hassling you."

"I mean no disrespect," Roice began with a soft laugh. "Though when you have fathered as many children as I, it becomes harder to frighten you."

"Easier in some ways though, I imagine," I said.

"Aye," Roice began to collect sheets and extra blankets from the servant's cart. "I reckon so. The weight on your heart does not lessen with age."

"Speaking of which," I said with a gesture of my hand, "how are Pammara and the new baby?"

"Both are well," Roice said with a gentle smile. "I enjoy the few stolen moments I get to spend with them."

"I must express I bare guilt when I think of them," I said somberly. "Jasper is only a few months old and I have had you here most of that time."

"The Ascension's important," Roice said with a parental tone as he met my eyes and returned the linens to the cart. "Pammara and I understand that, Your Worship. Though they are sweet as babes, I will have their older years to see them grow."

Roice came to rest by the bedpost, his eyes widening slowly as he took in my face.

"Oi, are you feeling well? You look..." he paused as he searched for the words. "Frankly, you look as if the hounds have dragged you through the Seven Rings. Shall I fetch the healer?"

"I appreciate your concerns; however, we do not need to disturb Hazel at this time."

"Are you certain?"

I paused, swallowing a mouthful of bile before I could convincingly speak. "I feel fine, Roice."

"Spare me the theatrics... your face betrays your words."

"Roice, I am well. I am just feeling a little warm from a potion I drank... nothing to be concerned about."

"If you're certain..." Roice said slowly. "Regardless, I will leave you a goblet of water before I depart. Is there anything else you require?"

"I suppose if you had a spare moment, I would gladly accept some water, help with rolling smokes, and a cup of mint tea."

"I could fetch that for you now," Roice said with a pleased expression, "though I'll have to run to the servant's annex in the West Wing."

"Very well," I said, finishing my smoke and beginning to start another. "There is a chilled bottle of wine in the ice drawer beneath the brewery. Could you pour me a glass to drink whilst I wait?"

"Forgive me, Your Worship, though perhaps you should wait for the water," Roice warned, "for the wine will not quench you completely."

"That is sage advice," I said, blowing out smoke to float in a loose cloud.

"Shall I see if Syler could sit with you whilst I'm gone? I just saw Frek enter her chambers and I know she is in bed."

"Thank you kindly, but I am well."

"If you're certain," Roice said, grabbing his torch from the cart and quickly heading towards the door. "Rest and relax, for I shall return."

The door closed quietly behind him with a click, allowing me a brief moment to slip out of my night dress. Sliding off the garment, I shucked it out from between the sheets, pooling it into a pile on the floor. I kicked off my shoes with practiced grace, listening as my heels fell in two solid thuds. Fluffing up pillows around me, I made a comfortable back support and leaned against the headboard.

My thoughts drifted to my sister as Roice's footsteps moved past her chambers towards the servant's annex.

He saw the wolf enter her chambers; I sighed in annoyance, my anger amplified with the pain from my potion.

Heat boiled in my stomach, making me groan in discomfort.

How can she be so cavalier? I wondered. *Her love for him blinds her, so I fear she will risk her safety.*

I shifted across my mattress, trying in vain to quench the throbbing through my chest and muscles.

She shall not heed my wisdom, I sighed resolutely. *Certainly, she must have inherited such stubbornness from our father, as Mother would never approve.*

I pulled the sheets up around me, beginning once more to smoke my spliff as Roice reappeared at the door. Clanking wheels and gears groaned under the cart he was pushing, overflowing as it was with flagons, herbs, smokes, and tea.

"I apologize, I saw Ol' Walter sitting in the hall and couldn't refuse him," Roice beamed as he patted the old cart tenderly.

"Of course, how could we refuse his service?" I mused, taking in the sight of the ancient cart. It had been around longer than half the people in the castle and was adored by nearly all of the servants.

"He is rather reliable," Roice chuckled before fanning a fist full of spliffs between his fingers and placing them on the bedside table. "I procured these from your sister. I had noticed she had made rose petal paper and I wanted you to have some."

"That is very kind," I said with a smile.

"I know it to be extremely tedious to prepare," Roice said.

"Aye, it is indeed," I said, "though I find the process quite enjoyable."

"'Tis for your love of challenging yourself," he said, removing the flagons from the cart and placing all but one in the ice box.

"I find it relaxing to melt the petals into a cohesive soul," I said.

"I could imagine." Roice indicated he was to change the subject with a wave of his hand towards the ice box. "Will you be able to get more water through the night, or shall I ask another to keep your cups filled?"

"I will be fine," I said, smiling through a ring of smoke. "I must thank you immensely for the offer, however."

Roice placed the cup of tea beside my bed atop the table. Reaching left, I snatched it up eagerly, gulping it down while the cup still steamed. The peppermint was so soothing I moaned aloud, blushing slightly when I noticed Roice was watching me with a bemused expression.

"Would you like another?" he asked with a grin.

"I believe I am well enough," I said, returning the empty cup and regretting how quickly I had drunk the tea.

"I hope this doesn't make you cross with me... though I don't believe for one moment that you are truly well."

"I am just warm," I said truthfully, "and a little nauseated."

"I shall leave you a servant's whistle, should you become in need of anything."

"Roice..." I withheld my judgements as Roice set the servant's whistle on the bedside table. "I appreciate your kindness, though I assure you, I am well."

"Very well," he said, stooping low to the ground and scooping up my dress and shoes. Taking them along with another pile of clothes, he disappeared amongst the fabric in the closet for several long moments. When his arms were empty, he returned to the laundry cart, gesturing at the remainder of the clean garments with an arching swoop of his hand.

"These are some items you requested for your journey. Where would you like me to put them?"

"You may pack them for me, if you could," I said, pointing to a small leather satchel that hung by a long strap off one of the bedposts.

"These aren't going to fit in there," Roice said, examining the pouch as he held it in his hands.

"Appearances can be deceiving," I said, finishing my smoke and placing the ashes in a clay dish on the bedside table. Handing him the small canvas pouch of moon buds, I added, "Would you mind putting this in there as well?"

"Aye," he said, taking the sachet from my hands. Roice began to load the items into the bag, astounded by the vastness I had hidden with charms and trickery. All manner of objects were suspended in the space within the satchel, ranging from weapons and potion ingredients to books, sleeping sacks, smokes, spare gauntlets, wine, and rations. When all had been loaded, Roice drew the bag closed, pulling hard on two leather strings to tie the pouch shut. The bag remained small in size, cleverly hiding everything I needed for The Ascension.

"Is there anything else I can do for you, Your Worship?" Roice inquired.

"You have done far too much already," I said, nodding in appreciation as Roice laid an extra blanket across the foot of the bed. "I think you best be on your way now."

"Aye, then I shall be taking my leave," he said, filling my mug to the brim with cold water. "All you have asked of me is packed and ready, and I wish you good tidings on your Ascension."

"And I wish good tidings to you and your family."

Roice smiled and nodded as he began to clear his carts, moving the empty wagons back towards the door as he prepared to take his leave. After pushing them both into the hallway, he returned into the room, selecting three gnarled cherry logs from the wood rack. He placed them upon the fire, filling the room with delicious smells and the soft glow of red flames.

"Love and light," I said in farewell, nestling comfortably into the sheets. Inhaling a deep drag of the floral-spiced smoke, I watched him move towards the door, noticing as his steps suddenly slowed.

Turning around unexpectedly, Roice met my eyes seriously, speaking softly in the glow of the fireplace. "Luck from the Gods and stars, Knomucca. I sincerely hope the Gods of Fate are smiling upon you."

"Your well wishes are appreciated, Roice. Enjoy your time with family, and stay wise."

"Love and light," he replied, bowing slightly and disappearing through the threshold.

IV

EVERETT

I woke with a start, momentarily disoriented with my surroundings.

I must have slept, I thought in disbelief, pleased to feel well despite how much wine I had drunk. Thank the gods... for they smile brightly upon this day.

The sun had not yet fully risen in the east, though long shadows accented the twilight filtering through the small window high above me. Bringing my arms inward, I pushed myself off my stomach, lifting my head to discover stiff muscles in my neck and shoulders. Swearing softly, I rolled onto my side, thankful to notice someone had placed a goblet of water near my loft.

Sitting up, I grabbed the water, drinking the entire cup in one swallow. Absently, I rubbed my neck, working out the pinched nerves and tight spots while allowing myself time to wake. My legs were unsteady, feeling shaky and sore as I rubbed the sleepiness from them. Lifting my arms above my head, I arched in a satisfying stretch, tilting onto my knees and crawling towards the bedside wardrobe.

Moving alongside the bed frame, I felt the metal shift and squeak. I grabbed the frame tightly to keep my balance, my body still heavy with sleep and wine. Making it to the wardrobe, I was grateful to have clean garb to freshen my appearance, for my clothes felt stale, and my body had a seasoned smell.

Realizing that I had slept in my shoes, I began to undress. Untying my boots, I freed them from my tight leather leggings, my skin breathing as I pulled them from my legs. A small stone wash basin was mounted in my wardrobe, allowing me to freshen myself whilst I began to dress. My undershorts were soon to follow, my manhood proudly exposed as I slipped into fresh trousers. Yesterday's jerkin was replaced with a heavy black tunic, grey woolen leggings, and a tightly knit cap.

I grabbed my traveling boots from a shelf on the right, then slipped them onto my feet. My tan canvas rucksack hung on a hook in the closet, packed with underclothes, tunics, and leggings to last me the next half a week. My dress armor and attire for The Ascension were loaded in a wagon with everyone else's, consisting of one of the nearly twenty carts of supplies we were bringing with us. A tightly woven, thin straw bed roll nestled in the corner of the closet. It rustled softly as I tucked it under my arm and stepped back from the wardrobe.

My hammer was mounted on the wall near my bunk, hanging beside my utility belt, armor, and a plethora of other weapons. Though my hammer was my favorite, I was a fluent swordsman, and I enjoyed winning games of throwing darts and daggers. I was fair with an axe and knew how to load a trebuchet, though I hadn't had to do so since my years as a squire. I could wield a mace and had even made weapons on the battlefield. However, my greatest underlying talents shone through during hand-to-hand combat.

I donned my armor, feeling heavy with the added weight of chainmail and iron. Removing my belt from the wall, I clasped it around my waist, grabbing a set of knives, a clean water skin, and two pairs of dragon scale gloves. Hanging them on the belt, I added my glossy, black leather smoking sack, filling it with herbs, onion skins, and matches from an abandoned servant's cart in the corridor. I slung my hammer across my back, keeping it close until the time came to use it.

Having all I required, I left the barracks tower, descending the ladder and emerging from the hall into the crisp early morning air. Returning to the courtyard, I followed last night's path back to Valvang, eagerly anticipating the morning meal that would provide me strength for the day ahead. The air smelled of fried meats, eggs, and greens, the aroma growing stronger as I entered Valvang from the door in which I had left only twelve hours prior. Half a hundred candles lazily lit the air, adding a coziness to the castle I was not excited to leave.

Scarcely any soldiers were seen breaking their fast, and I hoped this meant my men were already in the stables. I ate my food quickly and spoke to no one, inhaling four plates of sausages, mixed vegetables, cheesy eggs, and half a loaf of bread. Washing it down, I had three cups of water, feeling rejuvenated as the shakiness and soreness of last night left me. During my meal, I watched the western entrance to Valvang, hoping I would catch Knomucca as she came in for a quick meal to begin her day. She had previously disclosed her need for an angelfish eye. Despite my warnings against her traveling alone, I knew her departure was approaching. I only knew she would join us on our march on the morrow, her path intersecting with ours after a day's travel.

I added extra bread and meat to my rucksack, then grabbed sugar lumps from the servant's cart to feed my horse, Truff. Moving west, I followed a long granite hallway until it came to a fork. Taking the right passageway, I found an iron door. I pushed it open, stepping down a bulky wooden staircase as I made my way outside.

Walking along a narrow gravel path, I continued westward away from the castle. The walkway blended into a boundless field, expanding until half a league from the castle's inner wall. Altering my course, I shifted slightly north, cutting across a pasture that was wet with the morning dew. Far off, birds chirped from their perches, their nests resting high in the rafters of the stables that were now coming into focus on the horizon.

The smell of hay greeted me warmly upon my entrance to the barn. Chaotic chatter, clatter, and laughter bombarded me as horses were saddled. Turning left, I made my way down the main aisle, taking a sharp right down a hall towards my tack locker. Removing my saddle, bridal, and brush bucket, I closed the locker before thoroughly searching my rack of saddle blankets. On the bottom shelf rested a patterned blanket, the various colors fanning and spreading together to give the appearance of flames. Deciding on this cloth for The Ascension, I packed it in one of my saddle bags, along with a simple blue blanket that Truff would wear during the nights on our journey south to Riverside.

Leaving the tack room, I returned down the hall and continued left. I walked past dozens of horses, then veered right to cross through another winding hallway. The hall intersected with another large passageway, the corridor buzzing with the noises of soldiers and horses as I continued straight another thirty paces. A set of swinging doors appeared on my right, and I slipped through them, cutting across the riding arena and moving to the left.

Truff's stall was behind the arena and six rows over, snuggly situated between a pair of sassy Palominos. His rich brown fur stood out between the bright beauties, making him easy to find. Approaching the stall, I hung my tack on nearby hooks, then slid open the door to find him snacking on a stack of straw.

"Good morrow," I said, smiling as he lifted his head and perked up his ears. "It is nice to see you."

Truff lumbered towards me and shoved his face into my stomach, beginning to sniff and search for the sugar lumps he undoubtedly could smell. Flaring his nostrils and flapping the lips of his small muzzle, he nipped playfully at my fingers.

"Oi, you restless beast," I said in jest, producing the sugar lumps from my sack and allowing him to take them from my palm. I scratched his face as he ate, grinding my knuckles playfully into his broad forehead. Truff let out a hot breath and lifted his chiseled, wedge-shaped head, tapping me on the shoulder hard with his chin.

"Come along then," I said, positioning him on my left side before opening the stall door once more, "Truff, walk on."

The Arabian horse obliged, walking parallel to my body as I led him into the aisle. He didn't need to be tethered with ropes or halters, for he would always follow closely when it was commanded of him. Truff was pure bred and exceptionally intelligent; I had been fortunate to have received him as a gift from my father when I assumed the role of Commander. My father had named the horse Tree Root Truffles in honor of his favorite fungus, comparing the richness of his brown fur to the color of the decadent mushrooms.

"Woah," I commanded, sticking out my arm and stopping him in the aisle. "Stand and wait."

Truff sighed, sticking out his high arching neck in anticipation of grooming. I mucked out his stall and changed the shavings, then washed out his food and water buckets so they would be clean upon our return. All the while, Truff stood at attention, earning him another lump of sugar once I began to brush him. I combed out several small mats in his mane and tail before tightly braiding them. His hooves were spotless and did not need picking, though I had to use my hammer to secure a horseshoe that had come loose on his back leg. I finished washing, drying, and brushing his body, getting ready to saddle him, when loud voices began booming down the hall.

"This isn't funny anymore!" snapped a commanding female voice. "I am only going to say it one more time. If you can't carry it, leave it behind. The supply trains are already loaded, and there's no room for anything useless."

A second, rough-sounding voice retorted a hint of offense in his accented tones. "That's harsh. It isn't useless, and you know it."

"What I know is we would need half a dozen horses to pull it, and that would drastically hinder our progress-"

"Sergeant, please reconsider-"

"Oi... seriously? You're being ridiculous..." the footsteps and voices drew closer. "I cannot believe we are discussing this yet again."

Sergeant Kye and Chief Warrant Officer Bullet came around the corner, both dressed in armor and carrying their tack. Kye approached one of the palominos beside Truff, hung up her tack, then slung her halter from her shoulder.

"What are you two on about?" I asked, spreading a thin red saddle blanket I had found near Truff's stall across his back. My words were lost in the growing intensity of their argument.

"There must be something you can do," Bullet pleaded.

"My hands are tied," Kye said. "Besides, even if we have the resources to do it, we most certainly do not have the time."

"We could repurpose some of the horses... I could enchant some of their shoes to give them greater strength and speed... should expedite the trajectory a fair bit-"

"Aye, so they can run on without us and leave us in their wake? We are leaving the horses as they are." Kye rolled her eyes in annoyance, releasing a tense sigh with her words. "We've discussed this already... we're not taking the cannon!"

"Gods... still on about that cannon poppycock, are you?" I sighed, tightening the girdle of Truff's black leather saddle.

"And your packing list is the peak of pragmatism," Bullet seethed sarcastically as he stroked his beard, running his hand down the length, which was tucked neatly into the leather utility belt he was always seen wearing. "You hoard like a dragon... Hand me that parchment with the wagon inventory I saw hangin' in the tack room earlier before yah took 'er down..."

"Aye... Certainly..." Kye snatched the rolled parchment from her boot, passing it towards Bullet as she returned his sarcasm with a mischievous grin. "Any suggestion of supply to remove shall only prove fruitless and provide me little amusement."

"I reckon everything has a purpose and place," I said as I shifted Truff's saddle, though my words seemed to fall on deaf ears.

Bullet fetched an enchanted quill from his belt, drawing lines across the diagram before turning the parchment towards Kye once more. "We could move contents from the wagon of grains into the wagon with the dress armor... Certainly these garments do not require their own cart."

"They most certainly do!" Kye met Bullet's eyes with the defiance her youth would allow. "I cannot risk moving the grains into the wagon with the armor... should accident befall the garments I doth not wish to ruin anyone's appearance."

"Very well..." Bullet produced an abacus from his belt, tucking the quill into the thick white hairs of his beard whilst finishing his calculations. "Though I cannot agree that horses should be required to tend a cart dedicated entirely to nothing except cauldrons and wine barrels... certainly we could consolidate them into another wagon..."

"Bullet, enough!" Kye slid open the door to her horse's stall with such vigor that it wrenched closed once more. She released a breath before speaking, the impulsiveness of her youth disappearing as she composed herself. "I followed the list Her Worship gave me and added what I felt would be useful, practical, and appropriate-"

"Kye-" Bullet tried to speak, though the Sergeant continued.

"It took me months to prepare everything!" Kye made a gesture of emphasis with the sweeping of her hand. "I have already been asked to set a cart aside to allow us to bring along Kiyoko's ethereal harp and I shall not forgo anything else."

"Sergeant, stand down," I sternly commanded, stepping around Truff and into Kye's line of sight. "You're going to spook the horses."

"My pardons Commander..." Kye released another sigh, sheepishly reaching towards her horse with a gentle hand. "But the Chief's demands are unreasonable..."

"They are far from unreasonable," Bullet said, saluting me briefly before walking toward his horse. "But I am aware my intensity on the matter has been rather abundant."

"Abundant are the waters in the orchard ponds, this was all of the waters of the Luna Sea," Kye exclaimed in exasperation.

"Guard your tone, Kyreese," I said, using the Sergeant's full name to accompany my warning.

"Commander, I believe caution is warranted..." Bullet surveyed his surroundings before he spoke, dropping his voice to a low whisper. "I had that dream again..."

"Aye?" A tense breath escaped my lips. "Does Her Worship know about this?"

"Not as of yet," Bullet said, removing the quill from his beard and returning Kyreese her parchment. "It hadn't happened in months... thought I was bloody well rid of them if I'm honest until I dreamt it again."

"And you wish the cannon as extra precaution," I said, patting Truff firmly on the neck once his saddle was settled.

"Seems insane, doesn't it?" Bullet asked with a heavy sigh.

"Nay... it is not," I said gently, focusing on Truff's large eyes as a way not to betray my sudden sadness.

"'Tis good to know ya' don't find me of unsound mind," Bullet winked, his pine green eyes catching the torchlight and appearing grey.

"I doth not indeed," I said gently, moving back around Truff and untangling his bridal. "Of course, the idea of the cannon at our backs is quite tempting, though we would have had to depart a week sooner in order to maintain our schedule."

"I reckon 'twould have been a slow venture," Bullet agreed with a nod.

"Not to mention you haven't even designed a way to move the cannon safely yet," Kye interjected. "Say we agreed to take the cannon and the bastard tumbles over... we cannot afford a fortnight repairing the damages."

Bullet had earned his nickname from tinkering, experimenting, and inventing all manner of gadgets, gizmos, and weapons used by the folks around the castle. He was an Alchemist, his skill equal to that of Hazel in the Alchemist Guild as Master of Elements, yet falling beneath her rank as he was not of the clergy.

"Horses could manage it fine in the riggin'," Bullet said, "there is nothing to design or implement aside from the cart needed for the transport and I already prepared the materials and instructions-"

"It is too much to manage right now," I said softly.

"'Twas that blasted dream..." Bullet said, dropping his shoulders heavily. "Reckon that bastard swirled my tea."

"My advice is to meditate on whatever bad feelings you have and wash them down the river," I said, sliding the bridle over Truff's nose. "Certainly, dreaming of the portal's decay is quite foreboding, though I reckon there is not much else we can do besides what we have already done..."

"Reckon the notion is easier said than done," the dwarf sighed, beginning to brush and saddle his midnight-black miniature pony. Bullet, our Chief Warrant Officer, was assigned to run the security detail that guarded the connective portal between our castle, Morriraen, and the castle in the Underworld to which it was spiritually connected.

"Perhaps it's been too long since you left the castle," Kye said, lowering her voice in concern.

"Aye, I prefer to be by my lonesome," Bullet shot back. "'Tis better than hearin' the chattering of baby birds all day."

Kye's face reddened in fury, and she opened her mouth to respond, but I interjected.

"Has anyone seen Kiyoko yet?" I asked, deciding it was a good time to change the subject.

"The General appears to be late," Kye said with an exhale, attempting to balance her energies. She tied her bags and a silver battle horn to her saddle. "He's normally one of the first to arrive, and no one's seen him thus far."

"We were actually talkin' about that before we started arguin'," Bullet added, leading his now fully armored horse further down the aisle.

"How did you get from..." I started, trailing off as I decided not to bring their argument up again. "On second thought, never you mind. Just have Kiyoko find me when you see him."

"Aye," said Kye, gesturing to Truff, who obstructed the aisle and blocked the door to her horse's stall. "Would you like to wait for him outside? Lady Moonbeam and I are keen on enjoying the early morning sun, and you both are in the way."

"I think I'll see to readying his horse," I said, glancing around one final time to ensure I had all I needed for our journey. "Truff, walk on."

Truff followed down the aisle, walking alongside me as I redirected our path to turn back towards the riding arena. Kiyoko's horse was boarded just outside it, located two stalls to the right of the hall with the swinging doors. Leaving Truff in the arena, I made haste towards Kiyoko's tack locker, taking everything I needed back to begin grooming his horse.

Where are you, Kiyoko? I sighed as I picked mud and leaves from the hooves of his spotted mare. It is not like you to be so careless.

When his horse was ready, I consulted the sun's position, quickly growing annoyed as mid-morning soon approached. Briefly, I considered beginning our march without him, though the idea was ludicrous. His company and special gifts were too valuable to forego, and I would regret it if I left without him. I wanted to be proud and happy that he had enjoyed another, though my role as Commander made it hard to do so.

"That's a good girl," I said to his horse, patting Ballara firmly on the neck. "He will be here soon."

Finding a stool beside Bellara's stall, I decided to sit down. I dug through the bags and pouches tied to my belt, beginning to roll a spliff whilst I waited. Binding sweet grass, white sage, and coltsfoot in onion skins, I lit the spliff on a nearby torch. As I smoked, the stables drew quiet, the men moving with their mounts outside to spar and wait in the fresh air. Halfway through my spliff, I heard pounding footsteps and heavy breathing, punctuated with the familiar sounds of Kiyoko running and swearing.

"Everett... thank the gods." Kiyoko's plum-purple kimono swirled around him, his lightly curled hair ruffling in the breeze as he sped towards me. His cheeks glowed with a fresh pink hue, his complexion oddly animated for someone who had not been at breakfast.

"Finally..." I said, my voice deadpan. "The wheels of your carriage turn slowly, though it has finally arrived."

"I lost track of the morning and time got away from me," Kiyoko said shamefully. "Had to travel from the Orchards, and gods know I should have departed sooner."

"Well that is clear," I said, letting my disappointment paint my words. "Am I to assume you did not break your fast When you awoke?"

"I partook in the fruit of the Orchards as I came to find you," Kiyoko quickly said. "I would not jeopardize my sobriety or your faith in me-"

"We were meant to leave ages ago, Kiyoko," I said sharply. "This behavior is not typical of you and it doth not paint a pleasant shade."

"My deepest pardons, Everett..." Kiyoko met my eyes and apologetically held my gaze. "I miscalculated my path and failed when trying to rectify it... I had meant to find you in Valvang and even planned to have a flagon of water and your platter served upon your arrival as an attempt of pardons from my rudeness this night past... though I could not hear the cocks crowing from where I slept in the Orchards and I misjudged the rising of the sun."

"Misjudged it by a longshot, I reckon," I chided.

"You appear to be well rested," Kiyoko said with a smile. "Your dreams from this night past suit you tremendously-"

"Do not read me, Kiyoko," I spat. "You know I strongly dislike when you do so."

"The energy floats at your surface," Kiyoko said. "Should you not wish for me to access these intimacies, you shall have to actively disguise them."

Sighing, I finished my spliff in silence, resisting the urge to share the remainder with him as I partook in the crisping herbs.

"I am assuming your night was decent then, yes?" I asked, my anger and annoyance flitting just below the surface.

"It shall not become anything serious," Kiyoko said with an unreadable expression. "Though, I reckon I enjoyed myself all the same."

"Well," I began speaking quickly to cover my jealousy, "as your commander, I am angry you were late and we shall design the consequences accordingly... though... as your friend... it pleases me to hear you had a decent evening."

"It would have been more enjoyable had we spent the time together," Kiyoko said gently, meeting my eyes and holding my gaze.

"Perhaps," I said noncommittally, raising an eyebrow as I watched Kiyoko step around my left.

"Everett..." Kiyoko said with a soft sigh, "you should not have readied my horse."

"Time is of the essence," I said, unwilling to admit I rather liked that Kiyoko's mount had been readied by my hand.

"I should not have compromised your honor," Kiyoko said, kissing the pad of his left thumb and pressing it into my palm as he disappeared into Ballara's stall.

"Do not think me too kind," I said, rising as Kiyoko led his horse from her stall, "I debated leaving here without you."

"I would have deserved it," Kiyoko said with a sigh.

"You are too valuable to be without," I said softly. "Knomucca needs you... And so do I."

"The feelings are mutual," Kiyoko smiled, his aura brightening in delicious lilac, showing his relief as the tension between us settled.

"Aye," I said, following the aisle toward the riding arena. "Your consequences are still to come. I shall find Truff, and then we best set off."

As I retrieved Truff, we followed Kiyoko out of the stables, meeting the rest of the men in the yard. Cheers and profanities broke out in rumbling, thunderous waves, the troops jostling Kiyoko as they interrogated him on his whereabouts.

"Oi, enough!" I said sternly as I slipped into my saddle. "As penalty for your tardiness, General, you shall be charged with tending to the horses at our first bout of resting. And you shall clean up after their droppings should any occur whilst we leave the castle grounds." I saw Kiyoko's sly smirk through my periphery, likely considering the punishment light.

"By mundane means," I added, the smirk now on my face as Kiyoko's energy darkened.

A hush fell across the ranks as they looked to Kiyoko for his response. "As you wish Commander," he said softly.

"Excellent," I said with a nod. Facing forward, I elevated my voice. "Mount up! Fall in line!"

The clanking and clattering of iron exploded around me as soldiers flew onto their horses and quickly took up their ranks. Kiyoko appeared in his usual place at my right, suddenly and silently offering me a smoke, which I eagerly accepted. Formal as we were being, there was still room for fun and flexibility, as only a quarter of our regularly armed forces were traveling south with us. Most of the soldiers requested for this mission were officers or higher-ranking soldiers, allowing for less required structure and more freedom.

"Sound off!" I called, listening as the drummers began to play a bouncing cadence.

Squeezing my legs, I commanded Truff to trot, feeling exhilarated with his forceful lurch forward. Turning left, we marched through a half league of grasslands and fields before reaching the castle's inner wall, on which Knomucca and I had sparred many times previously. Servants at the portcullis set to work, lifting the immense oaken gate that would allow us to cross to the outer ramparts. Fields of crops were planted between the castle walls, making room for the vast orchards to be planted closer to the keep's towers in the center.

Marching through the farms, we approached the outer bailey. Upon our arrival, another formidable gate was lifted, and we began to cross the drawbridge. Enchanted waves in the moat below us smashed against the shore, nearly spraying gusts of freezing water across our horses as we passed. Kicking Truff, I commanded him to canter, following the path to take Moon's Road south away from the castle.

After a short jaunt, I slowed Truff to a walk, for a large, steep hill marked the true end of the castle grounds. Light snow had fallen during the night due to the realm's imbalance, gently sparkling the tips of the trees that began filling in the landscape around us. Kiyoko rode beside me on his horse, his energy rippling with the annoyance of his punishment. I sparked the smoke he had given me, noticing then the herbs had not been bound in their usual fashion within an onion's tasteless, paper-thin skin.

"Oi," I whistled my signal for Kiyoko, demanding his attention with a playful wave.

"Greetings," Kiyoko said as he lit a smoke of his own, the smell of mugwort floating towards me.

"You made rose petal paper," I said with a surprised smile. "When did you possess the stamina to make rose petal paper?"

"I will never confess," Kiyoko teased with a wink.

"The botanical blend..." I continued excitedly. "I can taste the sweet grass, lemon balm, and coltsfoot... though something appears to be tasting of... cocoa?"

"That would be the coneflowers," Kiyoko nodded with a self-satisfied smirk.

"And... honey?"

"Aye. Honey was used to bind the herbs for a bit more flavor and moisture."

"I will confess," I said, meeting Kiyoko's eyes, "had you gifted me such a delight before we mounted our horses... we might have caused tardiness for a different reason than you have thus far..."

"It pleases me to know you are enjoying it so." A blushing cherry blossom pink floated through Kiyoko's aura, so fast and subtle that I nearly missed it. "I wanted again to express apology for my rudeness in regards to Lorraine... and I know roses are your favorite,"

"Oi, trying to bribe me with fancy paper then, are you?" I teased as we approached the bottom of the hill outside the castle grounds.

"Perhaps," Kiyoko winked. "I will admit I hoped the rose petal paper would soften your mood towards me..."

"I shall only allow it fully to do so if you confess when it came to be," I quipped.

"I would wager the details are fairly logical to conclude," Kiyoko said slyly. "Lorraine and I had a roust in the gardener's hut this evening past while she was meant to oversee any nightly chores, and I made the paper whilst she tended to her duties."

I recalled that Kiyoko's recent dinner companion was an apprentice of the Head Gardener, and my mood soured slightly. However, I fought not to betray my feelings through my energy.

"The prospect of a rousting in the gardener's hut is quite intriguing," I admitted, taking another long pull on my spliff.

"Well... there is inspiration to be had, and much I could disclose to you on the matter..." Kiyoko said with a grin. "If you are certain you wish to hear it."

"I am," I said sincerely. "You can tell me anything."

Suddenly, Kiyoko's face fell, his eyes darkening with focus as his muscles tightened in his shoulders.

I feigned horror and seriousness, widening my eyes playfully. "Do I offend? Was your time together so wretched that you no longer wish to discuss with me about it?"

"Nay, Everett... you did nothing amiss," Kiyoko said, his voice sounding vacant, clashing with the previous laughter he had had in his eyes. Peering into the tree line, his face firmed and furrowed, his irises widening to my practiced eyes as I noticed him read the energies around us. "In all actuality, I was thoroughly satisfied."

"What do you see?" I asked.

Kiyoko paused, abruptly holding up a hand to silence me. "Put out your smoke," Kiyoko commanded, his sudden demand taking me by surprise. "Something feels amiss. There is something in the trees."

Kiyoko drew a bow and looked sharply left, aiming at footsteps that had rustled in the fallen forest leaves. Pine branches swooped low, covering the ground in thick needles and shadows.

"Show yourself!" Kiyoko demanded in a booming voice.

Drawing my hammer, I simultaneously snuffed out the spliff on my saddle and slipped it into my shoe. The sounds of a copper bell unexpectedly rang as bleating bellowed beneath the branches. A lone, scrawny goat lumbered out from the trees, wearing a bell tied with twine around its neck. Walking into our path, it suddenly stopped before continuing to graze on grass that grew between fallen twigs and leaves.

"Oi, Kiyoko, it's just a wee billy gotten loose," I said with a chuckle. "Must have wandered from the castle grounds during the night and run away."

"He certainly startled me," Kiyoko said, his face blushing red as he lowered his bow. "Shall we send a soldier back to wrangle it? The Harvest is upon us and our cattle are essential for the winter."

"We shall indeed," I said, cupping my hands over my mouth and summoning Bullet with a whistle.

Bullet broke from ranks, weaving through the troops to approach upon my left.

"You've summoned me, Commander?" Bullet nodded in a brief salute.

"I possess a task for you," I said, gesturing towards the billy grazing in the path. "Could you return this little fellow to the castle?"

"Aye, Commander," Bullet nodded, his dwarvish ancestry gifting him aerokinesis. He would be best suited to take the goat back to the castle and use his magic to make up for the lost time in returning. He would have to walk whilst leading the goat, though he would have little trouble joining the ranks well before we reached our campsite.

"Excellent," I said with a smile. "Your horse will be tended to until you return."

"Very well, Sir," Bullet saluted as he slid from the saddle.

Guiding the pony forward, he lined him along my right, handing me the reigns to manage in addition to my own.

"Ensure you return in haste," I urged. "Waste no time in returning the billy to the stockades and joining us at camp."

"Aye, Cap'n," said Bullet, fastening a lead from his belt to secure to the goat. "I shall await here until the party passes, then set off at once."

"Thank you kindly for this service."

Bullet nodded, tugging the goat off towards the side of the path with a firm yank. Kicking Truff, we began to walk, guiding Bullet's pony on my right with relative ease. Kiyoko clutched his bow, watching the goat suspiciously until it was out of sight behind the supply train.

"Oi, Kiyoko," I said timidly, "I do not usually question you or your gifts... though... you got spooked by a goat..."

"Aye," he said, turning away to hide his embarrassment. "I must still be feeling the effects of last night's encounter."

"I am even more intrigued," I confessed, deciding not to bring up my annoyance with his interruption of my smoking. "Shall we continue our conversation posthaste?"

Kiyoko's response was lost in the sudden sounds of struggle that broke out behind us. Swearing was met with the screaming of a slaughtered goat, cracking through the air as painfully as a whip. Jerking hard on the reins, I turned the horses, noticing soldiers at the back of the ranks fighting near the supply carts. Moving towards the commotion, I took in the sight of the figures in all black that were ambushing my men.

The goat that had stood in our path moments ago now lay dead in the grass, blood gushing from the slice in its neck and staining the ground scarlet. Frantically, I searched for Bullet but did not see him in the throngs of battling blades and bows. While searching, I found myself looking off to the right, analyzing the rippling insignia of a crimson goat's head emblazoned on black fabric. The flag flashed and disappeared, leaving me to ponder the origins of the treachery that had been shown.

Placing my thumb and forefinger in my mouth, I blew an alarming whistle. The war horns sounded a thunderous alarm, signaling the forces to return the attack. Worried for Bullet, yet annoyed I had his horse, I securely tied the reigns of our mounts together and abandoned Truff's saddle.

"Truff, protect Archie," I called over my shoulder, aware my words were indistinguishable in the noise and chaos of battle.

Swarms of rebel soldiers emerged from the trees, howling war cries as their archers along the tree line took aim. Arrows whizzed past my head, striking the spot where I had previously vacated. Diving forward, I lunged into the throes, using my momentum to swing my hammer upwards. My hammer cracked through three skulls in a single, forceful strike, splattering blood in all directions.

Moving left, I shoved through the onslaught, narrowly dodging swords, shields, and staves that swung toward my face. Hordes of rebels rushed me, forcing me backward past the supply carts and up the hill. Desperately, I defended my position, smashing my hammer into a seemingly endless swarm of rebels.

"Their numbers are too great!" Kiyoko shouted somewhere in the distance. His voice was faint through the sound of blood rushing in my ears.

I glanced over my shoulder briefly, my anxiety growing as the hill crest drew closer. The steep incline was the first of the castle's defenses, and to lose its advantage could signal our defeat. Three rebels to every one of our soldiers was indeed poor odds, yet I swung my hammer with all I could muster in attempts to keep them from gaining ground. The blood-stained field slipped beneath my boots, denying me a stable stance to push back the enemy.

Gritting my teeth, I tried in vain to hold my ground and keep the rebels away from the castle. For every rebel slain, another took its place, and soon, I found myself retreating over the hill and onto Moon's Road to fight with more stable footing. Further up the road, I discovered Kye amongst a score of other soldiers defending the bridge near the outer bailey, overpowering ranks of rebels with the crack of her whipping hair. Her leather-lined braid was an extension of herself, moving swiftly through her enemies. An alarm began to sound in the southern watchtower, cutting harshly through the cacophony of battle.

Bringing my hammer up and over my head, I smashed it solidly into the head of an oncoming rebel, dropping him instantly. Pivoting left, I swung in a swooping arc, disposing of another two rebels that had come from my left. Their bodies flew backward, crumpling to the ground, showering my armor and face with blood. Spinning rightwards, I extended my hammer, feeling the vibrations as I delivered deadly blows to the men that had encircled me. Twice as many rebels took the places of the fallen, my waning energy causing my strikes to become wild and sloppy.

Rapidly lunging, I thwarted the attacks of another group of rebels. The power of my swings propelled my body forward, causing me to clench my core to keep from falling. Shifting my footing, I regained my balance, only to be knocked to the side by an enemy soldier charging me aggressively. Reaching out his hands, he seized my neck, forcing the air from my lungs. Stumbling to the right, I rammed his body into a cluster of his comrades, trying without success to break free.

Pain shot through my chest, dropping me to my knees. Thrashing wildly, I fought for breath, attempting to pry thick, meaty fingers from my throat. My vision blurred around the edges, the sounds of combat fading into far-off cries of battle and pain. My chest burned, and my head throbbed, the lack of air causing me to have hallucinations of a shadowed ship and a rusted red river.

Far off screams of terror broke through my awareness. Intense heat at the back of my head sent my heart pounding, gifting me with the strength I needed to pull free. Falling forward, I collapsed onto the road, my chin digging into rocks that lined the path. Harsh coughing sent me reeling, my chest bursting with pain as I gulped in the air. Rolling onto my side, I witnessed my attacker being ripped to pieces by angry, flaming corpses. Hot tears stung my eyes, and I wiped them away, suddenly scrambling to my feet to avoid being crushed by the burning, dead men above me.

Twisting right, I recovered my hammer from the grass, watching the corpses rising from the dead. Turning back towards the castle, I spotted Knomucca, her bloodied, wraith-like hands pressing hard into the ground, her ever-present gauntlets lying in pieces beside her. Briefly, our eyes locked, and I was met with a sad smile, her face quickly vanishing behind the brutal battle. The pain in my chest worsened as I dwelled upon her sadness, praying that the rebels she had resurrected would aid in her victory.

The remaining rebels screamed and shot flaming arrows, knowing fire was the only true weapon against the undead. Yet their fear still drove them back, their eyes fixed on the processional of past comrades, now possessed by the desire to end their lives. Our armies charged down the hill, my troops leaving no one alive as they chased the rebels towards the supply wagons.

An uneasy feeling took root in my stomach, fueling my steps as I followed in pursuit.

Soldiers, horses, and corpses clashed around the supply carts, evading flaming arrows whilst they fought for their lives. Fire danced across the treetops, its proximity to the supply wagons making me very apprehensive. Alchemist fire had been brought in case of emergency and was very volatile.

"Oi, fall back! Get away from there!" I bellowed as I ran down the hill.

Whistling the command to retreat to the castle, my demands were eclipsed by screams and deafening explosions. The ground shook, and the wagons caught fire, the impact of the flames destroying the living dead and many of the retreating rebel forces. A second wave of green flames ignited further down the line, engulfing more carts as it spread. Flaming shrapnel collided with nearby carts, igniting them in a bright green blaze, the inferno threatening to consume all of our supplies.

I sprinted towards the supply train, tempting the emerald flames with my flesh as I reached into the fire to save what supplies I could. Troops of The Gods' Guard ran to my aid, pulling the salvageable wagons to safety. I grabbed everything I could and flung it into the grass, growing discouraged as the fire consumed yet another cart. Swearing loudly, I quickened my pace, gambling my hands in a game of chance as I prayed I would not lose them to the flames.

Sudden, powerful gusts of wind fanned the verdant flames towards my face, sending me toppling backwards. I rolled to my feet to avoid desecrating where the dead lay. Overhead, shadows obscured the sun, and I followed their movements with my eyes. Thornin hovered in the sky above the carts, beating his powerful wings in obedience to Knomucca's whistles. Controlling their movements, Thornin's speed increased until a windstorm extinguished what had become a pyre for the ranks of the many dead.

I turned my back to the carnage that had been lain upon the hillside. Unscrewing my water skin, I drained the water in three gulps, desperately desiring more. I found a sturdy tree to lean against before unfastening my boot, fishing out the half-smoked spliff that I immediately set to lighting. My muscles throbbed, my awareness of my injuries darkening my mood.

I wished I could sit, though I knew I could not, for much required my attention before setting off south again. Pinching the smoke in the corner of my mouth, I pressed forward, tracing my steps toward the supply wagons to assess their damage. The wagons of explosives were no longer standing, their heavily enchanted wheels and support beams resembling a wooden exoskeleton. Barrels of wine had fueled the flames; the casks had burned open from the heat and now lay empty. Many rations were burned beyond recognition, though the food carts at the edges of the convoy had been spared. One of several alchemy carts had been singed to a pile of green, smoldering ashes. The wagon had contained some of Knomucca's fragile potion elements for the Elixer of Life and ingredients for other complex potions.

Approaching voices from my right caught my attention. Turning towards the sound, I spotted several soldiers walking towards me, accompanied by the Head Healer, High Priestess, and Head Alchemist, Hazel.

"Greetings, High Magister Hazel. Good of you to find me," I called the approaching group.

"Aye, Commander," Hazel came to a halt with a forced salute. "What has the damage been thus far?"

"It pains me to relay such upsetting news," I started. "Your wagon of fragile elements has been destroyed by the rebels."

"By The Creator's mercy," Hazel said, peering around me and placing her hand over her mouth. "Was nothing spared?"

"Indeed, the bastard's been blown to smithereens."

"Commander, how am I expected to proceed?" Hazel spat, venom in her voice, her shadow dark in her eyes. "I need my herbs, crystals, and tonics to administer medicine to the injured."

"You are going to have to improvise. Send soldiers, servants, and apprentices to scavenge what you can from the kitchens and silos. Have you seen Bullet? He can help retrieve botanicals and wine from the stores."

"I have not seen him," Hazel said. "I will try to be more observant, however."

"Aye, set to work then," I ordered, pulling deeply on my spliff to cover the sudden jolt of pain through my chest.

"You ought to consider coming by once things have settled," Hazel suggested, the edge in her voice softening with a light touch on my shoulder. Pulling my eyes fully away from the carts, I took in her framed brown hair and calculating eyes, the shadow no longer darkening them.

"I appreciate your concern," I waved her away with a gentle hand. "I have smoking herbs... I shall be well."

"The dismissal of your wounds is frustrating," Hazel said in the tone of a scolding mother. "Smoking herbs are not the cure for everything."

"I disagree," I said flatly.

"Commander..." Hazel's eyes softened, her tone becoming lighter. "Your wounds could use tending."

"I am certain they could," I said confidently, "though there are other matters that require my attention."

"Simply come find me when you are able," Hazel said. "You are clearly in need of my care."

"I am well," I said, pulling softly on the spliff in my hand.

"Stubbornness doth not suit you, Commander," Hazel chided. "I shall see you in a while. It is fated."

Turning on her heel, Hazel strode away, walking purposefully back towards the hill.

"The rest of you," I barked, pointing a finger at the soldiers who had begun to follow behind after Hazel's departure. "Find Sergeant Kyreese and assist in emptying the carts. Everything that is salvageable needs to be packed on the remaining wagons in exactly one hour. After which, have her provide me with an update on our inventory. Am I making myself clear?"

"Clear as quartz," said Lieutenant Tyfis with a salute.

"Find as many extra hands as you need to assist you. We have lost far too much time and we need to assemble on the road as soon as possible. Lieutenant Tyfis, before you begin, find apprentices of The Healer to attend to those who are busy with the wagons. And would you mind, too terribly, keeping an eye out for my horse?"

"Aye, will do. I'll be setting off then," Tyfis said, lowering his salute before vanishing north up the hill with the throng of soldiers.

The rest of his escort encroached on the wagons, immediately beginning to scrap wood, unload supplies, remove bodies, and secure the horses. Pleased to notice the rest of our army had finally emerged from the castle, I left the wagons to delegate the more gruesome tasks to a group of first-year rookies sallying at the top of the hill.

"Oi, it appears you are looking for something to do," I declared, challenging them with a commanding glare in my eyes. "Fetch some shovels from the stables and get digging. We need to bury everyone in the castle cemetery and mark the graves of those we can identify. See to it the castle scribes in the library assist you in creating the epitaphs."

The cowering rookies scattered, scrambling towards the distant portcullis. I took a cleansing breath then inhaled my smoke, pushing my pain into the ground as I relaxed and centered myself. After ten deep pulls, my smoke was finished, prompting me to turn from the carnage of the battlefield and walk up the length back toward the castle.

I finally approached the drawbridge, veering west at seeing a servant's tent erected beside the moat. Casks of water, barrels of wine, herbs, spare clothes, and bread from breakfast were being distributed to the soldiers from behind a set of rickety tables. I grabbed the bags at my belt and fished through them, finding my onion skins and entering the tent. Dodging around the tables, I procured herbs, beginning to roll several spliffs from sweet grass, lavender, and nettles.

Three soft thuds caught my attention. Glancing up from my work, I noticed goblets of water and wine had been placed on the table beside me, bordering a platter of bread, nuts, and cheese. I longed for a hearty cut of pork. However, it is considered disrespectful to consume meat after a battle, for in the afterlife, it is believed soldiers will long for the delicacy.

To the First Warrior, I thought, striking a spliff in sacrifice and cleansing my spirits with smoke. I am grateful my life hath been spared.

Exhaling deeply, I rubbed my neck, grabbing the water to drink in an attempt to soothe my wounds. The nuts and cheese were inhaled after my blessing had been finished, my energy returning with renewed vigor and purpose. Preparing a dozen spliffs, I slipped them into my smoking sacks, glancing down at my appearance and deciding to change my garments. The tent had grown progressively busy with soldiers and apprentices coming and going. I stepped behind the privacy screen to wash my body, freshen my garb, and replace my armor. Stepping out, I retrieved my hammer and placed it on my belt once more.

After drinking almost an entire cask of water, washing my face, and refilling my water skin, I pushed through the canvas doorway. The sudden whinnying of a horse made my heart flutter, and I spun around to see Ajax leading Truff by the reigns.

"I knew we would find him," Ajax teasingly said to Truff, stroking the white stripe from his nose to his forehead. "Someone was looking for you, Commander."

"Hey there, Truff," I said, my heart pounding in panic as I realized he was standing there alone. "Where is Archie?"

"The Chief has him," Ajax began. "I helped to corral the spooked horses, and I wanted to make sure Truff found you."

"Is Bullet well?"

"Aye, he seems fine..."

"Thank the gods."

"Though it is rumored his set of castle keys has been stolen in the chaos."

"Excellent..." I said sarcastically. "Where is Bullet now?"

"He was with Kiyoko just now when I saw him," Ajax said, slipping Truff's reigns into my hands. "The pair of them were trying a locator spell but to no avail."

"Oi... lovely..." I said with an acrimonious sigh.

"It also might interest you to know Her Worship is over near Hazel's tent, if you fancied a word..." Ajax said with a wink.

"I fancy a word indeed," I said, patting Truff between the eyes and lightly biting his ear.

"Follow the curve of the trees towards the Western Watchtower and you will find her," she directed.

"Aye, thank you kindly," I said, tugging Truff's reigns. I said over my shoulder, "If you would not mind encouraging urgency at the supply wagons, that would be much appreciated."

"Aye... I shall do what I can until the Merchant's Banquet," Ajax called after me.

Curving right, the moat bent with the landscape, trees twisting outward beyond the battlefield. The air grew quiet as Hazel's tent fell into focus; the energy kept low to avoid overstimulating the recovering soldiers. Smaller tents dotted the field in a circle, allowing extra privacy to perform procedures or provide rest. Flames of blue, white, and orange danced in cauldrons outside of the tents, prepared to be used for cauterizations.

Off on the right stood Knomucca, heavily focusing on feeding Thornin fruit from the palm of her hand. Resisting the urge to run towards her with the news of Hazel's wagon, I kept my composure. I tied Truff to a post on Hazel's tent, tightly securing the reigns before I peeked beyond the canvas. Hazel did not appear to be inside, releasing me from the obligation to address her.

Retreating from the tent, I moved through the field towards Knomucca. The sounds of my belt clanging announced my arrival, coaxing Knomucca's eyes to rise from the face of her dragon. Fetching a smoke from my pouch, I offered it with a match, delighted in her acceptance with a nod and a smile.

"Greetings," I said, taking in her beautifully disheveled appearance. Her sopping clothes were shredded, the water plastering the remaining fabric to her skin. Long, deep scratches marred her legs, likely from having flown on Thornin without a saddle. Her gauntlets were clean, though her hands were bloodied, her face struggling to remain steady as she finally met my eyes. Through her windswept hair, I spotted a simple silver carnation, the emerald leaves carved in the shapes of elusively familiar symbols. "May I ask how you are faring?"

"Everett..." Knomucca began slowly, "I am grateful to see you, however, I am confused as to why I am seeing you. Were you and your troops not set to depart just after dawn?"

"Aye, Your Worship, we should already have the morning's travel behind us. Alas, the Gods of Fate were watching over you, for the events of the day hath delayed our departure."

"How do you mean?" she asked, shifting the Tora Berries to her opposite hand and pulling deeply on the spliff.

Beginning with the events of the night before, I disclosed to Knomucca everything from Kiyoko's maiden and tardiness to the goat and the banner I had seen fluttering in the woods. All the while, she smoked and listened, periodically interjecting with curiosities. When my words concluded, I absently rubbed my neck, my throat aggravated from all the talking so recently after their trauma.

"How bad is it, Everett?" Knomucca asked.

It was unclear whether she had been asking about my injury or the status of our soldiers and supplies. Deciding it was the latter, I began speaking. "I do not have the status on everything as of yet, however, it appears quite grim, Knomucca."

"If you are using such familiar terms as my given name, the situation must be dire."

"I like saying your name," I said, my chest throbbing once more as my heart began to pound. "It is not professional to use your given name. Do not associate it as bad whilst thinking of me."

"I like when you say my name," she said, stepping forward, her eyes studying my face. "Tell me, what action are you taking to expedite the departure process?"

"Soldiers are tending the carts, reorganizing supplies, and discarding the ruined wagons. The graves are being dug as we speak, and troops have been designated to bury the bodies. Hazel and the apprentices are healing the survivors, and servants have been providing replenishments by the drawbridge."

"Excellent," she said. "Very impressive work, Everett."

"There is some news I regret to report, however," I said, taking on a more somber demeanor.

"I have already been informed that Bullet lost his keys," Knomucca said, and the anger I saw flash through the emerald of her eyes made my heart ache.

"I am glad not to be the one to bear this news," I began, "yet there is something worse I am afraid..."

"What other misfortune has befallen us, Everett?" she sighed heavily.

"The wagon of fragile potion elements was destroyed in the explosion," I revealed, the words further souring my spirits.

Knomucca's face fell, her eyes darkening despite her attempts to disguise them.

"My potion elements..." her voice trailed off as she clenched her fists in frustration. Dark blue juice from the Tora berries stained her fingers, pulp from the soured flesh mashing to fall to the ground.

"Aye..." I said quietly, following her earlier boldness and moving closer to her. "I feel truly awful about it. Have you any idea how I may assist in gathering new ingredients for The Elixir?"

"At this juncture, I am uncertain," she confessed. "Though I shall take some time to reflect."

"I hope you find clarity," I said, producing another smoke from my pouch. "Take this and allow it to clear your mind. I am here if you need a shoulder to lean upon."

"Aye, thank you Everett," Knomucca said, grazing her fingers over mine as she slipped the spliff from my hand. "You are quite the gentlemen."

Her fingers lingered for the briefest of moments, her eyes drifting up as she lifted her face towards me.

"Anything for you," I said, struggling to talk through my nerves.

"Everett..." she paused, rolling the spliff into her hand before caressing my neck with a finger. "Your bruises..."

My heart fluttered, and my stomach lurched with her touch, momentarily distracting me from my initial reaction to her words.

"I am no stranger to bruises," I said.

An unreadable energy floated through her eyes, her finger tracing a path along my windpipe and jawline.

"These ones are different..." she trailed off, her voice tinged with relief and regret.

Her touch sent a shock through my body. I reacted without thinking, snatching her hand and staring intensely into her eyes. Leaning forward, I could smell patchouli, the sweetness I had always imagined would surround her when we finally kissed. Inhaling sharply, I resisted the urge to smile, focusing on enjoying every second of the bliss that was to come.

A hot puff of steam suddenly emerged from my right. My head throbbed with a fresh wave of pain, the force sending me staggering backward. Thornin had shoved his face between our bodies, greedily devouring the remains of the berries from Knomucca's right hand. Pressing forward, he wedged between us, turning sharply to search me for sugar lumps.

"Oi, no treats from me," I said, laughing at the dragon's affections.

Knomucca whistled sharply, forcing the dragon back with the shrillness of her pitch. Thornin glared as he backed away, baring his teeth at her rudeness. Sudden footsteps were approaching on the left, and I turned to discover Kiyoko purposefully striding towards us.

"Greetings," he said with a salute, quickly averting his eyes as he ignored how close we had come to kissing. "I am sorry to have to interrupt. Commander, your presence is requested at the wagons."

"He'll be along in a moment," Knomucca said. "We must have a word with you first, Kiyoko."

Kiyoko lowered his eyes, his face growing tense and nervous.

"Would you mind terribly if I partook in the herb?" Kiyoko asked.

"If you must," Knomucca said.

Lighting the smoke he had already been holding, he took a long drag before he spoke. "What is the matter regarding?"

Knomucca took a controlled breath before beginning. "Everett has divulged the events of the morning, and I have to admit I am not impressed."

"Aye, it was a horrible time to be selfish-" Kiyoko began regretfully.

"However," Knomucca said, raising a hand to silence him. "Had you been here promptly, we most certainly would have lost the castle. Everett has disclosed that you have already paid your dues... I think we can forget about what happened this morning, and wash it down the river, so to speak."

"I am in alignment with Her Worship," I said.

"Thank you for your leniency, Your Worship," Kiyoko bowed his head before continuing. "You should know I believe the rebels to be from the mountains, for the hooves of their horses wore protection from the snow."

"The theory is in parallel with the banner I saw," I said, quickly explaining the flag in the woods to them.

"Trickery and treachery are afoot," Knomucca said. "We must force our eyes open and remain vigilant. It displeases me to think there may be traitors in our midst."

"How would you like us to proceed, Your Worship?" I inquired, growing uneasy with the increasing threats towards my beloved.

"I shall leave for The Luna Sea in a short while," Knomucca began. "And you, gentlemen, shall ride with the troops straight through the night. We shall meet outside the city, Ostarie, halfway through our trip to Riverside to make up for today's lost time. I shall also be updated on our inventory once we settle at camp, whereupon we must revise our plan of action at such time."

"Understood," Kiyoko said in parallel to my salute. "If all is well and good, we best be setting off then." Pivoting right, we stepped away, suddenly stopping when Knomucca spoke again.

Knomucca nodded. "You best indeed, and make haste. We cannot afford any other tragedies."

"Stay wise." I said with a salute. "Until we meet again."

V

KNOMUCCA

The early morning sun rose bright in the east, painting warm streaks across my face. I woke with sore muscles and stabbing pains through my ribs, my head throbbing from a night of restless sleep. Visions of fire and screams plagued my mind, the nightmares that haunted my dreams becoming more frequent with my Ascension drawing so near.

Turning onto my side, I noticed servants had been busy at work, stacking cherry logs by the fire and laundering linens in preparation for my return at week's end. A tightly rolled spliff rested on the bedside table beside a goblet of water, prompting me to sit up and indulge to combat the pain.

Leaning over, I peered through the open balcony doors to discover Thornin's absence. On normal occasion, this caused me no stress, for it was part of his daily routine to disappear for several hours at a time to hunt. However, the need to collect my remaining potion elements weighed on my mind, and I prayed his hunt would be swift as to not delay us further. Sighing through my smoke I retrieved a roll of parchment, ink, and a quill from a drawer in the bedside table, deciding to practice my calligraphy whilst I had a few spare moments.

Writing was among the many disciplines I used to study the art of combat, and it was the practice I enjoyed most. Landscape painting, dancing, sparring, playing games of strategy, meditation, and study of ancient techniques all aided in my practice and mastery. These exercises encompassed a wide variety of skills, from precise movements and strokes, to strengthening memory and stamina. The importance of drawing wisdom from many sources influenced my studies, for the desire to be knowledgeable in all things was a feat I hoped to one day achieve.

After scrawling the names of my trusted companions, along with several herbs, flowers, and stones, an entire hour had passed. A sudden, sharp knock pounded upon my chamber doors, jarring me forcefully from my scroll work. Reaching forward, I seized the corner of the bed sheet, wrapping it tightly around my body whilst shifting to be more comfortable. Lighting a new spliff, I readied myself before acknowledging my unexpected company at the door.

"You may enter," I declared.

"Good morrow, Your Worship," an irreverent voice croaked from beyond the door.

I was surprised to see Marthen walking stiffly through the heavy iron doors. Marthen was Syler's personal servant, as close to her as Roice was to me. Her long green dress was woven from grass and leaves, rustling around her as she moved into the room. Elaborate, greying braids wound through a fragrant flower crown, wafting the delightful scent of chamomile through the air towards me.

"Good morrow, Marthen," I said, taking a brief pull of my spliff before returning my parchment, quill, and ink to the bedside table. "To what do I owe the pleasure?"

"Your sister was hoping you would join her for morning tea and pastry," Marthen smiled coyly.

"I would be delighted," I said, grateful for the chance to see my twin before setting off. "When will the refreshments be served?"

"Everything should be ready within the hour, m'lady."

"Excellent, I will head there posthaste," I said. "As soon as I'm decent, of course."

"In your own time," Marthen said. "I shall relay the message to Her Loveliness and finish preparing. We shall see you momentarily."

Marthen dipped low in a practiced curtsy, then turned on her heel and vanished through the doors once more. I finished my spliff before tossing aside the blankets and rising to a stand. My bare feet padded across the cold tiles, the sounds of my footsteps muffled as I entered the carpeted closet. Walking towards the back, I found a shelf of leggings, selecting a pair made of grey leather. Moving right, I approached the tunics, finding one with loose sleeves and a tight bodice sewn from dark purple wool. The tunic draped across my thighs, curving in the back to stretch taut. Behind me stood a rack of shoes and I wasted no time in choosing thigh-high, white leather boots.

In the center of my closet was an immense, spinning carousel of weapons hanging on heavy iron hooks for ease of access. Obtaining a thick, chain-link belt, I fastened it around my waist with a clunky amethyst clasp. A bouquet of poisonous throwing darts was first to be secured on my left, followed closely after by a diamond encrusted dagger. A pair of iron bladed knives were slipped into my boots, leaving room on my belt for an axe. A simple silver short sword was fastened to the belt on the right, balancing the weight once my khopesh had been added. I slung my hand-crafted bow over my shoulders, following a quiver of arrows encased in leather to counterbalance the weight.

A set of slim and sharp knives were attached to my wrists beneath my sleeves, held in place by thick leather holsters. Chainmail armor was slipped over my head, adding an elegance that my appearance had been lacking. My current pair of gauntlets were exchanged for a fingerless pair forged from iron, the knuckles and palms laden with amethyst and tourmaline crystals.

Lastly, I approached the back of the closet, removing a hidden wooden panel from the wall, revealing a nook of deep, black velvet. A shining silver sword glowed within its depths, as softly as a single star in the night sky. The sword had belonged to my mother, having been gifted it by her mother before her, and so on since the time when our family tree was an acorn. I drew the sword from its cradle, feeling the blades magnetism and allure as I slid it into the leather sheath. The hilt shimmered and the pommel glinted with a reddish hue as they were carved from carnelian. Lifting my hair, I slid the sword down the length of my spine, hiding the hilt as my hair draped around my shoulders.

Grabbing a servant's cart from the corner, I loaded the shelves with equipment to tie to Thornin's saddle. Seven quivers of arrows, a pair of dueling swords, three pairs of dragonscale gloves, two water skins of water, sacks of smoking herbs and onion skins, matches, a bed roll, three pairs of gauntlets, and an extra set of boots were stacked precariously atop Thornin's specially designed dragonscale saddle. A hollowed compartment for storage rested within the cantle, the opening secured by an iron lock and a heavy golden chain. The swell of the saddle housed a rose quartz blessed by my sister, matching perfectly with the peach moonstones and labradorite gem in laced stirrups. Iron clasps hung from the bottom of the saddle, providing areas to hang bags or weapons if desired. The saddle could sit double, and though there was room for cargo, the saddle was light weight, flexible, and sturdy.

Before leaving my chambers, I returned to my bed, grabbing my enchanted pouch to hang across my body. Emptying the bedside table, I filled another pouch full of supplies to roll spliffs, attaching it to my belt alongside another box of matches. Closing the drawer, I rose to a stand, noticing a book on the bedside called, "Unseen Creatures of Crossfire," which I had been in the midst of reading. Rarely did I travel without a book in hand, for I enjoyed studying when I had spare moments to myself. Decisively, I slipped it into my pouch with the others, adding it to the collection of tomes I was bringing along for reference or in case of anxiety induced insomnia.

After checking one final time that I had all I needed, I began pushing the cart across the chamber floor. Pulling the door open, I awkwardly wedged through, gaining more respect for Roice and the servants who could gracefully handle the carts. Turning right, I moved down the corridor, following the curve to the opposite side of The Western Donjon. Syler's chambers were across the tower, the pair of us having decided to keep the rooms assigned to us in our youth. The chambers were strategically located, high enough to avoid easy attack, but low enough to risk escape in the frigid, tempered waters of the moat below. My balcony provided the necessary accommodations for Thornin, his scales being too sharp and dangerous to keep him indoors. Though Syler did not have a familiar to house, she did have an immense love for the moon, constructing a lavish window seat in which she was often found relaxing to gaze upon its radiance.

Approaching her doors, I shimmied the cart parallel to the wall, passing around it in order to announce my arrival. Raising a fist, I pounded in code, alternating between the rhythms we used to communicate covertly.

"You may enter," Marthen croaked from beyond the doors.

Lugging the cart through the threshold, I entered into Syler's chambers. The rising sun painted pink and orange through the large eastern window, the glass panes slightly ajar to admit the chilly morning breeze. Syler's blanket and cushion covered window-seat was large and luxurious, woven of hemp and twine to form a wide and shallow oval. The shape allowed for lounging in any position with continuous enjoyment of the sky. When conditions were clear, the view was extensive, portraying distant settlements, smoke from far off chimneys, dense forests, and far off mountains.

Partially consumed cups of wine sat abandoned on tables beside the window seat and bookcases, the messy remnants of a needlework project waited to be resumed. A large, ornate fireplace took up the wall opposite the window-seat, smoldering ashes from last night's fire smoking lazily with the scent of pine. A decorated circular cake warmed on the coals, the chocolate topping melting down the sides in rich rivulets. Syler's enormous bed took up the northern wall, extending outwards to have views of both the fire and sky. A quaint dining table, ladened with tea cups and platters was nestled in the center of the room.

An impressive, elaborately carved stone altar rested between her bed and the fireplace. A heavy silver statue of a swan on prancing legs stood tall on a granite octagonal pedestal, its amethyst eyes and moonstone talons glittering in the soft morning sun. An incense stand smelted from gold, shaped like a rose was currently in use atop the swan's wings, making the air potent with the smell of lavender. Candlesticks of varying shapes, lengths, and colors surrounded the statue, casting a soft glow across the swan's intricate detail.

"Greetings," I said, leaving the cart beside the wall.

"Gracious Gods!" Marthen exclaimed. "Did you haul that monstrosity here by your lonesome?"

"Aye, 'tis lighter than it looks," I said, beginning to unfasten my belt.

"Whom may I fetch to assist you in removing that from the castle?"

"I can manage well enough on my own," I said firmly.

"How foolish! It is improper to allow you to proceed any further without proper escort. Where are the servants tending you in Roice's absence?"

"I am handling my own affairs for a while," I said, and not for the first of times. "And I am perfectly capable of escorting myself."

"Insulting," she snapped, sending a wave of annoyance to burn through my hands. "I will provide assistance for you in moving it."

Deep breath, I thought with my inhalation, whilst fighting not to answer unkindly.

"Pray tell... whom is available that I may retrieve?" Marthen urged.

I released my breath, feeling my hands burn as I formulated my thoughts. Often, I had to question if Marthen meant well, for she was far too strict in terms of convention.

"If you are going to force my hand... Maliche could assist," I said stiffly. "Most of my trusted are occupied in preparations for The Ascension, or tending to the Merchants Banquet, which is why I wished to handle the matter myself..."

"Wonderful," she said with a self-satisfied nod. "Whereabouts may I find Maliche this fine morn?"

"I know him to be tending to matters in the greenhouse," I said. "He should be adding the last moment decorations and adjustments to the table bouquets for The Merchants Banquet this evening."

Maliche, the castle's head gardener, rose to his position after transferring from the militia. Upon his fifth year of service as a soldier, Maliche had been assigned to Chief Warrant Officer Bullet to provide security for the castle's connective portal to the Underworld. One night, as a cruel initiation prank, some of the soldiers decided to play a game of Slayer. Slayer involves using comical spells and weapons for sport in killing the creatures that break through the castle's connective portal, and it has caused many close encounters. It is a game I admit I condone too frequently, though there are demons in the Underworld that I cannot control as of yet and I don't mind the help in wrangling them. A fight between Maliche and a six-headed serpent went horribly wrong, requiring all who were in attendance to intervene and save his life. Maliche lost everything beneath the knee of his left leg, resulting in his retirement and manifesting his influence to become a gardener to escape the confinement of the castle.

"Excellent," Marthen said. "I shall send a message to him once I find a spare moment."

"Very well," I heaved a breath.

I hung my belt on the handle of my servant's cart to be polite. Wearing a sword on your hip during an invited meal was believed to bring unfair fortune, and I did not wish to attract any unwanted energy.

"Silver on your side, in darkness thrive," Syler's voice rang through the closet curtain. "Sage decision in hanging your belt."

"Aye... best not to gamble my fortunes," I said thoughtfully.

"My wise sister," Syler said, moving through the room to throw her arms around me by way of salutations. "I am delighted you could join me."

"I found the invitation to be a pleasant surprise," I said, warmly returning her affections.

Releasing our embrace, Syler made an inviting gesture towards the table. Golden stemless goblets with handles on the sides sat atop lace covered hexagonal plates. A ceramic tea kettle adorned a spinning silver platter bordered by a plethora of spices, garnishes, and herbs. Four tightly rolled spliffs fanned outwards from a simple copper ash tray, decorated deliberately with matches in a latticework pattern.

"The table looks beautiful," I said, waiting for Syler to sit before I could do so.

"It is you who looks beautiful," Syler said with a smile. Marthen pulled out her chair and Syler folded into it, draping a silken cloth into the lap of her sleeveless, golden-yellow dress. "Your energy is quite... intimidating."

I smiled, politely declining Marthen's assistance with a wave of my hand. Upon taking my seat, my hands began to itch and burn, the discomfort they brought from my decaying soul made me feel suddenly insecure.

"You are quite kind for the compliment," I responded in a timid tone.

"May I offer you ladies some tea?" Marthen interjected. "We have a lovely lemon that would pair deliciously with the chocolate pastry."

"Perhaps a cup of chamomile... And please, bring the gin," Syler said with a sly grin

"And jasmine for myself," I said, adjusting the position of my gauntlets to quell the itching before perusing the herbs in the center of the table.

"Very well," said Marthen, beginning to fill small silver bowls with honey. Scooping the herbs from their jars, she rolled them in the golden sweetener, coating the plants in a generous layer to sit and settle before she continued. "I shall return with the gin, and I shall deliver the message to Maliche."

"Splendid," Syler said with a smile. "I appreciate your service."

Marthen curtsied before turning confidently and retreating through the chamber doors with practiced grace.

"Thank the Gods for this respite from her presence," Syler said, chuckling softly as I smirked at her from over the tea kettle. "She is far too formal, and could do to loosen some stitches."

"You'd be correct, of course," I said, playfully scrunching the silken serviette from atop my platter in my fist and throwing it at her face. "Though she was our mother's servant, so best don your mask of politeness."

Syler laughed, snorting as she returned my assault with one of her own. "Perhaps she could tend to your affairs once you are home instead of Roice for a while."

"I already disclosed that I will be handling my own affairs," I said, a little too quickly. "Roice is taking time away to be with family, and I am planning to pay him handsomely to retire and stay with them permanently."

"Oi... someone is awfully defensive..." Syler teased through my blushing. "Knomucca, I see right through you."

"As I wished you to..." I said, desiring to quash the discomfort in my hands. Standing abruptly, I fished the stickied honey and herbs from the bowls on the table, plopping them into the mugs. "May I serve you, sweet sister?"

"That would be delightful, my twin blessed of fire," she said, her sudden formality jarring given her earlier complaints.

"It is my pleasure, my twin blessed of water," I said, finishing the phrase after an awkward pause.

Lifting the tea kettle, I poured the water, releasing billows of fragrant steam as the herbs and honey steeped. Moments later Marthen returned through the door, her brow furrowed in outward annoyance at the sight of my filling our glasses.

"You ought to have left that task to me!" she scolded, angrily slamming the bottle on the table. "It is below your station."

"Fetching gin for us was perfect," I said through the burning of my palms, placing Syler's tea in her hand and pouring in copious amounts of the gin. The fruity distilled juniper berries blended perfectly with her fragrant chamomile, and paired delightfully well with the subtle sweetness of my green jasmine tea.

"You simply must serve the cake," Syler suggested, stifling a giggle.

"There is no need to patronize me," Marthen muttered, retrieving the cake from the hearth and carrying it to the table. "It was disrespectful to send me on an errand and serve the tea in my absence."

Syler smirked mischievously, daring me from across the table to interject at Marthen's passive aggressive mumbling.

"I simply wanted to serve my sister tea," I stated flatly, sitting straight against the back of my seat to take a long drink. My hands continued to burn through my annoyance as I held her gaze.

Marthen's face flashed with anger, her knifework as forced as her smile whilst she cut the cake into slices. Taking our plates, she filled them with the dripping fudge cake, the inside dough swirling with vanilla and cinnamon circles.

"You've outdone yourself," Syler said with a smile as sickly sweet as the cake, obtaining papsal from the table to apply in case of poison.

Mirroring her motions, I layered on the seasoning, smiling to myself when the cake proved to be safe. "This looks delicious. I am quite fond of cinnamon."

"It is one of The Creator's many gifts," Syler said, lowering her head in a silent prayer before continuing. "I wanted everything to be special, so we could celebrate our Name Day, just the two of us."

"Shouldn't we have waited until after The Ascension to celebrate?" I asked, resisting the urge to sigh in bliss from the richness of the cake.

"Nonsense," Syler said with the shaking of her head. "The Ascension should not be allowed to dictate how and when the pair of us find enjoyment from our Name Day."

"I suppose you are right," I said, watching as Syler took a delicate nibble from her cake and washed it down with tea. "Your frivolity is quite inspiring."

"You flatter me," Syler said as her face fell. "It is a ruse to cover my nerves. Beginning my next adventure without you puts me at unease."

"I admit I too find it bothersome we are being separated," I said, enjoying the warmth of my brew to combat the breeze from the open window.

The briefest of tears formed in her eyes, though her composure stabilized quickly as she finished her slice of cake. Pushing her empty cup and platter to the end of the table, Syler spoke in a strained tone. "Marthen, would you please begin in cleaning this up?"

"I would be delighted," Marthen said with a self-satisfied smile, loading the empty plates, cups, kettle, and herbs onto a servant's cart. When the table was cleared, Marthen rose to her full height, and spoke with an eager tone. "Could I interest you in anything else?"

"We shall retire with smoke by the window. Perhaps you could bring us some wine?" Syler asked.

"Very well," Marthen said, gracefully pushing the cart and leaving through the doors once more.

Picking up the ash tray with the spliffs, I walked over to the window-seat and placed them on a small side table between us. Obtaining a familiar patchwork quilt, I curled my legs beneath it, finally adjusting my gauntlets before taking a spliff in my fingers. Striking a match and lighting the herbs, I inhaled deeply, tasting the subtle hints of nettles and coltsfoot through the sweet grass. Syler selected a smoke and sparked a match, lighting small flames at the end of her spliff, which extinguished with a sudden and fast breath.

"Oi, all hands on deck," I teased, as smoking was a rarity for my sister. Our mother had strongly disliked smoking, thinking it a disgusting habit, unbefit of elegance. "I've noticed you have recently been partaking in the herb more often. Is there something plaguing your mind?"

She lowered her eyes shamefully. "I will admit my thoughts have been rather... turbulent," Syler mumbled.

"I understand how you're feeling," I said, exhaling a ring of smoke on the breeze.

"Mother has been on my mind," Syler confessed, lowering her spliff, smoke trailing along the ends of her words. "I wonder what it's like where she is... and I wonder what wisdom she would have for us now."

I paused as I reflected on my sister's words. After a moment, I smiled and said, "I suppose she would tell us to trust our intuition."

"I wager she would." Syler quietly agreed.

"Our instincts are the most powerful weapons we possess," I said, dropping the ashes of my finished spliff from the window. "Mother would always say... hold faith in yourself and your choices, there is nary a safer place to carry our loyalties."

"Mind your manners," Syler said with a chortle, as she overexaggerated flicking her spliff into the tray between us. "You'll send Marthen into yet another tizzy."

"Oh, how tragic that would be," I said sarcastically, stifling a laugh.

Syler smirked and giggled before returning to our mother's wisdom. "An apple with the sunrise keeps a lady her wit... a barrel of wine with supper, and her secrets she shall admit."

I was delighted to see my mother's smile flash for the briefest of moments behind Syler's eyes.

"Her absence weighs on me more each day..." Syler said wistfully.

"I, too, wish she were here," I said. "She was always so elegant and mindful... Having her sword as all that remains of her shall never feel like enough."

"It never will be enough," Syler said heavily. "Although... I may have an idea for how I can help."

Rising suddenly from her seat, Syler abandoned her near-finished spliff and blankets, her movements jarring since I had begun to drift and relax. Crossing the room, she approached her rose quartz altar, opening a set of hidden doors near the bottom left. Removing a jagged panel, Syler retrieved a wooden box, sliding the stone back in place before returning to her seat.

"I have been wanting to give this to you for quite some time now," Syler began, removing the simple square lid from the box with the twist of a knob. "I know you were gifted Mother's sword upon our Name Day... the day she died... And I think Mother would want you to have this also... if she knew how you felt about Everett."

Setting aside the lid, Syler placed the box between us, showcasing a silver carnation hairpin with emerald leaves. Ridges on the gems swirled into ancient runic symbols - balance, unity, duality, love, and eternity bound together seamlessly into cohesive harmony.

"That... Is that Mother's betrothal broach?" I gasped, taking the box into my hands.

"I found it in her chambers after she died, whilst we were cleaning out her things. I remember her telling us about how our father gave this to her," Syler said wistfully.

"Aye, he thought a woman of her beauty was worthy of such an immaculate treasure," I said in the rehearsed words of Mother's stories.

"Aye... so Father crafted her the broach from silver, infusing it with his blood as devotion to never dishonor her..."

"Father broke his promise!" I snapped before pausing to calm my nerves. "They were never married... we were born and Father left Mother during the Witching Hour and she was left to care for us by her lonesome."

"It is challenging to understand why he left," Syler said soothingly. "There is much to which we are ignorant in regards to the situation."

Though I heard her words, it did little to soothe the fury growing within me. Smoke trickled through my fingertips, the smell of burnt cedar filling the air. Syler's eyes widened as she noticed the box, black fingerprints now scorched into the sides.

"Cool your forges," she said, hastily plucking the box from my hands.

"Mother never did tell us who our father was," I spat angrily. Breathing in deeply, I pressed forward. "We don't know half of who we are... that information could be crucial in some way to surviving the remainder of The Gods Trials, and it has been denied to us!"

"Mother had her reasons not to tell us," Syler said. "Fear not... She shall not have died in vain. Perhaps she was ashamed, perhaps her pregnancy was the result of an unwanted encounter. Only Mother knows why she has held the truth from us all these years."

In lieu of words, I reached forward and snatched my final spliff, lighting it in hopes of calming my rage.

"Knomucca, take the pin. Please. Wear it in your hair during the upcoming days and carry our mother close to you. And when you are ready, when you finally find the right time, give it to Everett."

"Give it to Everett?" I repeated Syler's words in confusion, lifting the pin and holding it in my hand. "Would he appreciate a gift such as this?"

"The carnation is of a simple design and the leaves match the color of your eyes. I suspect he will be honored in your giving it to him."

"Perhaps..." I mused, squeezing the pin gently between my fingers before slipping it into my hair.

"He could fashion it to his lapel," Syler teased with a giggle.

"Syler... this is a betrothal broach. That would suggest..." I replied in a quiet, contemplative voice.

"That would suggest you will have to ask for his hand in marriage," Syler said defiantly. "Enough with this foolishness in keeping your feelings silent.

You were made for each other. If you wait until after The Ascension, you will be a goddess. You know what happened to The First Warrior when he chose love over The Power."

"Anteyus betrayed The Power," I said, raising my hand in a silencing gesture. "I have no intentions to trace his footfalls. I will Ascend and fulfill my responsibility to the realms. Then, after an acceptable amount of time has passed, I will ask Everett to marry me."

"You think that by Ascending you will be allowed to marry Everett?"

"As long as I am protecting the balance of the realms, what does it matter how I spend my private time?"

"Knomucca, you have misinterpreted the legends of The First Warrior. He did not betray The Power; he chose love and was cast into Hell. If you don't tell Everett how you feel about him before you Ascend, you will Fall from Grace.

"Fall from Grace?" I asked in exasperation. "How could I Fall from Grace when I would be willingly accepting The Power and protecting the realms. I won't tell Everett how I feel until after The Ascension."

"Knomucca, you are not understanding. After you Ascend your duty is solely to the realms. You cannot indulge in mortal weakness by pursuing Everett."

"Marriage is a holy union," I said, springing to my feet and beginning to pace. "I think that supersedes all else."

"How daft can you be, Knomucca?" Syler asked with rising frustration. "Do you seriously believe The First Warrior did not think the same?"

"I don't recall hearing anything similar in the legends," I said defiantly.

"Throughout my years of study in becoming Goddess of Love, there is much lost to history that I have learned. In risk of repercussion, I will share this knowledge with you in the hope you abandon this fool's errand. 'Tis true that Anteyus sought marriage as the answer to his plight; however, The Creator thwarted his attempts to be wed well before any plans of ceremony could have been executed."

"There has to be a way," I said, running her words through my mind. If The Creator had kept the information from us that Anteyus had tried to be wed, there would have obviously been a reason why, and there would have been more truths He was hiding.

"Sweet sister, just tell Everett how you feel and avoid the risk of Falling from Grace altogether."

"I cannot, and probably should not," I said. "Our Mother gave up everything to grant me the gift of innocence for as long as she could. I owe all that I am to her. And what about everyone else we have lost? Kiyoko's wife, Rejj, Everett's father..." With a sweeping gesture of my hand, I indicated thousands of others. "There is no one else I can trust to look after them."

"Knomucca, you are playing with fire."

"Then it is fortunate I have been blessed by it."

"Our mother may have blessed us in the elements when we were born," Syler sighed. "That will not guarantee you immunity against them."

"All will be well, sister dearest."

"I am not fond of your plans," Syler scoffed as she noticed a cup near her seat. She lifted it to her nose and sniffed before shrugging and drinking the remnants. "But suit yourself. You have to trust in the decisions you make."

"Aye, and I must trust my intuition," I smirked.

"Oi, you are frustrating. I implore you to heed my warnings and consider what I've said," Syler's words slowed as the morning's intoxicants began to take hold. "I fear if you are not careful then The Creator will not be pleased."

Just then, the chamber doors fell open, admitting Marthen back into the room.

"Your timing is excellent," Syler hiccupped, her voice raising unnaturally as she lifted her cups to be filled.

"Have I missed something?" Marthen asked, taking in Syler's lack of composure and feeling the tense energy in the room.

"Simply sisters squabbling," Syler said, snickering.

"You know I believe such behavior unbefitting of a lady," scolded Marthen. "As is a lady being so deep in her cups before the Sun has even fully risen."

"It doth not matter what you believe," I snapped as fire seared beneath my skin. My heart pounded, angry at Syler for causing me to worry that despite all I had strived for, studied, and sacrificed, that The Creator would force me to deny my feelings for Everett.

Marthen wrinkled her nose in disgust, purposefully ignoring Syler's increasingly wild gestures to indicate her empty cups.

"You are appalling," she said. "I have some laundering to finish before Syler departs for The Far North in the morrow, perhaps I shall tend to that until the pair of you are separated, and your sister has her wits about her once more."

"That would be wise," I said, giving in to the pain through my hands, clenching my fists angrily.

"I know not what He in His infinite wisdom saw in the pair of you," Marthen mumbled as she stormed from the room, slamming the door behind her.

"I have no more patience for her," I snapped as I shifted my gauntlets into place. A blissful sigh escaped me as the pain in my hands finally ceased.

"That is as clear as the sky on this fine day," Syler said, gazing out the window and taking note of the sun's position. "Knomucca, it is after mid-morning. I have much else to attend to before the Merchants Banquet this evening, and I fear I must be getting back to work."

"How do you expect to be productive with your mind addled by the morning drink and herb?" I asked.

"It is only when you are not focused that you can see with the clearest of eyes," Syler said. "Regardless, 'tis nothing a cold bath would not remedy."

"And you thought I was being foolish," I sighed, extinguishing my smoke in the ashtray and returning to my cart of supplies. "Nevertheless, I should be sparring in the yard with the rookies whilst I wait for Thornin."

"Perhaps it would be good to exert some energy," Syler said.

I retrieved my belt and began to fasten it around my waist, balancing the weight and avoiding dragging any of the weapons on the ground.

"I hope there is no ill will between us," Syler said, hugging me once more after I readjusted my gauntlets. "I only spoke from my heart, and from my knowledge of our realm's lore. I want you and Evertt to have happiness together." Touching the pin, she added, "Love is strongest in the end, Knomucca."

"I have been struggling with this for years," I admitted, placing a hand on my sister's face so I could stare into her eyes. "I will find a way to protect the realms, do right by our mother, and marry the man I love."

"I sincerely hope so," said Syler, kissing my cheek. "If anyone can find a way, I believe it to be you."

"Thank you for the flattery," I said, winking.

"Stay wise, Knomucca," Syler said with a forced smile.

"Love and light," I said, giving my sister one final hug.

Opening the door, I pushed the cart through, forgetting Marthen's offer to have Maliche move it for me. Returning to the silent, empty hallway, I continued around the Western Tower. Halfway back towards my chambers, I took the servant's corridor, beginning to descend down spiraling circular ramps constructed from magic, masonry, and complicated mathematics. The cart rattled, the squeaking of the wheels echoing down the passage.

Partway down the corridor, the hall split in three directions. Following the path straight would lead to Valvang, whilst turning left and right led to a grand ballroom and servant's annex, respectively. A large oil painting marked the western wall; the shadowed silhouette of a galleon sailed sophisticatedly across the sea. A slender, black tree with gnarled roots was etched across the hull, its wide leaves interlaced with runes in a language I could not identify.

The ship belonged to Ozwal the Great, a death god prospect that almost Ascended nearly one thousand years ago. During a scouting voyage to the eastern islands, Ozwal mysteriously disappeared, rumored to have been seduced and murdered by Naiads protecting their home. His voyage was in search of a pinta berry, a rare fruit said to restore youth that grew sparsely on tropical trees. Ozwal desired to give this treasure to The Creator as an offering, attempting to procure it for his draft of The Elixir of Life. Like Ozwal, I, too, was drawn to the sea to obtain elements for The Elixir, driving me to possess the angelfish eye for its renowned powers of strength and courage. It reminded me I had the power to navigate through all circumstances with the help of my intuition and resourcefulness.

Centering the cart, I continued straight, slowing my momentum as the ramp's slope steepened. The sounds of the cart's clattering against stone filled my ears. However, it did nothing to mask the growing screams and clanking metal filtering through the embrasures that adorned the hallway. My heart began to race with the feeling of dread as I recognized the sounds of battle. I urged myself to quicken my pace despite the slippery stone beneath my boots and the additional weight of the cart pulling me forwards. A sudden gust of wind burst from within the righthand passage, the forceful energy jarring me backward as my cart smashed into solid stone.

"Your Worship," said a strained and out-of-breath voice.

Peering around the cart, I discovered Bullet, the shortness of his stature making it impossible to see him over my precariously packed cart of supplies.

"Bullet?" I said, confused. "What in the seven hells is going on?"

"Your Worship, I got here as fast as I could. There has been an attack!"

My mind began to recenter as I attempted to organize my scrambled thoughts. My words came rushing forth, and the slew of commands I had ready for Bullet all wanted to escape simultaneously.

"Explain yourself," I demanded, the first of many commands.

"To put it simply, the troops found a goat loose in the woods and I was charged in returning it to the stockades. Whilst waiting for the guard to pass, I heard a disturbance behind me, witnessing scuffling as rebels attempted to steal more goats from our lands. I tried to sound the alarm to warn the troops we were not alone, however, I was ambushed and barely managed to get away. The goat hath been slain, and my bags, which contained my set of keys to Morriraen, have been stolen."

"Bullet," I began, taking a deep breath to find my center. "I have several tasks for you. First, alert Syler about the battle itself and in regards to your keys. She will have to enact our security protocols to ensure the castle remains safe. Though she is currently deep in her cup, you will need to obtain for her a ginseng potion from the brewery."

"Aye," he said, nodding. "What's next?"

"Maliche and his apprentices are responsible for my cart. See to it that they have it waiting for me by the Western Wall when this is over. I will leave it in this corridor, though out of plain sight, whilst you are fetching them so they may find it."

"Understood," said Bullet. "How else may I be of assistance?"

"Ring the alarm and assemble the remaining forces."

"Aye. Will that be everything?"

"At present," I concluded. "Though you should perform a locator spell with Kiyoko to find your keys once things settle, and find me once the battle is over."

"Aye, you have my word," said Bullet. "Until we meet again."

"Thank you for your service," I said.

Bullet saluted, dashing down the corridor with such speed he was invisible. A sharp wisp of wind followed close behind him, swiping past my face like a cold and fleeting phantom. Hoisting the cart to the left, I wedged it in the corner, tucking it out of sight behind a large pair of potted ficuses.

Equipped with an extra quiver of arrows, I retraced my steps back to the oil painting I had passed moments before.

Sliding my fingers down the left-hand side of the frame, I found a rounded, wooden knob. Pushing it inward, I then twisted to the right before pulling hard to unlock the door beyond the painting. The canvas swung forward silently, giving me access to a tight and narrow gap. Wriggling through, I pulled the painting closed behind me, making my way through the dark passage that slowly widened as I reached the Western Parapet.

Sprinting south, I followed the screams of soldiers and horses, using a scope beside the crenellations to assess the chaos below. Down the hill near the supply trains swarmed a hoard of fighters; rebel soldiers dressed in black rushed forward with their attack. Blood sprayed from bodies to stain the soil, soldiers and rebels sliced with swords in a struggle for survival.

"Gods," I whispered, pushing aside the scope and dropping to my knees.

After adjusting my quivers, I drew my bow, squeezing a metallic trigger near the strings to increase the tension. The weapon expanded from a short bow to a longbow, the second layer of enchanted yew sliding outwards by way of gears. The bow had been Bullet's design yet enchanted by Hazel, giving it the ability to adapt for any use whilst looking modern and fashionable. Springs on the sides were used to collapse the bow to its original size; the fluent transition allowed for its perfect use during combat.

Rapidly, I strung arrows to my bow, firing them into the onslaught as quickly as I could. My first quiver was spent in seconds; despite all ten arrows meeting their target, the number of rebels was still overwhelming. Loading my second quiver, I steadied my aim once more, sniping the rebel's dead that crested the top of the hill. Anxiety flooded through me whilst I exhausted my arrows, my emotions reeling as I returned my bow to my back.

"Shite..." I swore again, taking a deep breath to prepare for what would come.

Gritting my teeth, I burst forward, using my momentum to vault over the crenellations. The air whipped around me as I plummeted from the palace, my stomach aching in anticipation as the moat quickly approached beneath me. Painfully, my legs smacked the water, the weight of my armor curling my body forward as I submerged beneath the surface. Fighting to relax, I moved with the currents, swimming against the freezing waves that desired to crush me against the castle.

Reaching the shore, I hoisted my body forward, slipping on the slick, sheer stone banks that lined the water's edge. Wedging my fingers deeply in the rock, I obtained a stable grip, using my arms to lift my body from the unpredictable waters of the moat. Kicking my legs hard, I propelled upwards, plopping my chest and face on the gravel ten feet above the water's surface. Gasping for breath, I flung my legs to the side, rolling onto the grass whilst coughing and fighting for balance.

The frigid air bit harshly across my skin; my clothes and armor were sopping wet, the weight pulling me down as I scrambled to a stand. I tried not to panic as I sprinted southward, fear coursing through me as the battle encroached on the crest of the hill. Drawing my mother's sword, I stood my ground, defending the top of the hill from the rebels who broke through the barraging battle. Swiping my sword sideways, I sliced through the onslaught, showering my armor in blood.

Familiar faces flooded up the hill as our front lines began to crumble. Through the throng of rebels, Kye raced towards the drawbridge, defending her position by the moat to keep the rebels from gaining ground. Lieutenant Tyfis guarded the flank on my left, countering the attacks of the endless stream of rebels that rushed towards us. The bell in the Southern Watchtower began to boom, relief washing over me with the prospect of Bullet sending reinforcements.

The battle pulled me off Moon's Road and onto the grass, the change in terrain momentarily disrupting my balance. Bodies fell like a heavy summer rain, drenching the ground with blood to nourish the earth. Rebels and soldiers lay equal as one, dead in the grass with empty eyes and blood crusted on their faces.

Their numbers are too great, I shuddered, raising my eyes and spotting Everett fighting further down Moon's Road, past the cusp of the hill. He swung his hammer in a sweeping arc, clearing crowds of the enemy in a single strike. Corpses fell in circles around him, their ranks replaced with the rush of reinforced rebels. Suddenly, Everett was slammed from the side, trying in vain to dispose of the assailant with an iron grip around his neck. Enemy forces swarmed forward, surrounding Everett as he thrashed to break free.

"Gods," I swore harshly, disengaging from the rebels as I sprinted across the grass.

I moved to the outskirts of the battle, using Tyfis as a reference to gauge the distance of the oncoming troops. Sheathing Réalta, I squatted in the soil, taking deep breaths to clear my mind. I pressed my palms to the ground as I attempted to anchor myself, meditating through the screams and clashing and forcing them into muted blurs. My heart pounded with immense force as I sensed Everett's energy, fear threatening to slice through my manifested calm as his life essence dulled and his soul began to slip. A sense of urgency flooded through my veins, my heart hammering harder with the slowing of time as I rode the rush of power.

"Cypress," I whispered.

The clasps and chains of my gauntlets shattered violently, breaking into sharp, jagged pieces. Shards of metal embedded into my flesh, blood rushing forth to pool around my palms. My power flowed through the earth, feeling the souls descending into the Underworld, their now empty corpses waiting to welcome my influence. The burst of energy caused my hands to transition as the corpses littering the ground began to reanimate. Shakily, the bodies rose to their feet, shuffling towards the rebels as they charged up the hill.

Focusing my energy, I fueled the corpses, controlling them with my blood and rage to defend the castle. My hands throbbed, and my vision blurred from the continuing blood loss. Unrecognizable voices began delegating a deluge of demands, their words summoning a fear within me as dark as storm clouds.

"The dead walk among us! Archers, archers, summon the fire!"

Clenching my fists, I summoned my final burst of strength, resurrecting a tumultuous wave of fallen soldiers. Arrows kissed by fire flew fast from rebels in the forest, enemy archers using trees to perch and snipe my thralls. Forcefully, I drove the bodies forward, fighting through the flames that began to consume them. Piercing screams drilled through my head, the cries of the burning corpses grinding against the terror of the rebels. Enemies began to fall as the bodies returned to the earth, and the surge in defeated soldiers provided a clear line of sight to Everett.

Locking eyes, I somberly smiled, allowing myself the feeling of relief and a centering breath before returning my focus to the battle. Fighting troops and corpses brawled through the fields, corralling the rebels down the hill and away from the castle. Clambering to a stand, I yanked the remnants of my gauntlets out of my skin, blood pouring forth once more as I quickly pulled on the extras hanging on my belt. Flames shot across the sky and ignited the trees, embers alighting on the grass to hinder the rebel's escape. The corpses conquered the remaining rebels, turning the advantage in our favor as the enemy retreated down the hill. Tyfis began frantically shouting to the left, sprinting south after Kye with fear in their eyes.

"Fall back!" Tyfis screamed. Panic-induced bile rose from my throat, encouraging me forward to chase after him. His tone became desperately urgent, spiking a new wave of fear that drained the color from my face. "Back away! Fall back!"

Suddenly, the ground shook, taking my balance and knocking me from my boots. Overwhelmed with dizziness and blood loss, I winced against the screams and pain that rushed my senses. Crawling forward, I found my balance, reattuning to my own body before opening my eyes. Rubbing away the tears, I focused upwards in a daze, springing upright as Thornin appeared on the eastern horizon through the smoke.

Shakily running forward, I followed the growing flames toward the supply wagons, my eyes stinging with a new wave of tears from the heat and smoke in the air. Charred and blackened bodies marred the battlefield, and a second wave of igniting carts destroyed the remaining corpses that rushed forward. Splintering, burning wood broke free of flaming carts to slam against wagons further down the line, launching a fresh wave of emerald flames through the supply trains.

"Save the supplies," Kye was shouting somewhere to my right, igniting a surge of soldiers to join in the effort of rescuing valuables.

Gods-, I thought, dashing back towards the top of the hill.

Behind me, the fire went up in a woosh, urging my steps forward in a crazed, panicked sprint. At the cusp of the hill, I stared into the sky, seeing Thornin gliding closer over a line of trees to my right. Placing my thumb and forefinger in my mouth, I blew a piercing whistle, watching as the dragon shot forward and swooped low toward me. Stealing my strength, I burst forward, leaping towards him as he dipped low to the ground. Clinging to his leg, I began climbing, fighting to hold my grip as he took to the clouds again. Swearing softly, I shimmied up his body, my clothes and skin ripping from scales as sharp as broken glass.

Emerging victorious, I mounted the dragon, tossing my right leg across his back to stabilize my balance. Reaching forward, I grabbed the spikes that protruded down his neck, holding on tightly as I whistled another slew of commands. Darting forward, Thornin dove in a wide arc, turning south to fly over the trees down the hill. Positioning my body flat against his back, I whistled loudly, feeling as Thornin tilted vertically and began to pound his wings.

Thornin increased his speed with another whistled command, creating thunderous gusts of enchanted wind. Peering around him, I was thankful to notice the smoke thinning, the air once again clearing as the fires in the carts and trees slowly diminished. Blasting a final sharp whistle, I demanded Thornin exert all his strength, squeezing my arms and legs into his rocking, jagged scales in an attempt to stay astride. After several long, tense moments, the fires were extinguished, relief escaping from my eyes in a wave of hot and silent tears.

Guiding Thornin right, we flew towards the Western Bailey, landing past the bend near the Western Watchtower. Gently alighting on the grass, his monstrous wings rustling in the breeze as he fell quiet. Swinging my legs from his back, I hopped to the ground, feeling my feet give way as I landed in the grass. Giving in to the exhaustion, I allowed my body to crumble, landing on my back with arms and legs sprawled out.

Inhaling deeply, I began to meditate, focusing on my breaths and releasing the tension from my body. Exhaling through my mouth, I felt my muscles lighten, the stress and anger of the last few hours dissipating away through the earth. My spirits lifted as I revitalized my energy, the sizzling scratches across my skin lessening to a dull ache as I relaxed. The cuts on my hands throbbed with my pulse, both slowing to a comfortable calm as my breathing lengthened.

Bustling voices of apprentices and servants began filtering through my awareness. Footsteps thudded across the ground near my ears, the sudden closeness jarring me painfully back to the present and into my battered body.

"Knomucca, is all well?"

Syler squatted beside my head, her neck craning forward as she stared into my face.

"Momentarily," I said, fighting the urge to close my eyes.

"You look wretched," Syler smirked, flagging down a passing servant in bright green Alchemist robes. "Fetch some Tora berry wine and fruit from the kitchens, if you would be so kind."

"Right away, Miss," said Bettylee, an Alchemist's apprentice, disappearing around the trees to vanish into the castle.

"Knomucca, why don't you try to sit up?"

"Piss off," I groaned.

"Come now," said Syler, unfastening the smoking sacks at my waist and beginning to roll spliffs. "Let's make you fresh as a daisy."

"Where were you, anyhow?" I asked, flopping my arm lazily over my face to block the sun.

"Shooting arrows on the Southern Bailey," she said.

"That was as useful as teats on a bull when I tried it," I spat, uncovering my face and beginning to sit, "and it's no secret I am the better archer."

"Shove off," snapped Syler. "Summoning Cypress always sours your mood."

"Oi... you'd be correct, of course..." Taking a deep breath, I exhaled and found my center, "I apologize, Sweet Sister."

"Aye... you best grovel," Syler laughed, slipping the smoke between my lips and lighting it with a match. "Though you possess more thorns than a rose bush, at present, I still love you."

"I am undeserving," I said, rubbing the blurriness from my eyes as another set of footsteps approached on the left.

"Greetings, m'ladies," said Bullet, saluting as he approached.

"Thank you for your swift actions on this day, Bullet," I said, hiding my pain behind a smile.

"It was my pleasure," Bullet waved away my words. "I am only wondering how I can be of further assistance."

"You informed my sister of your missing keys, I presume," I asked, watching as Bullet dipped his head low in a nod.

"I'll search for them best I can," Syler sighed. "Though I may have to engage Morriraen's emergency protocols if the portal proves temperamental or we are unable to locate them..."

"Those precautions are a last resort," I warned severely. "There shall not be a castle to return to if you activate the gargoyles..."

"I understand how severe this is, and I do hope it does not come to that..."

"Bullet, have you and Kiyoko had success with the locator spell?" I asked.

"Not as of yet, m'lady," Bullet said, shaking his head. "I thought it more prudent I found you first."

"I appreciate the gesture," I said. "Though we cannot afford your keys to remain unaccounted for. Yourself and the General should attempt the locator spell straight away... it is crucial we find your keys post haste."

"Understood," Bullet said.

"And see to it that Hazel has the Knells search the corpses thoroughly. Before performing their death rites, ensure that they check for your missing keys, or any other indicators of their loyalty," I continued. "Please make sure the outcome is communicated to me by any means necessary. Once I find my strength, I shall be departing for the Luna Sea. You may ask Everett for my itinerary as needed."

"Aye," Bullet said, saluting once more. "I do have one additional item to discuss with you if I may have a brief moment of your time."

"What is on your mind?" I asked with a deep breath.

"This night past... I dreamt of the portal's decay. The stone surrounding it cracked from a strike of brilliant light, and the entirety of all the realms were exposed to one another. There was darkness... chaos... the void... and a door with broken hinges casting shadows across the lands."

I released a silent breath, saying nothing, watching as my sister's eyes briefly flashed with alarm and horror.

"Is this the first time you have had this dream?" I asked, certain I was not to like his answer.

"Nay, it's been reoccurring." Bullet said sadly. "Are we certain it is wise for me to abandon my station and attend the journey southward when this vision has entered my knowing?"

"I trust that Colonel Arynne is plenty capable of looking after things as your second in command," I said gently. "You are needed to assist in navigating the portals for The Ascension should any problems arise... we shall need to have faith that whatever is meant to come from these premonitions shall resolve in our favor."

"Sage words, indeed," Bullet said reassuringly. "That will be everything... Thank you for your time."

"I appreciate your telling me," I said as I held his gaze. "Even if the news should continue to make me feel uneasy."

"Bullet," Syler spoke suddenly before his departure. "While searching for Kiyoko, could you also find a servant to retrieve as many bottles of Torra Berry wine as they can from the cellars? I wish to gift Knomucca with their rejuvenation should she require Cypress again."

"Certainly," Bullet said, saluting quickly and gesturing to his left. "If all else is well, I shall set off straight away."

"Very well, stay wise and take your leave," I said, watching as Bullet swirled in frigid wind and bolted across the field.

"Why must you ask him for more wine if you have obtained some for me already?" I asked, attempting to withhold my annoyance.

"I suspect you will be needing more than you wager," Syler said, adjusting in the grass as servants coursed busily around us.

"I pray you are incorrect," I said, releasing a cleansing breath.

A calm moment passed between us, broken by the appearance of the green-robed apprentice. Bettylee stooped low, gifting Syler two goblets, a bottle of Tora berry wine, and several of the blue-spiraled berries themselves.

"Thank you kindly," Syler said, dismissing the apprentice with a wave.

Seizing a glass, she began to fill it, stopping when the dark blue wine reached just beneath the rim. "I shall be watching to ensure you consume every drop to fully rejuvenate your spirits. You nearly approached the limits of your strength, and I can see it in your face."

"I did exert a vast reserve of energy," I said between sips of wine. "It is rather tiring."

"I am glad you have agreed to bring more Tora with you," Syler said with a sad smile. "If you are required to continue conjuring Cypress... or are encountered with a forced visit to Heimaaila, it may become beneficial to indulge as to keep your spirits freshened..."

"I shall bear that in mind," I said, growing concerned with the swirling worry far off in my twin's eyes.

"Very good," Syler said, reaching forward and flicking the growing ashes from my forgotten smoke. "Your spliff is fading to naught but ashes... best not let it go to waste. The only thing mother hated more than smoking herbs was wasting them."

"You would be correct, of course," I said, inhaling deeply as I allowed myself to relax.

"Aside from your freshened spirits, there are other benefits to procuring more of the Tora berries," Syler said, rising unexpectedly to her feet. "If you find yourself in need of a smile, you can feed the berries to Thornin until he turns purple."

"It is quite amusing," I agreed pleasantly, enjoying the sour wine as it splashed against my lips. The Tora berries calmed the itching and fire that burned through my palms, bringing a temporary wave of relief that made me sigh with bliss.

Syler slipped a handful of the berries to Thornin, smiling as he nibbled on her fingertips. A silence fell between us among the organized chaos of the servants scrambling to set up tents.

"Fair morrow, M'Ladies," a familiar voice said, my stomach falling nervously as I tore my eyes from my sister.

Looking upwards, I was anxious to discover Hazel carrying a pair of metallic trays laden with food in her hands.

"Greetings, kind Priestess," Syler said, turning away from Thornin upon her arrival. "That looks delicious, Hazel."

"My cousin has been hard at work preparing sustenance for the troops," Hazel said with a satisfied expression.

"How would we manage without our Chatza?" I asked rhetorically, taking on a pleasant tone with Hazel whilst in the presence of my sister.

"I'm certain she would appreciate such high praise," said Hazel, placing the trays of cheese, nuts, greens, bread, and Tora berries on the grass. "I noticed you had to summon Cypress. I wanted to make sure you had Tora berries as soon as possible."

"That is very thoughtful," I said, struggling to conceal my trepidation in her presence. "As you can see, Syler has me well taken care of."

"You should feel plenty rejuvenated then," Hazel said. "None of this fainting or sickness from using your spirit magic this close to The Ascension."

"I have not lost my wits from my magic in quite some time," I said, the bitterness in my words threatening to taint my tone. "I was inexperienced, ignorant, and juvenile."

"Indeed," Hazel said, her eyes sparkling with an air of innocence.

"Though... I cannot ignore how fortunate I am for your discovery of Tora berries having helpful medicinal properties against metaphysical ailments."

"I am honored I could serve the realms," Hazel said with a smile. "When you are finished, please return the tray to the station on the opposite side of my tent, if you would not mind."

"Aye, we shall," I said, keeping my voice calculated as I continued speaking. "Have you been informed yet about Bullet's keys?"

"We shall search for them best we can," Hazel said, fidgeting unexpectedly as she glanced towards her tents.

"You may freely leave if you must," I said, flicking the ashes of my spliff into the breeze as Hazel suddenly met my eyes.

"Knomucca... have you spoken to Everett as of yet?"

Hazel's countenance was without emotion as worry and terror struck through my chest, my spliff a convenient distraction to mask my nerves.

"Not as of yet," I said. "I do need to speak with him; however, I was attempting to regain my strength first."

"Perhaps that is wise," said Hazel, the shadow heavy in her eyes. "Wouldn't want him to see you looking so wretched."

"Is all well?" asked Syler, her voice jarring me from the rage that began to swirl inside.

"I'm certain all shall be well," said Hazel, the darkness dissipating from her irises as she took a cleansing breath. "I apologize for my rudeness, but I must be tending to the apprentices and soldiers. Are you in need of anything else before my departure?

"I appreciate the offer, though I have nothing else," my tone failing to conceal the scalding emotions that boiled within me.

"Are you certain there is nothing else?" she asked, the darkness returning to her eyes as I met them.

"Perhaps there is one other matter you could tend to for me," I began, deciding spontaneously to challenge her frame of mind.

"What might that be?" Hazel asked eagerly.

Fishing the broken gauntlets from my enchanted pouch, I handed them to her. "If you have the means to repair these, I would appreciate it."

"I shall see what I can do," she said, slipping the gauntlets into the pocket of her robes. "Please, M'Ladies, if there is any other way I can assist, I shall be in my tent."

"Aye, very well," I said, shifting into a comfortable position and pulling a tray of food into my lap.

"Stay wise, M'Ladies," Hazel said, giving a curt nod before taking her leave.

"Love and light," said Syler, returning her nod in respect.

Hazel swept briskly away through the grass, veering purposefully towards her tents.

"How strange," Syler said curiously. "Hazel did not attempt to examine your wounds or threaten to pull rank should you decide not to adhere to her treatments... I certainly hope all is well with her..."

"It is rather odd," I said, feigning ignorance to the shadows in her eyes.

"Is that why you gave her your gauntlets to repair, instead of burying the broken pair in the box beneath the willow tree?"

Syler's question pierced me, nearly causing me to drop the tray I held in my lap.

"We mustn't speak of such things," I said sternly. "One never knows whom might be listening."

"Nonsense," Syler teased. "We are mired in chaos... not a soul is aware of our words."

"I suppose that is true," I said, glancing in a cautious circle before continuing to speak. "I have nearly perfected the art in enchanting the gauntlets myself as to no longer require Hazel's assistance..."

"That is quite impressive," Syler said, her eyes sparkling mischievously as she uttered a short laugh. "Hazel is akin in age to our mother... it is proof you could use time away from the books if you are achieving an elder's mastery with your current years."

"How do you know about the willow tree?" I asked cautiously, attempting to draw my sister's attention away from my growing abilities.

"I spend a lot of late nights in the orchards," Syler whispered. "I've seen you disposing of your gauntlets there."

"Oi," I swore softly. "I suppose your station as a socialite keeps you from your chambers at all hours."

"Suppose you could use a little rowdiness," Syler laughed as she patted my arm. "Break free from the books you are always studying..."

"Leave me be," I said, finishing my smoke and ashing the remains into the breeze.

"Will you confess your motives?" Syler asked. "Why did you give the gauntlets to Hazel instead of burying them?"

"There is nothing left to confess," I mused. "I noticed her lapse in behavior and am simply testing her judgements."

"Your distrust of people frustrates me," Syler sighed. "Not all can prove to be as loyal as the Commander and his General, yet not all seek your failure and deserve such scrutiny."

"Believe what you will," I said, dismissing my sister's criticism. "Though even the deadliest of snakes hide under lavender bushes."

I turned from her gaze, sprinkling my papsal across the dish before beginning to eat. The salted nuts paired deliciously with the creamy goat cheese, and my body continued to strengthen from the nourishment. Whilst eating, my thoughts strayed, returning to my earlier encounter with Bullet in the hall, anger pulsing through my veins with each heartbeat. The circumstances of the morning replayed in my mind with every bite. They quickly replaced the anxiety regarding my upcoming conversation with Everett.

"Eat, Knomucca," said Syler, gesturing to the goat cheese spread across my bread. "Why has your face suddenly turned so grim?"

"Never you mind," I said, finishing the bottle of Tora berry wine and choking down the last of my food despite my nerves.

"Hazel is right," Syler said unexpectedly, stacking her empty tray atop my own. "Try not to fret, all shall be well and good."

"Time tells all," I said, taking the trays in my hands and summoning the will to stand. "I shall be back momentarily."

"Take the time needed," Syler said, absent-mindedly running a hand through her hair as she watched my departure.

Struggling to move, I walked forward, seeing Hazel's tent amidst a circle of small, separated pavilions constructed for patient privacy. Walking along the back, I wandered to the opposite side, my legs sore and tingling from tiredness. I placed the silver trays upon the cart, the shelves threatening to spill over from the mountain of cups and cutlery. Returning to my path, I felt my body growing stronger again, the shakiness leaving me after good food, Tora berries, and smoking. My cuts throbbed, burned, and pulsed, the momentary absence of fatigue allowing me to realize just how injured I had become.

Around Thornin's body, I spotted Syler, her head hunched forward in hushed conversation. Thornin turned his head towards me as I approached, the shifting in his movements failing to alert Syler to my return.

"I am begging you, Syler, please. Don't do this."

"She needs it more than I do, Frek."

"I disagree," he barked. "How long are you going to keep pretending everything is fine?"

"Everything is fine," Syler snapped back. "I've asked you to stand down once already, Frek, and I am not going to do it again."

As I approached, I paused beside a pile of extra Tora berries in the grass to scoop some in my hand. "What are the two of you on about?" I asked, handing Thornin several of the Tora berries.

A silence fell among them as they lurched in fright, simultaneously whipping their heads towards me. Syler's expression softened as her eyes met mine.

"Never you mind," said Frek with an air of irritation. He turned on his heels and unexpectedly strode off.

"Perhaps you should keep feeding the berries to Thornin," Syler said, kissing my cheek and pulling me into a tight embrace, perhaps tighter than I expected from her. As her lingering grasp held me firmly to her chest, I felt the vibrations of her voice as she added. "These last few hours have been quite emotional, and perhaps him cycling through the various tones of violet will gift you a much-needed smile."

"That is sage advice," I said. "Stay wise, my twin blessed of water."

"Love and light, my twin blessed of fire."

Syler patted Thornin's nose and then moved away, disappearing behind a slew of soldiers and servants heading towards Moon's Road. Once she had departed and I had finished conversing with Everett and the General, I turned to speak to Thornin.

"I must check on the status of your saddle and heal my wounds. Wait here," I ordered.

Thornin slunk into the grass and laid his body flat, taking the time to bask in the sun. I was thankful that no one would bother him in my absence, so I left him to relax. I veered left to walk the outer path of Hazel's pavilions toward the Western Watchtower.

Maliche stood beside the tower's access ladder, talking to an apprentice beside my cart that I had left in the hallway. A calloused hand rested on his hip, his shirtless torso gleaming with sweat in the midday sun. His fair eyes and self-assured smile made my knees wobble as I approached.

"Good morrow, Maliche," I said flirtatiously.

"Greetings, Your Worship," he said, his husky voice rumbling through me.

His simple grey leggings complimented his body nicely, fitting tightly into his knee-high leather boots. As a gardener, he preferred comfort over appearance, and boots provided the support he needed for his prosthetic leg. The dark spruce wood was carved to match his other finely muscled calf, the top secured into the bones with enchanted iron nails.

"Thank you immensely for retrieving my cart for me," I said seductively, approaching him and tracing a finger across his collarbone.

"It was my pleasure," he said with a wink, his smile drawing me in.

"My pardons," the apprentice bowed his head. "I should take my leave.

"If you could, please take my cart over to where Thornin is laying, on the opposite side of Hazel's tent," I said, never breaking my gaze with Maliche.

The apprentice bowed once more as he grasped the cart handle and began to push it away over the field.

"Maliche... I require your assistance in satisfying some particular... needs," I leaned in closer, my breath against his skin.

"Did I not satisfy you enough last time?" Maliche asked smugly. "Or are my charms simply too enticing to resist?"

"I cannot deny I enjoy your charms," I said, slipping my arm around his waist, pulling him close to me, and stroking him slowly. "Perhaps we should seek Hazel's tents for privacy?"

"It would be one among many pleasures," Maliche purred; the bewitching allure of his voice tightened my body excitedly.

I turned towards Hazel's array of tents, looking back over my shoulder to wink at him before striding across the grass. Maliche followed me to one of the medical tents, swiping aside the canvas to gaze inside. After a moment, he held open the flap, allowing me to enter.

"It appears we have the place to ourselves," he smirked.

Ducking through the gap, I took in the surprisingly spacious tent. A circular wooden stool stood beside a feather cot. On the far side was a simplistic brewery containing a cauldron and a rack of hanging knives waiting to be used.

"Perfection," I said, seizing Maliche by the shoulders and pushing him backward onto the cot. "I desire your assistance in doffing my garments."

"With pleasure, m'lady," he said, reaching his hands forward and unfastening my belt.

Laying my belt gently across the stool, he returned with ravishing hands, unphased by the blood, cuts, and bruises across my skin. His fingers flew furiously to tear off my leggings and boots, taking care to keep the knives inside them.

"Excellent," I moaned in anticipation. Shoving Maliche backward, I began to climb atop him, my hair brushing across his neck as I crawled toward his face.

"How would you like me to satisfy you?" Maliche whimpered.

"In ways that will keep you from talking," I panted, spreading my legs as I straddled his face.

"Vixen," Maliche teased, nibbling on my inner thighs playfully.

Sliding his tongue across my skin, he began to explore, licking and biting towards my center. Cupping me low, he pulled my body close, flicking his tongue in slow, deliberate circles. Tossing my hair behind my shoulders, I arched my back, slipping my armor and tunic swiftly over my head as I relaxed. Maliche's fingers glided over my breasts, my left hand trapping his right in place hungrily. He teased me immensely in tracing the owl inked on the right of my ribs.

"Perfection," I moaned.

Rubbing and grinding myself against him, I enjoyed the quickening strokes of his tongue. I slid my hands eagerly down his arms and over his neck, meshing my fingers into his hair as I yanked his head in a rhythm of my liking. My eyes lulled back with a wave of pleasure, my breathing beginning to deepen as the pressure built. I cried out, clenching fistfuls of his curly dark hair as I rode atop him.

Pulling harder, I pressed against him, my thrusts growing in speed and urgency. I shook the bed violently, burning through the day's frustrations. A hot, delicious tingle burst forth in orgasm, my lips parting in satisfaction as I rode the pleasure. Energy built and swirled inside me, the surge rushing painfully forward whilst beginning to heal my wounds. Reeling to the side, I lurched with exhaustion, catching my balance with my elbow as I nearly collapsed from the bed.

"Your Worship..." Maliche's voice grew panicked. "It appears to be happening again."

"Aye, I am aware," I said, untangling myself from Maliche to watch as my wounds closed and my bruises healed.

"I thought you said that was an isolated incident," Maliche accused.

"It was..." I said slowly. "Though greater needs prevail..."

"Knomucca, this is dangerous." Maliche's voice held surprising concern. "Have you mentioned this to anybody else?"

"I have mentioned such to the spirits of the wind," I said facetiously, "to grant them cause to carry my burdens away with them."

"Knomucca," Maliche's face soured. "It is unwise to keep this solely within yourself."

"Where I keep my secrets is none of your concern," I said sternly, rising to my feet and beginning to fill the cauldron at the brewing station with a nearby jug of water.

"Your Worship," Maliche lowered his voice gently, "you really ought to talk to one of your trusted... perhaps Syler, Hazel, or Everett-"

"Maliche!" I threw up my hands to silence him, "The situation is well tended."

"They will not think differently of you," he said, suddenly sitting up.

"They could," I snapped bitterly. "I do not know the source of this power and cannot control when it comes."

"If you act alone, you most certainly shall be damned," Maliche said. "I am pleased I could help you release your frustrations, though I do not wish to help you keep this secret."

"Maliche," I inquired. "Would you consider yourself to be my friend?"

"Most of the time," Maliche teased.

"Then do me the decency of keeping this to yourself."

"I cannot promise I shall be able," Maliche said. "Though I confess that I care for you... this notion you possess that you must conquer the realms alone is complete insanity."

"It is what I must do," I said.

"Perhaps it is a burden that is to be shared with the Creator?"

The tone in his words boiled my blood, annoyance surging through my hands in a white, hot wave. Glaring intensely, I began to speak, my voice level and as cold as shards of ice. "If you find yourself with loose lips, you would do well to think before divulging what you know."

"Do not preach to me on the matter of loosened lips," Maliche said angrily, flying to his feet.

"Get out," I growled low, my aura darkening as black as my shadow.

"That was my intention," Maliche sneered. "Since I can see this encounter was one-sided."

"Very well," I snapped, relief washing over me as he stormed from the tent.

With water in the cauldron, I began to aggressively scrub my hands, using salt and lavender to rid them of blood before adjusting my gauntlets. Finding soap in the brewing stand, I quickly cleaned my body, using a cloth to rinse and scrub away the grime of the morning.

"Gods..." I whispered, thinking of the interaction that transpired with Maliche.

I stared at the newly healed wounds on my arms; the ability to manipulate intimate energy this way was a fairly recent gift. Sighing, I wished I had never received it, knowing that practitioners of this craft were often burned at the stake for using energy that was seen as impure by The Creator. Of all the creatures in the Underworld, the Succubi that used this magic were some of the most hated, along with Incubi and Kapas.

Shuddering, I yanked open my enchanted pouch. Angrily, I exchanged my torn clothing, procuring a deep red tunic sewn from cotton. My leggings were exchanged for ones of white leather lined with wool, matching perfectly with the boots I returned to my feet. After sliding my knives back into my boots and donning my armor, I adjusted my hair, shifting the carnation pin more securely near my roots. Attaching my weapons belt to my armor, I was composed once more. I retrieved Everett's gifted spliff to light before exiting the tent.

Over half the day had quickly come and gone; the sun's position behind the clouds made it hard to gauge the exact hour. Returning to Thornin, I was pleased to find he hadn't vanished from boredom. The cart containing his supplies and two extra bottles of Tora Berry Wine were beside him and ready to be loaded.

"Half mast," I whistled to Thornin as I dragged deeply on my spliff.

Thornin rose from the ground, squatting to shorten his height by half. Hoisting the saddle from the cart, I stepped onto Thornin's haunches, lifting the saddle higher to place it on his back. I tightened the chain around the barrel of his body, my hands subconsciously moving through the steps from years of practice. I used additional straps to obtain leverage and security via the spikes on his neck. Cautiously, I loaded my supplies, organizing them to fit snugly in the cantle before snapping the compartment closed. With my final preparations, I tightened my belt, donned a pair of dragonscale gloves, and finished my spliff. A chill rolled through on the breeze, and my body shivered, encouraging me to pull a midnight black cloak from my pouch to drape over my shoulders.

Climbing into the saddle, I stared longingly toward the castle, praying with renewed strength I would return home.

"Off we go then," I said, more to myself than to Thornin. Whistling sternly, I commanded him to take flight, holding on tightly to the saddle as he lurched upwards. Jumping forward, he leaped into the air, ascending into the sky straight from where he had stood. Thankful for this talent, I guided him in a wide circle, whistling commands to leave the castle behind and begin flying east.

VI

EVERETT

Following Kiyoko, I turned away from Knomucca, leaving her behind to contend with her dragon. Concentrating on the day ahead, I fought to control my emotions, my heart slowly settling after the nearness of our kiss. I exhaled a breath I hadn't known I was holding, annoyed with myself for becoming so flustered. Absently, I massaged my head where Thornin had struck me, swearing to myself whilst reflecting.

"Is all well, Everett?" Kiyoko asked gently. "You have gone quiet."

"All is well," I said, fighting to keep my voice from sounding grim.

"I have ears to lend if desired," he said encouragingly. "It might help to voice how you are feeling."

"Perhaps later on this evening," I said, guarding my emotions.

"Those last several moments appeared quite promising," Kiyoko teased with a wink.

"Hush, Kiyoko... snap your trap and leave me be," I laughed, punching him playfully in the shoulder. His eyes turned hungrily towards me before his brow furrowed with a serious thought.

"I wish you would loosen your spirits," he said gently. "It is acceptable to discuss the matters of our hearts should we need to-"

"You are relentless," I chuckled softly and shook my head with a breath. "Later on, my friend, later on."

Kiyoko nodded as a brief silence fell between us. Stealing a glance at him, I took in his pristine appearance: his neatly fluffed brown hair, the rose of his cheeks, and the lack of grime on his clothing. Had he an opportunity to freshen his appearance since the battle? The energy around me swarmed with unease.

"Considering the intensity of the battle, you appear to still be quite well kept," I said, meeting his eyes.

"Do I?" Kiyoko said, with a wry arch to his eyebrow.

I ignored his attempt to deflect my thoughts. "I searched for you between the waves of attack, but I could not sense your energy."

"I was near the wagons, attempting to defend the priestess's quarters and her supplies, given how crucial they are to Knomucca's success," he said, returning my stare.

"Even during the blast of alchemist's fire?" My eyes narrowed, contemplating his words. "You appear to not be burned."

"Perhaps you would like to take a closer inspection," Kiyoko said, stepping forward, placing a hand on the hem of his kimono and slowly raising it.

"Nay, that shall not be necessary," I said, placing a hand atop his.

As our hands touched, a spark shot between us. I looked deep into Kiyoko's eyes, the brown flickering with specs of sunlight. Something lay beneath his controlled expression that I could not detect. Sighing, I took a step back, composing myself.

"Regardless," I said sincerely. "I am glad that you are well."

Returning across the grass, we found Hazel's tents, my spirits brightening with the sparkle in Truff's eyes. Sudden, sharp whispers cut through the canvas walls like knives, the intensity of the arguing energy dragging me in to listen.

"You are behaving as if this is absolute," snapped the familiar voice that I knew belonged to Frek.

"It is absolute. I have known for quite some time now, Frek."

"Did you ever consider how I would feel about this? Do you not understand how my life will change?"

"Your life? How about my life?" the second voice parried, the rising tone revealing Syler's identity. "I am terrified, and alone."

"Syler, my love... you are anything but alone," Frek said sincerely. "There are many who care and are always around you. Even... you shall come to learn... at this very moment."

Suddenly, the canvas door of the tent flew open, brushing a soft wind across my face. Frek emerged from the other side, staring harshly and suspiciously into my eyes.

"Greetings," I said, allowing my blush to paint my face.

"Good day, Commander," said Syler, saluting nonchalantly. "May we assist you with anything?"

My face flashed with embarrassment, my words scrambling to simultaneously break free. "I was just... we were..."

"We were just wondering after Hazel," Kiyoko said, his calm energy easing my discomfort. "Would either of you happen to know her where abouts?"

"Nay," growled Frek, his annoyance of our interruption plain in his eyes.

"Darling," Syler placed a hand across Frek's back, soothing him gently. "Take a deep breath and quench your iron."

Frek obliged, though his eyes never softened.

"What I am certain Frek meant to relay," Syler continued without losing her stride. "Is that Hazel is performing a procedure at present and shall be back whenever she is finished."

"That is good and well," Kiyoko said with a smile. "Come along then, Everett, perhaps we shall return towards the wagons until the Priestess is ready for us-"

"Oi, that shan't be necessary," said Syler firmly. "General, I have been searching for you."

"How may I assist you, Your Loveliness?" asked Kiyoko.

"I had wished to speak with you in regards to Bullet's keys..." Syler took a breath before she continued. "Were the pair of you successful in using the locator spell?"

"My attempts were fruitless," Kiyoko admitted with a frown. "I shall confess the spell did not divulge any useful information."

"How can that be so?" Syler asked. "You are immensely gifted-"

"The rebels had impressive shields," Kiyoko said gently. "The dynamics of an upcoming Ascension, full moon, and unstable energies of the realms can allow them to cloak themselves thoroughly... if they possess the iron in their will to do so."

"Is there anything I can provide that could assist you, if you were to try the spell again?" Syler asked hopefully. "Perhaps you could indulge in sweet grass, or allow me to provide power behind your words..."

"I would rather avoid such risks during this fragile time," Kiyoko said. "I exhausted the resources I felt comfortable in using, and I would rather not stimulate my gifts with all else swirling at present."

"Another day comes to pass where I grow envious of the wisdom you possess, Kiyoko," Syler praised with a smile.

"Your kindness is abundant," Kiyoko replied with a salute.

"I appreciate your efforts," Syler continued. "Though it saddens me to learn Bullet's keys remain unaccounted for."

"I reckon we shall have to go through the Hells to find them," Kiyoko said dramatically. "Whomever possesses them certainly shan't release them without struggle."

"Gods have mercy," Syler said, running her hands absently through her curls.

"Was there anything else I could do to serve you?" Kiyoko asked with a salute.

"Only to accept my upcoming token of appreciation," Syler said. "I pray you linger for a moment whilst I fetch a gift for you."

"I shall admit you have captivated my interest," Kiyoko nodded excitedly. "Do what you must, and we shall wait for you."

Ducking further into the tent, Syler disappeared for several moments, giving me the time to unfasten Truff from his post.

"Frek, how are you fairing?" Kiyoko asked gently, the subtle shifting of his eyes indicating tension in Frek's energies.

"Well enough," Frek snapped. "Though it is considered impolite to listen to a private conversation."

"Perhaps you should speak somewhere more secluded," I challenged, disliking the tone he bore towards Kiyoko.

"Gentlemen, mayhaps we could settle our spirits," advised Kiyoko with a wave of his hand.

Frek scoffed, his energy softening slightly as he released a tense breath.

"Wolfman," Kiyoko chose the endearment he had designed for Frek. "In three night's time the moon shall be full once more... and I beseech thee to mind thine temper."

"I have tried best I can," Frek said.

"Perhaps some energetic healing this full moon would encourage you to relax whilst I negate your transition."

"That is not a matter to be taken lightly, Kiyoko," Frek said. "It would risk negative impacts to my energy if you disrupt my cycle."

"I suppose that is wise," Kiyoko said.

Frek scowled hotly as Syler emerged from the back of the tents.

"All is well, I hope," Syler said with a radiant smile.

"Aye, Your Loveliness," I said gently. "All is well and good."

"I possess Tora Berry wine for you, General," Syler produced a bottle of the deep blue vintage, handing it across the threshold to Kiyoko. "I forced my sister to indulge in some already, and now I shall do the same for you."

"You are kind in thinking of me," Kiyoko said sincerely. "Though I was fortunate to fight with steel and not with spirit."

"Keep it with you anyhow," said Syler. "The Cypress spell is bound to have consequences... Knomucca cannot truly expect to call upon the dead so closely to The Ascension without angering certain entities..."

"Perhaps it would be wise to partake," I suggested, smiling as Kiyoko agreed with a nod.

"We could share a glass, Wolfman," Kiyoko told Frek. "Mayhaps it would help to soften your transition and provide a moment's relief."

Frek rolled his eyes by way of reply.

"Commander," Syler spoke to prevent an awkward silence. "Could I have a word?"

"Certainly," I said, fastening Truff's reigns to Hazel's tent once more. "Shall I follow you inside?"

"That would be preferred," she said with a nod.

Frek held the canvas door open out of obligation, sliding rightwards to admit me access to Hazel's tent.

"Kiyoko had a marvelous idea," Syler said to Frek as she entered the tent. "Indulge... have a glass of wine with him whilst you wait."

"Very well," Frek said, gesturing his farewell with a hand and closing the canvas.

Hazel's tent lacked its usual grandeur, having been decorated and furnished with improvised materials. Bottles of botanicals and herbs, tinctures, and a plethora of instruments I did not recognize hung from a firm wire rack against the far wall. A stack of books haphazardly overwhelmed a small circular table, their leathery black covers dully reflecting the torchlight. A rickety wooden table housed a pestle and mortar, stone goblets, dyes, and the recipe for an aloe salve sprawling on a crinkled piece of weathered parchment. Narrow beds took up the back wall, covered in thick blue blankets and lumpy pillows.

Syler pulled a wooden stool out from under one of the tables.

"Would you care to sit?" she asked.

"I would rather stand, if that is acceptable," I said.

"Absolutely," Syler said, the resemblance to Knomucca in her intonation nearly made me lose focus.

"To what do I owe the pleasure?" I asked.

"I had merely wanted to ask if you spoke to my sister as of yet," Syler said. "Hazel had mentioned there was some unsettling news."

"Aye, we hath spoken," I said.

"May I ask about the depressing matter in which you shared with her?"

"It is rather unfortunate. Hazel's wagon was destroyed in the flames."

"Oi, Gods. Knomucca's potion elements..."

"Aye."

"The reason for Hazel wishing you would divulge this information is now clear," Syler said. "Everett, this is truly horrible."

"Indeed," I began. "I have expressed a willingness to assist in gathering new elements, though I suspect she will do it alone."

"I suspect you are correct," Syler said. "Assert yourself, Everett. Assist her regardless of her desires."

"That is my intention," I said.

Syler met my eyes with an unreadable expression. "She needs you, Everett. Swear to me that whatever happens, you shan't abandon her."

"I never would," I said.

"Be careful making such promises," said Syler.

"I would promise it with my blood," I said, placing a hand over my heart.

"I wager you would," she said, her expression softening. Syler rose to a stand, seizing her stool and returning it beneath the wooden table. "I apologize if this is rude, but I must be getting back to my work."

"Aye, the Merchants Banquet is this evening, is it not?"

"It is, indeed."

Syler edged towards the threshold, pressing her hand to the canvas before abruptly turning back to face me. Throwing her arms unexpectedly around my shoulders, Syler held me in a brief embrace.

"Luck from our First Warrior, Anteyus," Syler whispered.

"I had been ignorant towards your fondness of him," I admitted.

"You know it is forbidden," Syler whispered.

"Your blessings are appreciated," I said. "I foresee all shall end well with The Ascensions."

"My blessings are not in reference to The Ascensions," Syler confessed, pulling away from my arms.

Frek suddenly stalked into the doorway, his mood darkening instantly.

"Come, my sweet, let us be off," Syler said, taking Frek by the hand. "Stay wise, Commander."

"Love and light," I replied, following them towards the door.

I pushed through the canvas watching as Syler and Frek tore across the castle grounds. They walked stiffly towards the castle continuing to whisper angrily as they moved. Turning my attention towards Truff, I untied his reigns then led him from Hazel's tent.

"Let us find Kye," I said, gesturing for Kiyoko to follow me towards the drawbridge.

We reached the hill's summit, the remnants of the battle lingering amidst the grass. Rusted red blood splattered through the fields, marking the outline of the soldiers who had fallen. Confiscated weapons sat in a heap beneath a tree, waiting to be recycled, gifted to new owners, or stored. Shrubs and plants were smashed from battling boots, their leaves and roots ripped and scattered across the ground. Fallen bodies waited to be buried, the stench of death perfuming the air as an unwanted, autumnal aroma.

Crossing down the hill, we entered the organized chaos of soldiers dealing with the smoldering wreckage of the wagons. Parts of the convoy had been moved further south down the road, distinguishing the salvageable wagons from what had been destroyed. Burnt and blackened wood laid in large stacks along the trail, taken from the heaps of ashes. Supplies for our journey lay sorted along the path; countless necessities that had been spared were set aside. Wheels of the fallen wagons teetered beside the heaps of wood, waiting to be returned to the castle for later use.

Finding a nearby tree, I secured Truff to a low-hanging branch. Ducking around him, I scanned the chaos for Kye, spotting her down the road in a heated discussion. As I walked through the remnants of our destroyed convoy, apprentices and servants swirled busily, narrowly barreling into me with a mix of profanities and rushed apologies.

The tension of Kye's emotions became palpable as I approached her. Clutching several parchment pieces in her hands, she rifled efficiently through them, barking demands at anyone who fell too close.

"Oi, that will have to be scrapped," Kye was saying as I came up behind her. "Put it with the goods returning to the castle, and coordinate with the servants who are removing them. Lieutenant, see to it that the scraps of wood and remaining rubbish from the wagons are being brought up as well."

"Aye," said Tyfis, stepping around me and disappearing further up the hill.

"And where in the seven hells is Everett?" Kye roared.

"He is right behind you," said Kiyoko.

Kye spun sharply, meeting my eyes with anger. "Gods... 'bout time you got down here."

"Hold your tongue, Kyreese," I snarled, using her full name to indicate my annoyance. "There were other matters to attend to, we came once we could."

"My pardons, Commander," said Kye, softening her tone. "The damage from the fires is severe, and you shan't like what I must tell you."

"I am aware of the status of Hazel's cart," I stated, holding up a hand.

"Aye, that is only the beginning," Kye said, gesturing for Kiyoko and me to follow her further down the path. "As you may recall, we initially had twenty wagons of supplies we were bringing with us. Of those twenty carts, only seven were salvageable."

"Gods... Only seven?" I asked in shock, centering myself to prevent my breath from betraying the worry in my eyes.

"Aye, seven... Excluding Hazel's personal sleeping quarters."

"What is housed within the remaining carts?" asked Kiyoko.

"For our journey we will be bringing two carts of rations, one cart of wine, the wagon containing our dress armor, two wagons of metal tools, and one cart of feed for the horses."

"Gods..." I sighed and swore with feeling.

"Aye. Currently, Bullet and Tyfis are now assisting apprentices and servants in shuttling supplies and extra horses back to the castle. We cannot bring everything that has not been burned with us. There is simply no room, and there is not enough time to repair or build new carts."

"Very well," I said.

"Soldiers have helped in loading excess herbs, wines, rations, and anything else we can take with us into the remaining wagons. Maliche and his apprentices are needed to cleanse the blood from the grass and tend to the landscaping. Although, nobody can seem to find Maliche... neither of you would happen to know his whereabouts, would you?"

"I have not noticed him," I admitted, watching as Kiyoko nodded in agreement.

"Very well."

"How may Kiyoko and I assist?" I asked eagerly.

"We cannot depart until Hazel has examined you. Please go and find her."

"Aye, we will set off straight away." I said, turning with Kiyoko and moving back towards the piles of scrap we had previously passed.

"Excellent," Kye called after us with a salute.

Briskly walking, we moved back up the path in search of the Priestess. Kiyoko's energy soured, his face flushing with a sickly green.

Kiyoko sighed, soothingly massaging his forehead and hair. "Perhaps we should find herbs to cleanse the castle grounds... the amount of negative energy lingering is beginning to make me ill."

"Perhaps it would be wise for you to partake in your mugwort," I began.

"That would indeed be wise," Kiyoko said, averting his eyes as they began to water.

"I could prepare a spliff for you," I soothed. "If you would like."

"You possess mugwort?" Kiyoko asked, exhaling deeply as he massaged his face.

"You know I always do," I said gently. "I am never without it, for fear you shall be in need."

"I have spliffs prepared," Kiyoko said with a smile. "Though I shan't forget you offered."

Chuckling softly, I watched as Kiyoko struck a match and began to smoke absent mindedly whilst looking in the distance. The bitter smell of mugwort balanced the aromas of sweet grass and lemon balm perfuming the air.

"Oi, look," he said, gesturing with his chin.

Following his gaze, I spotted Maliche moving angrily down the hill. Storming forward, he barked aggressively at the plethora of apprentices that followed close behind him. Swearing in sharp tones, Maliche corralled his apprentices further down the path, passing alongside us with barely any acknowledgment.

"Commander... General..." Maliche greeted automatically as he walked by. His eyes flashed with an unreadable expression, his lips forming a straight line.

Kiyoko silently saluted, nodding from beside me with a spliff in hand.

"Maliche," I said with a nod, watching as he and his cohort rushed past.

Turning towards Kiyoko, I watched his smoking, waiting to ensure Maliche's absence before speaking.

"Any idea what he's on about?" I asked, noticing Kiyoko's eyes softening as the nausea left him.

"I am uncertain," said Kiyoko, finishing his spliff as he failed to meet my gaze.

"Kiyoko, what did you see?" I asked, annoyed with his sudden silence.

"His aura was green with envy when he saw you," confessed Kiyoko. "Parts of his energy contained orbs of blue... I reckon he was feeling unsatisfied..."

"How do you mean?" I asked.

"How do you think I mean?" Kiyoko inquired.

"I am uncertain," I said, furrowing my brow.

"Oi, keep it moving, keep it moving," Bullet barked, materializing from a plume of frigid wind. "Gods know we are short on time."

Turning sharply, I whistled my signal to summon Bullet. In his arms rested piles of clothing and bundles of herbs he had been in the midst of collecting to return to the castle. Acknowledging me with a nod, he wove through the mass of servants, standing at attention in front of me though he could not salute with his arms full.

"Bullet, I am glad to see you are well," I said. "Pray tell, what hath occurred once I charged you with the billy?"

"I was ambushed," said Bullet. "Rebels had been stealing our castle's goats and when I tried to sound an alarm, I was attacked. I escaped to the castle and retrieved the twins along with our extra forces, though due to their preoccupations with The Ascension and Merchants Banquet, our reactions were delayed."

"Where are these stolen goats?" asked Kiyoko.

"I'm uncertain," confessed Bullet. "I would wager they are long gone by now. Probably wherever they're keeping my gods-be-damned keys..."

"I am sorry that the locator spell proved to be fruitless," Kiyoko said. "Whomever possesses them has very impressive shielding capabilities..."

"Aye... reckon so," Bullet said with a chuckle. "Your brain's no tree trunk, if you are struggling to find them then there must be a reason."

"Indeed," I sighed, unsure how to cast the worry for the stolen keys from my mind.

A sudden swarm of soldiers stirred behind us, snatching supplies from the grass and rushing past.

"All shall be sorted soon enough," Bullet said softly. "My pardons for the worry I hath caused, Commander."

"All is well and good," I said, silently praying to the First Warrior that the loss of Bullet's keys would not return to haunt us.

"Hazel and the Knell have also been alerted," Bullet continued. "And the corpses are being searched before they are prepared for burial."

"It pleases me to hear you say so," I said.

"Oi," Kye snarled suddenly and sharply from behind us. "Why in the seven hells are you standing around? Samarin and the other nobles shall start arriving for the Merchants Banquet any moment, and we need to get this refuse off the road."

"Sergeant," I glared. "Mind your tone."

"Kyreese," Kiyoko soothed. "I understand the energies around us are imbalanced, but you would do well to quench your iron. There is too much at play to risk further disruptions."

A mischievous sparkle suddenly floated through Bullet's eyes. "Perhaps if we were to have had the cannon..."

Kye furled a fist, hammering Bullet directly in the jaw. The blow staggered him backward, his supplies scattering as he landed on his hindquarters.

"Sargent, that was out of line!" I growled.

"Well, he-" Kyreese started.

"No," I said. "Despite the pain that paints your past, any future outbursts of this sort shall result a demotion of your rank."

Kye opened her mouth to speak but quickly closed it.

"You should take a moment to collect yourself," I asserted.

She angrily stepped around Bullet, scooping up scattered goblets and rations before storming off towards the castle.

"I do suppose I deserved that," said Bullet, rubbing his face in embarrassment.

"Aye, you most certainly did," Kiyoko chuckled. "However, with the Ascension drawing so near, the energy of the realms is unstable. This, combined with our high emotions, could lead to anarchy and the collapse of the realms."

"Indeed," I agreed. "Kyreese needs to remember her rank."

"I, too, shall keep my actions in mind," Bullet said, returning the remaining supplies to his arms once more. "Commander... General... I best be setting off."

"Very well," I said, dismissing him with a salute.

Bullet burst away in a cloud of wind, the grass and leaves left rustling in his wake.

"How can we assist in displacing some of the excess energy?" I asked, turning towards Kiyoko.

"Soldiers could partake in the herb, meditate, or drink Tora Berry wine if there's extra."

"I reckon we'll find something for them," I said gently.

"Everett," Kiyoko's eyes dulled as he continued speaking. "If we cannot displace some of the tension and imbalance, I fear I shall be forced to absorb some of it."

My eyes widened. "Kiyoko... such action never bodes well for you."

"I am certain it is daft and dangerous to absorb energy this close to The Ascension," Kiyoko began somberly. "Though I do not know what other options befall us. The elements themselves may revolt against us if we are not cautious."

"Gods," I said sincerely. "I shall promise to you, Kiyoko... I will do all I can to keep you from having to turn down such a path."

"Be careful making such promises," Kiyoko said firmly. "There are far too many uncertainties ahead, and forces stronger than our own..."

"I would promise it with my blood," I echoed my earlier words to Syler. "I care far too much for you to condone such behaviors."

"The events of the day thus far, the upcoming Ascension, and the stress of our fellow comrades hath made me realize my tardiness this morning was most certainly as a result of amplified emotions and perceiving the realm's imbalance," Kiyoko said, a shadow flickering through his aura.

"Though I do sympathise that the energy is overwhelming for you, I would prefer you did not use it to justify making questionable decisions."

"In any case," Kiyoko continued, ignoring my scolding. His words were momentarily lost in the returning rush of servants and soldiers gathering supplies for the castle. "The most important thing we can do is remain calm, focus on the challenges ahead, and mind our tempers."

"Aye, it is a task sooner abandoned than completed," I concluded.

"It must be done," Kiyoko said, showing worry in his eyes for the first time. "For the good of the realms."

I sighed again, breathing through the worry coursing through me. Midday had already come and gone, the early afternoon bringing a chill that would last well through the night. Heavy clouds had rolled in from the east, the promise of early autumn rain greying the sky.

"It looks as though it is like to storm," said Kiyoko, gesturing with a hand towards the sky.

"I hope you are mistaken," I said while thinking of Knomucca, who was flying in the direction of the clouds. Closing my eyes, I lowered my head in a silent prayer. Focusing my energy, I sent blessings to Knomucca, along with prayers to the First Warrior so that she would remain safe.

"Everett!"

The sound of my name pulled me out of my prayer. Turning around, I spotted Hazel descending the hill, her bright green robes flowing around her as she sped through the grass. Apprentices garbed in black robes flanked either side of her, forming a living shadow edged by the white filigree on their cuffs.

"Commander... General..." Hazel nodded respectively as she approached. "I possess the morning's update."

"Aye, proceed," I said, noticing the smooth stone goblet she held in her hands.

"All the critically injured have been tended. Everyone is safe and cleared for travel, except for Greeves who has been moved to the Red Wing of the infirmary whilst we are gone. I have chosen apprentices to care for him until we return, however, I do not anticipate him seeing the light of the coming dawn."

"Let us hope that the bell of Heimaaila does not yet toll for him," I said with a heavy breath, placing a hand over my heart.

"How many soldiers were lost?" Kiyoko asked from beside me, shifting his weight awkwardly and taking a deep breath to avoid meeting Hazel's eyes.

"Forty-eight were claimed during the battle, and an additional seven perished despite our attempts to save them," Hazel said. "The Knell has begun the funeral preparations for all of those that were lost. They have also been dispatched to inform the families of the fallen."

"Is there anything that we can do to assist?" Everett asked.

"No," Hazel said firmly. "Those that are a part of my Knell have been selectively chosen and undergone specialized training over several seasons. They are more than capable of performing the tasks required."

"Have you at least had any luck in the search for Bullet's keys?" I asked hopefully, looking for any light in the growing darkness. My spirits saddened as Hazel shook her head.

"Nay, Commander," Hazel said. "We searched all two hundred of the fallen rebels quite thoroughly."

"Will that be everything?" I asked, eager to dismiss her and return to Truff.

"Not quite, Commander," Hazel said as she thrust the goblet forward. The ghost of a smirk flashed across her face. "I brewed you treatment for your injuries-"

"That is well and good," I said.

"You do not look well," Hazel's voice was harsh and urgent.

"I feel fine," I said, disliking the assault from her words and her tone.

"Everett," Hazel said, releasing an exasperated breath. "Your skin hath been tinted in purple bruises... your neck appears to be swelling... your voice sounds terrible..."

"My voice is different?" I asked quizzically, turning to face Kiyoko, who stood beside me quietly.

"You are noticeably injured, Everett," Kiyoko said gently.

Hazel pushed the granite goblet into my hands, using the distraction of Kiyoko's words to force the stone between my fingers.

"I will be monitoring you throughout our travels this eve, Everett," Hazel explained. "I want to be certain travel on horseback will not be problematic, and that your vital energies remain intact and stable."

"Aye, very well," I said, resisting a sigh.

"You will need multiple treatments to ensure there is no damage," Hazel continued, adopting a serious expression.

"Is there warrant to worry for long-term effects?" Kiyoko asked, panic dulling his aura subtly as sadness floated through him.

"There certainly could be," Hazel said, nodding. "You are going to need rest and relaxation... I would advise against smoking, however, that is as cruel to ask of you as it would be in asking a fish to live without water."

"Everett could stand to limit his indulgences," Kiyoko said, his voice cleverly coding the concern coursing through him.

"It is worth considering," Hazel agreed with an ecstatic smile. "The added heat of smoke and fire could aggravate his injuries."

"It is true, herbs for smoking are one of the many gifts from The Creator," Kiyoko said before I could voice the words for myself. "Yet I shall do all I can to convince Everett to exercise restraint."

"Excellent," Hazel said to Kiyoko, speaking as if I were no longer standing between them. "I must also again push with severity the importance of resting as much as possible... another kiss with death and Everett may not be so fortunate as to keep his life. Has all I have said been made clear?"

"Clear as quartz," Kiyoko said, his energy shifting as he turned from Hazel to face me.

"Perhaps you should drink then," Hazel said, also turning towards me, her eyes flashing briefly in unsettling darkness and shadow.

Scouring, I peered into the goblet suspiciously, examining the contents of the cup I now held in my fist. "May I inquire as to what I shall be consuming?"

"Tora berry wine, honey, peppermint, elderberry syrup, echinacea, and chamomile flowers."

"Excellent," I said, comparing her spoken word against the familiar smells of the botanicals I recognized from my many nights spent in the orchards. Taking a long drink, I relished the deliciously cold brew. I enjoyed the blissful, soothing liquid as it forced me to acknowledge how injured I had become.

"Will you have the required ingredients with us in order to continue preparing the treatments?" Kiyoko asked.

"I have placed all the ingredients for the tonic on the wagons myself," said Hazel.

"Very good," I said, taking a sip of the potion as I attempted to relax.

"Will that be everything, Priestess?" Kiyoko asked as I took another drink, gifting me a moment's peace to indulge in my goblet. "Or was there more to discuss with us?"

"I desire a word with you, General Kiyoko," Hazel said.

Kiyoko watched my lips eagerly as I drank from my goblet, his eyes briefly faltering before he turned away.

"What would you have of me now?" He asked.

"Did you receive any Tora Barry wine from Syler?" Hazel questioned, oblivious to the intimacy he shared with me with such few glances.

"Aye... indeed," Kiyoko said with a warm smile.

"It was quite kind of her Loveliness," I interjected with a nod.

"Aye, her generosity is as abundant as the evergreens," Kiyoko said.

"It was I who requested that she bring the wine to you," Hazel said suddenly.

Kiyoko arched an eyebrow curiously. "How unexpected."

"I concocted it myself," she said almost too excitedly, resting a bandaged hand lightly on his arm as she swayed with her movements.

"And why should I deserve such a delicacy?" He questioned. "You prescribe this wine to those who are metaphysically affected after a battle..."

"I know this morning has taken its toll on everyone," she said. "This is a new recipe I am perfecting... It will benefit anyone who consumes it..."

Hazel pulled her hand away from his arm. Kiyoko's aura crystallized, the energy solid as stone. Hazel trailed violet-purple light into her palm, stretching the crystals from Kiyoko's spirits. The bitter scent of mugwort floated through the air. A red light pulsed and snapped through my mind's eye. Darkness flashed through Hazel's irises, her skin paling briefly as she fought to maintain her composure.

"I am certain it will be quite delightful," he said almost melodically.

Hazel disguised her movements, sliding her hand cleverly into her sleeve as she shifted her stance. A sharp, purple thorn vanished through her palm, disappearing quickly. Her face briefly contorted with pain, a dark shadow flooding through her aura.

"Indeed," she said, her voice level.

"I have finished my treatment," I said, lowering the goblet from my lips.

Kiyoko snatched the goblet from my hands, his movements making me jump with surprise. He held the goblet in his palm, stretching his hand outward towards Hazel.

Hazel's irises filled with shadows as she eyed Kiyoko suspiciously. Kiyoko's aura rippled red in aggravation, his fingers flexing subtly around the stone. Reaching towards him, Hazel avoided touching his skin, tentatively grasping the outer rim of the goblet as she tugged it from his grip. Thrumming, pulsing strings of purple floated back from Hazel, and through the goblet, the energy tinted red with blood as it floated into Kiyoko's hand. Her fingers twitched and convulsed around the goblet, and her eyes twinged briefly with a moment of pain.

"Thank you," Hazel said curtly as she returned the goblet to her robes.

"My veins flow thick with mugwort," Kiyoko's voice was charming and hypnotic. "I would not forget how bitter of a smoke it can be."

"It is not a concept I am familiar with. I find smoking herbs to be a poor use of plants," Hazel said, her eyes resuming their clarity as she rebuttaled against his words. She turned to face me, "I hope you found the tonic to your liking, Commander."

"I did indeed," I said, feeling Kiyoko tense suddenly at my side as if he had forgotten me. "I appreciate your preparing it for me, Priestess."

"'Twas my pleasure... Since you have finished, I shall take my leave," Hazel started with a small sigh. "I must be finalizing preparations for our departure, and doth not want to be the cause for additional stress or delay."

"That would be wise," I said, wishing I had not needed to ask the question that followed. "When shall I be receiving my next treatment?"

"I shall see you sometime before dawn," Hazel said after a short pause. "Though if the pain becomes too much to bear, please find me sooner."

"Aye, thank you immensely," I said, saluting as Hazel prepared to walk away.

"Stay wise," Hazel said, returning my salute with one of her own.

"Love and light," I replied, watching Hazel and her apprentices return to their previous path up the hill.

Waiting until Hazel fell from sight, I turned towards Kiyoko suddenly as I was consumed by the need to speak. "What were you trying to prove by taking my goblet like that?"

"I needed to protect myself. Hazel tried to siphon my energy," Kiyoko said, shrugging innocently despite his yellowing aura.

"Are you certain?" My eyes widened in sudden shock. "Kiyoko, that is a serious accusation..."

"You would doubt my words and their implications knowing the weight of their water?" Kiyoko's face fell as offense tinged his aura in grey.

"I did not mean to plant seeds of doubt or disbelief," I said to him gently. "I merely grow fearful and concerned... Your head could end up on a pike, should the wrong ears catch wind of your words against The Priestess..."

"I am aware..." Kiyoko said somberly. "Yet it is the truth... she attempted to gain access."

"How did you respond?" I asked curiously. "You did not seem to be in peril."

"My wards aided in my defense and alerted me to her scandal," Kiyoko began with a soft smile. "I then retaliated, pushing towards her a rather painful shade which she shan't have liked."

"Did your energy enter her body?" I asked, weighing the decision to confess my observations.

"She tried to feed on my vital life energy," Kiyoko said with a heavy sigh. "She would have succeeded too, had I not reacted so defensively."

"What are we to do should she attempt this again?" I asked, shaking my head to clear it before Kiyoko began to speak.

"It is not a matter I am concerned with," Kiyoko said with a malicious smile. "When I removed my energy from her veins, I did not make the withdrawal particularly pleasant."

"Yet another delicacy she shall regret to forgo," I said, echoing Kiyoko's earlier words with a flirtatious smile. Tingling warmth cascaded down my spine and legs, my body responding to the memories of such pleasure that I knew could be felt from Kiyoko's energy manipulations.

"Aye, such sadness," Kiyoko said, allowing a short silence to float between us.

"We must decide a course of action," I said firmly. "I do not feel right concealing such information from Knomucca."

"If we are to present this incident to her, we will need evidence," Kiyoko said, his expression serious.

"Aye, that is wise," I sighed heavily.

Sadness lingered within the depths of his eyes. "We shall need patience until the moment to prove our conviction presents itself."

"Wise indeed," I said, exhaling my frustrations.

"Do not worry, I shall protect you." Kiyoko soothed with a hand across my shoulder. "Though, reckon we must hold the snake at an arm's length... praying all the while it doth not strike us."

"Such a notion churns my stomach," I said.

"We shall get it sorted."

"As we have now met with The Priestess it is now time to depart." My words blurred and muffled in the clattering of a fresh wave of soldiers that emerged down the hill. Kye led the officers through the grass towards us.

"Oi, gather 'round." The officers assembled in attention, saluting as they waited for me to address them. "This hellish morning is finally behind us."

A chorus of "huzzah!" rang through the ranks with a wave of thunderous cheering.

"Aye, we hath done Our Worship proud, and defended Morriraen with honor. The blood spilled in our soil shan't be forgotten, and lives lost on this day were given in sacrifice for the good of the realms. Although we may be able to consider the battle a victory, it hath come with a price. Nearly a full day's travel hath been lost to us, and most of our supplies hath been destroyed. There will be modifications made to the roles at camp, along with extra travel to make up for lost time. We must do all we can to allow Knomucca flexibility in retrieving her ritual elements... if we cannot grant her the time to do so, our tasks shall become far more complicated. Are we in accordance?"

"Aye, sir," responded a smattering of soldiers, accompanied by a salute.

"Excellent," I said, taking a swig from my water skin to soothe my aching throat. "Are there any concerns?"

My words were met with silence.

"We shall be setting off," I said, "Attend to what you must quickly and fetch your horses - the daylight is fleeting."

I sought Truff's tree, ducking behind the widened elm before untying his reigns from the branches.

"Truff, walk on," I said, leading him beyond the supply wagons to begin forming the ranks.

The clatter of armor clanked across the breeze as soldiers obtained their horses and assembled in formation. Kiyoko took up his usual place at my right, discarding the remains of a smoke that smelled of mugwort and lavender before climbing into the saddle. Slipping my boot into the stirrup, I hoisted myself onto Truff's back, adjusting my luggage as I shifted to be comfortable. The troops filed into their positions, clambering onto their horses and waiting at attention in front of us to allow Kiyoko and me to take up post at the rear. The supply wagons at our backs were each rigged to half a dozen horses to accommodate our hastened pace.

I placed my thumb and forefinger in my mouth and commanded attention with a whistle.

"Fall out," I demanded, flicking Truff's reigns sharply.

We lurched forward, leaving the castle Morriraen behind us. The path smoothed to flattened stone as we moved from Moon's Road to Castle Way at the forest entrance. The birdsongs had returned to the trees, the chaos of the battle finally settling enough for them to return home. Fresh tracks from deer and coons scattered alongside the path, the panic in their prints evident as they fled into the forest.

It was then I noticed our movements had gone unaccompanied by drums or brass. Whistling my signal to summon Kye, I quickened my pace, allowing her space beside me as she broke from the ranks.

"Greetings, Commander," Kye said with a sly smile and a salute. "To what do I owe the pleasure?"

"Where are our musicians?" I asked, disliking the procession's eerie silence that a good set of trumpets could help to resolve.

"Syler feared their company may have encumbered us..." Kye said seriously. "She requested they assist in providing entertainment for the Merchants Banquet instead of accompanying us to Riverside."

"Aye, perhaps that was wise," I said, understanding Syler's intentions with knowledge of our diminished supplies. "May I ask what her suggestion is for how we provide music at Riverside if it is asked of us?"

"Come now, Commander," Kye said, rolling her eyes. "We have many talented musicians amongst our ranks...and although Kiyoko's harp was destroyed in the fire, I am certain he has an instrument – or several – stashed in his saddle bags."

Glancing back toward Kiyoko, I was pleased to find him in good spirits, bouncing merrily as he relaxed into the rhythm of the ride.

"I suppose you're right," I said.

"I thought I mentioned all this earlier," said Kye, holding tightly to the reigns as she retrieved the pieces of parchment from her satchel.

"Afraid not," I said, maintaining a steady trot as we spoke.

"My pardons, Commander," she said, shuffling quickly through the parchment and returning it with a frown.

"Sergeant, the task of sorting the wagons was quite monumental. You did fine... please, allow any frustration you may still be carrying towards the situation to wash down the river."

"I appreciate your words, Commander, though unfortunately we will be dealing with the repercussions for days."

"Aye, understood," I said, taking a deep and cleansing breath to clear away my growing nerves.

"Will there be anything else?" asked Kye, sitting up straight in her saddle.

"Nay, Sergeant," I said, gifting Kye a salute. "Return to ranks,"

"Aye, Commander," Kye said, sprinting forward on her horse and returning to her line placement.

Pressing onward, we marched through thickening trees, the foundation of the path growing treacherous as we moved further from the castle. The eastern breeze tugged at my sleeves, the sky darkening with clouds as we entered the forest. The path narrowed, forcing the ranks into two-by-twos, and the far-off sounds of the Snake River entered my awareness from the left. Whistling sharply, I commanded the troop's horses to canter, gripping tightly to Truff's reigns as we sped south. The trees cut closely across the path, their branches smacking against our shoulders as we pressed forcefully forward.

Our horses' hooves pounded across the ground, thundering through the crisp autumn air. Curving rightwards, the path wove deeper into the trees, the road narrowing as it neared the river. Whistling loudly, I slowed the troops to a trot, feeling Truff's footing waver as we transitioned from stone to dirt. The path wound suddenly left, our elevation rising as we climbed a small yet steep hill.

Gradually, the ranks slimmed to a single file, shaving our orderly formation down to a steadily flowing stream. The Snake River hissed and sputtered through the dense trees, the reflective water peeking through the branches. The path rose precipitously, the incline cracked and broken with jagged roots and protruding sticks. Whistling harshly, I slowed the troop to a walk, focusing on Truff's footing as we stepped on the slender, unstable soil.

Steadily, the path bent rightwards, jutting through a small clearing and around a thicket of trees. The Snake River cut through a shallow gorge bordering on our left, the current flowing lazily between rocks and fallen branches. As we moved along the well-worn path, the tall grass turned to neatly manicured shrubberies along the edge of the river. Enchanted lanterns hung on swooping pine branches, lining the path and illuminating the way to the Snake River Trading Port.

Six wooden boats surrounded a stripped birch pier, the wood obstructed from the elements by a rolling canvas shade. Smatterings of brick houses were clustered along either side of the river, a large wooden drawbridge connecting them. Across the channel, a small stone bell tower and lighthouse, surrounded by horse stables, shone with oil lamps during the dark days that promised storms. Beyond the bell tower, several acres of land had been converted into farms, the fields enchanted to be raised above the height of the river to protect the crops from damage and flooding.

The River Fleet elves who ran the port peered through the windows of the brick houses as we approached. A small, slender elf with disheveled hair ran across the grounds to the bell tower, pulling on the large rope thrice, the rhythm indicating our arrival to the guard. The creaking and slamming of doors sounded as a handful of soldiers assembled near the port entrance. All of the River Fleet had trained as soldiers in the Gods' Guard before being assigned to the port, responsible for handling the realms' trade, as well as escorting guests to and from the castle, either providing steamers to far-off destinations or carriages to Morriraen.

A shadow moved behind the shacks as a man appeared at the front of the guard. His ebony skin glowed in the torches that surrounded the threshold. A thick-handled harpoon was readied in his left hand, and a wooden pipe held in his right. He adjusted his cerulean cloak with a practiced finesse, fastening it with a heavy silver emblem and an iron chain down the front. The medallion was carved with the crest of Morriraen, tinted a blue as translucent as the river.

"Salutations, Captain Southwell," I called from my horse.

"Greetin's, Commander," Lyle Southwell saluted. "Were we not expectin' to see you earlier?"

Nodding courteously, I slowed Truff to a walk as I began to speak.

"Aye, that is so," I said, remembering I had set a point to check in with him earlier in the day when I thought we would be passing through.

"Is everythin' well?" Lyle asked, folding his arms over his chest and taking a puff of his pipe.

"Actually, things are not well," I said, producing herbs from my smoking sacks and gesturing towards the elf's pipe. "If you allow me the honor in freshening your pipe, I can update you on the events that hath delayed us."

"Color me intrigued," Lyle mused, closing the space between us with a series of rapid steps. Lyle placed his smooth wooden pipe into my hands, stepping back as he met my eyes with a grin.

"I read you as a lover of nettles," I wagered, fishing through the leather sacks until I found the herb.

"I simply request no lavender," Lyle said. "Gives me a right awful headache, that shite does."

"I can understand that," I said. "The smell and flavor are quite potent."

"I find lavender to be an acquired taste. I do possess sweet grass and mugwort if you wish," said Kiyoko, appearing suddenly on my left. He tossed his smoking sack to me as he guided his horse around us. "I apologize if this is rude, though I reckon I shall ride ahead. Please return my pouch to me when you are finished."

"Excellent," I said, tugging on the strings to open the rough leather satchel.

Kiyoko's smoking sack was mended and worn from years of use; the braided hemp strings were held with labradorite to keep them from fraying. The delicate repairs I had made over the years to the cracks in the leather that had threatened to wash away the symbols of his coven and homeland now circled the crest like a halo. Tiny mesh compartments within the smoking sack neatly housed a plethora of herbs, onion skins, and matches for rolling spliffs, along with miniature jars and flasks that held small drops of honey. My smoking sacks had the same inner design, yet by their enchantments, remained glossy and new in appearance, as they had been a gift from Knomucca once I assumed my post as Commander five years prior.

"Such a bond you share he trusts you with his smokin' herbs," admired Lyle. "Consider me impressed."

"It is a great honor," I said, inhaling the scent of fresh greenery that wafted from the pouch.

"Aye, so it is indeed," Lyle said, accepting his freshly packed pipe and a match from my hands. "Thank you immensely, Commander."

"My pleasure, Captain Southwell," I said, tying Kiyoko's smoking sack to my belt and retrieving a spliff from my own that I had rolled previously.

"Anyhow, Commander," Lyle prompted, pulling deeply on his pipe. "I believe you owed me a story..."

"Aye, it was quite deplorable," I said, choosing my words deliberately. Lyle and his river fleet need not know certain details of the morning, such as Kiyoko's tardiness or the nearness of Knomucca and I kissing. "We had fallen behind in schedule from finalizing our departure preparations and witnessed an attack on the castle."

"Morriraen was attacked?" asked Lyle, his eyes widened in surprise.

"Aye," I let out a disheartened sigh. "We lost fifty-five soldiers to those treacherous bastards."

"Oi," Lyle loosed a heavy breath. "Do you have any inklin' as to who orchestrated the attack?"

"Not as of yet," I admitted. "We believe the rebels to be from the mountains, though we do not have enough evidence to support such accusations at present."

"Creator have mercy," Lyle gasped with horror. "The sun hath not smiled brightly on this morrow."

"Aye," I said, "we hath fell behind in our travels and need to do all we can to arrive in Riverside promptly, whilst allowing Knomucca time to accomplish what she must."

Lyle's face changed to one of puzzlement, his hand reaching upward to scratch his symmetrical, silken beard. Opening his mouth, he attempted to speak through the smoke that billowed from his lips, though his words fell silent.

"What troubles your mind?" I asked, growing uneasy with the tenseness of his body.

"I wondered..." Lyle sighed slowly before he continued. "I wondered when I last saw Her Worship... I cannot recall if I have encountered her since the summer began, nor do I remember seeing her for Lughnasa."

"I know it has been several weeks," I admitted. "She has been very occupied with tasks for The Creator and they hath consumed much of her time."

"I knew it had been some time since I last saw her..." Lyle said with a frown. "Commander... is it still your plan to pass around Kyraulh?"

"Aye," I said with a nod. "Though I am considering purchasing some goods from the markets if my Sergeant deems it necessary."

"Oi, avoid the markets..." Lyle said with a swooping hand. "Though you and the General may want to send a guard through the village..."

"I shall admit your words confuse me," I said, ashing my spliff into the growing wind.

"Durin' the last few weeks there's been a lot of civil unrest... and an unhealthy amount of rumors bein' spread 'bout Knomucca."

"Rumors?" I asked, "How do you mean?"

"People are sayin' her spirit magic is corruptin' her. They're sayin' she's becomin' more demonic, that she's learned to manipulate the intimate power of pleasure."

"What rubbish," I scoffed, though I could not deny the notion of her bringing me bliss from such power sounded quite thrilling.

"Is it that farfetched to wonder?" asked Lyle, speaking quickly. "Her hands are like that of a monster's. There are the whispers about her taste for hearts, an' the servants that have gone missin'..."

My eyes darkened. "What exactly are you accusing her of, Lyle?"

"Oi, I ain't accusin' her of anythin'," Lyle justified, placing a hand on his chest defensively. "I'm tryin' to warn you that there's a stirrin' in the seas and that's why I brought it to your attention."

"Very well," I said, narrowing my eyes as I studied his expression. If the morning's events had taught me anything, no one was above suspicion.

"I've held this post most o' my life," Lyle continued quickly. "I possess nothing but respect for Knomucca. You may not know this, but I lost my mom when I was just a lad, and I know her soul has been well cared for under Knomucca's watch... I ain't lookin' to start any trouble. I was just wantin' to lend my support, that was all."

"I am a man of action," I said seriously. "If you are trying to be of assistance, you could gather a fleet and resources, then meet us at Riverside on the night of the Equinox."

"It shall be done," Lyle said, the bowl of his pipe emptying of herbs.

"Luck from the stars," I said half-heartedly, assuming that his words would not hold their water.

"There is one other thin' I should probably mention," Lyle continued. "I had thought it was just odd... though now, I fear it may have a deeper meanin'."

"Pray tell," I said, refilling our herbs.

"This night past... 'twas around the hour of the blue jay and I was dead asleep, some rookies were earnin' their stripes with the older grunts durin' the night watch and I had had a piss poor day and needed to be alone. Suddenly, I was roused from sleep from the ringin' of bells, though it wasn't the bell of the watchtower."

"What kind of bell was it?" I asked, dragging deeply on my spliff.

"When I yanked myself out of bed, I grabbed a torch and came outside, though the path and boats were barren and empty. It had sounded as though there was the ringin' of several copper bells. Like the ones that you'd tie to a billy when tracking 'em."

"Interesting," I said. "Though you saw nothing?"

"Nothin'," Lyle confessed. "I even asked the crew about it this mornin' and of course they were all too pissed last night to remember a thing."

"Damn the rookies," I chuckled, discarding my spliff and drinking some water.

"Although," Lyle interjected, "the crew did mention the gate for the goats had been left open and now the corrals are empty... and nobody is fessin' up to it."

"Perhaps you heard the billies sneaking off," I teased.

"Or perhaps I heard 'em bein' stolen," Lyle said, smacking the bowl of his pipe against his palm to knock out the ashes. "Either way, it's over with now."

"I sincerely doubt that," I said, bunching Truff's reigns in my hands in preparation to take my leave. "If there is any way we can be of assistance please send word. I must rejoin the troops."

"Aye, will do," he said with a salute. "Thank you for the update, Commander. Also, the herbs were quite delightful."

"They were indeed, Captain," I said. Darkening my tone in seriousness, I met Lyle's eyes. "Keep in mind what I've said about showing your loyalty if you wish to lend your support to Knomucca."

"Stay wise, Commander," Lyle said.

"Love and light," I replied, kicking Truff in the sides and pressing forward.

Waving in farewell, I returned to the path, following the gravel and grass as the trail stretched to the left. Glancing over my shoulder, I noticed Lyle jump into a small boat in the river, pulling away from the dock and gliding towards the lighthouse before disappearing behind the hanging branches.

Turning in my saddle, I faced forward, flicking the reigns to continue our trot. Moss-covered boulders marked the border of the trading port, the rocks surrounding a Cenotaph in front of which Kiyoko was kneeling. The statue marked the end of Morriraen's infrastructure, and we would not encounter any others until reaching the village of Kyraulh, four leagues away.

It was normal to see Kiyoko meditating at this statue, his indulgence often delaying him for several moments. The Cenotaph was in dedication to his wife, Paedie; the monument was built here by Knomucca and Kiyoko three years after her death. Knomucca had met Kiyoko on the Snake River, each traveling to Morriraen on the monthly ferry. Kiyoko had wanted to join the army one year after his wife had died as a way to direct his rage, driving his desire to travel to Morriraen. The pair of them had spent many nights on the same craft, Kiyoko often crying and drinking far too much until he vomited.

My heart aches for him, I remember Knomucca saying. Her servants, who had attended her on the trip to and from Bethes, had carried Kiyoko drunk from the ship back to the castle. Could you imagine losing your soul mate?

Nay, I cannot, I said, meeting Knomucca's eyes with a solemn smile. It would be a miserable pain.

Knomucca smiled, brushing away the silent tears that rolled down her cheeks. He needs a family, Everett. He is crushed and broken and does not have a home. He is lost... and incredibly sad.

We will look after him for a while, I promised. The hurt in her eyes had been unbearable, and I desperately desired to embrace her.

Pausing atop Truff, I watched as Kiyoko held a small white candle in his palms, the wick drowning in a pool of hot wax. Upon my approach, Kiyoko blew out the candle, inhaling the fumes as the smoke wafted through the air. Collecting himself, he reached forward a hand, grasping the slender stone fingers of his wife's memory. Pulling away, he fanned three neatly rolled smokes across his palm, smiling as he left the candle at the statue's feet before rising.

"Kiyoko, I am sorry to have disturbed you," I said, relaying my conversation with Lyle moments before and returning his smoking sack.

"Thunder strikes when it is raining," Kiyoko said, taking the pouch and placing his newly acquired smokes into it. "The theatrics have only just begun, I am afraid."

"Aye," I said, releasing an anxious sigh.

"Your encounter implies the rebels are moving from the south," Kiyoko said. "If they arrived at the trading port before the castle Morriraen..."

"Perhaps they are not from the mountains, and we are mistaken..." I mused.

"How do you explain the hooves of the horses, or the crimson banner?"

"Crimson is easy to camouflage amongst the colors of autumn and perhaps the coverings of the hooves are meant to serve as false evidence."

"And the goat?" Kiyoko charged. "Are the mountain goats not a crest of the nobles that dwell amidst the peeks?"

"It is as you mentioned," I began. "The Harvest is upon us and our cattle are immensely valuable... our people would suffer from their loss and the winter months would be far from pleasant."

"It is a plausible theory," Kiyoko said with a shrug.

"One you are not in agreement with," I said, understanding how to read his body after nearly ten years of companionship.

"Someone is clearly attempting to plant a false trail to spread influence," Kiyoko said, approaching his horse and slipping once more into his saddle. "And make no mistake, should their plans wreak havoc there shall be vultures waiting to consume our remains."

"There is not time for such discussions now, we shall continue this at camp," I sighed, flicking Truff's reigns and passing around Kiyoko in a trot.

"Come along then..." Kiyoko said with a soft smile. "We best get a move on. The troop was left to ride ahead, we best not allow too great a distance to lapse between us."

"Aye, perhaps that is wise," I said, commanding Truff with a whistle and bursting into a canter.

A smattering of trees dotted the tall, weedy grass, and branches overhead knocked close to my face as I directed Truff south. The Snake River drifted away through the trees, the sound of the pulsing water reminding me of its presence to the east. The path's terrain roughened as we left the trading port behind us, the height of the unkempt grass gradually climbing to reach the shoulders of our horses as we entered the deciduous forest. Holes, rocks, and roots jutted from the ground as we sped forward, the uneven earth threatening to tear us from the saddle as we kicked our horses to a gallop.

Bursting forward, Truff pounded across the earth. My fingers tightened into the reins, and my legs and muscles clenched forcefully to keep me balanced. Leaning forward, I cracked the reigns, feeling elated as the wind whipped through my dark auburn hair. Spotting Kiyoko in my periphery, I was delighted to see him and Ballara galloping close behind.

We pushed further through the trees, the outer edges of the supply convoy coming into focus as we closed the distance with the troops. Desiring subtlety, I gently pulled back on Truff's reigns, whistling calmly to begin slowing his gait. His strides steadily transitioned to a canter, following then to a perky, bouncing trot. Slowing further, he flattened his pace, trotting leisurely as he recuperated.

"Aye, well done Tree Root Truffles," I said to him, patting his neck.

The supply wagons bumped and rocked across the ground, swaying and squeaking on enormous wooden wheels. Keeping pace with the convoy, I smiled as Kiyoko approached on my right, signaling with a hand before darting around the wagons. Nodding in response, I guided Truff around the convoy on the left, passing the seven wooden carts pulled by massive horses.

Flicking the reigns, I allowed space between myself and the carts, not wanting to risk spooking the horses pulling the supply train.

Weaving through the trees, I took a position at the front of the convoy, pleased to see the ranks had remained in my absence. Kiyoko fell in line at my right, saluting as we joined the troop. The forest felt eerie as the wildlife scattered from our ruckus. Clouds overhead covered the sky in darkness, causing the troops manning the convoy to light torches and lanterns.

Kye broke ranks and laced through the soldiers, veering past on my left and approaching the convoy.

"Oi, cut the number of torches in half," Kye demanded.

My eyes flickered, having been enjoying the glow and assistance the light had provided.

"We can attempt to make more at camp," Kye continued. "We still must ride through this night, and we will most definitely need extra light as the days grow shorter."

A voice responded in the distance, the words and tones muffled by the noise of the carts and horses.

"Until we reach camp tomorrow eve, I fear we must ration our supply," Kye stated.

Another unidentifiable response floated across the breeze.

"Oi, you are going to have to improvise... do the best you can," Kye said, turning away from the carts and moving back towards the ranks.

Raising a hand, I stopped her with a whistle, flagging her towards me with the flick of my finger.

"Aye... obviously you were listening then," Kye said, rolling her eyes.

"I am not in the mood for any more surprises," I said sternly.

"If there are more surprises on their way for you... it is most certainly not up to me," Kye said with a smile. "As for the wagons... well, that is a more complicated matter."

"How do you mean?" I asked, intrigued by her words.

"Several apprentices of the convoy lost their belongings in the wagons that burned, and they're very displeased. I offered them the opportunity for me to assist in replacing what I could, however, they refused."

"Aye..." I sighed.

"Now of course they're bothered by having to be without certain luxuries, though they had refused when I had the time to cater... and now, I am no longer able to do so."

"I understand," I sighed again.

"They are too thick to get it," Kye spat.

"Sergeant, relax," I said. "You know you must practice controlling your temper. As the youngest Sergeant in the history of the Gods' Guard, there are many eyes constantly upon you."

"I'm aware," Kye said, taking a deep breath.

"I am available if you need my assistance in handling anything," I offered compassionately.

"Your support is appreciated," Kye said with a nod. "Though how would it look if I could not handle my own affairs?"

"It would show you understand when it is important to ask for help," I said with a fatherly tone.

"You may have saved me once, Everett," Kye said seriously. "Though I do not wish to make a habit of it."

"I can see the fire within you," I smiled encouragingly. "Nevertheless, I am here all the same."

"Thank you, kindly," Kye said with a nod. "If you don't mind then, I shall be returning to ranks."

"Aye," I said, saluting as Kye bounded forward and took her place in line.

The path south rolled beneath our trotting hooves, the day passing quickly into the twilight. Large oaks gave way to grassy plains that caressed the edges of Snake River as it spilled over jagged boulders. The water sprayed in large gusts, the current swooping towards the arching stone bridge that allowed for passage into Kyraulh.

A shudder ran through me as the wind bit across my face, the cold coaxing me to retrieve a woolen black cloak from my rucksack.

"Oi," Kiyoko whistled, using his signal to get my attention.

Whistling my acknowledgment, I turned Truff to the right and walked towards Kiyoko.

"Given everything that has happened, how would you like to proceed?" Kiyoko asked.

"Perhaps you should ride ahead with the troop and I can investigate Kyraulh on my own," I suggested.

"That would be daft," Kiyoko snorted.

"We need to keep everyone moving," I said, obtaining a spliff from my smoking sack and fighting through the wind to keep it lit. After taking a long drag, I held it out for Kiyoko.

"Aye," Kiyoko said, accepting the smoke as it was offered, "though we are requiring ourselves to ride through the night, and thus we may have a few spare moments to use strategically."

"How do you mean?" I asked, confusion tainting my cloud of smoke.

"Everett, if what Captain Southwell said is true, and Kyraulh has turned its allegiance elsewhere, we may need to have the Guard at our backs."

"Wise, indeed," I admitted.

"As long as we make it to camp by tomorrow eve, our schedule should remain intact."

"I certainly hope so," I declared. "For I desire to assist Knomucca in retrieving her potion elements, though I shall admit I am uncertain as to what she should need..."

"We shall have to be creative," Kiyoko said with a smile, returning the smoke to my hands once more. Whistling sharply, he commanded the troop to halt, the trill echoing forcefully through the frigid wind. "All shall be well, Love. All shall be well."

"If I only had a smoke for every time those words hath been spoken on this day," I said, annoyed, finishing the spliff. "I would have quite the bouquet."

"It saddens me to feel your frustration," soothed Kiyoko, following his previous whistle with another, requesting the troop take cover in the nearby trees. "We shall skip across the stones with one foot at a time."

The troops broke rank to take cover amongst the foliage. Horses pulled the wagons back into the field of oaks, tucking them away from prying eyes. The wind whistled through the trees, and the rustling leaves around us provided the perfect opportunity for me to address the company.

"Earlier, I mentioned there would need to be some adjustments to our itinerary along the way to Riverside. Sergeant Kyreese, General Kiyoko, Chief Warrant Officer Bullet, and I have business that needs to be attended to in Kyraulh Village. You may take this time to rest and water your horses."

"May we be of any assistance?" asked Corporal Sanderson from her horse on the far left.

"The rest of you must remain hidden, lest we need you to come to our aid. The troop falls to Lieutenant Tyfis. To reiterate, you are to take this time to rest and I best not hear of any sparring. Is that understood?"

"Aye," replied the guard.

"Excellent, we best be setting off then," I said urgently. "At ease, soldiers."

Kye broke from the crumbling ranks, weaving her horse between soldiers dismounting from the saddle to stretch. The scents of various herbs filled the air as the troops began to smoke and share herbs. Bullet wandered into the trees on the right, lacing past the muffled chaos before appearing beside Kiyoko.

"Greetings," Bullet signaled a salute.

"Greetings," I replied, noticing Kye saluting from atop her horse to my left.

"Oi, before we set off," Kiyoko began, raising his hands in a gesture of peace. "Will there be any complications between the two of you?"

"I will be fine as long as he does not mention the Gods damn cannon," Kye said with an angry look towards Bullet.

"I wasn't intending to," Bullet smirked. "I think you made yourself clear as quartz last time."

"Perfection," Kye said, choking up on the reigns of her horse. "I am glad we have an understanding."

"As am I," I said, nodding to Kiyoko as he lowered his hands. "Come then, we best be setting off."

Turning rightwards, I guided Truff south along the path once more, following Snake River towards Kyraulh's connective bridge. Carved square abutments bordered the arching stone, the spotted surface sparkling above the rushing river water. Small twinkling lights hung across the wrought iron lattice work above us, bringing warmth through the now stormy sky while the torrent below sprayed freezing water.

The hooves of our horses clopped across the bridge, our loose formation tightening to two abreast as we marched across. Kye joined me at the rear as we swiftly trotted forward, the sounds of our horses muffled by the wind and rushing river. Rain began to fall as we moved beneath the overhang, the lights above extinguishing with a sizzle as the raindrops landed upon the tiny, ornate flames.

Oi, wonderful, I thought bitterly, fearing for Knomucca and her ventures at sea. I sincerely hope the Gods hath not abandoned us.

Shaking my head to clear it, I followed Bullet as he and Kiyoko descended from the bridge and took the road towards Kyraulh. The path transitioned to small pebbles and dirt, the border lined with fluffy bushes and stout stone pillars. Glass lanterns alight with flames rested upon the columns, illuminating the trail towards the village. Wrought iron chains connected between the pillars along the path, the metallic links clinking softly as the rain kissed the circular, clasping rings.

Crunching along the path, we followed the lights along the winding path towards Kyraulh. Warn down paths were smattered amongst stucco houses, along with wooden barns, brick smithies, tall cylindrical silos, and tin-roofed taverns. Neatly planted farms bordered the outer rim of the village, the fields barren and brown as the planting season had drawn to an end several weeks prior.

The village square was bustling for a stormy, late-summer evening, with lively folk celebrating the upcoming Autumnal Equinox. Carved turnips and pumpkins rested atop shelves beneath the carts of street vendors, flickering bright with candles that had been dropped inside them. These lanterns were placed for protection against the demons and vengeful spirits that were said to walk amongst the living at harvest's end.

On warmer and dryer days, performers would flood the town square, collecting coins in hats as they banged on drums and danced. Children would run and frolic through the streets and alleyways, paying no heed to travelers entering the settlement. As I looked down the paths, the streets were quiet, the rain forcing heads low and eyes downcast as the townspeople drew their hoods tight from the rain. Nary a rebellious flag or banner was hung from any establishment, nor did I observe any obvious signs of treachery.

"Oi!" Kiyoko turned gracefully in his saddle, summoning my attention with a whistling over the wind and rain. "I reckon we pay Floyd a visit."

"I would enjoy the warmth of a whiskey," I admitted, nodding my approval as we veered west from the town square.

A small stone inn with large windows and a thatched roof appeared up the road on the left. A driftwood sign above the door reading "Ironsides Inn", was illuminated by two glass lanterns. A small wooden fence jutted from the righthand side of the building, providing the perfect place to dismount and tie our horses.

We situated our horses and drew our hoods as we moved towards the inn's entrance. The gravel crunched beneath my boots, and the path was slick as we walked to the iron door. The high-pitched pings and clicks of circling bats cut creepily through the growing wind, the storm's increasing strength driving us to hustle quickly inside.

Ironsides Inn was surprisingly calm for a night so close to the Festess. The scattered dining space was filled with villagers sitting at blocky rectangular tables, drinking hot soup to warm themselves after a hard day's work. A massive target for throwing darts and knives was hung on the eastern wall, surrounded by thick leather padding and burning torches. An immense stone fireplace took up the northwest corner, the flames dancing above the bar as potatoes warmed on a spit. The skull of a wolf rested upon the twisted iron mantle, its sharp teeth casting shadows that stretched across the walls.

Moving towards the bar, we found stools. We slid onto them, easing into the cozy conversation of the townsfolk around us. Kye took the stool at my left, Kiyoko to my right, and Bullet furthest to the right. The serving wench approached in a low-cut corset, pressing her voluptuous breasts against the bar as she bent to retrieve glasses.

"Fair evening, Shara," Kiyoko smiled.

"Merry meet," Shara beamed, placing heavy ceramic mugs on the counter with a thud. "Blessed Festess."

"Blessed Festess," we replied, returning the common greeting heard around the sabbat.

Lowering my hood, I shifted upon the stool, resting my elbows on the counter. "Say, Shara, could we trouble you for some whiskey?"

"Aye... s'pose I can fetch that for yah," Shara smiled, ducking beneath the bar to retrieve a decanter of dark brown whiskey. Exchanging our mugs, Shara replaced them with stout, flat-bottomed glasses, pouring in the smooth, sunning spirit.

"Yah're gonna love this," Shara leaned across the bar and slowly filled our glasses. "Oi, lemmie hear if yah can guess the secret ingredient."

"Excellent," I said, lifting the cup in a prayer of gratitude. "To the Harvest, the Gods, and Knomucca."

"Here, here," my company responded, taking long, deep pulls of the whiskey.

The brew was sweet, yet hot like fire, the intense heat surprisingly soothing against my injuries. Hints of vanilla peaked across my tongue in glorious saccharinity, making me intensely wish I could share a glass with Her Worship.

"Gods, Shara, this is divine," Kiyoko praised, quickly draining his glass. "Is that vanilla I taste across my lips?"

"'Tis indeed," Shara smiled.

"Aye, 'tis just what the soul needs on a night so cold and dreary," Bullet added with a nod.

"Oh... 'tis quite nice," Kye said with burning red cheeks. "It's got... quite the heat..."

I let out a hardy chuckle as I watched Kye struggle to remain composed. Her eyes began to water, and she coaxed the sleeves of her cloak upwards to pat them dry.

"I'm glad yah like it," Shara said excitedly. "Floyd brewed this batch to enter in the Equinox competition that takes place at week's end."

"Best of luck to him," Kiyoko said with a smile. "I pray this brew should gift him first prize."

"He's a shoo-in I reckon," agreed Shara as she rotated the potatoes cooking on the fire.

"Speaking of Floyd," I interjected, setting my glass solidly on the counter. "Do you happen to know where we might be able to locate him?"

"He's out back handlin' a shipment," Shara said, returning to the counter and beginning to polish a set of mugs. "He'll be takin' a smoke after that... I could let 'im know yah were here if you'd like."

"Aye, that would be appreciated," I said, finishing my glass of whiskey and sliding the cup forward. "If you would mind replenishing our glasses and providing some harvest bread, we would be happy to indulge and wait for him."

"'T'would be my pleasure," Shara winked, leaning low as she filled our glasses once more.

Returning the whiskey below the counter, Shara quickly finished her work, polishing cups and cutlery with a rag before replacing them on the shelves behind the bar. Opening a bulky wooden box against the far wall, Shara retrieved a loaf of decoratively knotted bread, bringing it to the counter to cut with a large knife. The top was coated with nuts and a tempting orange glaze, the sides drizzled with chocolate stripes that demanded to be paired with the vanilla in the whiskey.

"Enjoy," Shara said, quartering the loaf and dividing the pieces onto thin wooden platters.

"Did Floyd bake this as well?" Bullet asked as he eagerly accepted his plate.

"Aye... that he did... the man really should slow down," Shara said with a chuckle. "Though, yah know it wouldn't be Floyd if he didn't make harvest bread."

"Are there any lemon logs stashed anywhere?" I asked hopefully as I bit into the exquisite pastry.

"Oi, Everett Rosewood!" Shara gawked at me with a horrified expression. "We serve lemon logs for Lughnasa and the Summer Solstice... You know Floyd won't serve them once the leaves start changin'-"

"Nay, we ought to have some on hand," Kiyoko interjected as my heart began to flutter. "I stashed several in the back rooms for him after the Lughnasa Festess..."

"That is awfully thoughtful of you," I said, reaching my hand across his shoulders and caressing his back in appreciation. "Thank you kindly, Kiyoko."

"I know how much you enjoy them," he said, briefly acknowledging my affection though gracefully leaning into my touch. "I hid them fairly well and just secured their presence When I was here last... and I helped Floyd set for the Festess not but four morrows prior-"

"Tuckin' them under the rice sacks was not one of your most secure hidin' places," Shara rolled her eyes.

"Floyd found them then I reckon," Kiyoko said as he shook his head.

"Not 'im," Shara laughed.

"Don't tell me the new bastard Floyd hired found them then-"

"Aye... I came in durin' the mornin' hours to help, and he was eatin' them with a cup of heated cocoa," Shara said. "Found them while he was getting' orientated I reckon."

"Who is searching in the hidden depths of the rice bin when they have first been hired?" Kiyoko projected across my thoughts. "Someone who is awfully curious..."

"Sounds sensible enough to me to enjoy them with a mug of heated cocoa," I said to Shara, fighting to maintain a smile. However, I was saddened by the lack of my favorite pastry. "I hope he found them to his liking."

"He seemed to," Shara said, rotating the potatoes again.

Down the bar, Bullet smiled as he dipped his bread into the whiskey. Widening my eyes in delight, I marveled at such genius.

"Oi, I think that'll do'er then," Shara said, rinsing the knife she had used to slice the bread and returning it to the slitted wooden block on the far wall. She turned over her left and snatched her bright red cloak off a hook near a slim side door. "Will yah be needin' anythin' else before I retrieve Floyd?"

"Nay, thank you kindly," I said, following Bullet's example and dipping my bread into the whiskey.

"I'll return in two shakes of a dragon's tail," Shara said, donning her cloak and vanishing through the side door.

We enjoyed our bread and whiskey whilst waiting for Shara and Floyd to return. Several long moments passed before they stumbled through the small wooden door carrying large canvas sacks.

"Gods, Floyd... give me those," Kiyoko rose from his seat and snatched the bags from Floyd before he could object.

"'Tis not your night to work," Floyd said as he shook his head in protest.

"You need to be slowing down," Kiyoko said with a stern sincerity I often heard him use with me. My heart fluttered with his intonation, the concern in his voice warming me alongside the festess whiskey. "No sense in having you carry such a weight when it compares to that of a newly birthed calf-"

"Oi, lad, shut it... I'm fine, really," Floyd said, his age betrayed by the exhaustion in his voice. "Is that why yar here? Ya think ya need to abandon yar previous obligations and assist a dying old man?"

"Well, at least yah're admittin' it now," Shara winked as she returned her cloak to its hook.

"Oi, ya looked better with that thing on," Floyd sassed, pretending not to notice as we laughed. Shara blushed, her embarrassment turning to a giggle as Floyd released a billowing laugh. "Blast... don't mess with me girl."

Smiling broadly, I took a large swig of my whiskey, finishing the remainder of the spirit and pushing my glass forward.

"Oi, Floyd," I interjected bravely. "Could I trouble you for one final glass of your Festess whiskey?"

"Oi, Everett, I didn't see ya there," Floyd said as he yanked a large knife from a block on the wall and slid it through the canvas rucksack. Bags of potatoes and fish toppled out onto the counter. "Ya better not be here to drink me under the table."

"This is your strongest batch of whiskey yet," I confessed.

"That'll be a pleasure," Floyd said, abandoning his work and fetching the Festess whiskey from beneath the bar. "What're you doin' here anyway? As far as I had known, I wasn't seein' ya this Festess."

"We weren't expected to be here," Kiyoko said with a heavy sigh.

"Ya made me hire a useless barkeep who didn't come to work today," Floyd continued. "And when he does show up, he doesn' do nothin'! Just stands around starin' off into the ether."

"Sorry that he is not worth the coin," Kiyoko said. "I would give much to be gifted the chance to linger here for the Festess and aid in serving such splendor... though we should be halfway to Riverside by now, yet our travel hath been slow and troublesome."

"Aye... may the Gods have mercy on the remainder of yar travels," Floyd said. "Well, what are ya doin' lollygagging here then?"

"We actually need to speak to you about a private matter," I said.

Floyd nodded and shouted as he pounded on the counter. "Oi, everybody out! I'm closin' up early."

Turning in my stool, I watched the villagers quickly finish their food and drink, tossing their coin in the center of the tables. Rising from their seats, they threw their cloaks over their shoulders before departing into the rain.

"That was unnecessary," I said seriously, the clamor clearing my mind of the drink.

"Oi, I was lookin' for an excuse," Floyd said, pouring himself a glass from a new bottle of whiskey. "I'm tired and need to sort the perishables anyhow."

"Floyd... you purchased fish?" Kiyoko asked in surprise from my left. The rest of the rucksacks had been opened, and the piles of goods on the counter had been sorted, Kiyoko and Shara working to put them away swiftly.

"Aye... I did indeed," Floyd said after his long sip of whiskey.

"We are serving them for the Festess," Shara said with a smile. "A whole fish upon the new year brings prosperity and abundance-"

"We're aware," Floyd said with a chuckle.

"We never have fish," Kiyoko said, adding salt and basil to the fillets before wrapping them in sturdy cloth. "You always call the fishmongers 'a roost of coin swipin' cocks.'"

"Aye, and the amount of coin they took doubled due to the Equinox festival," Floyd grumbled, producing the stool he kept on his side of the bar and sliding onto it.

"Aye... they gouged yah," Shara said as she disappeared through the side door with a basketful of grain.

"Gods, Floyd," Kiyoko sighed, placing the wrapped fish in a pile at the end of the counter for Shara to handle. "May I ask how you suddenly have the coin for fish, yet these two summers past I worked entirely without pay?"

"Oi... harsh Kiyoko," Kye said, pushing her empty bowl of stew towards the end of the bar.

"Nay, I understand his curiosity, and I am happy to explain. In all honesty, it is incredible news."

"Aye? You possess good tidings?" Kiyoko asked seriously.

"I am about to come into a large sum of coin," said Floyd upon finishing his whiskey.

"Happy day," I said, raising my empty glass in celebration.

"How do you mean?" Kiyoko asked. "Your Festess whiskey is fair, though you have never taken first prize in the past."

"I am certain this season shall be different," Floyd said.

"So, nothing is certain," Kiyoko snapped.

"You merely discussed my Festess whiskey, and I simply wished to disclose my opinion," Floyd said.

"Then where is the coin coming from?" asked Kiyoko with a softer tone.

Floyd waited to reply, producing a smooth wooden pipe from his cloak and sliding it across the bar towards me. He watched as I packed his pipe with sweet grass and returned it to him with a match.

"I'm sellin' The Ironsides Inn."

A silence fell among us, interrupted by Shara's footfalls as she shuttled supplies to the back room.

"When?" I asked, taking a spliff and match from my smoking sack.

"After the Equinox festival," said Floyd.

"May I ask how this came to be?" Kiyoko asked, turning to face Floyd.

"Kyraulh was very popular this summer past," Floyd began through a cloud of smoke. "Some nobles from Poets Cove were spendin' some leisurely time here and the place became fairly busy. It turned out my establishment and hospitality impressed them and they offered to purchase it for a hefty lot."

"Who exactly offered to purchase it?" Kiyoko asked, leaning on the bar as he spoke.

"This fellow Samarin," Floyd said. "Charmin' bloke, he'll be payin' me quite handsomely."

"Floyd, do you know if he's offered to purchase anywhere else in town?" I asked, lighting my spliff.

"I couldn't say for certain," Floyd said. "Though I might have heard some rumors about a few other places being sold."

"Oi, we'll have to keep our eyes open," Bullet said.

"Floyd, there's something else," I said, taking a crisp inhale of my spliff. "Have you been hearing any rumors about Knomucca?"

"I was afraid ya were gonna ask me that," Floyd said, loosing a long sigh.

Another silence passed with raindrops on the roof and Kiyoko tending the dishes, replacing the clean cutlery and glasses on the shelf before grabbing a bulky broom.

"There have been whispers about her this summer past," Floyd said seriously. "Combine this with her recent absence and it doth not paint a flattering portrait."

"What are people saying about her?" I asked.

"They're sayin' she's a whore," Shara stated, resting her palms on the bar as she spoke.

"Oi, Shara," Floyd scolded, tossing a nearby rag towards her face.

"It's what they're sayin'!" Shara said. "They think Knomucca is a demon and a whore."

"Why is she being accused of being a whore?" Kye spoke up then, her face angry. "I suppose she has had a few indulgences, though nothing that would classify her as a whore."

"They are sayin' she can manipulate intimate energy," Floyd said delicately.

"How do you mean?" Kyreese asked.

"The rumor is there are castle and townsfolk Knomucca seduces, then uses their energy somehow to heal wounds or grant herself sobriety," Floyd explained.

"Who is claiming to have been seduced?" I asked curiously, as my spirits saddened.

"I don't recall any names, I can barely remember yours as is..." Floyd waved away my words with a hand. "Though with her hands the way they are and those rumors that circled a few years back about the servants that went missin'... people are startin' to have questions."

"Questions asking if she is some sort of monster!" Kye said, wrenching my spliff from my hand and inhaling deeply.

"It shan't be an easy task in clearing her name," I admitted. "Even I will confess her hands are intimidating, and I do not fully understand them."

"She does not talk with us about what she endures in the Underworld," Kiyoko said as he returned the broom. "She is forbidden to discuss anything, and believe me, I have attempted to push her boundaries before... when I was in a darker place."

"Aye, before ya started workin' here," Floyd sassed again.

"You know I appreciate you giving me a job," Kiyoko said with a wink. "Even if it was because Knomucca asked you to."

""Twas my pleasure to gift you a job... and I'd do the same again."

Kiyoko smiled, his face glowing softly from the flames within the fireplace.

"Dear friend of her mother's I was. I'd give much to spend one more afternoon bakin' with Cornalla whilst she shared with me her secrets of sweetened apples or pressed fresh blackberries..." Floyd said, rising to his feet. "Y'all want my advice? Ride on, get where yar s'pose to be, and consolidate the support Knomucca already has. For the time bein' there's naught ya'll can do here, the wheels have already been set in motion."

"I suppose that is wise," I said. "Perhaps we could leave a small guard here, though our resources should not be divided whilst we have so much of the journey left ahead of us."

"Exactly," said Floyd. "Yar better off ridin' on."

Suddenly, the door slammed open, blasting a gust of cold from the freezing wind outside.

"Greetings, Floyd, my pardons in being tardy. The wind is really quite fierce."

"Oi, Bashrol, I didn't think ya were gonna make it in," Floyd said. "Folks, this is the useless barkeep I mentioned, Bashrol."

"Charmed," I said, spinning in my stool to observe him.

"Bit harsh, don't ya reckon," Bashrol said with a light-hearted laugh. "Are these the lads you're always on about?"

Bashrol stepped further into the tavern, his long grey cloak draping around him as he moved. His hood looped over a leather black tricorne and hung across his face to protect him from the wind and rain. A silver broach held his cloak in place; the upright, rounded petals of an oleander glimmered with a slight tint of shining scarlet.

"Aye, the same," Floyd said. "The works been done for the evenin', so guess ya best be clearin' off."

"I wager I shall need a room," Bashrol said, his cloak and boots sopping from the rain. "Home is quite far, and I dare not make the venture with the elements so vicious."

"My rooms are all occupied in anticipation of the festival," Floyd said. "Though there might be somethin' at the inn to the north opposite the bakery."

"I'll keep that in mind," Bashrol said, nodding respectfully as he turned towards the door. "Blessed Festess."

"Blessed Festess," we responded politely.

"Until we meet again," Bashrol waved, pulling the door open and vanishing like the Festess whiskey.

"Useless bloke," Floyd spat. "Didn't even think to offer himself for workin' or tryin' to find somethin' to accomplish... just blindly accepts there was no work for him and leaves."

"It's not as if he can read your mind," Kiyoko said, absently fidgeting with the sleeves of his kimono.

"I suppose we better be setting off," I said, finishing my smoke and smearing the ashes in an empty tin.

"Aye, yar girl needs ya," Floyd said.

"This was very rejuvenating," Kye said, standing from her stool and tucking her immense braid into her hat.

"'Twas indeed," Floyd said, taking another pull of his Festess whiskey and coughing sharply. "My pardons for not bein' able to assist in clearin' Knomucca's name, though what is best now is to focus on gettin' to her Ascension."

"Agreed," I said, rising from my seat and checking that all my bags, flasks, and weapons were hanging in their proper places. "It was nice to see you, Floyd."

"Oi, lads, the feelin's mutual," Floyd said, taking our hands and shaking them firmly.

"Stay wise," said Kiyoko, his tight handshake lingering for a longer moment.

"Love and light," Floyd said with a smile, the emotion on his face causing my eyes to well with tears.

Moving towards the door, we emerged into the rain, the thick cold drops washing away the streaks of sadness on my cheeks. I longed for another Festess together as a family, desperately craving the normalcy of a holiday free of worries from The Creator. How I wished we could throw knives, play cards, sing songs, and drink, smoking spliffs until sunrise without fear of losing friends in the battles that were yet to come.

Happy Festess, I thought, my mood glooming as the fires above the door finally extinguished in the rain, *Happy Festess, indeed.*

VII

KNOMUCCA

The castle Morriraen fell away as Thornin took to the sky, the freezing wind snapping through my hair and cloak as we flew to the east. The landscape rolled and blurred into green-brown smears; the trees, fields, and paradises I had called home were consumed at my back in the fading woodlands. Wind echoed through my ears as we propelled forward, my view of the ground diminishing through a veil of heavy clouds. The damp and cold air was thick with the promise of storms, their arrival estimated during the coming evening.

Gentle Flophenne, please... if you can hear me... I know The Creator has asked that you keep your distance with The Ascension so near... Though I beseech thee... prevent it from raining...

As if to taunt me, my prayers were answered with slamming cold wind, the frigid surge coaxing me to tighten the hood of my cloak. Sighing and swearing, I wrapped the black woolen fabric around my shoulders, tying the front closed with a heavy black string.

"Seven Hells..." I choked into the wind, wishing I had the warmth of a whiskey. Though I had tended to my wounds after the battle, a pain still raged through my torso. The bone-chilling cold, along with the grueling pain, began to weigh down my spirits dangerously.

Leaning forward in the saddle, I reached my hands outward, grasping tightly to a set of spikes protruding from Thornin's neck. Whistling sharply, I requested Thornin to fly lower, desiring clarity while guiding us toward the Luna Sea. Down below, the silver of the Snake River cut through the trees, the winding, curling track of the river resembling the path of a serpent for which it was named. Large, dense forests bordered the river, the branches of the trees flattening to grasslands as we soared overhead.

Hamlets and villages were speckled across the countryside, interspersed with swamps, mountains, and lakes. An expansive desert stretched and rolled away in the distance, the hot white sand bordering the edge of a vast forest to the north. Syler's journey to the Northern Ascension Temple in the desert oasis would force her to cross through the biome in The Far North. She would pass the mountains of dragon colonies that thrived in the desert heat, their dens high in the Northern Mountains that splattered through the desert landscape.

Suddenly fearing for Syler's travels, I decided to meditate, centering my energy as I pushed positive blessings toward her journey. Focusing on my breathing, I concentrated on manifesting my intentions, praying and wishing Syler would not have such obstacles to overcome. My spirits began to lighten as I started reenergizing, the physical and emotional exhaustion from the day flowing from my body as I released my stress into the wind. The pain in my chest and the cold within my body fought against my desire to remain relaxed. The practice overall improved my mood, though failing to remove these physical ailments.

Exhaling a final, cleansing breath, I returned to my body and awareness. Off in the distance, the sea began to take shape, filling in blue amidst the green of the forest and mountains. The water stretched in an endless expanse towards the horizon, the heavy grey sky reflecting off the raging waves that smashed against the white pebbled beaches. Freezing wind howled across the open water, spraying mist, rocks, and debris onto the shore.

Gods... how I wish it would not storm, I observed, noticing the late mid-day sun was nowhere to be found amidst the swollen black clouds.

The winds and waves would prove to be problematic. Whether on dragon-back or row boat, fishing in the reefs for an Angelfish would not be possible in such severe weather. I groaned at the thought of diving into the surf to retrieve what I needed. Though the water would still likely be warm from the summer sun, flying through the frigid winds of the growing storm could invite illness. Knowing this could be disastrous to my plans, I began to weigh other options.

'I fear as though I should need a vessel and crew,' I thought, remembering from my studies of Ozwal the Great that there were strategies in place to assist in sailing through storms. I had not wanted to recruit a crew or employ any vessel to obtain my Angelfish.

I don't see what other choice I have... Thornin doesn't fare well in storms, and assistance in finding the reefs would greatly expedite the matter... I reckon it is settled then...

Stroking Thornin's wings, I guided him to the right, changing our course to fly southeast. The coastline curved into cracked and crumbling stone; intense vines and greenery clung to the rocks and blossomed in fragrant purple flowers. Big plateaus of stone jutted out from the shore's cliffs, erosion claiming chunks of the rock in jagged, spidering holes. The briny smell of the seashore was potent even through the heavy winds.

Up on the right, a system of shallow, moss-covered caves materialized through a wall of thick foliage. Sharp calcite stalactites jutted through the fluffy green plants, the entrance to the den obscured though easy to find from memory. Bushes with prickling pares tangled in moss and vines, the flowers of the ripening fruit swarmed by bees as they finished collecting the remaining year's pollen.

Flying closer, we approached the edge of the caverns, my cloak snapping fiercely around me as I commanded Thornin to halt. Confidently whistling, I was pleased when Thornin ceased flapping his wings, hovering at the cliff's edge before gently alighting on a platform of rocks.

"Aye... that's a good lad," I said, whistling in praise.

Hopping from the saddle, I arched my body in a satisfying stretch, cracking my shoulders and knuckles before shaking loose my muscles. The pain in my chest and ribs persisted, bringing with it a slow-burning heat that thrummed through me.

That must be the Dragon Armor potion, I thought, remembering the discomfort from this night last and suddenly craving the taste of peppermint. *I am glad to see it is doing something... even if only to cause me pain.*

Sighing deeply, I turned my attention to Thornin, noticing him regarding me curiously.

"It appears it is like to storm," I told him, never entirely certain how much of my spoken word he understood. "I know you fear the thunder, and I do not wish to cause you stress. I shall have to pursue my Angelfish another way... take this time as your own, though you should seek these caves as shelter from the storms."

Thornin blinked, nipping playfully at my fingers. Temporarily, he soothed the persistent discomfort that accompanied my decaying soul through the gauntlets; my smile was full of genuine relief as I relished in the reprieve.

"Everything shall be well," I continued, accepting his playfulness as understanding. "We must meet the troops either before or at camp on the morrow... the sooner we make it back to them, the better off we shall be... though we still possess plenty of time, even with the prospect of storms."

Thornin nuzzled his nose into my palm, sighing a breath of smoke, which warmed me pleasantly.

"Though... I shall admit embarking out to sea with storms on the horizon is incredibly daft, not to mention the worst of omens... Should something happen, and I do not return by midnight of the second night, you are to find Everett at camp. He shall know what to do from there. Understood?"

Thornin sighed again, his tail flicking restlessly.

"Oi, I suppose that is all then," I said, placing my fingers in my mouth and whistling a series of commands. "Go, hunt and return here before the storm worsens. On the second midnight, find Everett."

Thornin exhaled abruptly, powerfully flapping his wings before lifting into the air. Turning leftwards, he began to fly north, undoubtedly seeking the warmth of the desert to hunt and refresh his spirits. With a heavy sigh, I watched him leave, praying I would find him here in a day's time and that he would not need to search for Everett alone.

"Love and light," I said as Thornin disappeared into the clouds. After adjusting my gauntlets, I pivoted on the stone, beginning my ascent up the cliffside.

Roots and rocks jutted upwards from along the mouth of the caves, the dwelling located partway beneath the cliff's edge yet several meters above the rock shelf. Grasping onto roots enlaced with thorns, I was thankful for my dragonscale gloves, my grip tightening as I climbed. Shoving my feet onto the rocks, I pulled my body upwards with my arms, feeling my muscles tighten as I clung to the sheer edges. Stretching my arms, I reached as high as possible, barely grasping the fingerholds above my head.

Scraping my boots against the rocks, I jumped, my hands caressing the side of the cliff as I searched for a place to hold. The top of the cliff came into focus, my gaze quickly faltering as the wind sprayed my eyes with a smattering of dirt. Swearing softly, I wiped my face, using my annoyance to summon my final burst of energy. Lurching onto the tips of my toes, I jumped again, flinging my arms upward to grab glossy ivy vines clinging to shrubs at the top of the cliff. Heaving and grunting, I pulled myself upwards, catching my breath before beginning to crawl through the greenery.

Taking a moment to rest and check that my gauntlets remained secure, I sat on the edge and dangled my legs over the side of the cliff. The view was breathtaking and expansive, the grey-layered sky quite picturesque, blending into the immense waves on the horizon. The tide slammed against the boulder-bordered coast, water spraying in all directions. A set of brave ducks wandered across the shore far below, emerging into the waves as they readied to dive and hunt.

Exhaling a cleansing breath, I marveled at the scenery, indulging in a relaxing drink from my water skin before rising to my feet. I wove through the remaining plants and vines, stepping through clumps of the moss and ivy growing from the cliff's edge. Moving across fallen trees, I emerged onto a slim and graveled path, appreciating the stable footing and familiar lands. The trail marked the beginnings of the Luna Sea roadways and infrastructure, the first of the permanent settlements along the coast located nearly two leagues away.

Tightening my hood, I prepared to walk towards Belleview, the first of the cities on the southeastern coast. The wind at my back hustled me forward, the small pebbles, sticks, and branches in the path crunching beneath my boots as I began to pick up my pace. A cluster of trees appeared on my left, providing cover from the coastal winds.

Hiking southeast, the path gradually widened and smoothed into clay as the coastline became more inhabited. Small stucco houses, sparse farms, and thatched stables punctuated the horizon, delightful views of the water and sky visible through their thin glass windows.

The two leagues passed quickly, disappearing into the wind. The temperature dropped once more as the trees around me began to thin, and a cold breeze howled and slammed into me from the left with the exposure of the coastline. The clay of the path transitioned to a cobblestone road, widening to accommodate merchants and their wagons into the city. A massive, wooden portcullis loomed in the distance; the gate was proudly lifted to allow visitors for the upcoming Equinox celebrations.

Marching forward, I tightened my hood once more against the growingly aggressive wind. A steady stream of travelers began filtering towards the portcullis, their path intersecting my own. My identity went unnoticed in the chaos and noise, my pace slowing as I slipped into the crowd. Under the disguise of my cloak, I was simply another ordinary tourist eagerly anticipating Festess bread, drink, and song.

Screaming and playing children ran frivolously through the rising crowd, their eyes alight with freedom and mischief as they readied for the coming holiday. Hustling towards the gate, I joined the throng of merchants approaching from the south, admiring the carts overflowing with harvests' abundance. Bands of travelers on foot or horseback funneled through the portcullis, their conversations, and laughter thrumming excitedly.

Crossing through the portcullis, I entered the seaside city of Belleview, moving beneath the raised wooden gate. The cobblestone path flattened into smoothed stone bricks cemented together with clay and alternating basalt squares, forming the city's main road. Carved pumpkin lanterns hung high on large brick pillars, their light casting circles on the ground below.

Sweet, dewy petrichor floated across the breeze, and the rain's aroma was pleasant despite the hindrance it would cause.

The city bustled with voices and movement, the prospect of storms failing to quash the Autumnal Equinox celebrations. Musicians flooded the corners of the streets, strumming iron strings, playing reed flutes, beating drums, and singing. Performers in leaf-woven dresses danced through decorative bonfires, twirling their hands high above their heads as they juggled bright orange flames. Merchants and vendors encircled the onlookers, enticing the drunk with roasted turkey, squash soup, sunflower pastry, and large mugs of Festess whiskey.

Up on the left, the path split to the east, curving away from the center of town and leading towards the docks. Regretfully, I left the carousing of the townsfolk, following the road behind the cobblers, thatchers, and smithies. I passed bakeries warmed with the scent of fresh bread, their doors open to encourage patronage during the cold evening hours. A scent reminiscent of my mother's harvest cinnamon cake tugged at me, nearly pulling me from my journey. Garlands hung in the windows of apothecaries and sanctuaries, and wreaths braided from basil, rosemary, and lilies were placed for protection against the dead and evil spirits.

As I ventured away from the main city square, the streets fell quiet, the bricks of the lesser-traveled path uneven and jutting out at odd angles. Small sand dunes poked through the distant pebbled beaches; tufts of grass and pink-flowered shrubs atop them had been strung with orange glass candles. The trail to the beach was alight with lanterns carved from turnips, dangling amidst torches twisted from straw and wax. Drunken couples kissed in the glow of the torchlight, oblivious to the travelers and exhausted fishermen who walked the path beside them. The intensity of their passions warmed my body immensely, persuading a smile from beneath my hood as I tried not to think of Everett.

Further, down the shoreline, a set of six spruce docks illuminated by torches appeared through a haze of wind and rain. Taking a narrow gravel path, I began descending a short and steep hill, moving rightwards to follow the curve of the coast. Merchants and fishermen shuttled past along the left, pulling heavy iron carts loaded with fresh fish, shells, coral, and struggling crustaceans. Sailors and skippers followed closely behind the carts, celebrating that their work was done and sharing flasks of whiskey.

Continuing towards the docks, I emerged onto a large, smooth platform of rocks. The piers jutted forward from the immense piece of stone, the platform created to keep the waves from destroying the coastline. A small guard shack stood tall alongside the right of the docks; the absence of smoke tufting from the chimney indicated that the shack was currently empty. Carved turnips rested alongside the doorway, their insides alight with candles to repel demons and negative energy. The practice of carving turnips, instead of pumpkins, along the shore was born from the belief that they would keep the spirits of lost sailors at bay.

Turning from the guard shack, I scoured through the docks, starting furthest from the guardhouse and walking to the left. Illuminated wooden signs above the piers detailed city maps, general trading lines, and convenient river routes, their bold black markings pointing in all directions. The Luna Sea was only a portion of the realm's abundance of water, connected to the Baulhtunac Ocean by three narrow straits thousands of leagues to the east. Even the mouth of the Snake River fed into the Luna Sea, the river originating from the hot springs and melting snow high in the Southern Mountains.

The wind smashed the waves against the docks, pounding the anchored boats angrily into the side of the piers. The platform remained solid beneath my boots, though the surface had become slick as the waves sprayed across the stone. Searching through the docks, I contemplated the vessel I needed, discounting barges, catamarans, and rowboats on the left. Sighing, I turned my attention rightwards, observing a plain oaken sloop docking two piers over.

Wandering through the torchlight, I lingered on the pier's edge, watching a familiar fisher climb from the small and shallow craft.

Oi, that's Captain Southwell, I mused, confused to find him abandoning the Snake River Trading Port.

Lyle pulled a heavy hemp rope from the boat, dropping an immense iron anchor into the water with a splash. Freeing another coil, he tied his sloop to the dock, grabbing one of the carved turnips hanging on the pier to place on the stern for protection. Shifting to a stand, Lyle began walking toward the shore, his footsteps muffled by the roaring of the wind. A sudden, solid wave smacked into the edge of the docks, spraying cold water across the stone. Lyle turned sharply to avoid being splashed, nearly slipping and smashing into the ground where I stood.

"Oi, easy there," I said, snatching his elbow as it neared my face.

"Aye, pardon me," Lyle said, swerving slightly as he regained his balance. The heavy pin that fastened his cloak clanked loudly, the silver glowing orange in the overhead firelight. "I owe you my apologies; I hadn't seen you there."

"For this you owe nothing," I replied, maintaining my grip on his elbow while lowering my hood. "Though for your absence from the trading port... for that you owe an explanation."

"Syler- how surprisin'," Lyle said with a smile.

"Captain... you have me mistaken," I said, releasing Lyle's elbow and turning over my shoulder. Lifting my left sleeve, I revealed the moon's phases inked across my forearm, the linework glossy and shiny in the torchlight.

"Oi, Knomucca... How daft could I be? Of course, it's you... the Merchants Banquet is this night and I recall Syler was to play hostess..."

"Aye... that would be correct," I said with a nod.

Lyle paused and searched my face, blushing as he fumbled to speak. "It's quite dark and I was... well I..."

"You were hoping it was her... perhaps I am right to assume you have met her here before?" I mused boldly.

"Aye, you'd be right in assumin'," Lyle said. "It's that obvious, then?"

Raising my hands in a gesture of peace, I spoke through a hardy laugh. "Only to me. Though, please feel inclined to spare me the details. I shan't wish to know the source for why you have mistaken us."

"Very well... I appreciate you respectin' my privacy," Lyle laughed, stepping around to face me while standing clear of the spraying waves.

"Of course," I said with a smirk, following out of range of the misting water.

"I do feel right awful in havin' mistaken you for your sister," Lyle said with a chuckle.

"Wash it down the river," I said, playfully clapping him on the shoulder. "Although... I need to venture out to the reefs in order to obtain an Angelfish... perhaps you could accompany me..."

"Oi, ain't it like to storm?" Lyle asked, arching his back as he scanned the sky.

"Aye... wager it will," I said, producing a black woolen cap from my pouch and securing it atop my head. Though the wind was harsh and frigid, drawing my hood felt disrespectful somehow.

"Could we partake in the Festess whilst we wait for the storm to pass?" Lyle asked.

"Afraid not," I said, lowering my head guiltily. "The matter is incredibly time-sensitive. I would have flown to the reefs atop Thornin, though he has a horrible fear of thunder."

"Oi, beast like that's afraid of thunder?" Lyle teased.

"We all have our burdens," I said seriously.

"I s'pose that's true enough," Lyle chuckled. "True enough, indeed."

"Well, how about it then? I have coin I could pay, or if there is something else you would prefer, we can discuss your price."

"If you're offerin' to pay," Lyle smirked, "I'd appreciate some of your finest smokin' herbs... the troops at the port rather like them, and they sell for a good lot to tourists When we shuttle them to and from the castle..."

"How lucrative," I smiled.

"Indeed," Lyle said with a nod. "Learned this when I discovered they keep fair-quality herbs in the guard shacks at docking ports. I'm hopin' to find some lemon balm..."

"I have quite the variety of herbs on my person," I disclosed, glancing toward the thatched shack to my right. Remembering the turnip lanterns at the threshold, I grew suddenly nervous, feeling insecure about challenging talismans that repelled demons after what had happened with Maliche earlier. "If you agree to assist me, then we really must set off."

"Oi... if you're requestin' my services, I s'pose you got 'em. Though, I'll also be needin' to find some friends of mine... I was comin' to collect them anyhow and I s'pose I'll be needin' a crew."

"I s'pose we will," I began. "Seeing as how you left all your troops at the trading port."

"Aye... reckon I'll be explain' soon enough," Lyle said, smiling as he began to step around me. "I'll just take a moment in the guard shack, then we will find the folks I'm lookin' for."

"Excellent," I said, hiding my nervousness as we approached the guard house.

Pounding across the platform, I followed Lyle towards the shack, allowing a slight distance to lapse between us. Crossing onto a thick whicker rug, I approached the threshold, holding my breath anxiously with every step forward. The light from the lanterns illuminated the dark spruce planks of the shack, casting dancing shadows along the walls and floor. Cinnamon and vanilla candles had been lit inside, wafting amazing smells into the crisping air.

The turnip lanterns beside the threshold glowed menacingly. On the left, the carvings through the husk were crisp and neat, the elaborate runes manifesting protection, life, earth, fertility, and stability. The righthand lantern depicted a familiar folklore; whoever carved this lantern had no fear of ramifications or judgment. The turnip proudly displayed etchings of The First Warrior's axe, runic symbol, and lover's knot cut deeply into the ghostly white shell.

Oi, I thought with a slight chuckle, *Everett would admire such boldness.*

Though I assumed Everett was fond of The First Warrior from the tattoo on his right calf, the notion was never openly discussed between us. I would wager Everett's entire family tree worshiped Anteyus, for Everett was deeply devoted to his family and valued their beliefs and practices. Though the desire to broach the subject with him often tempted me fiercely, I knew I could never ask him of this directly. It was forbidden to give one's faith to gods who were not Ascended by The Creator, and I did not wish to endanger him or his family.

Such subtle rebellion lightened my spirits, making me feel less nervous about walking through the threshold. Stepping forward, I attempted to pass between the lanterns, gasping sharply as an unseen thrumming pulse shook my body viciously. My hands writhed in pain, aching against the gauntlets restricting my life force.

Oi, Gods... I thought angrily, suspecting that summoning Sypris and using my healing magic had amplified the talisman's intensity.

Stumbling backward, I suppressed my panic, stealing my strength as I burst forward again. Pushing through the pain, I shoved between the lanterns, feeling victorious as I entered the guard house. The tiny hut was clean and orderly, though presently unoccupied. A small woolen bed was nestled tightly in the corner, resting beside a small iron brazier and a hook for hanging clothes. A large desk took up the back wall, standing beside a whicker cabinet and padded leather chair. Candlesticks were lit in each corner of the desk, the delicious smells intensifying as I entered the room.

"They usually keep the herbs over here," Lyle said from the opposite side of the room. The door of the cabinet stood open on his right. "There ain't as much as usual though I reckon you'll find somethin' that sparks your interest."

"I suppose I shall take a look while we are here," I said innocently as I adjusted my gauntlets after encountering the lanterns.

"There are rose petals," Lyle said, fingering through the sachets of herbs within the shelving. "...Should you find such temptation suitable."

"Rose petals require a bit of preparation in order to smoke them how I like," I said, shaking my head decisively. "I should like to find something with a little less maintenance."

"There's lavender, peppermint, mullein, ginseng, mugwort..."

"I would appreciate some peppermint," I said, grateful for the opportunity to continue nursing the pain from the Dragon Armor potion.

"Aye, this might be lemon mint, actually," Lyle said, smelling the herbs before passing a small mesh sachet into my hand.

"Aye, I wager you would be correct," I said, inhaling the scent of the chilling, citrusy herbs.

"You wantin' anythin' else?"

"This should suffice," I said, tucking the small pouch into my smoking sack.

"Oi... just a moment..."

Lyle placed a small canvas sack from the upper left shelf into my hand. Lifting the pouch to my nose, I opened the small strings, deeply inhaling the fresh pine scent of the superior-quality sweet grass. Notes of oranges and cloves made the sweet grass smell spicy, the aroma pairing perfectly with the flavors of the Equinox celebrations.

"Oi... Gods," I said with a blissful sigh. "Sweet grass is my favorite... how incredible this plant smells of earth, fruit, and spice all at once."

"Aye, 'twas grown with great care," Lyle said.

"It smells absolutely divine," I said, placing the pouch in my smoking sack. "The aroma is strongly of oranges and cloves."

"Aye, cloves are one of The Creator's many gifts," Lyle agreed. "I obtained a second pouch for myself for upon our return... I would love to partake in some now, though I wish to venture for your Angelfish with a clear mind and spirit."

"I can respect that," I said, "and I appreciate your prudence."

"Oi," Lyle dismissed my comment with a wave of his hand. "I reckon I've got what I need, then."

"Very well," I said with a nod, allowing Lyle to cross the room and pass by on the right. "Where to, now, Captain Nefarious?"

"I s'pose we ought to be findin' the blokes I'll be needin' to help us," he said, pausing briefly at the threshold before continuing. "We might not be able to partake in the Festess on this night, though I hope my mates who undoubtedly have aren't too down in their cups to be of use. If tradition prevails, I should know exactly where to find the bastards."

"Excellent," I said with a laugh, briefly thinking fondly of my own traditions I held during the Autumnal Equinox celebrations. What I wouldn't have given to be warming by the fire at The Ironsides Inn, drinking a glass of Floyd's Festess whiskey, and defeating Everett in a game of throwing knives. "Perhaps you should lead the way, Captain, and I will follow behind you."

"Perfection," Lyle said, saluting with his left hand before pressing into the rain.

Sighing softly, I pushed through the threshold, fighting through the pain pulsing between the turnip lanterns. Lurching forward, I rushed through the path of the talismans, nimbly swerving rightwards to fall in line beside Lyle. Lyle shot me a look of amused puzzlement before pulling his hood tightly to politely overt his gaze as he noticed me adjusting my gauntlets. Maintaining my composure, I walked confidently beside him, keeping pace as we returned across the smooth stone platform.

"Where is it we will be going exactly?" I asked, following as Lyle stepped from the immense slab of smoothed rock.

"To the Misty Well," He explained simply. "They have the best Festess Whiskey."

"I have been craving a good whiskey the last several hours," I said with a smile. "I could use one to brighten my spirits... all this talk of tradition is making me think of home."

"Aye, reckon you've people you're missin'," Lyle said, gesturing for us to return up the narrow gravel path. "Oi, I nearly forgot to mention Your Worship. I just saw Commander Rosewood hours before arriving here in Belleview."

"Is that so?" I asked nonchalantly. Stepping across the gravel on my previously traversed path, we moved past the distant sparkling sand dunes, returning on the route toward the center of town.

"Affirmative," Lyle began. "He had set a point to check in with me as the Gods' Guard passed through the tradin' port, though he didn't end up arrivin', until several hours later than expected."

"Aye, we ran into some trouble at Morriraen," I grimaced. "It was quite terrible."

"They were on their way to Kyraulh last I saw 'em... reckon they should be arrivin' there any time now."

"Thank you kindly for the update," I nodded in gratitude. "And I appreciate you watching for the Guard, Captain Southwell."

"Even though I run the port, I was a soldier first," Lyle said as we entered the increasingly crowded streets. "I was worried when they didn' come through, though I'm glad everythin' is well."

"All is well for now," I smiled before asking, "What has brought you here?"

"Your Commander..." Lyle began. "When he passed through, he suggested a way for me to lend you my support."

Lyle gestured for us to turn left. Moving south, we looped along the bustling town square. The sky was dark with heavy clouds as the wind and rain gathered speed. Celebration and revelry echoed over the roaring wind, laughter stronger than any storm threatening to ruin the festivals.

"He said to gather a crew and supplies and to meet up with the guard at Riverside," he explained. "After reflectin' on the matter I decided to lend my support...in honor of my mum. I lost her when I was a lad, she never survived the birth of my younger brother. It wrecked my father it did, but I know her soul has been well watched over under your care."

"Lyle, that is truly awful," I said, understanding the pain of losing a mother.

"One night when I was really down in my cups, I fell asleep and my mum came to me in my dreams, wrapped in glowin' white light. She let me know she was happy where she was, that it was warm, and she knew true peace," Lyle said.

"That's beautiful, Lyle," I said, understanding from my years spent in the Underworld that it was possible to manifest visits with the living through their dreams if one was determined, persistent, and visited the Dreamweaver.

Our moment was interrupted by hordes of passing drunks shrilling and screaming with laughter. "We are just about to The Misty Well, if you allow me to finish escortin' you there, we will arrive in just a moment."

"Excellent," I said, moving again alongside Lyle and emerging onto a widened brick road.

The Misty Well rested on the corner to the north, its red woven roof bright amongst the surrounding bakeries and butcher shops. Twisted iron tables outside were overflowing with occupants, their center umbrellas decorated with small twinkling candles casting yellow and orange flames through the stormy sky. Loud music poured through the open wooden door; the clanking of drums, metallic thrum of iron strings, hooting of horns, and piping of flutes flooded invitingly through the threshold. I was thankful the doorway had been absent of demon-repelling lanterns. However, wreaths of sunflowers, chrysanthemums, fountain grass, and basil had been hung in the windows to honor the Harvest and abundance from The Creator.

"After you," Lyle said politely, gesturing with a hand and urging me through the door.

"Aye, thank you kindly," I said with a smile, stepping past him and entering the tavern.

The inside of the inn was festive and lively, the pub packed tightly with patrons at every table. Tall cylindrical candles hung from the ceiling in an array of oranges, reds, yellows, and browns, their flames shining through metallic candelabras shaped like turnips and pumpkins. Fallen leaves lay scattered across the floor and tables, the air inside smelling of trees and pine-scented fireplace logs. Circular tables dotted the smoothed wooden floor, leaving openings near the back to dance and an area on the right for throwing knives. A massive stone counter with stools and a raised flat stage took up the remainder of the pub's space, the stage currently in use by a musical group wearing lumpy orange hats.

"Oi, I see 'em over there," Lyle shouted above the noise, pointing towards the back of the dining area.

"Perfect," I said, leaning left to avoid passing serving girls carrying trays of wine and whiskey.

"Aye, looks like they're playin' cards," Lyle delighted, eyeing the passing goblets longingly.

"Sounds entertaining," I mused, following as Lyle wove through the crowds standing beside the tables.

Shoving his shoulders outward, Lyle plowed through the crowd, followed close behind by my footsteps and unheard apologies. The music and laughter made it hard to hear the words of people passing, and our interruptions were quickly forgotten as drinking and games ensued. Moving left, Lyle guided us to a table beside the counter, approaching a small band of three engrossed in a vicious game of Shepherd's Claw.

"Oi, Jorden, clean out your ears... I already said I played seven before this..."

"I don't believe yah, Ilesa," said the fellow to my right. "I already played the hook, and if not for Tahar reversing my fortune I would have lost by now."

"Oi! ridiculous..." Ilesa threw her cards angrily on the table through the taunting laughter of her companions. "I have yet to make it past the second round and you blokes drag on for hours..."

"Ay—" Lyle nudged me gently as he pointed to Ilesa's cards. "Do you reckon you can spot her error?"

"Certainly," I said, "she connected the river as a double when she needed a straight."

"Aye, seems logical," Lyle said with a nod, "though I s'pose double doubles or a triple would have been sufficient as well."

"Aye, reckon that'll do'er," said the fellow to my right, hearing us speaking behind him as the music lulled between songs.

"Oi, some rat the cat dragged in," Ilesa said with a shrill laugh, her bright blue hair glowing silver in the candles.

"Greetin's... Happy Festess," Lyle said, roughly embracing the broad man with bushy blonde hair who stood abruptly beside me.

"Oi, is this Syler yah brought along... thought you were s'pose to be occupied..."

"Jorden, don't be a moron..." Ilesa scoffed, "ain't it obvious that's Knomucca?"

Jorden met my eyes, his big blonde brows falling beneath his mass of hair.

"Aye shit, you're right," Jorden laughed heavy and hard, "y'all look the same except for the eyes."

"Forgive my brother," Ilesa said to me with a nod, "he's rather oblivious sometimes, and has had far too much to drink."

"All is well," I said with a smile, noticing that that had been the second time this evening I had been mistaken for my sister.

"Though perhaps if Lyle properly introduced us, there wouldn't have been cause for awkwardness," sniped Ilesa.

"Oi, Knomucca," Lyle rolled his eyes in feigned annoyance. "By now you've gathered that blueberry tart calls herself Ilesa... this bloke standin' here goes by Jorden, and that fellow over there is... Tahar was it?"

"Aye, 'twas indeed," said the scrawny young lad in a red plaid apron.

"No offense mate," Lyle said as the music began to climb once more, "you don't look like the type to be drinkin' with these bastards... your dress is far to proper."

"I had only meant to join for a quick game and eat lunch," said Tahar, "though the game dragged on and the whiskey flowed..."

"He should have been back to work hours ago," Ilesa said with a laugh, "'bout to hustle him I was though now I s'pose I can take his money the ol' fashion way."

"I can never quite tell if your serious," Lyle said, my hands thrumming painfully through the gauntlets as I shifted my body to watch Ilesa. Her deep blue eyes sparkled playfully, betraying nothing of what truly lurked beneath them.

"'Tis part of my charm," Ilesa giggled, pouring herself a glass of wine from the pitcher to her left. "Could I interest you in a glass, Knomucca?"

"I'd prefer a spliff and a whiskey," I said honestly. I was aware I should venture for my Angelfish promptly, though first, I desired to warm my spirits.

Lyle clapped his hand on Tahar's shoulder, "perhaps if this bloke is s'pose to be workin' here he should get on behind the counter then."

"There are other waitresses," Tahar said with a grin. "I'm enjoyin' my time with the lady here and I don't wish to be interrupted."

"Actually Tahar... some whiskey would be divine," Ilesa said, smiling teasingly as she scooped the cards from the table, "why don't you fetch us some and we can think of another game to play."

"Oi, very well," Tahar sighed, sliding from his seat and bringing along his full cup of wine.

"Your Worship... Jorden... why don't you both take a seat?" Lyle said, nodding to each of us politely. "We can take a brief moment to indulge in the herb and honor the gods while discussing why we are here."

"That would be delightful," I said, claiming Tahar's previously vacated seat and procuring a smoke from my smoking sack.

"I'll be standing if that's satisfactory," said Lyle, shouting over the laughter and applause that swirled through the tavern around us. "Ilesa. Jorden! Knomucca needs an Angelfish and requests that we escort her out to the reefs."

"When are yah lookin' to do this?" Jorden asked as he met my face from across the table.

"I'm hoping to depart once my smoke is finished," I said, obtaining a match and grasping it between my fingers.

"Allow me," Ilesa said, gracefully plucking the match from my fingers and holding it in her hand. Dragging the match across the rough stone table, Ilesa sparked the small flame, placing it at the end of my smoke as I deeply inhaled the herb.

"Oi, how sweet," I said, deciding it was best to respond in kind and not betray my sudden alarm at how quickly she had stolen my match.

"Aye, you're lookin' to leave soon then," Jorden said. "'Tis awfully unfortunate... as my sister so rudely stated I have been drinkin' for the last several hours and I've become quite comfortable."

"I can see that," I said with a smile, admiring the plethora of empty cups, pitchers, bread baskets, and goblets spread over the remainder of the table. "I'm envious of the day you must have had... I'll admit mine has been rather tedious."

"You'd be right in assumin' we've had our share of laughs," Ilesa said as she shuffled her cards. The deck flawlessly flowed from one hand to the other, the cards buzzing and thrumming as they arched, bridged, and collapsed, "You can imagine we wouldn't exactly be keen on leavin'."

"I could sober your spirits with a ginseng potion," I offered, watching as Jorden's eyes bulged in alarm.

"I'm not that lost in my cups," he said firmly. "Although.... ain't it like to storm any moment?" Jorden lifted his glass and finished the remainder of the goblet he found on his right.

"I wager it will..." I said, flicking the ashes of my spliff into an empty cup. "I am prepared to make it worth your while, simply name a price."

Tahar approached suddenly from the counter, depositing a round of whiskey on the table with a thud and sliding us each a glass.

"What are we goin' to play next," he asked as he hovered uncomfortably close to Ilesa.

"That's a mighty fair question," Ilesa said, the mischievous glint in her smile making me uneasy. "I was thinkin' Old Maiden or Four-Side Slam... either of those sound appealing to y'all?"

"Perhaps I should up the incentive," I said, leaning on my elbows as I lowered my smoke. "I can pay in coin or other expensive luxuries... I can provide smoking herbs or books or procure cinnamon-scented candles..."

"We don't need any of those things," Ilesa laughed harshly, "we are plenty fine on coin and herb... and the scent of cinnamon makes me gag."

"Respectable," I said, taking a pull from my spliff while I weighed my options, "I could perform a reading of flames or bones or find work for you at the castle..."

"If I'm being frank," Ilesa began, "we both know the one who needs a readin' of any sort is you... though I can see in your aura you'd be too stubborn to ask for one."

Ilesa split the deck in two, weaving the cards in an intricate archway through the air. Swiping a card from the center of the deck, she flashed it briefly before my eyes, sending a wave of anxiety to crash through me. Images of an angel shrouded in light stood amongst the graves of a cemetery, her body silhouetted in the sun that showed through the storming sky. Across the bottom of the card scrolled the runic symbol for "judgment," the glossy golden ink glittering menacingly as the card caught the light of the torches.

"Ilesa, that's enough," Lyle said, slamming his palms onto the table and commanding her attention. My gauntlets dug uncomfortably into my hands, though I resisted the urge to adjust them as I often did in the company of strangers.

"You, bar keep, get back to workin'," Lyle growled with a harsh bark.

Tahar turned away on his heel, shuffling towards the counter as he muttered inaudible words lost in the music.

"Oi, whilst I appreciate Her Worship attemptin' to settle her own debts between ya," Lyle continued, "it isn't her burden to bear. The two of you owe me a favor, and I'm here to collect."

"Sailin' into a storm is suicide," Ilesa said, shuffling the ominous omen she had shown back into the pile. "Couldn't we wait here awhile until the weather clears?"

"I'm afraid I've lost enough time already," I said, taking a deep drag of my whiskey and inwardly sighing with bliss. The brew was smooth with smokey tones, and the fire warmed my spirits immensely, and I craved a second glass.

"Ilesa... you owe me," Lyle said seriously.

"We both know why you're bein' so persistent Lyle..." Ilesa glared into Lyle's face as she collected her cards into a smooth leather bag. "Oi, fine, we'll be absurdly daft and forgo our Festess frivolity to join you."

"Aye, very good," Lyle said, obtaining Ilesa's untouched glass of whiskey and lifting it in the air. Shouting over the music, Lyle raised his glass in thanks, "To the Creator, the Harvest, and the turn of a new year."

"Here here," I said, alone in my reply as Ilesa glared and Jorden drank in silence.

"There's singin' at The Silver Spoon on this night," Jorden said with a sad sigh as he finished his whiskey.

"There'll be singin' on the morrow," Lyle said, setting his empty glass in the center of the table and collecting Jorden's beside it.

"Provided all goes well," Ilesa sniped, slipping the pouch of cards in the bright blue cloak tucked around her chair.

"Oi, don't be so dramatic," Lyle teased, taking the empty glass from my hand and collecting the remainder of the ashes.

Ilesa rolled her eyes, her blue cloak wrapping suspiciously around her as she stood.

"If everyone is finished, we best be setting off," I said regretfully, swiftly checking I had all my possessions before sliding from my seat.

Jorden lumbered to his feet, his body swaying slightly as he pushed in his chair. Opening my enchanted pouch, I obtained ten silver coins, leaving them in my empty glass with a satisfying clang before turning from the table. Jorden donned a heavy woolen cloak, wrapping it tightly around his shoulders as he followed behind me. Moving forward, I picked through the tumultuous crowd, the capacity of the inn far exceeding my liking as there was barely space to lift an elbow. Lyle wove through the chaos on my left, keeping close at my side as we approached the open door.

Leaving the tavern, we emerged into a sprinkling, misting rain, the promise of its increasing intensity imminent on the wind. Drawing my hood over my cap, I swore softly, taking a cleansing breath before whispering.

"Flophenne... please... I am putting innocent lives at risk in the name of The Creator and I do not wish them to come to harm. I'll owe you a favor, or a Dedication once this is over... just do what you can to protect them, please."

My whispers went unnoticed in the harsh and howling wind, the streets beginning to thin as the festivities moved indoors. Lyle stepped from my left and veered in front of me, walking in parallel with Jorden and Ilesa down the alleyway we had taken. Briskly walking east towards the docks, we hustled past butchers and bakeries, drawing their doors and shutters as they prepared to close for the evening. The short and straight street slimmed our formation to two wide, shucking me next to Ilesa, who fell in step at my left. Her bright blue cloak shined in the remaining lights of the street, her glow oddly comforting in the dreary evening sky.

The town square remained surprisingly active, the levity and spirit of the town's folk quite entertaining. Vigorous music, familiar in its bouncing cadence, repeated in an energetic chant, accompanying groups dancing around bright orange fires. Their lyrics were hard to decipher across the harsh wind, though the familiar notes of the piercing reed flute cut through crystal clear. As we edged along the square, Jorden began to sing, bellowing the Festess melody as he followed Lyle at his left.

Smiling with Jorden's Mirth, I began to hum softly, my silent singing slowly growing in volume as the melody progressed.

At seasons end ,
'Tis time again,
To celebrate abundance.
Creations gifts,
Harvest riches,
Granted through His eminence.
The year is done,
Another gone,
The winter yet forthcoming.
Through long dark nights,
Candles burn bright,
To signal his returning.
Creation gives,
Creation takes,
In an unbalanced cycle.
Gifting us life,

Creating all,
Yet all is for the taking.
At season's end,
'tis time again,
To celebrate abundance.
Gods of nature,
 harvest and life,
Ascendant through His essence.

The heavy wind carried away our words and melody, our purposed footsteps on the cobblestone soon the only clear noise in the rain. Torches along the path extinguished with a sizzle as the rain quickened, the heavy drops falling in splashes against the stone. Moving rightwards, we continued towards the docks, the town square falling away as we followed the road towards the white pebbled beaches.

Approaching the beaches, we moved rightwards, taking the slim and gravel path once more towards the docks. The lanterns hanging on the pier had been protected from the elements, and the sturdy, thick shells of the pumpkins and turnips concealed the candles within. Stepping onto the slick stone platform, I was anxious to see the angry and aggressive waves, the tide spraying freezing mist as the water smashed against the shore. The boats strapped to the pier rocked and dipped in the current, their momentum dragging a slew of quieted curses from my lips as I dwelled on what was to come.

"My sloop's too small to handle all four of us," Lyle shouted over the wind, "I was only expectin' to ask y'all to meet me at the Tradin' Port in two days' time and travel with us south towards

Riverside... I wasn't thinkin' I'd need my ship and thus I came alone in a singular craft."

"Aye, that'll be useless in the storms," Jorden said, speaking while I smiled at the notion of Lyle joining us in Riverside and a hunch that this had been Everett's doing.

"Oi, 'tis true," Lyle smiled, "we shall require a larger vessel if we wish to stand any chance against the waves."

"Perhaps the caravel on the second dock from the left," Ilesa pointed through the heavy grey. "Brother here and I were hired out on a job this mornin'... reckon nobody'll come lookin' for her with the storms and beginnin's of the Festess."

"I reckon you're right," Lyle said, following the platform left and moving with us towards the second pier, "the caravel would be the best option."

"Perfection," I said, gesturing Ilesa to walk in front of me as I took up my post behind her.

Slimming to a singular line, we pounded across the docks, the blocky spruce planks shaking beneath my boots as the waves crashed around us. Hustling forward, we made our way towards the end of the pier, fanning wide once more to avoid the spraying water as the dock expanded. Glass torches and lanterns hung on chain-link columns around the border, the bright lights illuminating the gently sloping bow of the vessel.

The caravel possessed the ideal number of sails and luxuries for making the voyage to the reefs tolerable through storms. The size was fair, spanning roughly eighteen meters from bow to stern whilst sporting a singular stem castle. The ship's main and mizzen masts were shrouded in tangling enchanted lights, the fires slowly extinguishing as the rain dipped into the candles. Trailing my eye along the underside of the hull, I noticed the name of the vessel, the looping black letters curving and stretching with the shape of the ship.

Sonnet Moon, I read with a smile, thinking immediately of our radiant goddess Senaya.

Instinctively, I turned to face the east, sighing sadly as I realized the moon would not be alight and guiding me through the heavy cover of thunder and clouds. *Senaya... I pray you are well....*

"This'll do nicely," Lyle said suddenly at my left, his voice loud even over the wind, "she's even rigged with storm sails already."

"Excellent," I said, turning to face Lyle while placing my back into the wind. "Captain Southwell, would you mind too terribly in leaving your broach behind on the post? Should something happen to us and the craft fails to be returned... I wish for the owner to know where they might be reimbursed."

"Very well," Lyle said with a nod, beginning to unfasten the heavy silver medallion hanging down his front.

The flat, shining circle was used to prove the elf's identity, as Lyle often handled trades, goods purchases, and guests' transportation to and from the castle. The medallion detailed his name, rank, and station; the words Captain Lyle Southwell - Snake River Trading Port were carved neatly into the silver and tinted black. On the opposite side scrawled the crest of Morriraen, woven brightly with a translucent blue resembling the river's waters.

"Thank you kindly," I said, watching as Lyle looped the long chain of the medallion in a complicated knot before letting it rest against the pillar on the dock's inner corner. His placement had been quite advantageous; the glow of the glass lantern hanging from the same column would catch the observant eye, though otherwise, it would go unnoticed.

"Absolutely," Lyle said, turning to see Ilesa and Jorden climbing over the misting waters into the ship's hull.

"Shall we then?" I asked, exhaling a deep and cleansing breath as I smiled at Lyle.

"We shall indeed," he said, following behind me as I boarded the caravel.

Stepping onto the agile deck, I climbed over the side of the boat, the wind snapping viciously as it blew off my hood. Tightening my cap, I moved to the starboard side to allow Lyle to clamber aboard, the ship swaying gently as we walked across the sturdy hull. Housed in the aftercastle was an iron brazier and a slim, narrow starscope resting atop a set of carved and exposed beams. The ship's main and mizzen masts loomed like sentinels, their heavy wooden spars thrumming solid and secure as the wind jingled through the rigging.

Lyle whistled, commanding our attention over the fierce and howling wind. Moving portside, I fell in line between Jorden and Ilesa, the pair wandering from the forecastle as they ignited the brazier.

"Jorden," Lyle began as he spoke with a nod, "I'd like you to be my dock hand."

"Aye, Captain," Jorden nodded, cracking his knuckles as he set to raising the anchor.

"Ilesa... I'd like you as ship cadet, and Knomucca... you'll take First Mate."

"Aye Captain," I said with a salute.

"You'll be on the main and mizzen masts, respectively, with Jorden and I mannin' the rutters and other operations."

"Very well," I said.

"Seems acceptable to me," Ilesa said.

"Oi, perfect," Lyle continued, "Once the anchor is lifted, we will leave the harbor and head northeast. Travelin' at an angle should grant us an attempt to stay on the edge of the storm whilst makin' our way towards the reefs."

"Understood," I said. "I appreciate you having a plan... and I sincerely hope you all know how grateful I am for your help."

"I'm only doin' this for the Captain here," Ilesa said with a harsh note. "Your sister is well and everythin'... though as far as I'm concerned you owe me a favor for assistin' you like this."

"I can respect that," I said with a shrug.

"And what do you say we throw in one for my brother here, too?" Ilesa said with a smirk as she feigned nonchalance.

"Consider it done," I said, "although, I suppose I will be owing him a night of singing... it is hard enough hearing our voices now as they are or I would oblige whilst we traveled."

"Aye, shame indeed..." Ilesa rolled her eyes subtly as she adjusted her hood. "It's been a pleasure doin' business with you, Knomucca."

"Oi... Anchor's away," Jorden yelled suddenly, followed by Lyle whistling the signal for such so we could remember it.

"Cadet, First Mate, report to your sails," Lyle said, matching his command with a series of repetitive triumphant whistles.

"Aye, Captain," I said, saluting briefly and turning towards the hull's center.

Climbing onto the forecastle, I approached the smaller mast, the mizzen mast located nearer the stern than the main mast in the center. Walking around the tall looming beam, I began to examine the hemp ropes of the rigging, thankful for the light the brazier provided through the wind and rain. Working swiftly, I unfastened the taut tan canvas of the sail bag, unfurling the breezy, silver cotton sail and allowing it to catch the wind. Feeling along the mast, I secured the halyard, freeing it from a spike that held it fixed in place during the off hours.

Opening the rope clutch at my hip, I released the lock on the boom, easing out the mainsheet and allowing the rigging lines to relax as the sail flapped beside me. Grasping along the bottom of the sail, I quickly folded the foot, swiping my hand through the reefing lines and connecting them to accommodate the raging wind. When the sail was stretched, and the lines were readied, I stood at attention beside the mizzen mast, noticing Lyle pulling on the tiller as he turned the rudder away from the docks.

"Casting off," Lyle commanded with a whistle. Using a heavy metal trolley with wheels, Jorden pushed the caravel, the launching trolley in combination with the wind lurching the boat forward unpleasantly. Fighting to keep balance, I grasped tightly to the steady, swaying mast, watching Lyle guide the boat, directing the craft as the wind propelled us forward.

"Hoist the sails," Lyle shouted, jamming the tiller to the portside as the waves rammed against us.

Seizing the halyard, I jumped at the mast, using my downward weight to pull the rope. The extra force allowed the sail to rise faster, the tension increasing as the sail neared the top. Pulling the halyard, I wrapped it around the winch, tightening the ropes in place as *Sonnet Moon* sped forward. Looking upwards, I noticed horizontal wrinkles flowing through the sail, requiring several cranks from the winch as I tightened the tension in the ropes. A long, vertical fold flapped parallel to the mast, disappearing and smoothing into the fabric as I adjusted the mainsheet and boom vang once more.

"Hold her steady," Lyle said, pulling the tiller as he turned the rudder again. The boat straightened out, pulling away from the docks as they fell behind us.

"Oi, First Mate, slacken the mainsheet," Lyle called, his command nearly inaudible in the roaring wind.

"Aye, Captain," I said, reducing the tension in the rig and loosening the sail. The wind fell tightly at an angle at the starboard, the swell of the waves rising and falling as we pulled away from the harbor.

"Perfect, tie her down," Lyle said, quickly followed by clinks of the winch and my locking the boom once more.

Gliding north, we ran with the wind, the illuminated coastline of Belleview blurring in the grey evening as we sped toward the reefs. The angry, cloudy water foamed with heavy waves, the craft slicing through them with every dip and lull.

"Oi, Cadet, ready to tack?"

"Aye, Captain, tackin'," Ilesa shouted, adjusting the rigging to turn the main sail into the wind, "transitionin' to beam reach."

"Aye, copy that, maintain starboard tack," Lyle said, handling the rudder with Jorden at his left.

The hull shifted slightly, aiming the boat northeast in a truer direction towards the reefs. In the distant east, thunder rumbled with the far-off flash of sky-splitting lightning, my spirits plummeting with the waves as the rain poured. The wind chilled and choked my breathing, making it hard to focus on manning the sails while fighting for my breath.

Sailing onward, we sliced through the swells of the waves, every crest and dip lurching my heart into my throat. The silhouette of Belleview was no longer visible behind us; the lights of the piers had vanished in the stormy grey evening. Clusters of trees along the coastline were covered in darkness, the brazier only providing enough light to support our venture forward. The land and trees around us helped calm the spraying and destructive waves, though their temperament soon fouled as we entered open water.

Suddenly, the boat began to curve portside, the waves threatening to drag us head-on into their rising, foaming swells.

"First Mate, spill the wind," Lyle whistled sharply.

I reacted without thinking, slacking the tension in the mainsheet and angling the sail into the wind. The wind began to push around the sail, avoiding hitting the sail directly and allowing the caravel to straighten.

"Excellent, tie her down," Lyle said as I cranked the winch and sheets back in place.

Riding the wind, we continued northeast, working as one to keep the boat steady. Gruff, sonorous thunder crashed in another rolling wave, the lightning moving closer than when it had previously struck.

"Cadet, ready to tack?" Lyle shouted again, "Broad reach, portside tack."

"Aye, tackin'," Ilesa responded with a whistle, tugging on the rigging as she manipulated the sails into the wind.

"Slackin'... slackin'," Lyle shouted, his voice panicked and nervous.

The caravel swerved heavily to the left, the bow threatening to submerge directly into the oncoming waves.

"Straighten her out, Cadet," Lyle said urgently, Jorden abandoning him at the helm and sprinting across the hull towards Ilesa.

Yanking the halyard and sheets, the pair of them talked in rushed words, the sails turning straight as the boat curved away from the waves.

"Nice work," Lyle praised, though his congratulations had been given prematurely.

Sonnet Moon began to curve rightwards, overcorrecting to aim stern side into the waves.

"Tack, Cadet, tack!" Lyle shouted harshly.

Sudden waves smashed the boat hard, launching a freezing sheet of water across the hull and over the bulwark.

"Get it under control or we're goin' under," Lyle demanded.

Jorden and Ilesa yanked at the rigging, pulling the sail parallel with the mast. Loosening the winch, I slackened my ropes to accommodate them, my sail shifting slightly as the wind rushed around it.

"Back off Knomucca," Lyle hollered harshly, "tighten 'em up! Tighten 'em up!"

Yanking the winch, I fell to the side, whacked by the boom as waves smashed over the gunwale.

"Tighten 'em up!" Lyle screamed again as I locked the boom and rigging in place.

The boat straightened, slicing angled through the waves as water filled the hull. Propelling forward, we began to sink lower, allowing the waves to crest the gunwale and continue flooding the caravel.

"We are goin' under," Lyle said, my body quickly snapping to alert as Ilesa began to scream.

Removing my cloak, I fought through the cold, shedding the excess weight as the bottom began to fill with water. Rushing forward, I abandoned the mizzen mast, approaching Jorden and Ilesa as they desperately clung to the halyard.

"What can I do?" I asked over the wind.

"There's nothin' you can do here," Jorden barked as Ilesa cranked on the winch, "In fact, you've done more than enough already."

"We are nearly to the reefs as it stands, and the sand barges-
"

My words were silenced with a burning to my cheek, anger flowing through me with the awareness Ilesa had slapped me.

"Pray to your twisted Gods you make it there alive," Ilesa said as another wave crashed onto the hull.

The platform beneath my feet suddenly gave way, and the harsh sizzle of the brazier extinguishing filled my ears as Ilesa clung to the mast. Lurching sideways, I was thrown into the battering waves, my lungs filling with air as I careened over the gunwale. The soberingly cold water filled my ears as my head submerged, the distant yelling of names and screams lost as I was dragged beneath the surface.

Fighting to gain control, I spun beneath the waves, kicking my legs out harshly as I pounded towards the surface. Cresting the water, I searched for the caravel, spotting the sinking masts straight ahead against the flash of lightning.

"Captain! Ilesa! Jorden!"

I began shouting as I swam forward, clawing through the relentless waves as they pounded against my face. Coughing sharply, I fought to tread water, pumping my legs as I searched for the craft. The peaks of the sails dipped beneath the surface, *Sonnet Moon* falling beneath the water with a rush of my tears. The waves pushed and pulled at the weapons hanging from my belt, the weight dragging me under as I desperately searched for my crew.

They're gone, I thought through my tears, struggling to keep my head above the water. In vain, I called their names again, opening my mouth and swallowing the angered sea. Coughing and spitting, I exorcised the water, only to take in more as my head sank beneath the surface. Falling deeper, I swung my arms desperately, thrashing towards the surface as I only plummeted downward. Sucking in water, my lungs began to burn, the awareness I was going to drown imminent as my head began to throb.

Not like this, I thought somberly, *Gods... please... not like this. I'm letting everybody down, Syler, Everett...*

Reaching desperately upwards, I summoned my final strength, rising several feet before my breath shortened. Brief moments of euphoria filled me as I struggled for air, my vision blurring into warm shapes and colors as I slowly slipped away.

VIII

EVERETT

"**M**y heart would break should Floyd part with the Ironsides Inn," Kiyoko said, watching as the lanterns above the door extinguished in the rain.

"He may not have a choice in the matter," Kye said gently, lightly touching Kiyoko on the arm, "you heard what he said... he's dying."

"And another that I love shall then be lost," Kiyoko said.

My heart ached as I heard the wistful sorrow in his voice.

"'Tis a part of the natural cycle," Kye said, tightening her hood against the wind.

"Perhaps we could purchase The Ironsides Inn ourselves," I suggested to Kiyoko with a gesture of my hand. Turning as I spoke, I approached the fence where we had tied the horses. "We would possess control of his legacy and could assist in keeping Floyd comfortable until he crosses over."

"Brilliant," Kiyoko said sincerely, "We can run a tavern in addition to our remaining military responsibilities."

"I would lay a wager, we are iron enough to handle it," I mused, collecting Truff's reigns tightly in my hands.

"I would be lying if I did not convey that the idea is quite tempting," Kiyoko admitted, leading Ballara around the fence and sliding his tatami slipper into the stirrup.

Returning through the village, we marched along the widening roads, the sky dimming from the lack of lanterns in the rain. Heavy wooden shutters were pulled over the windows and doors, keeping out the storm and intruders alike. The energy of the Festess flowed through the cracks in the shutters, spilling forth the sounds of laughter, clanking goblets, and music to warm the streets. The three days post and prior to the Equinox were always the most exciting. Though I was glad the commoners could have a night free of worry, I couldn't stop myself from growing envious.

Turning right from the main road, we followed the cobblestone path from Kyraulh. The bridge across the Snake River materialized through the grey of the evening sky. Water whipped in white foam waves downstream, spraying and spreading over the bridge and edges of the banks. Trotting forward, we merged onto the slick bridge, my pace slowing to a fast walk to avoid Truff losing his footing. Water splashed against the sides, spooking Truff as the waves crashed across his hooves.

"Woah, easy there fella," I soothed, gripping the reigns tightly as Truff began to whinny.

The rain swirled and slammed my face, the exposure of the open water unkind through the freezing wind.

"Walk on, Treeroot Truffles," I said urgently, feeling uneasy as the growing waves rushed towards us.

Truff hesitated, lingering slightly before lurching forward. Following too closely behind Bullet, we hustled the formation over the bridge, the sudden tremors in Truff's body leaving him as we reached solid land.

"That's a good lad... well done Truffles," I told him, using his name in this rare form to convey my pride. Reaching down, I patted him on the shoulder to steady him.

Rounding on the path, we returned to the resting ranks. Soldiers lingered beneath the thick branches of trees, concealing their bodies and horses from the rain. Thankfully, my orders to cease sparring had been obeyed despite the notion that strong pumping blood would keep the body warm. A circle of soldiers smoked in the trees nearest the supply train, watching it closely to prevent further incidents.

Whistling over the wind, I commanded the troops to gather in formation, watching as they left the comfort and protection of the trees. Circling around my horse, the soldiers stood at attention, waiting patiently for me to address them even as the rain poured from the sky.

"We shall be leaving a small guard of you behind in the village. Those of you selected will be briefed on your purpose by the General before the rest of our force departs."

A smattering of replies broke through the ranks, and their concerns, questions, and comments about the deviation from the plan were silenced with a terse whistle.

"Corporal Sandson, you will lead Bruitis, Raenor, Joen and Shoeman back into Kyraulh. Enjoy the Festess, though don't drown in your cups. You are there with purpose, and that best not be forgotten."

"Aye, Commander," Corporal Sandson said, saluting crisply and adjusting her hood.

"Oi, be gone with ya then, and report to the general," I said, watching as the troops I had selected broke from the ranks and ventured from the trees.

"The rest of you," I continued gruffly, adjusting my composure as the rain weighed down my cloak, "take a brief moment and collect yourselves, for once we are yet again southbound we shall not rest until morning."

The remaining troops quickly disbanded, vanishing again beneath the trees for a final smoke and piss. Answering my own call of nature, I returned to Truff's saddle with a fresh cloak and lighter load, appreciating the apprentices of the convoy who bewitched my cloak to dry it. Soldiers assisted in pulling the supply train from the side of the path, tending to the horses with sugar lumps and blankets in an attempt to keep them steady. Taking my position in front of the wagons, I whistled over the heavy wind, cupping my hands over my mouth to ensure my spoken words were heard.

"Ready your horses... fall in line..."

The ranks began to assemble through the rain, scattering cylindrical glass lanterns through the rows to provide light. Kiyoko appeared through the trees on the left, cutting in front of the ranks as he positioned his horse at my right. I exhaled a breath I hadn't known I was holding, for the comfort of Kiyoko at my side always put me at ease.

"Fall out," I demanded with a whistle, feeling as Truff staggered forward to lead us at the head of the ranks.

Pushing south, we moved alongside the river, watching as waves whipped and rolled over the rocky banks of the shore. The hissing current was deafening. The raging, foaming water thundered through the rain, pounding against the shoreline. The trail beneath the horses began to loosen and fill with water, the once tightly packed earth shifting as drops puddled in the dirt. The leaves on the trees were weighed down by the sheets of rain, the wind shirking them loose angrily from their branches. The miserable rain fell heavily against my skull, pounding into my head even through my hood and hat.

"Everett," Kiyoko yelled over the storm, "There's trouble at the wagons."

"I don't hear any trouble," I countered, straining my ears through the harsh wind and rain.

"Something is amiss," Kiyoko said, his intonation indicating he had read the trouble with his energy.

"You were confused by a wee billy just hours previous... are you certain we ought to investigate the wagons?" I teased with a chuckle and a wink.

"Oi," Kiyoko punched me playfully in the arm, sending a burst of warmth through my pounding heart, "bite your tongue... or else I may have to-."

"Nonsense," I said, rubbing my arm in mock annoyance and tugging on Truff's reigns. "I believe you when you say there is a disturbance... you know I shall always be supportive and behind you..."

"An exquisite notion indeed," Kiyoko said with a wink, following beside me as he turned his horse.

I chuckled hardily, allowing Kiyoko to enjoy my smiling as I guided Truff to the side. Weaving through the ranks, I noticed the convoy had slowed amid the lines of soldiers. The horses were spooked and refusing to walk, whinnying softly as they tried to turn around. Soldiers and apprentices were leaping from the convoy, slamming their bodies into the sides of the carts as they attempted to move them.

"Commander... General... I was about to come searching for you," Kye appeared through the rain on foot, carrying a hanging glass lantern in her hand.

"I am assuming the wagons are stuck," I said, fighting to remain composed.

"Aye, they won't budge," Kye said, taking a deep and cleansing breath before she spoke.

"With the added weight in each cart they certainly shall sink faster," Kiyoko said, shaking his head and turning towards me.

"What can be done about this?" I asked, weighing my options.

"Not enough," Kye said, taking another immense breath. "I expanded the wagon harnesses and have recruited all available horses... shy of our enchanters imperviating the wheels, for which we have not the time, I cannot think of anything else."

"Gods," I swore angrily, noticing Kiyoko calmly at my left. Absently, he twisted Ballara's mane, leaning his head slightly forward as he thought. Taking a calculated breath, he began to speak, his words slightly distant as he focused and strategized.

"Nor do we have the time to wait until the weather clears... perhaps Everett and I best help push the wagons," Kiyoko said.

"That would be appreciated," Kye said as she adjusted her hood, "I could hang on to Truff and Ballara for you gentlemen as Lady Moonbeam is working in the rigging."

"Thank you kindly," I said, sliding my boot from the stirrup and jumping from the saddle.

I turned my back to the convoy, whistling with all my might to slow the troop to a crawl. Placing my fingers in my mouth, I blew another slew of whistles, communicating through my tones and trills that I needed extra hands at the convoy. At my belt hung a pair of dragon scale gloves, and I quickly slipped them on, appreciating the warmth and grip they would provide in moving the wagons.

"That is a sage idea," Kiyoko said. He pulled on his own pair of dragon scale gloves that he had received from Knomucca as a recent Name Day gift. Like my own, they had been made from Thornin's underbelly, an endeavor that could take the better part of a year to collect enough scales to achieve.

"Let us put distance between ourselves and the river," Kiyoko said, saluting Kye and gesturing for me to follow him.

"Stay wise, Kyreese," I said, echoing Kiyoko's salute with one of my own and moving swiftly behind him.

"Love and light," Kye called over the wind, turning slowly through the mud and leading the horses toward the troops.

Light would be excellent, I thought, leaving Kyreese at my back.

The heavy foliage blocked the worst of the blistering wind and rain as we passed through the tree line. The mud slipped and sloshed beneath my boots, splashing in heavy glops to stain my cloak.

Wonderful, I sighed in annoyance despite the somewhat improved conditions. I longed for the rain to cease and release us from its tyranny.

We approached the rear of the convoy, finding apprentices sallying and bickering about how the task was to be executed. Rage flooded through me instantly, boiling my blood, as I glared down upon them through my hood.

"Oi! The lot of ya, piss off," I snapped, thrashing angrily at the apprentices as they instantly began to scatter. Darting out my hand, I seized the collar of a passing rookie, bringing him roughly to stand at attention as his hood fell to his back.

"Ruffalo, bring me Tyfis and Corporal Bean."

"Ah-ah-aye," the rookie sheepishly squeaked to my order, quickly passing around me and disappearing with the others behind the carts. I could not help but notice the glint of fear in his eyes as a result of my outburst.

"Everett... mind your temper," Kiyoko scolded, moving toward the furthest left wheel of the wagon, "or I shall be forced to mind it for you."

"Useless pricks," I muttered, remembering the rookies who had been behaving in the same manner earlier atop the hill outside Morriraen. Still, I felt a hint of shame for letting the situation get the better of me.

"Either put your annoyance to use, or wash it down the river," Kiyoko hissed.

"It is my intention to demonstrate my strength," I teased, standing nearest to the back right wheel of a wagon. I focused on the task to distract my thoughts from my guilt.

"Excellent," Kiyoko said, nodding as I settled into place. "Ready then?"

"Oi... Aim! Mark! Strike," rang out across the convoy.

Squatting down, I prepared to lift, hearing Kye and others command with a whistle to set the convoy forward. Wedging my fingers under the lower frame, I grabbed the studs, heaving upwards to lift the wagon from the mud as the wheels began to turn.

"We need more traction," Kiyoko heaved between labored breaths. "Planks or something similar could provide the friction we need to move."

"Any spare wood we had was likely used to repair the wagons after the attack," I sighed, wishing my rage alone could move the carts.

"Commander... General..." a winded voice came suddenly from the right. "I was told you had been searching for me?"

Lieutenant Tyfis saluted upon his approach, sporting Bullet at his left instead of the Corporal for whom I had asked.

"Aye, we were indeed," I said, my irritation with the apprentices beginning to bubble once more, "though... I had not been asking for the Chief, nor do I see the Corporal..."

"I had wished to lend my support instead," Bullet said, hopping off his miniature pony. "I was beginning to fall asleep in the saddle and needed to stretch my legs."

"How can one sleep through the rain?" I marveled, nodding as Bullet took a place at the wagons to my left.

"It relaxes me," Bullet said despite Kiyoko's teasing stares. "My tunic and cloak are impervious to water... a simple enchantment I could have gifted to all if only the time and supplies had permitted me so."

"We shall survive," Kiyoko said as he shook his head in amusement.

"Everybody ready then?" I asked, releasing a tense breath.

"Aye," said Kiyoko amidst the others and their nodding. "Best set to it... Aim! Mark! Strike!"

Gradually, we inched south, shifting the convoy as far from the river as the trees would allow. The first of many leagues took nearly four hours, the troop traveling assiduously so as to leave no room for error. The constant lifting, pushing, and heaving were strenuous on my body, and I relished in the notion that when we finally stopped to make camp, I could earn a full night's rest. The second league passed as slowly as the first, the early evening hours turning into the night with no break in the weather.

"This is miserable," Tyfis said with a grunt.

"I find it on par with baking fresh bread," Kiyoko said playfully. "There are far worse tasks to be fulfilled in my opinion."

"I would give my prick for a glass of whiskey," Tyfis said heavily. "My bones are in desperate need of respite."

"I know the feeling," I said with a chuckle. "Though I reckon Kiyoko is wise, as per his usual. Events could be worse than they are."

"Certainly that is so," Tyfis lifted the wagons and shoved them. "As they could be when one finds a snake in the hay bales."

"I reckon you are allowed to gripe," I said gently. "However, if you simply focus on your work, all shall be well."

A silence fluttered through us, my spirits momentarily lightening from our bantering as we pressed onward.

"Perhaps we could use a song," Bullet suggested. "In the motherland when the work was hard we would whistle a tune to coax forth a smile."

"It is almost the Festess," I agreed, shrugging my shoulders. "I suppose a song could be nice... I shall provide the tune, and the lot of you can provide the vocals."

"Aye, it is perhaps best given your wretched singing voice," Kiyoko teased, taking a long drink from his water skin while I resisted the urge to bash it against his face.

"We cannot all be as gifted a bard as you Kiyoko," I glared. "You gift the Gods with beauty when you play them a song... I gift them with a whistle instead of my word."

"It is sweet all the same," Kiyoko said, his eyes crinkling slightly as he realized he had annoyed me. "You lead us Everett... when we recognize the melody we shall join you all the same."

Sighing away my anger, I pushed against the wagons, debating with myself about what I wanted to whistle. Slowly, the rhythm began to move me, the short linear notes escaping my lips as my company began to sing.

With seventeen years to my name,
I first set out to sea.
After years of hell and labor,
I sailed back home to thee.
The seas could not drag me under,
My spirits sailed and roamed.
Though I've had many adventures,
I'm lucky to be home.

The hearth is where I'm happiest,
A harvest of plenty.
Home after hellish nights at sea,
growing the family.
Her tears have threatened to drown me,
as I once again leave.
Though at the hearth with my maiden,
is where I'd rather be.
Whiskey shall keep my company,
and smoke will pass the time.
Through the many nights and labor,
I'll watch the nights pass by.
And though there will be adventure,
My spirits sail and roam.
I would rather be beside her,
I'd rather be at home.
A sudden silence fell among us as I fought hard not to blush.

"Beautiful choice, Everett," Kiyoko said, taking a long breath before he continued. "I'll admit I was expecting something a bit more atoned to the Festess."

"I was feeling moved," I admitted, thinking of Knomucca from the stirring lyrics and pushing positive blessings toward her.

"Wondering how Knomucca is fairing, I reckon," Bullet said unexpectedly, peering into the sky to avert his eyes. "I, too, have been thinking of her the last several hours... I hope she's well."

"As do I," I agreed with a sigh, disliking the notion it could be an entire day's time before I saw her again.

Trudging onward, we continued to push the convoy, kicking mud and debris from the wheels. Around the hour of the wolf, the rain finally began to clear, lifting my spirits with the weather, though I remained drenched and freezing. The second village along the river came into view to the southwest, its gates set further back from the riverbanks than that of Kyraulh. Heaving the convoy forward, we emerged onto a wide gravel road leading towards the right to intersect with Ironhaven, about a league from Snake River. Passing over the road, we scraped the mud free from the wagon wheels, unencumbering them and smoothing out the rims to allow the carts easier movement. Whistling briefly, I instructed the Guard to take a small rest, gifting myself a brief moment to stretch and indulge in a smoke.

"How are your injuries?" Kiyoko asked suddenly, leaning beside me against the back of a wagon. His arm rested against my own; the soft cotton of his kimono lay gently against the wool of my cloak.

"I am well," I said, offering him the spliff as I pulled a drink from my water skin.

"Are you being truthful?" Kiyoko asked calmly.

"Aye, Kiyoko, I am..."

"Such a blessing grants cause to rejoice," Kiyoko said, meeting my eyes and gently searching my face.

"There is no need to disbelieve me," I soothed, affectionately brushing my thumb across the corner of his mouth. Certainly, there is pain and discomfort... though I shall soldier onwards with pride, strength, and good spirits as I have been blessed to do so."

"I admire you," Kiyoko said, briefly resting his head against my shoulder. "Ever the hero... ever mine anyhow-"

"What is unfolding here, Commander Rosewood?"

The sudden shrillness of my spoken name nearly made me jump, threatening to tear my heart from my chest. Kiyoko's head remained firmly pressed against me; his boldness and lack of embarrassment made him all the more impressive in my eyes. Hazel appeared suddenly on the left, rounding the corner angrily and holding a goblet in her hands.

"Merely having a rest," Kiyoko said as he lifted his head from my shoulder. "Everett provides much more comfort than a boulder or a wet tree-"

"Aye, that I do," I agreed, swallowing my annoyance at her interruptions of my time with Kiyoko. "How may we assist you then, Priestess?"

"Did I not ask that you relax as best you could whilst we continued towards Riverside?"

"Oi, all hands were required to pull their own weight," I said, accepting the spliff from Kiyoko and inhaling deeply.

"Certainly somebody else could have done this instead of you," Hazel said.

"I'm assuming you've come for my treatment," I said, changing the subject as I gestured to the goblet she held in her hand.

"Begrudgingly," Hazel admitted, "I am providing this dose of your tonic sooner than I would have liked. I don't have the herbs to support you exerting yourself Everett, and you'd do well to heed my warnings."

"I feel well," I said, taking the goblet from Hazel's hands and deliberately drinking it slowly despite its deliciousness.

"It has crossed my mind to persuade Kiyoko to bleed your energy dry... knock you on your ass for a few days until we reach Riverside."

Sudden panic smashed through me like angry waves, for I disliked the implications from Hazel's words that she knew of Kiyoko's gifts.

"Oi," I snapped, deciding to divulge a truth I knew her to suspect. "It would be a lovely idea, then whilst I am sleeping like the dead you can contend with Kiyoko as he attempts to sacrifice half the fleet to the Underworld."

"You're being dramatic," Hazel said. "Certainly he would appear high strung, yet he would be able to control himself should he merely try to do so."

"It is not so cut and dry," Kiyoko said as he pressed his arm against me. "And I reckon I would decline, anyhow."

"Not if I could persuade you," Hazel said, her voice holding a suggestive tone.

"Kiyoko cannot so easily be convinced," I said, remembering how difficult it had been to persuade him the one and only time he fed from my energy. There are moments of that night I could not completely remember. Though that night had occurred three years prior, Kiyoko still would not divulge what truly happened.

"Come now Everett... we mustn't be thick," Hazel said as a shadow flashed behind her eyes. "Knomucca is requiring much of you, and I must deliver you to Riverside in fine health and fortune... certainly the most suitable way to do so is to subdue you whilst you conserve your strength and have Kiyoko restore your energy upon our destination."

"Why must you jest to unleash such grimness upon us, instead of trusting that I shall seek your treatments and wisdom should I find it necessary?" I said, trying to brush my growing curiosity towards her darkening countenance away.

"I trust in your loyalty to Her Worship, much as I trust the sun shall rise in the morrow..." Hazel said with a suspicious gleam through her irises. As for your communicating that you are feeling unwell, I trust in that about as much as I trust that frogs have wings."

"You wound me," I said, shaking my head as I returned the empty goblet to Hazel. "I hear what you are saying Hazel, I sincerely do. Though, you cannot expect me to sit astride and watch the rookies handle the work."

"I expect you to know when you are being daft," Hazel said. "There are necessary tasks you must accomplish, yet there is plenty else you can trust others to fulfill whilst you take the time to recover."

"I do prefer to get my hands dirty and not sit from high places, though it may not be your preference," I said defiantly.

"Your stubbornness is infuriating," Hazel's anger flashed once again in a shadow beyond her eyes. "You barely listen at all... it must be for your sculpted muscles that Knomucca wishes to keep you in her trusted..."

"Mind your place," I said sternly.

"With all due respect," Hazel narrowed her eyes as she continued speaking. "I am not one of your soldiers you can demand orders to and be rid of when you don't wish to see them. My words bear weight... and you'd do well to remember that."

"There is no need for the theatrics," I said, placing my fingers in my mouth and conveying with a whistle to ready the horses. "I appreciate you tending to me, though I am not in need of you. If I anger you, then perhaps you best take your leave.... I reckon we ought to be using the time to march onwards instead of exchanging such unpleasantries."

"If you insist," Hazel said, spinning the goblet in her hands and regarding me curiously. "I've done all I can for the moment anyhow..."

Turning slowly, Hazel left us in the back of the convoy with Tyfis and Bullet resting atop nearby boulders.

"Oi, come along then," I said, whistling a command to move out the ranks once more.

Wrenching the wagons south, we continued through the woodlands, veering southwest as Snake River began to curve. The trees slowly fell away as we emerged into a vast prairie, expanding to the east and west for many leagues. On a clear day, the Baston Mountain Range would become visible on the distant horizon, looming over the connecting streams that fed into the Snake River. Yet, as I looked up on this stormy night, the clouds obscured my view of the peaks.

"How much longer do we need to push the wagons?" Bullet asked amidst the silence that had formed. "The ground won't dry till the morrow and we'll be encountering mud along the riverbend for several more leagues."

"I say we get to Woodroe, then take a rest," Kiyoko spoke as he shoved the wagons forward. "It is two leagues away and by then most of the hours of the night shall be behind us."

"We cannot afford to take a rest until well after dawn and are outside the city," I said.

"I thought you might say that," Kiyoko smiled mischievously. "Yet I think it may be prudent to allow the troops to rest."

"What are you on about?" I asked, raising an eyebrow suspiciously as I attempted to decipher his meaning.

"The forests around Woodroe are home to the Rose Lily, the oldest apothecary in our realm dating back to the time Anteyus, The First Warrior."

Kiyoko knew that with my family's history, mentioning Anteyus would spur my interest. Anteyus was chosen as the original Death God Prospect before humanity's Fall from Grace. Legends told of a time before the Fall, when Crossfire was in harmony, the elements of spirit and nature flowing together as one. Yet the creation of humanity led to a shift in the physical world. Humanity proved to be selfish, thoughtless, and all too willing to take the lives of one another – an act against nature believed only to be worthy of the Creator. Anteyus was selected to accept the Power of the Death God and ferry lost souls to the land of the dead.

Anteyus had prevailed through the Gods Trials, Ascended, and accepted the blood of The Creator to become forever immortal. Though humanity was flawed and harmony forgotten, Anteyus sought comfort and companionship from a squash farmer who lived in the west. The pair of them became inseparable; Anteyus found it difficult to be parted from his lover to return to the Underworld. His desire to remain in the land of the living and his ever-growing absences disrupted the balance of nature.

The Creator was furious, for Anteyus had failed the realms. The Creator demanded that Anteyus leave his lover and remain in the Underworld, where he was forbidden to ever leave to return to the land of the living. Anteyus refused to abandon the man he loved and challenged The Creator. In doing so, he lost everything. His soul was ripped clear from him, and he was banished to the void between realms.

Turning towards Kiyoko, I sighed deeply, reaching out with my energy with a request to speak directly into his mind.

"Kiyoko... I am not certain I understand..."

"Everett... The Rose Lily is ancient, perhaps there is something within its walls suitable for Knomucca and the Elixir of Life..."

"Kiyoko... ever so brilliant..." I quipped sarcastically. "We would be doubling back on our path and lose valuable time travelling."

" It is worth the diversion, and we could obtain more herbs for Hazel's treatments." Kiyoko said aloud, unwilling to alert the others we had been conversing in secrecy.

"We will need to move quickly," I said.

"Quench your iron, Everett... All shall be well," Kiyoko said, finishing his water skin and continuing to push the wagons.

We moved through the night, the whistling, sweeping gusts of wind blocked mostly by the mass of the wagons. My body warmed from work, yet my skin remained cold, my nose and cheeks reddening as I fought the elements.

"Bullet," I said, midnight finally approaching as the mud thickened beneath our boots.

"Aye Commander," Bullet said, his face betraying the exhaustion he fought to hide from his voice.

"You usually have a spare whiskey..."

"Aye, normally 'twould be so," Bullet began. "During the ambush earlier this day, when I lost the bags that contain my keys, I also lost my spare whiskey."

"Those blasphemous heretics..." Tyfis said, the first words he had uttered in hours, which was not abnormal for him.

"Aye, and my extra clothes, my coin, my pipe, my spare tinker's tools..."

Sighing deeply, I gave into the day's anger, kicking the wheels of the wagon aggressively to free the clinging muck and leaves.

"I would settle for a smoke if the wind were not so unpredictable," Kiyoko said. "Yet we cannot always obtain what we wish. Instead of feeling bogged down from the day, we should focus on what luxuries lie ahead for us at camp."

"Aye, as to force us to ignore our remaining misery," I said with a final boot to the front wheel.

"Everett," Kiyoko warned with gentle sternness. "Your temper..."

"Wash it down the river," I said with a cleansing breath. "I am back in control now."

Gradually, the river sloped to the southwest, the origin of the river high in the Southern Mountains. Snake River, formed by many streams and tributaries, would eventually form the Luna Sea. Following the river, we drifted southwest, crossing through a thicket of trees as we passed into a tranquil meadow. On a hot summer's night, fireflies and lightning bugs would paint the sky to the tune of chirping crickets. Old Woodroe would soon approach in nearly a quarter league, the Witching Hour nearly upon us as we pressed towards the other side of the clearing.

"I dare say I shall sleep like a baby when the time finally comes," Bullet said with a laugh, attempting to lift our spirits even as his steps began to drag.

"I fear I shall sleep miserably all the same," I said with a sigh, for my insomnia never seemed to allow me a full night's rest, no matter how much energy I had exerted. My condition developed after the loss of my father four years prior, and now I was unable to allow myself proper rest as I did not wish to relive my life with him.

"I am envious of your insomnia at this moment," Bullet said with a yawn. "For there are still many hours ahead of us before we are certain of sleep."

"We could find you some ginseng from the Rose Lily..." Kiyoko suggested. "Even I shall admit, I am struggling to keep my eyes open and I have spent many a night occupying a sleepless Everett."

"That you have," I said, remembering those nights fondly as I met his eyes with a smile.

"I appreciate the offer," Bullet said. "Though I don't believe the ginseng will be necessary."

"As you wish," Kiyoko said, hunkering down and pushing the wagons as we continued forward.

The infrastructure surrounding Old Woodroe formed a path beneath our boots, the mud changing to a flat and smooth road made slick from the rain. Releasing the wagons, I followed closely behind them, standing at my full height to stretch my arms and back after having been hunched for so long. The path followed the river, keeping us parallel to Snake River yet diverting our direction from that of true south. The Witching Hour fell upon us with gusts of cold wind, the rain having left us, though the wind remained relentless.

Far through the trees, the portcullis to Old Woodroe was bright with hanging lanterns, and the gates lifted to lure visitors to the partially deserted town. Broken music and shrill laughter were carried on the wind, the few townsfolk partaking in the Festess despite the quiet that normally filled the village streets at night. The town thrummed with a low moan, emanating phantom grey energy from the gates. Shadows spilled from the portcullis, gathering along the riverbank as the running waters raced before them, blocking their path.

An unsettled feeling floated through me, churning my stomach. Exhaling deeply, I reached my energy towards Kiyoko once more, grateful when he lowered his defenses and allowed me to enter his mind.

"Kiyoko," I glanced towards him sneakily, noticing him walking behind the wagons on my left. "It is the witching hour... I fear it is unwise to enter the village at night... You know the legends."

"Aye..." He said with a nod. "Fear not the phantoms of the sick and lost.... I shall protect you."

"I have no doubt," I said with a gentle smile. "Though the prospect worries me all the same..."

"All shall be well, Everett," Kiyoko soothed. "It is a necessary risk, and I worry more for the incompletion of Knomucca's Ascension than I do over troubled spirits."

"When did you become so comfortable with the dead?" I asked suspiciously.

"Since the loss of my Paedie," he said, avoiding my gaze. "Let us not worry until we must."

Kiyoko closed his mind to me, raising his defenses with a gentle push. Tyfis and Bullet lumbered along beside us, a comfortable silence covering our company like a familiar blanket. The wagons creaked as the wood settled with the shift in temperature, the noise echoing across the wind and the cover of sweeping pine trees.

"When would we like to halt the troops?" Kiyoko asked, turning to face me as he finally broke the silence.

"I suppose we can this moment," I said, stretching one final time while dreading the inevitable climb back into Truff's saddle.

"Excellent," Kiyoko said, placing his thumb and forefinger in his mouth before whistling a command to halt.

"Everett, Kiyoko..." Bullet turned suspiciously towards us, using our names to convey his emphasis. "Could I have a word?"

"Of course, you can, Chief," I said, dismissing Tyfis with a salute.

"I would like to accompany you to the Rose Lily."

"Perhaps you ought to stay with the troops and rest," Kiyoko suggested.

"Nay, I helped Hazel build the wagon for Knomucca's potion elements and I may recognize some of them if I see them in the apothecary," Bullet began with a proud smile.

"Your face is slack with exhaustion," Kiyoko said. "You could meditate for a spare moment while Everett and I collect a small band to set along with us..."

"I am certainly dead on my feet," Bullet said. "Though I can manage a little while longer. And perhaps we ought to request Hazel and Kyreese to attend as well. Hazel is obviously knowledgable in regards to the Ascension, and Kye is in charge of the convey and may remember something."

"Very well," I said, thinking it may be wise to keep the Priestess close.

Whistling thrice, I summoned Kye and Hazel to the back of the wagons, conveying my final command that the troops could freely relax. Partaking in Kiyoko's spliff, we waited until they approached, Hazel appearing annoyed as she witnessed the lot of us smoking.

"Oi, what is all this about," Hazel asked, crossing her arms. Kye rounded the wagons to Kiyoko's left with Truff and Ballara in hand.

"We need to venture to the Rose Lily," I began once we had become reunited with our horses. "Knomucca's potion elements need replacing, and the Rose Lily may possess something she requires for her recipe."

"Has she divulged any elements she wishes us to procure for The Elixir of Life?" Hazel asked, her eyes far too eager as she searched my face.

"Not as of yet," Kiyoko said, his aura fractured into sharp yellow spikes. "We were hoping you and Bullet might remember what you preserved for her within the wagons. We could retrieve some of her previously chosen elements in an attempt to recreate her previous draught... otherwise I fear we shall simply have to improvise..."

"Aye, creating the prescribed recipe..." Hazel's words were muttered beneath her breath, her eyes clouded as a shadow flooded across them. The shadow bled from her eyes into her aura, darkening the swirling pool of energy around her. "Reckon we could obtain the elements to brew the approved draught..."

"Indeed," Kiyoko said slowly, his aura hardening against Hazel's darkness.

"Aye... I best go with you," Hazel said.

"Delightful... come along then," Kiyoko said as he patted his horse. "We must waste as little time as possible."

"Aye... If we must," Bullet said with another yawn.

I chuckled hardily as I clapped Bullet on the shoulder before mounting Truff. Guiding my horse by the reigns, I followed Kiyoko to the left of the convoy, finding the ranks dismantled and disassembled in the cover of the trees. Whistling softly, they encircled around us, standing at attention as I began to speak.

"Soldiers, you have earned a short rest whilst we venture into Old Woodroe to replenish the lost supplies. You may feel inclined to do as you wish... though again I must ask you refrain from sparring. Tyfis will oversee the watch. Have I made myself clear?"

"Aye," replied the Guard, signaling in salutes as I turned Truff towards the village.

"Excellent..." I said with a nod, sighing briefly as I wished I could also relax. "Rest well and rejuvenate."

The company moved in behind me as we formed the ranks. Truff and I stood alone at the front, noticing as the trotting of Kiyoko's horse fell in place behind me. Hazel stood beside him, waiting impatiently in her saddle. Bullet and Kye made up the back of the ranks, the five of us turning on the road and moving towards the portcullis.

The smooth stone road was loud beneath the hooves of our horses, the noise pleasantly welcome in the quiet of the night. The air swirled heavily around us, the energy suffocating as the shadows grew. My hands tightened around Truff's reigns as the urge to gallop away from Old Woodroe filled my spirits.

Near the portcullis, the trees were laced with orange candles, casting shadows into disorienting patterns across the ground. A warm tingle floated across the back of my head, accompanied by the bitter scent of mugwort. A distant knocking shook my aura, the knowledge Kiyoko wished to enter my mind, filling my senses.

"I wish to speak with you before we enter the city," Kiyoko whispered through me, his words interlaced with the distant tune of the iron strings. "Would you be willing to stop for a moment?"

"Certainly," I said, closing my mind against him with a gentle push. Turning towards the ranks, I spoke aloud. "I need to speak briefly to the general... please wait for us outside the gates."

Hazel rolled her eyes as she passed, her white horse glowing through the darkness as she rode from my left. I watched as she moved steadily, seemingly unabashed by the gloom of our surroundings. Kye and Bullet regarded us curiously as they trotted toward the portcullis. Kiyoko approached me, stopping our horses closely together. His leg pressed against my own, his warmth a comfort despite the shadows.

"I wish to gift you with something important before we enter Old Woodroe," Kiyoko began, speaking softly so as not to be overheard. He reached into the pocket of his kimono, producing an inky black stone.

"What treasure is this?" I asked, searching his face.

"When I was a young lad, my mother worked hard to protect me, and teach me how to control my gifts... she gave me a piece of black schorl to help me learn to transmute energy, protect myself, absorb auras, and keep centered."

"How wise of her," I said, regarding the stone in his hand.

"How wise, indeed," he uttered softly.

He paused for a moment, hanging his head and fidgeting with the stone between his fingers. He lifted his hand with hesitation. "I- I want you to have it..." His voice broke subtly. His eyes were soft with a vulnerability and tenderness I had not seen before.

I hesitated, holding his gaze.

"You have so few possessions remaining from your homeland," I interjected. "Your kimono and your smoking sack... I cannot claim this piece of you."

"You have already claimed the most important piece of me," he said gently, grasping my hand and placing it over his chest. "I promised I would protect you... and I am honoring my word."

"Kiyoko, I-"

"Please, Everett, take the stone... I need for you to have it... I need for you to stay safe...."

I felt the beat of his heart quicken beneath my touch. His delicate fingers clasped around my hand, the warmth traveling across my skin. Gently turning my hand over, he released the heavy stone, the large, hard gem fitting perfectly against my palm. Shining vertical lines cut across the piece of schorl, the dark, opaque rock blocking out the light through its center.

"Thank you, Kiyoko," I said, leaning in my saddle to close the gap between us.

"Oi, are you two just about finished?" Hazel interrupted before our lips could touch.

"Aye, quench your iron," Kiyoko replied over the wind. "Come along then, Everett. This schorl shall shield you from any malevolent spirits that wish to harm you."

"I cannot thank you enough," I said sincerely, placing the stone in my cloak and following behind him as he kicked Bellara to a trot.

Ducking through the raised portcullis, we entered Old Woodroe. The earlier storm had freed the trees, pillars, and benches of their Festess décor. Wreaths, sunflowers, and smashed squash lanterns were scattered across the ground. Shredded bouquets littered the puddles in the streets, yet the immense pumpkins that had been carved at the entrance to the town remained bright with yellow light.

Following the main road, we slowed our horses to a walk, treading carefully across the debris from the storm. Music and laughter flooded through the closed shutters, the doors closed to keep the warmth in and the shadows out. The wind slammed against loose doors and empty merchant's carts, the howling gusts adding an element of eeriness I strongly disliked. I was thankful for the heat of Truff beneath my body, yet the weight of my heavy, drenched cloak and fatigue caused me to wish to be done with this night.

The melodic grinding of iron strings floated on the breeze, the whistling and howling of the wind cutting through the darkness. A loud thwack of a door slamming shut to our right caused us to jump. The wood creaked and groaned as if hordes of dying were crying out in pain, begging for us to help. The sound of heavy footsteps rustling the leaves along the path drew my attention to the left. I strained to look through the darkness for who was there, but no one was visible. As if sensing my unease, Truff whined and pulled back against my commands. Following his gaze, I saw a figure pass through the trees, a long cloak flapping in the wind as he moved.

"Oi!" I called out, wrangling Truff to move forward.

I paused by the tree line, looking from left to right, but the figure had disappeared. For a moment, I questioned if what I had seen even existed. As I moved to return to the group, a set of cerated grooves in the tree caught my eye; three long, thin scratches resembling the talons of a heron ran along the bark of the tree.

"Is all well?" Kiyoko asked, approaching my position.

His sudden approach caused me to startle, which I tried to disguise as turning to face him. Taking a deep, steadying breath, I reached towards him with my energy, pushing against his defenses to enter his mind. Sensing my urgency, Kiyoko opened up to me, and I shared the image I had seen with him. A panicked expression flashed across Kiyoko's face before he once again willed his expression back to neutral. Closing his mind, he nodded as we both turned to rejoin the ranks.

I turned rightwards, leading the ranks down a small side street. Weaving across another central path within Old Woodroe, I began to see the Rose Lily taking shape through the darkened sky. The apothecary stood immense and mighty, stretching between multiple streets and alleyways. Smoke lulled lazily from the chimney, indicating with the scent of pine there was an occupant within. A small, square stockade stood empty across from the apothecary, providing the perfect place for us to leave our horses.

Kicking Truff, we leaped over the wooden fence, him landing within the palisades. Sliding from the saddle, I approached the gate, opening it wide to admit the ranks as they followed through. After Bullet and Kye crested the threshold, I closed the gate, standing just beyond it as my company began to dismount. Kiyoko left the pen first, followed by Bullet and Hazel. Kye took an additional moment with Lady Moonbeam as she had just recently pulled her from the rigging of the carts.

"Is everybody ready?" I asked as Kye slipped through the gate, signaling her apology in a salute and standing at my left.

"Aye, reckon we're ready," Bullet said, following Hazel's nod and Kiyoko's smile of agreement.

Assuming the ranks, we walked towards the door, crunching across the wet gravel path leading away from the stockade. Long oval puddles splashed beneath our boots, the water drenching the bottoms of our cloaks. Large pumpkins carved in the shapes of wide dragon mouths and jagged human skulls cast bright light across the ground. Petrichor was masked with the smell of cinnamon, wafting heavily from the brightly lit lanterns.

"Check the door," Kiyoko whispered through me, spreading warmth down my spine as I relaxed into his energy.

Reaching out a hand, I pushed against the door, discovering it to be unlatched and slightly ajar.

"It appears to be open," I turned over my shoulder, watching as the shadows created by the lanterns danced across Hazel's cheeks. Shifting my energies, I tugged against Kiyoko's defenses, whispering through him secretly as I continued to give instructions. "Perhaps you should reach out, see if you can tell what might be inside."

"I have done so already," Kiyoko replied. "All I can tell is they are asleep."

"Perhaps when we enter, we should announce ourselves," I suggested.

"I suppose that is wise," Kiyoko said. "I am fine taking lead, should that satisfy you, Commander."

"It does so greatly," I said, my body stirring from his offer to protect my front.

"Reckon we ought not to stumble in blindly," Hazel said, fishing through her robes and finding a small bundle of candlesticks. "Should we find the lanterns extinguished within, we shall need some light to find our way."

"Clever," Kiyoko said, watching as Hazel used the lanterns adorning the threshold to light the wicks.

"One for all," Hazel said as she placed a candle in each of our hands.

Stepping forward, Kiyoko reached towards the door, suddenly swearing loudly as he stumbled backward. A flash of blue light was accompanied by a piercing pop, the noise sending a ringing through my ears as I rubbed my head to clear it.

"What in the Seven Hells was that?" Kye asked in shock.

"The door is warded," Kiyoko gasped through me. "The talismans must think I'm a demon."

"Go inside, Kiyoko," Hazel said in a tone that was becoming much too familiar for my liking.

"Perhaps you ought to lead us... being that you are an Alchemist," Kiyoko said to Hazel. My anger towards her rose as she turned and avoided his eyes.

"Kyreese," I said with a gentle sigh. "Do us a kindness and lower one of these lanterns, would you?"

"Aye, Commander," said Kye, uncurling her braid from under her hat and shaking it loose.

Moving sideways, we fanned from Kye's radius, allowing her space to snap her braid like a whip. Curling her plait around the pumpkin, Kye gently lifted the lantern upwards, moving it from the hook beside the door frame and lowering it gently to the ground.

"Excellent," I said, saluting my thanks and rewarding her with a smile. "General, try thine luck again."

"Very well," Kiyoko said, reaching out a hand and slowly stepping forward.

The door to the Rose Lily fell open, swinging gently as Kiyoko moved inside. Following closely, I allowed Hazel to pass, slipping through the threshold between her and Kye as Bullet brought up the rear. Holding aloft the candles, we were surprised to find the inside illuminated as Kiyoko began to speak.

"Oi! Is anybody home? ... Greetings... Merry Meet and Happy Festess... Can anybody hear me? ... This is General Kiyoko of the Gods' Guard... We have come on behalf of Knomucca and need to speak to whomever is in charge here..."

A loud metallic bang came from the rooms in the back, with the resonance of a metal tin or tray falling to the floor. Grunting and muffled noise stirred from behind the thick granite counter, our shadows growing and sharpening as a second wave of lanterns was suddenly illuminated.

"Show yourself," Kiyoko demanded.

A disheveled man with untamed, greying hair peered from beyond the doorframe behind the counter before gingerly stepping forward. In his hand, he held a small vial of effervescing blue-tinted liquid. His green Alchemist robes appeared smooth and free of wrinkles, and his energy was bright and alert for someone awake in the wee hours.

"I was spectin' to be free of visitors... ain't it after the Witchin' Hour and nobody had come by all night."

"Greetings, kind sir," I said as I stepped forward. Opening my cloak, I flashed the emblem of Morriraen. The silver sword that divided the crest indicated that I was Commander.

The man's eyes widened, his face immediately fighting to pretend he hadn't betrayed his worry.

"I'm closed 'till sunrise," the Alchemist said, his eyes darting leftward as he slowly moved from the doorframe.

"I wish we could respect your limitations," I sympathized. "Though I am afraid we are in need of your apothecary-"

"I can't serve ya 'till sunrise..."

"We shall only be a moment," I said.

"I'm not wantin' any trouble," the man behind the counter said, his eyes flickering to the left once more as he again moved forward.

"Nor do we," I said, closing my cloak and lowering my hood. My black woolen cap rested snugly over my ears, my face exposed in the light of the lanterns as I met his face with a smile.

"Aya laddie? Then I'd suggest ya come back 'round sunrise."

"We will only take a moment to look around," I repeated, glancing towards Kiyoko, who was holding the hilt of his sword inconspicuously. "If we cannot find what it is we are searching for, then we shall take our leave-"

"Everett, perhaps I should handle this," Hazel interrupted, stepping from beside me and approaching the counter.

"Hazel?" The man's eyes widened, the horror impossible to disguise, as his body began to shake.

"Greetings, Duke," her shrill voice rang.

"Hazel... ya shouldn't be here," Duke said as he glowered.

"And where, might I ask... should I be?"

Duke opened his mouth to respond but closed it again without speaking.

"Hazel, how did you come to know this man?" Kiyoko asked, shifting his weight to stabilize his footing. His eyes changed, and I knew he was trying to read the energy in the room. His face contorted subtly in pain as he failed.

"There are other wards and amulets," Kiyoko whispered through me. My eyes never left Hazel as I accepted his words.

"Alchemy is a niche yet strong discipline," Hazel began. "A lifelong practice that can never be abandoned once begun. My roots are far from shallow... I've been practicing for many years and as a Priestess my studies have broadened me. One collects masters to help sharpen the mind and Duke was once one of those to me."

"Aye, the Alchemist's Guild is a small lot... we look out for each other," Bullet said suddenly from behind me, reminding me that I often forgot that he, too, was an Artificer and a novice Alchemist.

"What are ya lookin' for?" Duke asked, his eyes darting left once more as his hands continued to shake.

"Where's Terra?" Hazel asked suddenly, keeping her voice calm, though I noticed the change in her energy.

"Aye... T-Terra..." Duke quivered, nearly dropping the vial as his hand shook.

"Aye, your wife..." Hazel continued speaking as she moved slowly towards the right. "Was she called to perform a ritual for the Festess in another city? The pair of you are rarely ever separated... especially at your age. Yet when opportunity beckons... I myself had been invited to lead a ritual in Bellview, yet I had previous obligations..."

"Terra... aye, Terra... she must be asleep."

"We would love to see her," Hazel said, trying to adjust her line of sight through the doorframe in which Duke had emerged.

"Ya know, I'd rather ya return 'round sunrise... I dinnae want any trouble..."

"Duke, if you simply allow us a moment to find what we require..."

Suddenly, the door fell open behind us, followed by the clanking of iron. I pivoted to my right so that Kiyoko could be watching my back. A large band of rebels began to funnel through the threshold. At the rear, a man cloaked in scarlet pushed his way through to the front of the company.

"Duke, you miserable old man... Where's my tonic?"

The voice was charming and melodic, the familiar blue eyes churning like the sea as mischief sparkled through them.

"Commander Rosewood... what an unpleasant surprise."

"Samarin," I said stiffly, hearing the slide of iron behind me as Kiyoko adjusted his sword. "'Tis interesting to see you here... I assumed you would be enjoying the luxuries of Morriraen as you relaxed after the Merchants Banquet."

"My men are most certainly enjoying Morriraen and it's luxuries," Samarin said, the lanterns casting a menacing shadow across his face. "Duke, where is my tonic?"

"I did what ya said, now where's Terra..." Duke said, his voice shaking as much as his hand as he held up the vial in the light.

"Weez, bring in the wench..." Samarin laughed; the infectious amusement in his mirth made my skin crawl.

The side entrance to my right swung open, pulling in a sharp gust of wind to rustle the herbs and other ingredients on the shelves. An unmoving body was tossed carelessly through the threshold, falling into a heap on the floor. The body had been bound with woody, long-stemmed vines, sprouting pairs of velvety tentacles. Black lines spidered across the victim's skin where the tentacles dug deep. Her pallor was gray and muted as the vines fed on her life force, slowly bleeding her dry.

"Damn Spider Vines," Kiyoko whispered in horror, drawing his sword and glaring in hatred towards Samarin. He subtly shifted his stance back away from the vines, knowing how fatal they could be for someone of his nature.

"There's your pitiful wife," Samarin said satisfactorily. "I'll be collecting my tonic now..."

"Duke, do not give it to him," I interjected, watching Samarin as he avoided the direct light of the lanterns. His face was swollen, large red bite marks marred his cheek, and yellow and brown puss coated the edge of his skin.

"It would appear the Merchants Banquet was quite eventful..." I said boldly. "Or did you earn that bite from a wolf on your way here?"

"I beg your pardon?" Samarin asked defiantly.

"Your face," I said with a laugh. "If I did not know any better I would say my dear friend Frek had a bit of a nibble..."

"Snap your trap..." Samarin growled, the men around him simultaneously drawing their blades.

"You shall need all the luck from the stars you can muster," I laughed. "I am not certain what horseshit you think a tonic will fix... far as we know there is no cure to prevent the transition and there is a full moon in two nights' time."

"We will find the cure," Samarin said, pointing his blade toward me as he began to circle around the doorway. "Perhaps I should take me an Alchemist along with my tonic.... Being there are four in this room alone, it shouldn't be that hard to procure one."

"Piss off," I said, drawing one of the daggers from my belt as the room was too crowded for my hammer.

Chaos erupted in a swirl around me as the rebels rushed towards us. Kiyoko disappeared behind the shelves on my left, putting space between us to fight and keep our distance from the Spider Vines. The gleaming iron reflected the light of the lanterns as I thrust my blade forward, sticking the gut of the first rebel I could reach. Pivoting his body, I flung him from my knife, slamming him against another pair of rebels beside me.

Ducking around the displays, I forced my way towards the counter, desperately desiring to obtain the tonic Samarin had so badly wanted. Duke's eyes were wide in horror as he stared bewildered at his wife, never seeing the rebel from behind the doorframe with an arrow aimed at his head.

"Duke-"

The arrow through his head ripped the words from my throat. His body slackened towards the floor as I fought to react. Sprinting forward, I lunged towards the counter, my head smashing against the fist of the assassin who leaped to retrieve the tonic. Pain rang through my ears as I stumbled backward, the grip on my knife tightening from fear as I shook my head to clear it. Leaping from the counter, the assassin rolled to the floor, weaving through the aisles as he darted towards Samarin and the door.

"Stop them!" I shouted, scrambling past Terra on the floor as I attempted to chase after them.

Kye swung her hair fiercely, snapping it sharply against the rebels as she fought to clear a path. Barreling towards the door, I was tackled from the side, careening against a rack of hanging metal tools and long, sharp pokers. As I fell into the rack, I slammed the face of the rebel on my right into a hanging cast iron cauldron. Twisting leftwards, I spun the opposite rebel over my shoulder, throwing his body into the ground. Regaining my footing, I pushed against the rack, sending it crashing down on top of them. Kye's hair whipped across the room once more, knocking the tonic loose from Samarin's companion and sending it flying. Running forward, I leaped into the air, catching the vial firmly in my hands as I tumbled over a short wooden shelf.

"Get me that vial," Samarin hissed.

A fresh wave of adrenaline coursed through me as I crawled on my hands and knees. Sudden swearing and the clanking of iron sounded high above my head, my instincts forcing me to roll as I toppled beneath another rack of tools. Working quickly, I forced the tonic into my smoking sack, using the cover of the rack to adjust my grip on my blade. Rebels hurtled towards me with ravenous eyes as I calculated my attack.

"Shite," I whispered as I rolled from behind the rack, kicking it forward to crush the oncoming rebels. Glancing leftwards, I was gifted with a clear aisle to the door. As I ran towards the threshold, Samarin stepped in my path. I swung my knife as he approached, though my advances were blocked by his sword as he countered me. Dropping my blade, I risked a bold maneuver, seizing the elbow of his sword arm and easily disarming him. My foot hooked around his leg, throwing him off balance, as I wrenched his arm behind his back. I held him tightly against my body as I gripped his throat.

"Wait..." Samarin rasped as I considered snapping his neck.

"Give me one reason why I should not rip your head from your body."

"If you kill me now, you'll never find Syler..."

"What in the Seven Hells are you talking about?"

"Everett!" Kiyoko's voice came from my right.

Tightening my grip, I squeezed against Samarin's throat; his face flushed red as a fresh wave of blood pooled in the bite upon his cheek.

"Answer me!"

A sudden pain to the back of my head sent me reeling. Releasing Samarin, I stumbled as I fell to the floor. My ears rang as my awareness blurred, the scuffling of boots and screams cutting through the din like a blade being sharpened by a whetstone.

"Oi! Everett!" Kiyoko's voice was panicked. "They're getting away!"

Desperately, I fought to move, finding my body pinned beneath a heavy set of metal shelves. Arching my back, I shoved myself upwards, grunting loudly as I heaved the display from my back. It fell to the floor with an immense clang, freeing me to clamber to my knees as I twisted towards the threshold. The thick wooden door swung ajar, and the freezing wind of the night beyond blew through and smashed hard against my face.

Scrambling forward, I ran towards the door, hurling through it as I chased after Samarin. My cloak billowed behind me as I ran through the streets, my arms pumping fiercely as I fought to match his stride. The distance he gained only widened, his course complex as he wove through alleyways and streets.

"Samarin! Stop your running!"

Samarin only ignored me, running faster through a narrow side street as he led us north. Realizing then his plan to escape, I summoned my final strength, trying in vain to catch him as we ran through the cemetery that bordered Old Woodroe. In the distance, I watched as Samarin mounted a horse alongside a waiting companion.

"Pissant," I swore furiously, watching in anger as Samarin took the reins.

"Coward! Oi! Coward!"

Samarin kicked his horse, bursting forward in a gallop away into the trees.

"Burn in the Seven Rings, Samarin! BURN IN THE SEVEN RINGS!!"

IX

KNOMUCCA

Horrifying, broken images began flooding through my mind. Black veins spread across the flesh of a demonic goddess with an immense pair of shadow-sculpted wings. Her thin, bony hands with long fingers extending into claws reached out towards me. Mummified bats and corpses met their demise from those hands; the screams and shrieks from their decaying bodies echoed through my awareness. Scorching, roaring heat coursed through my chest and hands, pulsing in deafening pain as I swirled through the fire... fire... fire...

Gasping sharply, my eyes burst open, my lungs burning painfully as I began to cough intensely. Raising a hand, I was pleased to find it free of its gauntlet, my flesh the familiar dark shadow I recognized as myself in the Underworld. Clearing my throat, I pushed myself to my elbows, shielding my eyes from the sudden light that spiraled in from above.

"What in the Seven Hells?" I whispered, resting my head against the floor as I took a cleansing breath.

Pushing my energy outwards, I felt towards my physical body, reeling sideways suddenly as a wave of pain washed over me. Swearing in annoyance, I began again, deepening my breathing and leaning into the pain as I attempted to return to my body. The connection had been temporarily closed from the physical world, abyssal darkness blurring into my vision as I fought to center my energy.

"My body is unconscious," I said aloud, sighing in relief as I relaxed. "Thank the Gods."

Resting momentarily, I allowed myself to regain my composure, meditating briefly as I oriented to the Underworld. The additional energy needed to become corporeal here in Heimaaila required a great deal of discipline for me to manifest. Inhaling strength, I allowed myself to become rejuvenated, feeling my spirits lighten as I slowly opened my eyes once more. Firelight around me pierced and burned, my vision painfully stabilizing as I rose to a seat. I noticed the familiar scent of cherry logs burning in the hearth as I became fully aware of my surroundings.

My chambers within the Underworld's castle, Morrireaea, sharpened into focus. The similarities between it and its sister castle in Crossfire, Morriraen, always provided me comfort. Morriraen had been created as a place for all Ascension Prospects to live, access The Creator's resources, and, when needed, compete. The God's Trials created a bond between the two castles that would link them forever.

Despite the intricate construction of the castle, it was now a shadow of its former glory. To connect it to the land, The Gods built the castle using clay, preserved fruit, and stone from all across the continent. The structure was enhanced with obsidian from island volcanos and decorated with glass made from the sands of the beaches, then bound together with magic. All elements within the castle's center exist in harmony: the seas to the east, volcanos to the west, mountains to the south, and dragon winds to the north.

Since the time when Anteyus dwelled in Morriraen, it had been destroyed and rebuilt over half a dozen times. When Anteyus fell From Grace, Crossfire's energy became unbalanced. The shift in energy resulted in the destruction of the castle, creating a psychic imprint in Heimaaila, forming the twin castle Morrireaea. Despite the many similarities, Morrireaea is sick and twisted at its core. The air that lingers in it is haunted by the dead and is not a place for the timid and faint. Nor is it kind to those who are not welcome within its halls.

Taking a final breath, I rose slowly to a stand within my alternate chambers to face my altar, which loomed with a thick presence. Hundreds of candles were lit amongst the wrought iron latticework, casting delicate dancing shadows mesmerizingly across the stone. Another five-headed, wooden-chiseled hydra was the altar's main centerpiece; each pair of eyes within the serpentine skulls was carved from a different precious gemstone. The five heads were linked to each one of my five altars, allowing me to see the rooms they occupied by looking through the hydra's eyes. Incense burned from the inner walls of the hydra, smoke pouring forth from their open mouths as the scent plumed into the room.

An emerald-hilted dagger accented the jewel-encrusted border in the front right corner of the altar. Jars containing active spells, fueled by my energy to manifest specified outcomes, were tucked neatly across the back of the altar. Spells of protection, prosperity, and foresight were abundant, encased in ornate vases of square glass stuffed with lavender, basil, labradorite, and cinnamon.

Inhaling deeply, I began to cross the room, focusing on the sweet smell of the burning cherry logs. Moving with stable footing, I slowly approached my altar, reaching the smooth octagonal stone and placing my hands firmly upon it. Drawing a breath, I could feel my strength straining to return, pouring like molasses over bread. Focusing on the hydra, I stared into the emerald green eyes of the center skull as I moved my energy into the statue.

I relaxed and released a deep breath, leaning into the shift in spirit as I began to view the overworld. The emerald eyes of the dragon connected to the altar in my chambers at home in Morriraen. I expected to be welcomed with the familiar sight of my bookshelves, a burning fireplace, and an invitingly warm bed. My eyes strained, struggling to take in my chambers; the overwhelming presence of Spider Vines blinded my senses from the world beyond.

What in the Seven Hells...

A sudden, intense wave of sadness washed over me as I felt the unexpected pull of Syler's energy. Releasing my altar, I stumbled backward, breathing deeply as I was forced to clear my mind. A solid knock came from the chamber door as if containing the deep sound of a grandfather clock. Annoyance prickled across my palms as my concentration wavered.

"You may enter," I called.

The elaborately carved door fell open, spilling light from the hall beyond into the darkest corners of the rooms. A broken spirit with a crooked neck appeared beyond the threshold, holding his lopsided head in his slender and narrow hands.

"Greetings, Rejj," I said, towering over the frame of a lad who had barely come of age before death. Rejj possessed a Name Day one month prior to my own, the pair of us celebrating during his life with wine and exchanging literature before things became different.

"Good evening, Your Worship," Rejj's voice rasped, the pain involved in uttering a spoken word evident through the straining of the muscles in his neck.

"To what do I owe the pleasure?" I asked, fighting to camouflage the severity of the grating his rasping had against my ears.

"I could ask of you the same," Rejj began. "I was not expecting to see you for nearly a day or longer yet the sounding of the Knell Bell in the library announced your arrival."

"Aye," I said, thinking carefully of what to say rather than divulge the truth of the matter. "I possessed a few spare moments and decided to tend to some business."

"Very well," Rejj stood at attention. "According to my calculations, it is nearly the hour of the Wolf. Is all well? I noticed you had to summon Cypress... The Knell Bell was quite disturbed earlier this day with spirits being allowed to cross over..."

"Aye, we ran into some trouble at Morriraen," I said. "Do your records indicate anyone who did not return?"

"Nay, all appear to be present and accounted for... thankfully it seems as though nobody hath deserted."

"Excellent," I sighed, smiling with genuine relief.

"Aye... of course I wished I could have been more prepared in welcoming the returning spirits home to Heimaaila once their services were no longer required, though I reckon all ended well."

"I am pleased to hear that." I said, suddenly exhausted. I collapsed into a chair at the nearby table.

"Were you successful in attaining your Angelfish eye?" Rejj asked as he sat across from me.

"Nay. My ship was lost to the waves. It was storming at home moments ago," I said somberly. "Did the bell toll for Captain Southwell?"

"Nay. Only for those who left during Cypress." Relief washed through me. "Knomucca, are you well?"

"How I wish times were simpler and we were home for the festess. You should be there to see it, curled in your favorite chair with your copy of Tales from Brook Road instead of being forced to muddle through this madness."

"I don't disagree," Rejj said, sighing as he began to adjust the pile of parchments and books in front of him. "Do you still possess my copy in Morriraen's library?"

"It is in my personal collection," I said, smiling as I recalled the worn, green leather-bound book falling apart from a spine broken with use. "I keep meaning to repair it... though I cannot bring myself to do so."

"That is kind of you to admit," Rejj rasped, his eyes brightening with a blue glimmer. "Destroyed that book I did, writing in the margins, circling my favorite lines, folding the corners of pages... You wouldn't guess what I miss the most about it..."

"I would love to know, if you wish to tell me," I soothed, feeling anger and guilt at myself for the role I played in the unfair circumstances that led him to be in Heimaaila.

"The smell... when it lingered when you rifled through the pages... Gods damn, nothing smells better than the musky, sweet scent of an old book."

His words saddened me, for there were few things I held in higher regard than the sensation he had just described.

"You shall one day hold your beloved Tales from Brook Road once more in your hands... regaling yourself with his handsome, debonair charm. You shall read as he ventures across the realms, stealing from the noble to enable those whom are lacking. You shall dream of his adventures and sword fights, laughing against the power hungry who never cease squabbling with the nightmare of Heimaaila far behind you in a past life."

"Being reborn... it sounds too wonderful to be a guarantee."

"As long as I can Ascend, I promise you will be reborn, Rejj. I know we have discussed all this before... though I want to repay you for trapping your soul into the Seven Rings."

"You repaid me with my rescue," Rejj croaked, his aura flashing with the deep grey of anger lingering far beneath the surface.

"You should have never been placed in the position of needing my rescue."

"I've told you, I don't blame you for anything, Knomucca. The Power was new to you and I had just murdered your mother..."

"Aye... Though you killed my mother so that burden would not be upon me... that was quite selfless, and all you received was a haul to the gallows and three years in the Seven Rings."

"You weren't meant to take her life," Rejj rasped. "I was the one who overheard her in the library... The Creator demanded she die in order to relinquish The Power to you, even though it wasn't a part of whatever previous bargain the pair of them had struck..."

"Watch yourself, Rejj," I said gently. "I have not yet freshened the wards around my chambers, one can never be certain of who might be listening."

"It is what I heard... your mother in tears because He was not respecting His end to a bargain and then would take her soul," Rejj said, ignoring my desire for caution. He shook his head, the muscles in his neck straining and popping as it rolled to the side. "The Creator wanted your mother dead, and he wished for it to be done at your hand."

Rising suddenly, I quickly approached my brewing station. Obtaining patchouli incense, I lit them using the candles. Lifting the statue, I slid the incense inside a small wooden disk, placing the hydra atop the burning herbs to camouflage our sounds within the room. Returning to the table, I found my seat, regarding Rejj seriously.

"What compelled you to take my place?" I asked spontaneously.

"The way He was speaking to her, Knomucca... if you would have heard Him you would have understood how imperative it was He not get what He wanted."

"I partially understand," I admitted. "You lost trust in Him..."

"Aye," Rejj said, beginning to fidget slightly with the parchments on the table.

"Then why go through with it... why did you not fight to keep my mother alive instead of sending her here alongside yourself..."

"He had already made up His mind on the matter Knomucca... the dismissiveness and disregard He held in His voice... I knew He already saw her as a walking corpse.

"I'm not like you Knomucca... I have not the means to fight the Gods nor do I believe I hold true water against them. He wanted your mother dead, and had it not been by my hands on that day with the least amount of pain possible, then it would have been forced upon you... or done in a gruesome manner by a hired hand who could have done much worse."

Drawing a breath, I felt my spirits sadden. Rejj's words held a serious truth I had already contemplated thousands of times. "Truth be told, you did her a kindness... when Mum accepted The Power until I became of age, it rotted her from the inside. She was so ill by the end... her skeleton was separating from her body, and she was in perpetual pain. I often wonder if it was the Creator's punishment for her act of protective defiance."

"I had no idea," Rejj said.

"She hid her illness beneath luxurious fabrics and the remedies of Chatza and Hazel... Though I understood how poorly she was fairing, even more so now with my own soul decaying the way it is."

"Oi, everything is twisted," Rejj said.

"It is indeed," I said. Glancing downwards, I began to watch Rejj's hourglass, purple sand filling the bottom with the passing moments. "Rejj?"

"Knomucca?"

"I have never thanked you... for saving me from having to kill my mother. I am sorry I chose to put you to death; I should have never thought that was an acceptable course of action."

"It was the only course of action," Rejj rasped harshly as he met my eyes. "In the eyes of the public, I attempted to assassinate a Prospect... the penalty by law is death."

"Your arrow hit me by complete chance," I said. "It bounced from a sconce and ricocheted behind my ear... you were always an awful shot, the only bow you ever lifted was in the stories in your imagination."

"Brutal," Rejj laughed, the mirth painting his eyes with a yellow sparkle.

"Besides, you were aiming for my mother..."

"It seems as though we are finally to a place where we can find all this amusing," Rejj's aura shimmered mischievously. "Only took fifteen years... though I reckon we finally managed."

"Have you been able to find her?" I asked in anxious anticipation.

A silence fell between us, accompanied by the crackling of the cherry logs in the fireplace. The look on Rejj's face told me all that I needed to know. His expression softened as he shook his head. My breath caught in my throat as I fought not to show my disappointment.

Rejj turned his attention suddenly to the books and parchments at the table. "Knomucca, perhaps we should discuss the research you asked me to pursue..."

"Aye... Have you found reference in the records to any demon, aside from the succubus or incubus, who possesses a gift in manipulating intimate energy?"

"And you are certain The Creator wanted you to engage in this?"

"It is best I am prepared in all things," I said impulsively. "One never knows what knowledge of the realms He may ask before granting me the gift of His blood."

"I suppose that is wise," Rejj rasped, turning over the plain leather cover of the book to sift through the pages on which he had written. "There was little in the way of evidence... though I believe I have enough to paint a fairly convincing portrait."

"Please, enlighten me," I said with a smile, scanning my eyes down the parchment to decode the precise, looping characters of Rejj's manuscript.

"The word 'demon' made my research challenging... as you know the word comes from the Old Language, meaning 'one that has Fallen from Grace.'"

"Aye... it comes from the word demonagoria, the insult given to Anteyus after he betrayed The Power."

"Indeed... the term evolved from the journals of previous Death God Prospects, for several claimed to see his twisted and haunted soul screaming in the Void between the realms."

"Can you imagine... his appearance must have left quite an impression, for after their sightings the word became used to describe a monster of a terrifying nature..."

"I certainly can imagine... If my experience in the Seven Rings has taught me anything... it is terror knows no bounds."

Rejj took a long pause. Another wave of guilt slammed through me. I sighed as I attempted to refrain from dampening my spirits.

"Aye... reckon you were unable to find much on the subject then..."

"I said no such thing," his eyes flashed with pride. "There were a few instances of recorded magic where it is clear intimate energy was manipulated... though if you are searching for this gift in creatures akin to demons in the way we currently understand them, your options shall be more limited. However, if you are willing to broaden your mind..."

"Consider me curious," I said, rising from my seat to procure herbs and onion skins as I wished for a harmless task to perform while I listened.

"Well... vampires are first to come to mind..."

"Reckon that is logical," I said with a sigh, irritated that I had such oversight.

"Certainly... they feed upon vital life energies, often requiring physical contact with their victims. Though... 'tis worth noting that some can feed from the energy itself."

"Aye... suppose they can," I said, my mind briefly fleeting towards Kiyoko and his ability to absorb energy.

Rejj paused, releasing a bashful breath before speaking. "I can actually speak upon experience to the incredible sensation of a vampire bite when a feeding is consensual..."

"That promises to be an intriguing tale," I said with a soft smile. "However, perhaps one for another time."

Rejj flushed with a light blush. "Then, I'm afraid that is all they truly have to offer in terms of our research..."

"I suppose a small trickle is preferred over drought," I said with a sigh. "What other information have you gathered from the records?"

"The next topic I have to discuss is that of the Dreamweaver..."

"Aye, the Dreamweaver," I said, watching as Rejj turned to the back of the book. Spinning the volume towards me, Rejj pointed to the parchment upon the right, marking with a finger the outline of an alluring maiden wrapped in lace.

"The Dreamweaver, a maiden of folklore rumored to aid in restful sleep by sewing the eyes shut with thread."

I continued to read. "'To keep one's inner peace, thy shall be blinded to the evils of the world.'"

Rejj nodded his head with a heavy, rasping sigh. "She is said to spin webs of silk in the corners whilst you sleep to ward away bad dreams as they are caught in her traps."

"Legend says she is a fallen Prospect who failed to stay beyond the grave... even if she were to exist, she would not be the sort to manipulate intimate energy."

"Who is to say for certain?" Rejj continued. "Though, if she is to control our sleep, it is possible she could have influence over what intimacies are revealed in our dreams."

"I suppose that is true," I nodded thoughtfully. "Her talents may be worth remembering."

"You should know there is a ritual to summon her... should you ever want to test the limitations of your power after you Ascend."

"I shall keep that in mind," I said with a wink. "Sounds as though it could be interesting."

"Among the creatures who also use threads or webbing are the spiderellas. Half human and half spider creatures that reside here in Heimaaila. She feeds on the vital life energy of her victims caught in the webs she spins."

"Aye, spiderellas," I said contemplatively. "It was naive of me not to consider them."

"I initially would not have either, if not for a journal entry from a previous Prospect. She had an encounter with one, and regarded the experience of her depleting life force as... 'euphoric and terrifying.'"

My eyes trailed down the pages of Rejj's book, noticing the top of a strong, voluptuous woman with eight glossy legs entangled around her.

"They wrote 'she calls brave those in touch with their shadows... The huntress who waits to strike. The fates... The weavers of truth... The darkness in the night. Blissful is her bite, her pull enticing. Revealing what is unseen... In the self and in an hourglass turning. She is always weaving, and her spirit always yearning...'"

A shudder ran through me. Absently, I reached to the nape of my neck and ran my fingers along the spider that had been inked there. I remembered the thrilling and sharp bite of Everett's needle as he diligently worked, his breath hot against me. The intricate details complemented a spider's elaborate webbing and captured its grace and strength, displaying the discipline and control it required to keep a steady hand.

"Aye, they are rather inspiring creatures," I said in slight amusement. "I did have a thought. If we are broadening our scope, then I reckon we could discuss the Naiads..."

"Naiads? I don't see the connection."

"The Naiads are the ones believed to have caused the disappearances of thousands of souls, including that of Ozwal the Great." I declared. "I believe them to be psychic... it would explain how they are able to manipulate the minds of the sailors they imprison through their songs."

"I don't believe they are," Rejj shook his head as it lulled sideways. "There was this fable my parents used to tell whilst reading to the infants in the Warrior's Nursery... about a maiden lost at sea who turned partway to fish so she could find her way home."

"How charming," I said, absently fidgeting with my hands as it always felt strange to be free of my gauntlets for such a length of time as this.

"The fable ends with the lass finding a charming sailor and he grants her true love's kiss to free her of her binds as a fish."

"Being born of library apprentices has gifted you with stories even I have not yet had the pleasure of reading and I will admit I am envious."

"'Tis one of my favorite reads," Rejj's aura flashed grey with a mournful sigh.

"It seems like a tale worthwhile... though this fable doth not provide an absolution that Naiads are not persuading sailors to drown at sea."

"I suppose not... yet I am certain you yourself could recall a time when knowledge you gained through the books was not applicable. And therefore, when you tried to use it you planted seeds of doubt."

Pausing briefly, I leaned back in my seat, taking a breath as I attempted to recall any such situation. "I suppose there are the vampire wives tales... disclosing how mirrors lined with silver render a vampire unable to see its reflection as they have no soul to gaze upon."

"Aye, and through experimentation with Hazel the pair of you discovered that such tales are false." Rejj's aura sparkled with another thought, "perhaps other written information about our realms shall also be proven false, and the naiads will be proven innocent."

Rejj cleared his throat. "This talk of reading minds, moods, and auras and manipulating energies to use as their own reminds me of Seders and Sneaks."

My mind flashed to Kiyoko, the scent of Mugwort filling my senses.

"The reference is briefly addressed in the tome Unseen Creatures of Crossfire... as I do not have access to the literature at this time I cannot hope to quote it properly."

"I can bring you the volume the next time I project here," I said. "Though I have read the manuscript many times over... I cannot recall a moment within the text in which you speak."

"I reckon it's a story for when you return," Rejj took another sigh, settling deeply into his spirits. "I couldn't even attempt to recall the text in its actual word... it has nearly been two decades since I saw the book last."

"Yet the notion you remembered its exact location is quite impressive."

"Thank you kindly, Your Worship." The sudden change in formality abruptly centered my energy.

"I cannot thank you enough for your research," I said, referring to the hourglass, which was nearly full. The clock would turn over at sunrise, the bottom swinging fiercely as the hour would soon be falling upon us.

"It was my pleasure," Rejj sparkled in satisfaction. "I always enjoy the thrill of a good read."

"I know the feeling," I said, wishing I could be home in Morriraen with a glass of whiskey and a book about the cosmos. Suddenly, the room wavered as my spirit felt the need to return to my physical body. "I reckon I shall be entering my body again soon. Though, you mentioned hearing the Knell Bell, I am concerned for the fate of my crew."

"Crew? I thought you didn't want to involve Everett and the troops in obtaining your Angelfish."

"It was not them," I said, unable to deny the relief I felt, knowing they were safe.

"The Knell Bell only rang to announce your arrival, no other spirits crossed over during that time and I would certainly have recognized Everett."

"If the Bell only tolled for me then the others must have made it to safety."

"Let's hope so," Rejj said, turning to watch the hourglass, observing how the remainder of the purple grains spilled into the bottom. "When are you able to return to your body?"

"I am only unconscious, I could easily wake myself at any time."

"That is a relief," Rejj rasped with a smile.

The hourglass turned with the coming of dawn, flipping the newly filled pear-shaped bulb upwards to the top of its apex. A soft metallic chime began to play a familiar tune, and memory recalled Bullet's improvised lyrics in my mind.

Up with the crows,

The day soon begins.

Sleep has cleansed our spirits,

From the whiskey and the gin.

There's work to be done,

'tis far from a farce.

We shall drink much this evening,

Now up from your arse.

The chiming ended in a lingering vibrato, the hourglass repeating the song thrice before finally falling quiet.

"Dawn has fallen in Crossfire..." Rejj said. "I reckon you should be getting back to your physical body."

"Most definitely," I agreed. "Before we depart I had one additional question... how are the preparations for The Ascension Ceremony progressing?"

"All is well... the décor is set, I have been gifted with the seating arrangements, and have set myself to familiarizing them. The musicians are secured and Bullet should have confirmed with you the design for The Creator's Throne... assuming He decides to grace us with his presence."

"About that..." I hesitated. "I have decided to break tradition and request for Him to join us at our table."

The shock and horror was clear on Rejj's face, his eyes widening.

"Knomucca... He has facilitated many Ascensions... certainly He has expectations of elements that are not to be ignored..."

"It is not my intention to ignore them, only encourage His inclusiveness."

"Knomucca... He has taken much from those you love... yet you are flirting with the notion He is to sit politely at your table amongst your company?"

"There is nothing wrong with my company," I growled.

"You know that He won't see it that way. He will see it as you requesting He, with His awesome powers, dine at a table with not only Gods of His own creation but also the mortals beneath Him."

"Rejjren..."

"Nay, Knomucca, you heed my warnings. The Creator isn't going to be your friend or ally. He corrupts souls with His blood because He is sick and twisted. And if you think for even the shortest of moments your company will remain cordial around Him, then you are being daft...I can guarantee I shall do no such thing and I'm certain Kiyoko would be too overwhelmed with the intensity of His vibrations to feel anything other than the anger he has towards Him taking Peadie..."

"Rejjren... Kiyoko became a fixture in my life in the years that followed your death... I am confused as to how you would know such an intimate detail of his life... if there is something you are concealing about Kiyoko from me then you best choose now to be honest."

Rejj paused. "I only mean those who have lost much won't be keen on removing the stones from their souls."

Anger flashed through me, though I swallowed it down, pretending not to notice as Rejj lied to my face. I wished not to betray my advantage in gaining this information. However, I suspected that as a Sneak, Kiyoko possessed more gifts than I was aware of and that he hoped would remain hidden.

"The empire was not constructed overnight..." I paused as I briefly gathered my thoughts. "I expect it shall take some time... though I will have an eternity to balance everyone and it would be helpful if neutral ground was established."

"This desire is but a dream smoked through an emerald dragon... this is not something I believe you shall be able to achieve, Knomucca."

"I do not require your belief, only your support," I said.

"Well..." Rejj bent in a mocking bow. "Luck from the Gods and Stars."

"I do not wish to construct Him a throne, Rejjren." I released a tense breath before continuing to speak. "I refuse to acknowledge His true Power over me once I Ascend. I shall then be His equal... and I demand to be treated as such."

Rejj lifted his eyes. "I hadn't seen it like that..."

"Aye, and I wished to not have had to say it aloud."

"My pardons..." Rejj lowered his eyes in shame. "I shall admit my faith in you was momentarily lacking... the notion you wished for us to befriend The Creator sliced my soul in a way I cannot express."

"I would never ask that of you," I said seriously. "Your feelings are justified. I only wish to end this notion of superiority He is wielding so proudly over us."

"I admire you for that," Rejj said with a smile, the hourglass shifting as the early morning fell quickly upon us. "I suppose if you require my support... then by the stars you shall have it."

"I owe you much gratitude, Rejj." I said, regarding him fondly as he draped the strap of his satchel across his shoulders.

A silence fell between us as Rejj collected his remaining book, parchments, and hourglass, arranging himself neatly before rising from his seat.

"I reckon I shall be seeing you soon then," Rejj pushed his chair towards the table, sliding it smoothly. "Luck to you in retrieving your Angelfish... I hope you return to the troops soon enough, as well."

"As do I," I said, rising from the table and slowly approaching the bed.

"Peaceful rest and meditation, may the journey to your body find your spirits well."

"I certainly hope it does," I said, unwilling to admit I was nervous about finding my body upon my return. Thank you kindly for the rejuvenating conversation, Rejjren."

"It was my pleasure," Rejj said, approaching the door and forcefully pushing it open. "Stay wise, Knomucca."

"Love and light, until we meet again." I said, watching as the door firmly closed behind him.

I allowed myself to enter my bed, for it was easiest to return to my body from a state of relaxation and comfort. Sliding beneath the sheets, I pulled the blankets atop me, nestling down as I slowly began to meditate.

Focusing on my breathing, I allowed my energy to center, feeling the connection towards my physical body open as consciousness began to flood through me. Exhaling a deep breath, I felt my spirits lighten as I once more embraced the beauty of the sun.

X

EVERETT

The hooves of Samarin's horse pounded away in the distance, the sound of my heavy breathing filling the night air. Thrashing forward, I blindly stumbled through the trees, swearing in vain as I attempted to follow his path from the edges of the graveyard. Sharp and swooping branches cut across my face, tearing my cloak and snagging on my boots.

"Damned traitor," I swore aloud as I forced myself to finally turn around.

The light of the sconces in the graveyard was barely visible through the thick wood; the heavy shadows and drooping evergreens made the way nearly impossible to navigate. Slowing my steps, I was forced to return to my path, relying on my hearing, previous practice, and instincts to guide me forward. Most of my leisure time was spent hiking through the vast woodlands that surrounded Morriraen, gifting me the pleasure of moving fluidly through the trees with very little effort. My body swayed and lulled in the ebbs and flows of the forest, encouraging me to reach the cemetery after only a short moment.

I leaned against a mighty elm, allowing myself several moments to catch my breath and composure. Sliding down the rough and coarse wood, I rested my head against the tree, needing to rest a moment as the day's exhaustion weighed against me. Sighing sharply, I produced a spliff from my smoking sack to calm my nerves and settle. As I exhaled deeply, I released my tensions into the breeze, peering out onto the cemetery as I smoked my spliff and relaxed.

As I rested, I noticed the offerings that shrouded several tombs scattered throughout the graveyard in preparation for The Festival of the Dead occurring in the coming weeks. Bouquets of basil, chrysanthemums, and sunflowers graced the soil upon the graves, silhouetted in the lights of the pumpkin lanterns that shone through the nighttime sky. Painted ceramic skulls marked the tops of headstones, the totems providing guidance to the spirits who returned to visit from Heimaaila. Coins, toys, trinkets, and breads had been left upon these altars, welcoming those fortunate enough to return from the Underworld and granting them gifts from home.

The sight was quite relaxing. The soft glow of the candles stretched and wove gentle orange through my vision. As I was halfway through my spliff, I knew I mustn't linger, prompting me to draw a knife from my belt and set to marking my tree. Carving my family crest into the bark, I took note of the landscape around me, drawing a small compass to point to the east to indicate my traveled direction.

Suddenly, the leaves beside me began to rustle, the point of my blade flying from the trunk as I quickly swung towards my left.

"Everett... you feisty sidhe..." Kiyoko's voice purred in the darkness beside me. My heart pounded through my chest, and my reaction to his words was automatic as I laughed out a blush.

"Oi... find your jollies in messing with me do you..."

Kyoko tightened his grip on my wrist, sending a thrumming warmth down my spine.

"I do admit...I take pleasure in making you squirm."

"Is that so?" I asked, enjoying the spark that flashed through his eyes.

"Indeed," he purred.

"This is not a harmless game of wolves and sheep, or an attempt in catching the cockatrice. These trees are not of the orchards, and you scaring me nearly cost you your head."

"What a fine way to perish it would have been," Kiyoko traced his thumb across my wrist. "It is true, these trees are not of the orchards, though. Perhaps we could still use their sanctuary for a stolen moment."

"That is well with me," I said, my heart hammering. "And what game would you wish to play? If we are to be standing in the orchards. "

"We could still have a go at catching a cockatrice," Kiyoko slid his hand down my arm as he spoke.

"Aye? And what tricks do you possess to make me stone? Or will you instead use your beguiling smile to cheat your victory? "

"I reckon not," Kiyoko said with a wink, releasing my arm. "I am far from surprised you chose to hold this against me."

I laughed. "Perhaps I was being rash... regardless of how you appeared to me, I am grateful to have you here... alone."

"Wherever you go, I shall make like your shadow."

I blushed, turning away from him as I continued to mark my tree.

"I possess your dagger," Kiyoko said in a sultry voice. "I cleaned it best I could, though I know you to be particular about your iron."

"I suppose I am," I said, trying to focus on my details. "Perhaps you should join me in my tree carving... The iron is in need of a sharpening after its encounter, and the wood will provide a cleanse."

"I would love to," Kiyoko moved to my side, his leg pressing firmly against my own as he took in my drawing. "This is quite decent, even without you drawing by torchlight."

"I could draw my family crest blinded," I said, my knife slowly moving toward the bottom of the design as the heat in his voice made my muscles weak.

"Your devotion is endearing," Kiyoko said. His hand gently clasped my own, guiding my dagger to continue drawing.

"Kiyoko..."

"I have been wanting to show you something," Kiyoko said, silencing me with a mischievous wink and returning to the drawing. I watched as Kiyoko etched the crest of his coven through the bark, weaving the symbol flawlessly into the emblem of my family.

"I must say, the symbols of our lineage form quite a pleasing picture when combined..."

"I reckon they do," Kiyoko said, his eyes lifting from the carving and catching my own.

"What brought this about?"

"I have been tinkering with the design for a while now, ever since you asked if I wished for you to mark me with ink."

"You have a flawless, expansive canvass," I said with a smile. "I cannot deny I would find much pleasure in branding you this way."

"This is the only design I would desire to bear," Kiyoko said.

"I quite enjoy your design, though I have one criticism," I said, my gaze sliding downwards as I set to filling in the compass.

"And what might that be, Everett?"

"The compass... your distraction ruined the arrow and it is no longer straight."

"If you allowed me to do so, I could easily right your compass northwards for you..."

My blush was automatic, my body reacting against my judgment with the boldness of his proposal. "Now?"

"I don't see why not," Kiyoko plucked the spliff from my fingers, sending the blood rushing to my head. "As long as we returned to the Rose Lily in haste, no one would grow curious to our absence."

I leaned against the elm as my body quaked with the pain of excitement.

"I thought I should mention... I very much admired the way you tossed that shelf from your back," Kiyoko pressed the spliff against my lips, continuing to meet my eyes as I took an immense drag. "The sounds you made when you threw it on the floor reminded me of the many times you have done the same to me."

"Aye... we could reenact that if you desire," I said, releasing the smoke through my nose before inhaling it through tightly pursed lips.

"As you wish, sir," Kiyoko said with a mischievous smirk.

My breath caught in my throat as he finally began to kiss me.

Exhaling contentedly, I allowed a moment to pass between us, guiding my hands upwards into the gentle curls of Kiyoko's hair. The waves were soft between my fingers, my hands gently massaging his scalp as a moan escaped him. Hungrily, he parted my lips, biting my tongue playfully as my grip on him tightened.

"Wait, Kiyoko," I panted, his lips trailing a heated line across the wounds of my neck. My manhood stirred, the sparkling allure in Kiyoko's irises made it difficult to speak. "I am confused... just this night last, you were in bed with another... you were obviously angered towards me... though now you are seeking my company..."

"I bear no confusion, Everett," Kiyoko said, breathing heavily in my ear as his tongue ran across it. "I tried to wash my feelings for you down the river, though I could not escape them. I attempted to create space for you to sort yourself... though being without you hurts as a knife through the rib cage. I nearly lost you twice on this day, and I could not bear the thought of you leaving me without never having tasted you again."

"Kiyoko-"

Firm, confident kissing interrupted my speaking, the warmth of his lips welcomed after the heavy night through the rain. The smell of mugwort played across his skin, the taste adding a bitterness to him I rather enjoyed. I traced my thumb along his jawline, tugging his hair playfully and kissing him intensely.

"Gods... Kiyoko..." I moaned amidst the parting of our lips. "You are beginning to tread in dangerous waters..."

Kiyoko pulled away, smiling as he replaced our spliff between my lips. "You know I love you, Everett, and I know you to feel the same... I am no longer willing to gaze silently whilst you are frozen in the middle of your love for me and Knomucca. I needed to make my intentions known to you before you chose her, before you willingly and permanently discard what we know is immense between us."

"I love you both," I said sincerely, understanding at that moment that I bore no greater truth and wished to pursue them both together and equally. "If I admit the matter is complicated, would that suffice? Or are you determined to fluster me this entire venture?"

"I know I blindsided you... I know you do not wish to face your feelings and instead hope the gods will force your actions... though I have decided to take the matter into my own hands. I could never forgive myself if I allowed you to continue without your making a true decision, for avoiding your feelings altogether shall not hasten their disappearance."

Opening my mouth to speak, I took a cleansing breath, growing fearful Kiyoko would not accept my desire and need to love them both. Afraid he would not lend his support, I fell silent, shaking with the insecurity that I was flawed and unjust for believing I could be committed to the pair of them equally.

"The Ascension draws nearer every moment," Kiyoko said gently. "Only time shall divulge if we shall cross to the other side unscathed, and I knew if I wished to hold a place in your heart... I was to resort to boldness."

"Your words speak a great truth," I said, wishing I could explain there was a desire I worried I would never sort. "Though... in this moment, I fear I have not the strength to gift you mine-"

Kiyoko raised a finger suddenly over my lips, turning unexpectedly and sharply towards the right. Sergeant Kyreese stood amidst the glow of the graveyard lanterns, her eyes twinkling in delight as she took in the pair of us against the elm.

"Commander... General... "

"Kyreese," Kiyoko spoke without pause. "Your shielding has quite improved..."

"Aye, thank you kindly, General."

"I will admit," Kiyoko searched Kye's face before continuing. "I was completely blinded to your presence."

"You were very... focused," Kye said with a blush. "And I reckon my hair draws power as the moon nears full."

"Aye... indeed... that would certainly explain things."

A silence fell between us, Kiyoko shifting to his right to allow us to have proper distance.

"I followed the lot of you and left Hazel and Bullet at the Rose Lily..." Kye said as she shifted her weight uncomfortably. "I was worried in regards to how you were fairing, though I can see that was unnecessary."

"It would appear so," I said with a blush, retrieving my dagger from Kiyoko's hands and attaching it to my belt along with my spares.

"What came of Samarin?" Kye shifted her braid across her shoulders and adjusted her cloak. "Your lack of vigilance would suggest to me that he cleared off."

"Mind your place," I said harshly, recoiling as Kiyoko glared.

'She asks a valid question,' Kiyoko snapped through me silently. 'Do not over boil because you are embarrassed.'

"My pardons, Sergeant," I said, finishing the remainder of our smoke as a way to calm my nerves. I discarded the ashes, rubbing them into the woven crests of our lineage, taking in the sight of the entangled lines. "Samarin and his servant escaped on horseback through the trees to the west and I was unable to catch them."

"'Tis a pity," Kye said with a sigh. "Reckon it's good you were able to procure that vial from him though."

"Aye, reckon it was," I agreed with a nod before rising to a stand.

"And how did this come about?" Kye motioned with her braid towards the elm. "I have known you to mark trees upon your separation during previous occasion Commander, though I cannot recall a crest this intricate."

"It was of my own design," Kiyoko said with a smile. "A frivolous pastime through experimentation."

"It is quite pleasing to the eye," Kye said as she adjusted her gaze. "It would look quite stunning drawn in ink."

"I thought the very same," Kiyoko said.

"And how are you fairing, Everett," Kye began to speak, filling the quiet that hung between us. "That shelf upon your shoulders must have bore quite a weight."

"Aye, reckon it shall leave a bruise," I said, offering a hand to Kiyoko as I pulled him to his feet. Our eyes met again, and he held my gaze. The intensity of our previous moment still pulsed through the heat of his fingers.

"Shall I return alone to the Rose Lily? Do the lot of you need another moment to yourselves?"

"What an interesting question," Kiyoko flicked his eyes from Kyreese to regard me curiously. "How do you reckon, Everett?"

Frustration flared through me upon Kiyoko's words, the pressure to commit my allegiance to him unfathomable with all else at present. "I reckon we best follow you and retrieve our fellow comrades."

Kiyoko released my hand. Sadness and anger flashed through his aura, brightening only to my eye for the slightest moment as he loosed a breath.

"Oi, there you have it then," Kiyoko said as he hid the wounds I had dealt him. "Spare moments with me are not desired."

Kye shyly averted her gaze, looking away as she gestured at the pair of us standing tensely. "I don't wish to witness... whatever is going on here..."

"There is nothing to witness," I said firmly.

"Nothing to witness..." Kiyoko fought to maintain his composure, though I knew my words had wounded him deeply.

"I think I shall set off towards the Rose Lily..." Kye said.

"Excellent," Kiyoko said, stepping from my side and moving behind our Sergeant. "I shall be right along beside you."

Kiyoko turned to give me a pointed glare before he fell into line with Kyrese. The steps through the graveyard were grim and quiet, Kiyoko's tenseness apparent in the subtle tightness of his shoulders. Releasing a breath, I extended my energy outwards towards him, wishing to speak despite the sharpness of his anger.

'I only wish to converse with you if the matter regards our task at hand, or else I fear the pair of us need a moment apart to reflect,' Kiyoko's words stung like the thorns of a rose.

'You barely give me time to react then reply with anger...'

'Anger? Oh, Everett, you wish to see my anger?' Kiyoko's words snapped through me; the harshness pierced my head in pain and rang through my ears. 'I gave you pause to respond... I poured my soul to you, and you denied me your affections.'

'Kiyoko...the rest of the group was waiting at the Rose Lily. Before we realized how poignant our absence was, it was fine...but with Kye here, it was clear we needed to return...besides, that was hardly my entire reply.'

'Do not be thick, Everett... You had many moments to speak and yet you remained silent... In your choosing to return to the Rose Lily instead of choosing to remain behind to sort out your feelings, you gave your allegiance to Knomucca instead of me, yet again.'

'That is unfair, Kiyoko.'

'I disagree,' Kiyoko's energy sizzled silently through me. 'Certainly, our romance began with innocent intentions, though you have known of my devotion to you since Winter Solstice three years prior.'

'It is true I have known of your devotion, and you knew the same of mine. Though you never confessed it again. You left after you absorbed my energy and still will not confess what became of you.'

A tense silence hung in the air between us, as thick as fog. I looked sidelong at Kiyoko, his copper eyes masking the emotions I knew were roiling beneath the surface.

'Everett... I never moved onward. And whenever we speak of that night, it is because you are wondering where I went. Yet you never confessed your love to me again either. You only speak of your devotion to Knomucca. So, I indulged in your cowardice, I grew hopeful with the notion you would confess your truest feelings, and come to choose your happiness instead of remaining silent-'

'I have loved Knomucca for a long time, and yet I still fear what I know I feel for you. All I am searching for is happiness,' I said defiantly. 'Hurting you by leaving your partnership is not my intention.'

'Horseshit Everett,' Kiyoko snapped through me with a wave of hot purple. 'You are quick to wager what you have with me, for something you may never achieve with Knomucca.'

Sighing deeply, my thoughts fell silent. I realized that by doing nothing, I had unwittingly made a choice.

'Everett, let me ask you something.'

"Anything," I said eagerly, praying that his question would heal the wound growing between us.

'Do you love me?'

'More than anything,' I said gently.

'And do you love Knomucca?'

'Aye... equally the same and with all I have.'

'And if one night Knomucca confesses she shares this devotion for you, would you deny that your instincts would compel you to abandon all else and flock instantly to her side? Even if the pair of us had fully, deeply, and truly committed?'

'I shall admit... I would always wonder what those moments would be like-'

'Aye, Everett...thus I can no longer wait for you. I need to find that passion for myself, find someone that fills me with burning desire... I had everything with you... though I cannot waste my remaining years grasping at smoke-'

'Kiyoko... I do not wish to make you feel lost or alone-'

'Then perhaps you should have behaved differently, fought through your fears and insecurities instead of yet again choosing to run from me.'

'Kiyoko-'

'Nay, Everett, I have nothing else to discuss with you on the matter. I need space from you unless we are required to discuss matters that concern the realm... I need to allow myself time to process and maintain my composure.'

'Kiyoko, please....'

'The matter is settled, Everett,' the pain in Kiyoko's words tinged his aura. 'Tighten your shields and let me be, or the next time you intrude on my energy, I shall not respond in kind.'

Resisting the urge to plead for him again, I released a cleansing breath, pulling my energy securely around myself as my shields fell into place. Adjusting my hood, I wiped clear the tears that had begun to burn my eyes, watching Kiyoko through blurred vision as he moved silently in the darkness. Kye walked to his left in the space I should have occupied. My heavy steps across the cobblestone echoed through the strain of my heartbeat; the sudden gusts of frigid wind masked my sobs.

Dawn would soon be approaching and painting the sky; a faint, soft blue attempted in vain to lift my spirits. To the east, the Rose Lily materialized again, a thick and heavy shadow that shone through the soft and early sun. The talismans remained crooked against the doorframe, the candlelight muted in a haunting reminder of the earlier moments when my life was balanced. The door had been pulled closed against the elements, deterring unwanted spirits from crossing the threshold.

Allowing myself a brief moment, I paused beside the small stockade, standing alongside the horses we had corralled earlier that night across from the apothecary. Truff whinnied in greeting and eagerly approached the fence, granting me an excuse to check upon how he was fairing whilst creating distance between myself and Kiyoko. The pain shone through him in the anger of his steps, his slippers eerily silent upon the stone as he controlled the rage boiling beneath him. I knew from his tense shoulders he wished to strike me, loathing the rigidity of his body as he managed his moods through meditation.

I exhaled a long, sad sigh, absently patting Truff's nose as I watched Kiyoko walk towards The Rose Lily. Gradually, the muscles in his slender spine began to relax, his arms falling loosely to his sides as he shoved through the door. Sergeant Kyreese silently regarded me over her shoulder, adjusting her braid and saluting before following closely behind him. Releasing my aggression, I thoroughly scratched Truff beneath the saddle, smiling unexpectedly as he firmly nuzzled my hand.

"You always know how to dry my eyes," I said with a sad smile, tenderly massaging his favorite spot behind his ear with my thumb. Truff burrowed his nose into my glove, meeting my face with a heavy expression, sensing the anguish and distress in my energy. I slipped Truff the final cubes of sugar I had obtained from Morriraen. "Thank you kindly for the distraction, though I reckon I best be setting off towards the apothecary... I cannot digress any further..."

Truff lowered his gaze and followed me to the edge of the stockade. He watched as I turned and walked down the cobblestone path. The apothecary door remained open, creaking softly through the silence as a light breeze caressed the doorframe. Sighing heavily, I took an immense breath, centering my mood and energy after a tense moment of struggle. Glancing towards the pumpkin lanterns, I bravely stepped between them, gently nudging through the threshold into the chaos within.

Hazel and Bullet had been hard at work righting the shelves and displays I had bombarded during our earlier encounter with Samarin and his troops. Kettles, herbs, stones, and a plethora of tools I could not recognize littered the smooth stone floor. The shelf I had heaved from my shoulders had dismantled many others in its path. Centered in the room, Terra, The Alchemist, still remained upon the ground, the Spider Vines twisting and contorting across her purpling skin.

"Commander... General..." Hazel appeared from the room beyond the counter, carrying a large cotton blanket. "How kind of you to have finally rejoined us."

"Aye, the Gods hath smiled kindly upon us," I said, feeling pangs of comfort and sadness as Kiyoko took his place at my right.

"Is all well?" Hazel's hands fanned silently outwards as she flattened the blanket.

"Such terms are arbitrary and relative," Kiyoko said with a neutral expression, forcing my will to remain fixed on Hazel and unwavering towards him.

"Oi, you have quite the mood," Hazel ducked briefly beneath the counter, covering the corpse of Duke with the blanket. "Am I to assume from your lack of good nature that Samarin and his prick got off unscathed?"

"Aye, and I am certain they are most satisfied," I said begrudgingly.

"Kiyoko, you wield a bow most of the time, do you not?" Hazel said condescendingly.

"You would be correct," Kiyoko said with a chuckle. "I reckon you are wondering if my arrow met his arse..."

"I was going to put it a bit more delicately..." darkness flashed through the judgment in Hazel's eyes.

"I did not have a clear shot... I had trouble keeping pace with Everett as I needed to climb through the mayhem he caused and the pair of them were further along... had I decided to shoot Samarin, I most likely would have taken Everett instead and I had not wished to do so."

"Perhaps you should have risked it," Hazel moved from behind the counter. "Did you see where they were headed?"

"He and his servant fled through the western cemetery..." I said.

"Truly?" Hazel raised an eyebrow.

"Aye..." I said. "Had Truff been at my side, we certainly could have caught him. Though, as it was, we were clearly not successful.

"Unless Samarin possesses aid or refuge he is heading towards the swamplands-" Hazel started.

"He could just as easily divert northwards and return towards Morriraen," I interrupted firmly. "My pursuit of him had become necessary only as a result of him telling me I would not know where to locate Syler-"

"How do you mean?" Kiyoko asked with a gasp, shielding the chaos of emotion whirling beneath his eyes with the faintest flash of his aura.

"It is all the information I have at present," I admitted in embarrassment. "It is clear in his words something has happened to her..."

"You wait until this moment to divulge such important information when just moments prior I discover the lot of you canoodling and carving marks beneath the elm!" Kye said with much annoyance.

"Canoodling?" Hazel said, her face gleaming proudly with her accusation. "Commander... General... what doth our Sergeant mean by canoodling?"

"It is as it sounds," I admitted, my cheeks burning hot in a harsh pink blush.

"Though, frankly," Kiyoko spoke firmly from beside me, "the nature of our way and how we spend our time is of no matter to you."

"You would be correct, of course, if these were your own spare moments," Hazel smirked mischievously and winked her shadow-dark eyes. "Though I bare sudden worry, the pair of you shall lack the responsibility necessary to work together, should theatrics or complications arise."

"Theatrics shall most certainly arise," Kiyoko said, boldly puffing his chest. "Though no matter how thick Everett's skull becomes I shall always know the currents through it."

"I don't follow," Hazel admitted with a wave of her hand. "Though I reckon it won't much matter anyhow if events continue to progress poorly... as they have thus far."

"Indeed," I said, watching as Sergeant Kyreese hid her face behind her hair in shame.

A silence fell across the room, broken only by Bullet as he continued returning cauldrons to the shelves.

"Reckon we best move on to the more gruesome challenges of our conversation," Hazel said, approaching The Alchemist Terra as she lay paralyzed in Spider Vines. "As the lot of you can tell, there is still work to be done before we can determine the course of action... I would like to remove the Spider Vines, though I shall need some stronger intervention to do so."

"There are no physical elements powerful enough to free one from Spider Vines," Kiyoko said, shifting his weight and turning away from Hazel uncomfortably.

"I wish you the best of luck, though I fear we cannot be of assistance," I said, noticing Kiyoko's hesitation.

"Though her skin purples, she possesses a pulse, along with sporadic, shallow breathing. Spider Vines drain one's vital energies and grow stronger from the energy they consume," Hazel said, her eyes darkening.

"How long until she crosses over?" Kye interjected.

"It shall be long and miserable," Kiyoko sighed, his fingers gently massaging his forehead.

"Spider Vines enjoy their feedings, they'll consume her as slowly as possible to relish in her energy," Hazel said. Reaching into her robes, she produced a small metal tool, beginning to prod and tug on the vines that ensnared Terra. "If only you would have blessed Samarin with your arrow, ending the life of whomever cast the Spider Vines is guaranteed to break their binds."

"Oi, Hazel, leave 'em be," Bullet said nervously from across the room.

"I believe I can disrupt them... I have come close through previous experimentation..." Hazel reached into her robes once more, obtaining a small bottle from within before swirling the liquid.

"Hazel," Kiyoko's voice became urgent, forcing my gaze from the Alchemists and into his panicked eyes.

"I cannot simply ignore this opportunity," Hazel barked as she adjusted her grip on the surgical tools. "The vines are adhering to her flesh... the skin is melding into the plants and looks to be disintegrating..."

"Gods," I said in horror.

"Hazel, I beseech thee, in the love of all that is divine and good, do not pull at those..." Kiyoko inhaled slowly and deliberately from my right.

"Kiyoko, there are so few opportunities to learn about Spider Vines," Hazel snapped. "Unless you are aware of another way to rescue those taken by them, I shall do whatever I can to learn..."

Kiyoko's face was pained, as it often was when he was overwhelmed with energy. "You are going to aggravate them!"

A harsh flash of purple snapped through the air with a sharp sizzle. I lunged forward, thrashing in vain to catch Hazel as she lost her footing and was sent reeling. A growl leaped from the Spider Vines as a sudden, white-hot light shot from the sconces on the wall, leaving them extinguished. A pulse rushed through me as I felt my energy suddenly waver. The stumbling of the others in the room indicated that they had felt the same momentary loss of energy.

"Is everyone well?" I asked in the darkness, pivoting instinctively to shield Kiyoko and keep him at my back. "Roll call."

"Warrant Officer present," Bullet said from far to my left, his hurried footsteps skittering across the room as he abandoned the shelves. His silhouette moved to Hazel's side, lending her an arm as she faltered to a shaking sit.

"Present," Kiyoko said shortly.

A tense silence fell over the room.

"Sergeant, are you well?" I asked.

"Aye, reckon I'm fine," Kyreese veered from the right, her hair beginning to glow in the same violet shade of the Spider Vines. "Though, I am uncertain as to what is happening with my hair..."

"Oi, that was brutal," Hazel said suddenly, rubbing her head absently. She knelt over Terra once more as she continued to speak. "Perhaps if I were to-"

"You shall do nothing more," Kiyoko said sternly from my side. "Their demeanor shall only worsen if you continue to provoke them."

"Snap your trap, Kiyoko," Hazel hissed. A shadow consumed her aura; her eyes glowed briefly with an otherworldly red before returning to normal. "How would your morals allow you to leave this situation, knowing what we learn here could help others?"

"We could bring her to Knomucca," Kiyoko said in a low voice, his spine rigid. "It is possible her hands could possess the power to defeat the Vines-"

"You know as well as I that we could not hope to reach her in time," Hazel snapped as she eyed Kiyoko. "Although, you possess an ability we could learn a great deal from. You are uniquely gifted..."

Kiyoko's panic flooded through me. "Do you realize what you are asking?"

"Aye, Kiyoko... I know your secrets."

'She believes the only way to free her would be for me to absorb the energy...' Kiyoko panicked silently through me.

'Could you not simply use the energy for healing?' Surprisingly, my words floated easily through his mind's eye. 'Certainly, you have several physical ailments you could remedy with the energy intake...'

'It would not be enough Everett,' Kiyoko said sadly. 'Even if I were to satiate all my physical needs the extra energy would need to go somewhere, and I would fall the victim.'

My heart hammered through my chest with Kiyoko's words, his energy releasing me gently.

"I do not care for those secret conversations the pair of you have that you believe no one else notices," Hazel said.

"Mind your place," I interjected.

"Kiyoko, I am requiring you to use your talents to tame these Spider Vines," Hazel stood to her full height and faced us.

"He will do no such thing," I shot back.

"As High Priestess and Head Alchemist, I am taking command of this situation due to its medical nature," she said smugly. "I am ordering General Kiyoko to follow my commands. Not only will this be an opportunity to study the Vines in more detail, but it could save the life of a fellow Alchemist."

"You cannot do this-" I started.

'I do not need you to fight my battles for me,' Kiyoko said into my mind before continuing aloud. "I shall be risking the lives of others."

"You're going to have to work through your guilt somehow," Hazel said sharply. "Terra is an Alchemist, and an Elder at that, allow her to succumb to the Spider Vines without intervening and you might as well give Knomucca your resignation."

"Your words are painting Her Worship unjustly," I said in a harsh tone. "She knows of Kiyoko's gifts; certainly, this is not how she would like things to proceed."

"I agree with the Commander," Bullet said. "Even I understand the precariousness of Kiyoko's nature. This is not the solution that Knomucca would want."

"While you may believe that to be true, it is not the case," Hazel said defiantly.

"This is madness," I said in frustration. "High Priestess Hazel, are you officially declaring rank against General Kiyoko?"

"I am," Hazel said.

"Aye," Kiyoko spoke in a tone I failed to recognize. "Remember in the future you chose to do this... the blood that shall flow from my hands will certainly stain your palms as well."

"I don't care much about what all falls from this," Hazel said sternly.

"You are vile," Kiyoko said angrily, unable to calm his spirits or center his breathing. Vibrant, violent red seared my eyes as it raged through his aura. "All would do well to remember I did not wish to do this."

"You have my word," I said, feeling Kiyoko's body beside me as his eyes drifted closed.

"General, what is being demanded of you?" Kye asked, looking nervously between Kiyoko and Hazel.

"He is being told to consume the energy... take it in as his own," I said, trying to keep my voice level.

"What will happen to him?" Kye shifted her weight uncomfortably.

"Each type of energy reacts differently to the body," Kiyoko said. "We are never quite certain how the energy will behave until I have absorbed it..."

"There is no knowing what he could become," I interjected. "A compassionate healer, a distant stranger, or a violent lunatic."

"You're a vampire," Kye accused, her face paled.

"My kind are of their kin," Kiyoko nodded and opened his eyes to search her face.

"Why was I never told?" Kye's breathing grew heavier.

"There was never any need," Kiyoko said solemnly.

"Commander..." Kye said. "The troops have a right to know who... or what they are fighting beside."

"Perhaps you should wait for us outside before you find yourself court marshaled," I warned. "While I understand your past may make this a difficult revelation, it does not permit you to disrespect a superior officer."

Kye opened her mouth to speak but quickly shut it. She glanced towards Kiyoko before gritting her teeth.

"Nay, she must remain here," Hazel said. "Her hair could come of great use, and I do not wish to be far from it."

Kye visibly tensed.

"Hazel, the Sergeant is in no condition to assist. Let her escape her demons and wait for us outside," I said.

"Nay, Everett, she shall remain within arms reach."

"I agree with the commander, let her go outside," Bullet spoke defiantly.

"Bite your tongue, Baldrumlin Bharrum," Hazel spat, the use of Bullet's real name catching me by surprise. "You do not even like this girl. The entire castle could hear you bickering about the damned cannons while we were trying to leave the castle."

"The sapling and I may butt heads from time to time, though I do not wish her harm," Bullet said.

"Do not go against your elders," Hazel spoke angrily towards him.

Bullet turned helplessly to face me.

"Kyreese, you may go if you wish," I said again. "I shall accept any consequences for this discretion."

"Kyreese, you will stay where I can see you," Hazel growled. "Or do you wish for another bout of nightmares?"

"Hazel, may I remind you that while you may be the ranking official on matters such as these, you do not have the authority to mete out punishments for my troops. Kye can stay or go, it is her choice," I said sternly.

Kyreese stared down at the floor, her spirits falling quiet as she retreated into herself.

"Good girl," Hazel praised. "Now, I have waited long enough... Kiyoko, do what has been asked of you."

"You do not have to do this," I pleaded, moving closer to Kiyoko. Despite being bombarded by an influx of purple that made me instantly nauseous, I whispered my thoughts through him. 'Take my hand. Let me in Kiyoko... I can help you...'

"He does if he wishes for me to keep his secrets, for he is a man of many," Hazel retorted. "What will it be, Kiyoko?"

The doors to Kiyoko's mind slammed closed, his aura glowing sharply as he began to sing softly.

"With my words I beseech to thee,

Come to me through the roots and trees,

To the meadow of daisies and sweet peonies,

Beyond where harm and threat can find thee,

The in between is where lies your safety."

Kiyoko's voice was hypnotic and mesmerizing, the pitches vibrating in a calming allure I had trouble resisting. His arms fell to his side as he took an immense breath; the dark, loose curls of his hair fanned outward with the enchanted wind that consumed him.

"Kiyoko-" His name escaped my lips involuntarily.

Drowning out even my own thoughts, the Spider Vines began to scream, creating a piercing, unwanted cacophony against Kiyoko's lullaby. Slowly, the Spider Vines began to unravel from around the Alchemist, slithering and writhing across the floor towards Kiyoko. Acting instinctually, I drew my hammer, stepping directly into his path as the Vines crawled towards us.

"That's enough, Kiyoko!" Hazel shouted. Her voice was distant and barely audible over the blood rushing through my ears. "They have released her, you can stop-"

Slamming my hammer downwards, I smashed into the Spider Vines, watching in horror as they began to multiply. Thriving from the energy, the vines began to climb up the walls and across the shelves, growing in thickness and strength as they fed from Kiyoko's life force.

'Kiyoko, use your shields,' I pleaded through him, hoping my words would reach him despite his anger towards me. 'Kiyoko, please, raise your shields-'

The Spider Vines began to bark and growl, the tentacles across their membranes furling as I drove my hammer into them. The vines wrapped around the head of my hammer, encroaching across the iron and tangling my hands. The Spider Vines attempted to pierce my dragonscale gloves, sending an unexpected and painful spark across my skin.

"Do not touch them, Everett," Kiyoko shouted desperately. "By the Gods that be, do not touch them."

Shaking my hammer harshly, I freed the Spider Vines from the shaft, smashing into the shelves as I defended Kiyoko at my back. Bullet appeared on the left, using the dagger from his belt to stab the onrushing vines.

"They seem only to grow from our advances," Hazel shouted from across the chaos. "If we are not careful I fear we shall be over run-"

"So, much, purple," Kiyoko slurred from behind me. My stomach plummeted with the realization his mind was beyond him. "How particular... this shade tastes remarkably of cherries..."

"Bullet," instantly, the dwarf met my eyes, his dagger snapping from his sleeve as he fought to focus through Kiyoko's contagious humming. "We are in need of an intervention-"

"Are you certain?" Bullet's eyes sparkled with delight as I smashed the bramble of Spider Vines across the stone floor. "The Rose Lily is the oldest building in the realms... we have to act with care-"

His words were interrupted by a rush of hissing Spider Vines, their number only increasing as Kiyoko became one with their energies. Clearing through the demonic foliage, I regained Bullet's attention, speaking quickly as the Spider Vines lunged from the shelving.

"I need to get Kiyoko out of here," I shouted. "He is drowned in his spirits... it would be best for him to be outside."

'The Spider Vines shall hunt us,' Kiyoko said weakly through me. 'They have tasted my energy and shall crave more.'

"Bullet," I commanded over the hissing Spider Vines. "Up the ante!"

"I'll see what I can find," Bullet barked as he retreated through the aisles, lurching sideways as a thicket of vines lunged toward his face.

"Work in haste," I called after him, slinging my hammer across my back and lifting Kiyoko into my arms.

Adjusting his weight, I held his body against my chest. I began to weave backward and towards the left, carefully picking my way through the fallen debris of our earlier encounter as I held the Spider Vines in my sight. The Spider Vines snapped forward in quick strokes as they sensed my escape. In reaction, I contorted my body in horrid angles as I fought to avoid them. I tripped into a fallen cauldron, and I nearly dropped Kiyoko. I landed harshly on my knees before securing him in my arms once more and scrambling to my feet.

"Bullet, need some help here..."

The Spider Vines sprung, reaching outwards and raking across my boots. Fiercely, they began tangling up my leg, squeezing harshly and twisting like the bite of a snake. A primal scream escaped my lips; my instincts drove me to smash them with my opposite boot in a critical error. Grabbing hold of my feet, the vines fought to climb towards Kiyoko, his eyes wide in alarm as they blurred with panicked intoxication.

Shoving Kiyoko upwards, I forced him onto my shoulders, summoning a burst of adrenaline as I pulled from the Spider Vines. From the right, Kye's braid cracked suddenly like a whip, crashing through the wall of Spider Vines with a satisfying crunch. A wave of piercing screams curdled through my ears, sending pain throbbing across my temples as I forced my legs free.

"Much appreciated Kye," I called out, my heart pounding in panic as my words hung in the air over her gut-wrenching sobs. "Kyreese... Kyreese... are you well?"

I grew distressed by her lack of response, peering through the clutch of rushing vines as I searched for her whereabouts. The Spider Vines tangled and twisted across the shelving, thrashing at my face as I shielded Kiyoko from their sting. Barreling sideways, I repositioned Kiyoko across my front, turning my back towards the vines as I started moving rightwards.

"Kyreese, we are coming to find you," I said, heaving through the displays as I started towards her direction.

Kye's heavy breathing punctuated her sobbing, the sound guiding me towards her and into an isle of loose-leaf herbs. Curled up on the floor, Kye lay tangled in a heap of shelving and braids, her spirit pulsing with heat.

"Kyreese," I said, gently nudging her with a boot. "Kye... Oi... Kye... it's Everett."

"Everett," Kye rubbed the pain from her eyes. "Please don't make me touch them again-"

"Kye, we need to get outside," I said, sliding Kiyoko onto my right shoulder as I hoisted her small frame onto my other shoulder. "Up we go, lassie, nice and-"

Kye wrangled out of my grasp; a sudden horror flashed brightly in her eyes as she sprung to her feet.

"Get away from me," Kye growled, her hair alight with a harsh glow as her face flooded with anger.

"Kye, let me carry you," I said, fighting to remain calm. "I can handle the pair of you with ease, just let me lift you."

Reaching outwards, I grasped tightly to her waist, losing my grip as she wriggled away.

"Get off of me..." Kye screamed in alarm. "I said stop, go away!"

"Kye, it's me Everett, I -"

Sudden growling slammed into my awareness, the hissing moving from behind my back as I fought to help Kye relax.

"Burn in the Seven Rings!' Kye screamed, punching me squarely in the jaw and sending my head reeling.

"Kye," I spat, blood dripping from my lips.

Sprinting sideways, Sergeant Kyreese plowed through the shelving, knocking towers of tools, bottles, and plants to the floor as she fled. Kiyoko burst into a sudden fit of laughter, alerting me with his rudeness he was still conscious. Remembering the Spider Vines at my back, I moved in a wide circle, freeing them from my path as I began to chase Kyreese and search for the dwarf.

"Bullet, call out..." My voice was urgent, my instincts guiding me through the aisles in an attempt to determine his location. "Have you made progress?"

"Aye, though you aren't going to like it," Bullet said with a mischievous laugh. Beyond the aisles, Bullet stood with several glass bottles containing drenched and sopping cloth soaking in lantern oil, flour, and Festess whiskey. "And we will need to gain a fast distance."

Suddenly, the Spider Vines hissed and growled at my right, quickly following my path through the aisles as they yearned to consume Kiyoko.

"We shall be outside," I said calmly, whistling my retreat and shifting backward.

Bullet obtained a jar of beeswax from the shelves, coating the goop across the fabric before procuring a box of matches. Flinging it open, he worked with sure and steady hands, his smile from the upcoming pandemonium painting his freckled, bearded cheeks.

"You'll only have a short moment before I'm forced to act," Bullet said, sparking the matches across his belt and lighting the cloths.

"Understood," I called after him, keeping the Spider Vines in view as I turned down the aisles and followed after Kye. "Godspeed and stay wise."

"Luck from the Gods and stars."

Bullet's words fell on my back as I increased my pace, swerving through the shelves and fallen tools with the Spider Vines growling close behind. Kiyoko stirred suddenly with harsh, incessant laughter, the shrill tones piercing and distracting as I shoved us forward. Sergeant Kyreese sprinted fluidly through the aisles and displays, bounding over the fallen piles as she slipped gracefully through the door.

"Kye!"

Lurching to a run, I fought to match her pace, hearing the Spider Vines slither over my shoulders as they chased us toward the threshold.

"Oi, comin' in hot!" Bullet exclaimed from across the room, the smell of matches and whiskey perfuming the air as the sound of breaking glass filled my ears.

Heavy clouds of smoke floated through the air, and the smell of burning flour assaulted my nostrils as I fought onward. Summoning my final burst of strength, I hauled through the door, slamming my shoulder against it as waves of flames ignited behind me. Swearing intensely, I leaped through the threshold, hearing unsettling pops and snapping as fragile apothecary elements caught fire.

"Oi! We're heatin', up!" Bullet shouted as the door swung open in relief.

Grunting harshly, I plowed forward, forcing us past the pumpkin lanterns resting beside the doorway. Sharp, thrumming energy rebelled against me, threatening to push us backward into the flames within The Rose Lily. Bullet shouted in the distance, though his words were unintelligible. The Spider Vines screamed, and glass shattered as the fire continued to climb.

"Everett... your arms are so strong..." Kiyoko began to speak suddenly, shaking intensely as he continued to laugh.

"Oi..." I said with a sigh, yanking Kiyoko upwards as I tossed him over my shoulder once more.

"Everett... you know I've always enjoyed being frolicked this way..." Kiyoko's infectious laughter turned sharply into notes of bitterness. "You are quite daft to forgo such luxury, giving coin instead to the cowardice within yourself...

"Rest, Kiyoko," I panted, rushing forward in immense, calculated strides. "Steele yourself... Cling to me tightly."

"You know that's how I enjoy myself best," Kiyoko flirted as he bounced down my spine. "Perhaps I should seize your hair whilst I enjoy my mount atop you-"

"Not now, Kiyoko," I wheezed, his weight tugging uncomfortably at my cloak. "I beseech thee... close thine lips and rest."

We sprinted down the path, splashing through the puddles of the night's earlier rainfall and running towards the horses. Sergeant Kyreese pounded across the path, turning to notice us over her shoulder as a thunderous crash sounded at my back. The ground shook in tumultuous waves, unsettling our balance and knocking us head over foot. A sudden surge of heat crashed through the sides of The Rose Lily.

"Kiyoko!" I shouted, seeing him sprawled across his front with his face swimming in the puddles.

Crawling towards him, I yanked his body from the earth, dragging his feet across the grass as a fresh wave of fire consumed the apothecary.

"Kiyoko," I lightly slapped my hand against his cheek, feeling him laugh as he shook the rain from his hair.

"Oi, isn't she a beaut," Kiyoko said, his pupils wide in excitement as he admired the dancing flames. "They're sparkling Everett- Gods, I wish to sing to them."

"You will not," I said sternly. "Kiyoko, if you open your mouth and utter a single word to those flames, I will be forced to subdue you-"

"I'd like to see you try," Kiyoko teased.

"Kiyoko, please, gather your senses somehow," I begged. "When Knomucca sees you in this condition she is going to be furious!"

"Knomucca..." Kiyoko's body tensed for the briefest of moments, his abdomen suddenly shaking uncontrollably as he reeled in laughter. "I have no fear of Knomucca-"

"Kiyoko, please, take a breath," I pleaded, using the momentary distraction to free the ropes used to fasten my cloak. I began to talk into his ear, using a level tone to ground him as I set to binding his hands. "I can procure a Ginseng Potion for you or perhaps some mugwort-"

"Keep your herbs," Kiyoko said, a sudden grin smearing across his face as he turned towards me with a wink. "How are you fairing back there, Myne Hertis Rote?"

"Kiyoko," I said, releasing a long breath. "The last time you absorbed energy it was forced upon you by my hand... I saw a side to you that night that worried me and I vowed to never let it happen again... Hazel manipulated you and I shall remedy that best I can... though I cannot let you swirl the cauldron and make matters worse for yourself-"

"You did not force me, Everett," Kiyoko held my gaze though I was hyper-aware of his movements. "It was consensual... a Winter Solstice Festess where you desired my warmth."

"Aye... I remember," I said with a whisper.

"Even through the dead of winter, that night was quite heated," Kiyoko began despite my discomfort. "An abundance of smoke and whiskey fueled your curiosity, and you persuaded me to absorb your energy."

"Aye," I said slowly, hoping our conversation could distract him from being reckless. "Much of the events of that evening escape me, though the consequences bound us deeper together than that of blood or soul."

"It is the truth," Kiyoko said. "Though I no longer wish it to be so."

"You wound me, Kiyoko," I rolled my eyes.

A third, thunderous wave of fire broke from the Rose Lily. Distressed whinnying pulled my attention towards the panicking horses. Truff leaped suddenly over the wooden fence, charging across the grass as he fled from the fire.

"Easy there, Truffles," I called with a whistle, unwilling to risk releasing Kiyoko from my grasp for even the slightest moment.

Truff ignored my whistling, running eastward through the trees into the morning's rising sun and leaving me behind him.

"Truffles!" I shouted, holding Kiyoko tightly as he twisted and howled with laughter.

"Hysterical," Kiyoko cackled. "Perhaps you should free my hands and allow my freedom as you chase after him."

"It is as likely as rain in the desert," I said sternly, my agitation growing.

"Oi, release me, Everett," Kiyoko said, his laughter all but gone as his voice grew serious. "I consider you a friend... so I shall give you fair chance before I bleed you dry."

"First, you threaten our bond and now you seek my energy... You really must dislike me at present if you are threatening to consume me so-"

"On the contrary," Kiyoko said, his eyes filling seductively as I fought to resist their compulsion. "I remember how you tasted... quite the delicious combination of sunlight and coward-"

My anger consumed me, my head thrashing forward as I rammed it solidly against Kiyoko's skull. His words fell quiet as I rendered him unconscious, the flames and smoke spilling from the Rose Lily, tainting the tears in my eyes as Kiyoko drifted slowly to sleep.

XI

KNOMUCCA

My body woke with a tense and harsh snap, my eyes opening painfully to a blue sky, the sun blindingly bright. The sound around me was muted and defused, muffling through my ears as if they had been stuffed with cotton. The dank, briny scent of salted air flooded suddenly through my awareness, the taste catching in my mouth as a stifling choke. Heat from the rising sun radiated across my face, the desire to sleep immense and tempting as my body grew heavy with sluggishness.

*Perhaps I ought to close my eyes for a while...*My head throbbed as if from a night of heavy smoke and drink.

Unforgiving waves smashed across my face, jarring me from my stupor as a cough wrenched from my lungs.

"Oi," I swore intensely, wishing to close my sore eyes from the sun's harsh light.

I swallowed mouthfuls of the unsettled sea, the waves twice their normal height with the approaching full moon. I had awoken whilst floating upon my back, waves splashing across my face. My arms and legs found their rhythm after a painful moment, throbbing with heavy soreness from the time without my spirit.

My return from Heimaaila had taken much of my energies, exhausting my spirits thoroughly and craving me a fair feast and rest. Returning my ethereal spirit into my physical body tired me under normal circumstances, forgoing the notion of a night floating amidst the harshness of the sea. The morning's heat had made me sweat despite the waves, the chilled water failing to satiate the insurmountable thirst brewing painfully within me. My muscles were sore, and my head pounded from dehydration. The desire to feed as I had on my pleasures with Maliche to heal myself of such raw afflictions was so overwhelming I surrendered a heavy sigh of sadness.

"Gods, have mercy..." I said aloud, summoning the strength I needed to continue swimming.

Lifting my eyes, I forced my remaining strength to search the horizon. Water stretched in an endless expanse as far as my eyes could see, sparkling and shimmering with the brilliant gold of the early sunlight.

"Where in the Seven Hells..."

I peered through the dawn in the hope of familiar monuments, growing discouraged by the infinite sky that provided no clear indication of my whereabouts. My searching was hindered by the relentless and pounding waves, the salt burning my skin with every passing moment. Kicking my legs tiredly as I continued to tread water, I released a burdened breath and began to plot my course of action.

Reckon I ought to venture eastward, I reasoned. *I must continue the pursuit of my angelfish...And search for the sand barges while I collect myself...*

Floating forward, I pushed myself through the rising waves, moving through the ebbing currents as the waters carried me along. The wind snapped around me, reminding me of the sails from 'Sonnet Moon' and the disaster that had befallen us the night before.

"CAPTAIN SOUTHWELL!" I shouted at the top of my voice, summoning all the strength I could muster, searching for the sight of my comrades. "ILESA! JORDEN! Can anybody hear me?"

The sun remained alone in its reply, shining mercilessly through the rich blue sea and sky.

"Excellent," I swore sarcastically, a wave of anger washing over me and joining the swells of the sea.

My arms and legs cut through the unsettled waters, the weapons at my belt swaying heavily in the tides as I swam in search of the reefs. Waves lapsed across my torso, slamming behind my head in a painful cadence. Gritting my teeth in annoyance, I pushed my body forward, attempting in vain to ignore the added weight of my clothes, weapons, and boots, tugging heavily beneath the surface.

"Easy does it," I soothed gently to myself. "Little further now... any moment, we'll come upon the crew and reefs..."

Exhaustion flooded through me in bouts of nausea, forcing every ounce of will I possessed to keep myself from vomiting. The waves smashed as I turned my back towards their summits, using the tides to propel myself forward. Unlike sailing in the storms, I used the waves as an advantage to conserve my energies, adjusting my course as I swam towards the sun's rising in the east. There remained no signs of birds or other sea life, the sun my sole source of companionship as I trudged through the endless expanse of sea and sky.

"Oi... Gods... it is warm..."

Groaning softly, I fought to keep my head above water, swimming through the sea. Radiant, golden light shone down brightly through the clear blue sky, rippling and reflecting in glimmering prismatic shimmers. I struggled to keep my vision clear and focused, feeling warm and lethargic as the water stretched out endlessly before me.

"Carrying... too much... OFF," I slurred aloud, finding comfort in my voice amidst the pounding of the waves.

Fighting to stay afloat, I worked to unfasten the tools hanging on the hooks around my belt, avoiding my enchanted pouch as I did not wish to risk its contents. My pruned and raw fingers fumbled clumsily as I struggled to release my tools as offerings to Piscaro, the God of the Sea.

"Let them go, Knomucca," I told myself, my stomach dropping in sadness as I released my weapons into the water. "Enjoy the pain of my sacrifice, Piscaro."

Keeping my daggers and spare gauntlets, I forwent the blades at my ankles, kicking them free in attempts to grant myself easier movement. My white leather boots floated to the surface, horror flashing through me at the sight of their warped and sodden soles. The salt-stained hide bubbled and frayed at the seams, coaxing a sigh of sadness from my lips as I watched them sail free through the waves.

I wish Everett could have been given the chance to repair them, I thought, envious of their buoyancy.

As I watched the fraying seams, I recalled Everett creating them. His gift with the tattoo needle served him well in working leather, allowing him to craft everything from saddles to shoes. I could still feel his calloused hands as he passed me the boots, his fingers caressing my own as we parted. After he made them for me, I asked for a grimoire in which to inscribe the plethora of information from my studies. His diligent effort and craftsmanship were such that I dared not open the tome he sculpted for fear I should blemish his perfection and artistry.

The unforgiving sting of the salt from the waves dragged me from the past, plaguing my mind and spirits once more with my harsh reality. My eyes were sore as I squinted through the sun's reflection on the water's surface, wishing once more that I should have a parasol to obscure the heat and provide shade. Focusing on my thoughts of Everett, I allowed them to lighten my spirits as I fought through my exhaustion.

The sun ascended as I swam through the endless blue. No sign of reefs or sand barges was apparent, forcing me to verify my course eastward with the sun's position. A slight breeze had begun to spill across me, gifting me hope and partial rejuvenation with the refreshing air as the waves battered my back and shoulders.

How much further am I to traverse? I thought, focusing on each word to quash the exhaustion brewing painfully inside me. *I should have passed the sand barges by now...*

Raising my voice, I hollered for Lyle and his crew once more. The sun merely shone across my face, the heat adding an unwelcome catalyst to the insurmountable thirst plaguing my body and spirit.

Shedding the weight was not enough to grant me reprieve, I fretted, beginning to take long and deep breaths as I urged myself to stay calm. *I shall need aid in my floatation... or else I fear I may travel to Heimaaila only to never return...*

Pressing onward, I deliberated upon my course of action, beginning to weigh the possibility of opening my enchanted pouch to see what help its contents could bring.

I cannot open it, I convinced myself. *It shall certainly befall me a tragedy should it spill amongst the waves...*

The relentless mid-morning sun scorched down, causing a thirst I could no longer ignore. Reaching my hand downwards, I felt alongside my enchanted pouch, prying loose the water skin that hung from my belt.

"Excellent," I exclaimed with delight, fighting to tread water as I attempted to satiate my thirst. The freshwater across my lips was so refreshing it made me yearn for the extra water skins I had buried within the fabric of my enchanted pouch.

Gods... what am I to do? I wondered, fastening the empty water skin to my belt and holding my pouch in my hands.

I must risk opening it, I determined. *I cannot deny that I am in need of more water, and I must allow myself to have it...*

My fingers fumbled as I began to unclasp my pouch, freeing it from my iron studded belt and holding it aloft. A smattering of large waves topped with sparkling white foam careened towards me with such speed and aggression that it knocked me under. The undertow ripped the pouch from my grasp as I tumbled through the water. I watched in silent horror as it turned upside down, emptying its contents into the deep. Curses bubbled from my mouth as I rushed towards it, clasping it shut with a hand. Turning around, I searched through the contents of the pouch, now surrounding me in the water. Locating my waterskins, I quickly seized them while my daggers, potions, and spare gauntlets sank. The stale air in my lungs forced me to resurface and leave them lost to the sea.

"Gods be damned!" I swore to the sky, allowing the sun to witness my moment of grieving.

I began to catch what I could, stuffing various herbs, match cartons, and books back into my pouch, which I held atop the waves. Glancing to my left, I could not contain my instant happiness, seeing my bed roll floating across the waters. Hastily, I yanked the twine that contained the sleep sack, allowing it to unfurl and open flat. I smiled at the realization that I could use it as a raft to lie upon.

"Oi, how wonderful," I said aloud, pressing my cheek against the canvas duck cloth and releasing a laugh fueled by heat and exhaustion. "Losing most of my pouch's contents was certainly worth such a gain."

Kicking my legs, I sprawled my upper body across my bedroll, floating atop the waves as I propelled myself eastward. Desperately, I unscrewed the top of the waterskin, savoring its refreshing coolness as if it were the ambrosia of the gods. The morning passed, and still, I searched in vain for the reefs, Captain Southwell, or the crew.

The sun shed its unrelenting light, warming my skin and making my eyes feel heavy. My body dragged sluggishly through the water, my head drooping low against my makeshift raft. Sudden heat welled in my stomach, and nausea flashed through me, along with a shrill pain in my forehead.

A familiar energy pulled against my aura, opening my mind despite its defenses. A distant memory floated through my mind's eye, the unexpected vision forcing me to relive it in the present. My younger self, after my coming of age, had found the spare moments to enjoy a bit of light reading.

I enjoyed drawing my pleasure from the neatly stacked books lining the cherry-wood shelving throughout the study in which I found myself.

My third eye pulsed with pain as I relived those moments. A fire was burning brightly in the hearth, the imagery so vivid I could feel the warmth of the flames as if I were standing before them now. This particular reading den had once been my favorite, though its memory is now tarnished. The chairs were lined with comfortable cushions and blankets I would place upon my lap. At the same time, I worked or luxuriated in the realm's finest literature. I had enjoyed my studies, a talent bestowed upon me by my mother and best appreciated in the seclusion and comfort I had found in this alcove.

A book lay open across my lap, the pages illuminated in the soft glow of the light casting from the fire. I had begun reading the diaries and journals of the previous Prospects who had written them before they crossed over. I learned from the memories they had inscribed about their life and how best to house spirits until such omniscience would be gifted from The Ascension. A looping array of letters were scrawled over the parchment, my eyes concentrating intensely as I absorbed the words from the page.

"It was absolutely blissful," broken fragments of the written words flashed through my mind's eye, my voice whispering the secrets of the text through my dehydration and delirium. *"The warmth was exquisite, mounting to such unbelievable nirvana I had become temporarily blinded. I could have died from such pleasure... allowed it to consume me thoroughly and completely until my essence, my very being, craved nothing but such sweet euphoria worthy of my eternity..."*

A sudden knock came from behind the solid oak door, claiming my concentration from the well-written diary and grimoire of a late Isibol Yendese, her crossing falling victim to overindulgence from the luxurious sensation of a feeding vampire. "Hark, who hath called upon my door?"

"'Tis I."

Reacting upon fear ruled by instinct, I slid the journal beneath the knitted stuffed pillow to my right. His voice had hissed suddenly in unexpected fury, the memory harsh and unwelcome. The Creator glided across the threshold through the reading den of my memory, draped in a cloak of thin-flowing shadow. His face was obscured beneath a tightly woven veil, the fringe decorated with glittering gems sparkling like the flames in the hearth to His left. A twisted iron crown rested atop his cloak's long and swooping hood, concealing the multitude of gnarled and terrifying horns I would later learn adorned His scaled and speckled skin.

"Greetings," I struggled to maintain a level tone, unwilling as I was to alert him to my discomfort. "Benevolent One... how unprepared I find myself for your arrival..."

"Knomucca..." I had disliked it immensely when The Creator used my name. "Knomucca... how pleased I am to have finally found you."

"I have been here quite some time," I had said, having retired to my alcove in the late hours after supper in lieu of worship in the castle's sanctuary.

"I required assistance in searching for you," The Creator had said, stepping further into the reading den and allowing the door to close behind Him.

"I apologize if you found my location inconvenient," I had said, wishing I could return to my reading with a neat whiskey and be done with His company.

"You have advanced in your studies thus far," The Creator said, meeting my gaze though I could not see His eyes through the veil. "I have come to know you rather enjoy them and would have found you here eventually."

Leave me be... I thought, changing the words as a lackluster attempt to break from the original conversation and ground myself in the present. My third eye throbbed, my head splitting with pain as the Creator pulled me back to him.

"How may I be of assistance?" I recalled my words, returning to the normal flow of the original memory.

"I merely came to bend an ear." The Creator moved towards me, every footstep pounding painfully through my head. Nervousness and fear washed over me like the waves. I tried to pull away from Him once more, digging my fingers into my bedroll. His energy rocked against me.

"I shall admit I am intrigued," I had said, shifting to a proper posture in order to center my focus. Deftly, I slid a second pillow over the first, concealing the misshapen lump that had formed from concealing the diary.

"I have come to learn what you know of an event having occurred this Moon-day past." The Creator's words seared through my mind's eye. His lapse in noticing the concealed chronicle behind the pillows was a surprising foible.

"I am certain I shall not be able to assist you," thinking quickly, I had attempted to formulate a reason as to why I should no longer continue conversing with Him. "This Moon-day past I led sessions of the castle's parliament... I was in Valvang a majority of the day and took my meals amongst the company of Chatza in the kitchens when I had lulls in my work-"

"Oh, I am certain that you possess the information that I desire," The Creator had purred in a tone that churned my stomach. "For this event occurred during the nighttime hours, at a soiree hosted by Senaya..."

"Aye..." wishing I had had a diversion, I had taken a cleansing breath, having remembered the spontaneous gala with a sudden feeling of dread. "Had you desired an invitation? The whole lot was rather hastily planned, only half a day to decide the details, quite below a being of your stature."

"I heard that though the festivity was constructed quite suddenly, that it was an impressive success."

"Indeed," I had said, fighting not to betray the nervousness roiling my stomach like the angry tides.

"I heard you enjoyed yourself quite immensely," The Creator had said, my heart pounding furiously as I restrained from clenching my fists.

"How do you mean?" The words had flashed through me with renewed defiance. I had learned from our interactions that it was best to hold my tongue until the Creator had revealed his hand, or else my own words and actions could be turned against me.

"The rumors hath alluded to your overindulgence in wine and herb..." The Creator had glared through His veil with a tense push of His energy.

"I suppose I indulged," I had said deliberately. "Though I doth not understand my offense... the courts had concluded and my work was completed-"

"What else had you partaken in?" The Creator had asked with a souring tone.

"The restful sleep that comes from having spent an evening amongst good friends and wine..." I had begun slowly.

"What of your overly friendly interactions with the stable hand?"

"We spoke briefly," I had said cautiously. "He had been gifted the night free to attend and I pursued his conversation for a time."

"Do you agree that it was overly friendly in nature, and that you had not been sober when you sought his company?"

"I do recall a delicious cup of honeyed mead."

"Knomucca... answer me plainly."

"I have done so..." I had said, taking a steadying breath to quell the anger beneath my words. "I am accused of intoxication based only on the evidence of my flirtation with a commoner?"

"Bite your tongue, Knomucca," The Creator had hissed again in an unsettling tone. "You would do well to remember I do not repeat myself."

"My apologies," I had said with a concealed sigh. "I can confirm that I found the stable hand to be quite comfortable company... and I knew the wine to be of immense quality."

"So, you admit to overindulging then?" He had purred in satisfaction.

"I suppose I am," I had gulped. "I reckon I did enjoy a fair few glasses."

"Are there any other details you have omitted that you now wish to share?"

"I have nothing else I wish to confess-"

"Knomucca, enough with your antics!"

"To what exactly are you accusing me of?" I had asked, drawing my strength from the cherry wood bookshelves in the alcove of my memory. "I already admitted I had a fair lot of wine... what else is it you are searching for?"

"Where is the stable hand now, Knomucca? I am wishing to have a word with him..."

His question had made my stomach drop like a stone, my mind swimming as I scrambled to find my words.

"He set homeward at the night's end," I had said quickly. "Said he had to tend to his sister-"

"His family's dwelling is not an unreasonable distance from Morriraen," The Creator had challenged. "He should have reached home by now, yet nobody has seen him..."

"Nobody has seen him?" I had questioned, fighting to keep my face free of worry.

"Nay," The Creator had hissed. "Not since the pair of you were spotted venturing into the orchards alone... and well after the witching hour."

"That is rather odd," I had said, swallowing hard in a vain attempt to remain grounded. "Though I shall admit I have not ventured to the stables since Senaya's gathering and, therefore, have had no reason to check upon how he faired."

"Lies," The Creator had hissed, my spine prickling painfully, for I had failed to deceive Him. "I know you sought such seclusion to indulge in his body."

"I see not how anyone I have intimacies with is of concern to you," I had said, maintaining as much composure in my voice as I could muster. "Especially when it was consented."

"Consented?" The Creator pushed His energy harshly towards me once more. "You were seen entering the orchards together, though not returning from them in the same manner... I suppose your disposing of him was also consented?"

"I am uncertain what you mean," I said, fighting my deceit's futility.

"Do not lie to me, Knomucca," The Creator had snapped, his anger ringing through my head like a bell. "You were seen entering the orchards with him, then returning to the gathering alone in the early morning hours noticeably refreshed, whilst the stableboy was never again observed by anyone."

"Certainly, the circumstances doth not paint a flattering portrait," I had said, fighting against the intensity of his energy pushing against me. "Though I do not know what has come of him... I shall admit I indulged in the wonders of his body... though I am afraid I do not know much else-"

"I know you killed him," The Creator had said, His words threatening to crush me. "You fed on him, drained his energies, and wrenched his heart from his chest."

"You come to me with such anger and accusations, when I know taking the life of another bears no burden to you with your fondness for heartache and plagues-"

"Bite your tongue," The Creator had hissed as pain rushed through my mind's eye. "I am warning you... be silent when I am speak-"

"What is it that truly angers you?" I had snapped, allowing rage to cloud my judgment. "For my killing a stableboy you paid barely any mind to, or for enjoying the way he wielded his tongue and fingers?"

Sudden pain sliced across my cheek. Blood dripped from the heron talons that protruded from The Creator's sleeves where his hands should have been. My face stung from the burning scratches, the pain intensified by the hot sun above me. Panic threatened to choke me as I fought to breathe the salty air.

Revisiting a memory should not cause physical pain, I thought.

My fingers pressed against my cheek, the fresh blood staining my gauntlets. Nausea rippled through me, my head splitting in pain.

"This is not how it happened," I said aloud, staring at the deep red blood on my hands.

"Nay, I pardoned your language as an error of your youth, though you should know better now," He hissed, locking my gaze to His painfully. "How disgusting you are to me... the Gifts I hath bestowed upon you are not to be used for such inappropriate squaller..."

"It was an accident," I said, deciding I would admit my offenses as the tears brewed beyond my eyes. "I lost control... it was a mistake-"

"Disgusting," The Creator hissed. "You are always to be in control of your gifts and prove you have the strength to wield them. Such weakness is unbecoming. If you cannot handle my essence, how are you to handle my blood?"

"I shall attempt to do better," I said, knowing it was best to placate him. "I had not meant to cause any harm... it was simply an accident."

"Should I ever hear of your feeding from another's energy in this manner again I shall respond in a greater unkindness than I have thus far," The Creator loomed overhead, quickening my pulse, warm blood streaking down my cheek. "I hope I have made myself understood."

"Your words have rung clear as quartz," I said, resisting the urge to touch my stinging cheek.

"Very good, Knomucca," The Creator said as He adjusted His cloak. "You are quite impressive... I should hate for you to be unable to complete your Trials. Or those of your dear sister-"

"Syler..." Panic shot through me in a sobering spike of pain. "You leave her out of this, my actions bare no reflection on her..."

A sudden flash of Syler's face floated through the cresting waters. Her green, almond-shaped eyes tinged with pain and a fresh stream of tears. Her hand reached out towards me as I swam through the currents, my exhaustion perpetuating the fantasy that I had felt her through the turbulent tides. Her screams burned my ears and pierced needles through my eyes as the salt of her tears stung my skin. Syler began to speak in a choked whisper.

"Knomucca-"

The black tendrils of Spider Vines suddenly sliced across my mind's eye, my body shaking from the heat of the sun's glare.

"Syler," I called into the sky. "Can you hear me, Syler?"

The Creator laughed low, pulling me back into the study. He shifted to stand with His back to the hearth, His silhouette obscuring the warmth of the flames, muffled by the cold shadow of His cloak. The sun dimmed, and the sky grayed. Patches of darkness swooped and glided, swirling the currents around me into large waves. They collided and splashed with a force that pulled me under, leaving me to struggle against The Creator's attacks. I battled against the heavy waters, eventually cresting the surface to fight for breath. As I gasped, a wave knocked me forward, the air thick in my lungs. A sudden rush of wind passed around me, leaving me with a feeling of clarity as I gazed at the suddenly crisp and clear sky. Flocking birds traveled overhead, flying in flawless formation east through the brilliant path of the sun.

"Oi, *that* gave me quite a fright," I said, watching the birds soar above me.

Lifting a shaking hand, I examined my cheek, my stomach dropping as the salt stung the fresh scratches. A wordless horror stole my breath upon realizing what had just occurred.

"I must try to focus on good tidings..." I said, watching as a red-tailed hawk followed the path of the flocking seagulls. "A blessed omen it is to catch the sight of such birds."

I deduced from their migration that land would be a reasonable swim away. Kicking my legs with what final strength I could muster, I pushed myself forward, continuing to the east as the sun rose radiantly overhead.

Wee bit further now... I soothed to myself. *Any moment... all shall be well...*

I scoured the horizon through the sun's glare to trace the birds' path. The hawk circled overhead and flew sharply towards me, looping around my path before gliding eastward.

I kicked my legs and moved through the water, allowing the waves to propel me forward as my body rested upon my floating bedroll. The distant tides obscured my sights in every direction as I followed the hawk overhead. With the bird in my sights, I gained newfound strength and growing curiosity. As I swam for what seemed to be yet another eternity, the hawk led me to a distant island cresting on the horizon.

"Thank the Gods," I laughed in relief. "Please be not a mirage..."

I marveled at the notion of a distant shore, growing hopeful with the prospect of tending to my ailments and regaining my center. Above, in the sky, the hawk circled in a wide arc, returning on its path towards me before again flying eastward and disappearing from sight.

Bursting forth, the tides pushed me towards the distant shore as I paddled. The temptation of shelter and fresh water further fueled the strength I needed to bring the green palm trees into my sight.

"Thank you, curious bird," I said, the wind carrying my words. "In debt to you, I am indeed."

XII

EVERETT

Flames from the Rose Lily continued to fan upwards, dancing above the tops of nearby trees and threatening to set them alight as they had throughout the day. Heavy grey smoke obscured the early morning sunrise, painting the sky as if the day would fill with rain. Smoldering remains of the damaged apothecary fluttered through the air in wisps of ash, scenting the smoke in an unpleasant floral bouquet. The remaining horses whinnied in the paddock towards my right, their screams reminding me of the pain of Truff's escape towards the far-off wood to the north.

"Bullet!" I shouted, praying my voice would not pierce Kiyoko's dreams and disturb him. "Bullet! Are you in there?"

A silence fell upon the morning, punctured by the crackling of flames as the Rose Lily burned bright in the dawn. The cobblestone walls began to crumble from the heat of the fires, the thatched roof igniting with a harsh woosh and fanning smoke to the sky. Flocks of birds flew from the trees in fear as the flames drew closer, scurrying away through the leaves and branches with frightened chirps.

Bullet.... May the Gods bring you to safety, I thought, surveying the falling ashes and embers as I prayed that the grass and trees would not also burst into flame.

Stumbling forward, I moved in the direction of the Rose Lily. I hesitated, stopping abruptly as I knew I could not reach him. Kiyoko lay unconscious in my arms, breathing steadily whilst he rested. His chest rose and fell in a comfortable rhythm, his body warm through the fabric of his soft plum-purple kimono. His face was slack and relaxed, giving him an empty expression.

I hated Hazel for forcing him to absorb the Spider Vine's energy, knowing that although he had been gifted respite from the swirling energy inside him, it would return once he awakened.

"Bullet!" I shouted again, unwilling to accept the possibility that he had perished.

A sudden, swirling wind bit across me, glimmering and glistening energetically in a deep ice blue. Bullet emerged from the twisting wind, panting loudly as he hunched from exhaustion as the wind dissipated. His beard had been burnt, and his eyebrows were singed, the hairs atop his head smoking and frayed.

"Thank the Gods," I said delightedly, gifting him a nod. "I am glad you are safe."

"Aye..." Bullet said, running his fingers through the remaining strands of his hair as he surveyed the damage. "The blasted fire has nearly robbed me blind."

"That is just vanity. They will grow back... but you cannot be replaced," I said heavily, allowing a brief silence to pass between us as I adjusted Kiyoko to better bear his weight. "Show your war wounds with pride. It is a mark of strength."

Bullet held his silence, simply watching as the flames of the Rose Lily began to wane.

"Bullet, what happened in there?" I asked as I could no longer bear the silence. "Where is Hazel?"

"My initial round of fire was not enough to eradicate the Vines," Bullet began. A soft smile painted his lips, and I knew that he had enjoyed conjuring the flames that caused its absence despite the near loss of all his hair. "I had to get creative with some of the other elements in the apothecary, and my fires nearly grew beyond my ability to control them."

"Are they gone then?" I asked hopefully, holding Kiyoko tighter against my chest. The smell of mugwort danced across his skin and floated to my nose.

"I am uncertain," Bullet admitted. "The flames were becoming too hot and dangerous... I was barely able to use my gifts to move the air and escape."

"Gods..." I said with a heavy sigh.

"We shall observe the flames until they have extinguished, and if any of the Vines come through the threshold, then we will know the flames did not stop them." Bullet declared.

"I suppose that is wise," I said, exhaling a steady breath. "And what has become of Hazel?"

"To that I am also uncertain," Bullet hung his head as he continued speaking. "My attention was focused on burning the Spider Vines and I lost sight of the Priestess. She and the dead alchemists are gone, and I do not know what came of them."

"Gods," I swore intensely. "How do you suppose we find her?"

"Reckon she'll find us once Knomucca returns," he wagered.

"Aye... Suppose the shrew shall indeed show herself," I spat.

"My deepest apologies for losing her, Commander," Bullet said heavily.

"You need not give one," I said sincerely. "While the Priestess is a concern, the Spider Vines required your attention. You did what circumstances demanded. It is I who should apologize, I merely meant for you to cause a diversion, not risk your life."

"What were we to do, Commander? Escape the confines of the Rose Lily only to continuously run from the Spider Pricks until we reach Riverside? I think not."

"Wise indeed," I said, feeling Kiyoko stir as his breathing changed. "How are you fairing now that you are free of the flames?"

"I am as well and good as I could be," Bullet said, his voice lowering to a whisper. His eyes flickered towards Kiyoko before he absently scratched his cheek. "Though... I advise we do what we are able to keep the General in our sight. We don't need him runnin' off to cause trouble."

Glancing downward, I took in Kiyoko's slackened face. His once-piercing stare was subdued through his slumbering, his sun-kissed copper eyes laying dormant beneath the curtain of his thick lashes. His disheveled dark hair was strewn in waves about his shoulders, framing the carved angles of his jaw. His slender lips parted lazily as he rested, his devilish smile lost in his dreams.

"Aye... wise words indeed," I said with renewed anger towards Hazel. "We are certain to have a strenuous day ahead."

"Aye," Bullet agreed.

We watched as the bright flames from the Rose Lily began to diminish, grateful the cinders had kept the impending threat of the Spider Vines from breaching the threshold. Bullet stood vigilant beside me, his attention focused on Kiyoko and the smoldering remains behind him. His spirits were heavy and sad, his aura as frayed as the remains of his singed beard.

"I was but a short moment from searching for you," I admitted gently. "I was worried when you did not answer my summons."

"Admirable, and appreciated," Bullet gifted me with a salute. "All ended well, and your energy is needed elsewhere-"

Suddenly, the flames roared with renewed height, the heat emanating as they increased in intensity. The smoke poured thick and black from the apothecary, masking the early dawn in shadow. A cool, dark plum energy flowed from the tourmaline in my cloak, the scent carving through the charred remains of herbs and ashes in the air. A radiating pain shot through my head, my forehead ringing with Kiyoko's distant voice.

"Everett, help."

The flames gave another burst of light. The tourmaline froze in my pocket; the cold pervaded through the cloth and pressed against my skin. A loud, popping energy escaped the apothecary, reverberating in the morning light as the darkness faded from the sky.

"What in the Seven Hells was that?" Bullet asked.
"Hazel..." I began, trying to keep my voice level. "She must be taking post inside."

A burst of water enveloped the Rose Lily, and the flames extinguished with a sizzle and puff of smoke. Ashes and embers smoldered brightly, framed by the cracked and burnt brick walls that once housed the realm's oldest apothecary. Another eerie silence filled the morning, accompanied only by the sound of distant birds as they flew from the wreckage.

"What are we to do now?" Bullet questioned. "I reckon it isn't safe to venture inside, though someone needs to survey the damage. And repair plans shall be needed..."

"We have plenty of troops to see to the matter," I said sternly. "Dispatch a pair of scouts to take word back to Woodroe and inform them of the... mishap that has occurred here. Inform them to obtain the plans, materials, and builders required to restore the apothecary, and tell them the castle will settle the debt."
"And what of Knomucca?" Bullet asked.

"I am certain she will understand... eventually," I said.

"Shall I assess the damage first?" Bullet said.

"Nay, we have more important matters to attend to at present," I said.

As Bullet turned to leave, he paused and gestured towards the stockades. "Commander, it appears I won't be leaving you to your lonesome... there is the Sergeant."

Turning towards his gesture, I spotted Kyreese beside her horse, leaning against it as she rested her eyes.

Seeing Kye and the comfort that she drew from her horse sent a sharp pain ringing through my chest. The memory of Truff running past me and into the distant wood made my spirits sink with sadness. A sigh escaped my lips as I recalled the sound of his whinnying. I knew I could not relinquish Kiyoko to search for Truff, though my heart felt like it would tear for every moment I was forced to divide my attention.

"We shall find your horse," Bullet said in a tone that reminded me of my father, oddly knowing what was occupying my thoughts before I found the words. "At the first opportunity, I shall send soldiers to search for him..."

"Aye, perhaps Marsen, Tialon, and Noa," I said, my words falling flat.

"I shall see to it," Bullet nodded.

Sighing deeply, I continued to observe Kye as she rested, her aura sluggish and heavy as she leaned against Lady Moonbeam.

"What do you suppose Hazel meant... She would give the Sergeant another bout of nightmares?"

I paused, watching tension cloud Kye's aura. Her shoulders were clenched, and her breathing was erratic, her alertness compromised with her spirit's dissociation.

"It is not my place to speculate..." My words trailed away as Kye wiped a silent tear with her sleeve.

Bullet nodded. "Try to see if you can find out when you talk to her... Not to be indelicate, but any information we have can help us create defenses against the Priestess."

"Can you do that?" I asked.

"I could supply something temporary," he said. "Though it is the General who could provide more security... Should he come round."

I nodded as I exhaled a tense breath, watching Kiyoko's chest gently rise and fall.

"Very well...Is there anything else you wish to discuss?" Bullet asked tentatively.

"Nay..." I hesitated. "Please go and retrieve the remaining troops... Dispatch the scouts to Woodroe for the repairs, and the scouts to search for Truff. Upon your return we will need to make camp whilst we discuss how to handle Hazel."

"Very well," Bullet said. "I shall return swiftly."

"Until then, I ought to have a word with the Sergeant... make certain she is well," I said, scooping Kiyoko into my arms.

Bullet regarded Kiyoko before gifting me a salute. Turning rapidly around, he disappeared in a plume of wind and ran briskly in the direction of the troops.

I shifted Kiyoko in my arms, lifting him across my shoulders. Crossing the grass, I approached the stockades and gently opened the gate before closing it softly behind me. Lowering Kiyoko, I carefully placed him on the grass. His body stirred, the movement threatening his sleep.

"Stay asleep, Love," I whispered. I pressed a gentle kiss into his fingers before rising to a stand. I tucked him against the fence, making certain he remained asleep before I approached Kye.

"Kye?" I said gingerly. "Kye..."

Her breathing quickened as I drew near. Her aura had split and fragmented, the shards cracking around her third eye and the crown of her head. Long black vines wove through her energy, the tentacles squeezing her spirits tightly.

"Kyreese," I said, my words failing to reach her.

She groaned in discomfort, pain flashing brightly through her energy. Lifting her hands, she pressed them over her face, shielding her eyes as she began to cry.

"Oi, lassie," I said more urgently, placing a tentative hand on her shoulder. "Kye-"

Her eyes flew open, panic painting her aura. Lady Moonbeam flattened her ears and whinnied a low, protective growl.

"Lassie, it's Everett," I soothed. "I will not hurt you."

"Everett... I don't feel well," she said, fighting to keep her eyes open. Her skin's mahogany tint paled to a flushed pink. Her deep purple hair had loosened in its braid, the strands fading at the roots in a lighter hue. "I fear I may be ill."

"I shall help to right you," I said, squeezing her shoulder firmly in an attempt to ground her.

Her tears flowed down her cheeks, spilling into the broken strands of her braided hair.

"Lassie, tell me what troubles you," I pleaded.

"I cannot," she sobbed. "I fear I have not the strength."

"A falsity if I have ever heard one," I said, rubbing her shoulders protectively. "You are the realm's youngest sergeant. This alone shows proof of your strength."

The sobs racked her body, her shoulders shaking like angry autumn leaves.

"Kye, please, talk to me."

"Do you remember Orin?" She asked.

My heart fell through my stomach.

"Aye," I said regretfully.

She shuddered, wrapping her hair protectively around her.

"Why do you ask?" I fought to keep my voice calm.

Kye took a shaking breath and averted her eyes.

"Does this have anything to do with Hazel?"

She nodded slowly.

"I can protect you..." I said sincerely. "I have once before, and I will again."

"They'll keep hurting me," Kye said, tears streaming down her cheeks.

"Kye, you listen to me," I began, leaning in and searching her face. "He cannot and will not hurt you again. You were a defenseless child when he had his way with you-"

"When you saved me," she sobbed.

"Aye, lassie," I said with a nod. "But you are stronger now. You are a skilled swords master, and you know how to hold your own in any storm."

Kye's breathing began to slow.

"When we brought you home, Knomucca and Senaya helped you forge your hair... so you would never be defenseless again. You are not who you were when we first met. You can handle this Kye. I know you can."

Kye held my gaze but didn't speak.

"Sergeant, I need you to tell me about the nightmares," I stated, appealing to her pride as a soldier to invoke her strength.

"Nay-"

"Bullet and Kiyoko can create protections against the Priestess, but we need whatever information we can collect in order to do so," I said.

Kye stood tight and rigid before her body began to quake once more.

"Could we sit over yonder beneath the oak?" I asked.

Kye nodded slowly.

"Come along then," I declared, placing my arm protectively across her shoulders.

I steered her from her horse, moving her towards the gate of the stockades.

"Wait here a moment," I said, hoisting Kiyoko from the grass and draping him across me.

Returning across the grass, I opened the gate and guided the Sargent from the pen with a gentle hand. When the fence was secure, I led them across the grass, moving us towards a large oak. I watched as Kye sat and leaned firmly against the tree. I lowered Kiyoko delicately to the earth. I sat on the ground between them, producing my water skin from my belt.

"Here," I said, handing it to Kye.

She took it hesitantly and slowly began to drink. I fished through my smoking sack, finding a spliff tucked into the leather. I coaxed it to life with a match and inhaled the herbs gratefully.

Kiyoko stirred beside me, moaning softly in his sleep. I smoothed his hair affectionately, then leaned him against me so he would be more comfortable.

"You are quite sweet towards him," Kye said as she slowly sipped her water.

"I love him," I said, relieved I could voice the words aloud.

"I suppose you do..." Kye nodded, taking a breath before continuing. "Everett... I'm sorry I told the Priestess about your kissing him... I... It was wrong."

"Wash it down the river," I said, exhaling my smoke in the breeze.

"She knows people's secrets," Kye said, her voice barely above a whisper.

"Tell me about the nightmares," I said again.

Kye plucked the spliff from my fingers, inhaling deeply.

"In the dreams he's healed," she began. "He can walk, and his manhood is... functional. He finds me wherever I am... he threatens to finish what he started with me and he says that he'll kill you if you intervene again."

"Gods," I swore, horrified.

"Sometimes I relive that day... in the dreams... and I wake with the pain in my body he caused. Sometimes I try to fight free, but my gifts freeze away..."

"They are always with you," I said, preparing to ask a difficult question. "Does Hazel ever appear in the dreams?"

Kye took a long drag before she spoke. "In the worst ones... She experiments on my hair. She rips it from my head and cuts my body to be more suitable for him..."

"How do you mean?" I asked as delicately as I could.

"She cuts out parts of me so he cannot make me pregnant," she said.

A heavy silence fell between us, punctuated by Kiyoko's gentle breathing.

"That is terrible," I said. "I am sorry you have to witness such a horror."

Kye released a plume of smoke and nodded softly.

"These are merely demons in your mind," I comforted. "When I saved you from him, I left him for dead..."

"I pray he remains in the grave," she said.

Another silence fell between us.

"What's going to happen to the General?" she asked.

"He will wake, and we shall clear his mind," I said, not wanting to worry her with the prospect that he would wake violent and unruly.

"Could I rest with him a while?" she asked. "I know you and Bullet have some matters to attend to... But I do not have the spirits to assist until I have collected myself."

"That is well with me, he will sleep for several hours more," I said. "We shall find a place suitable for the pair of you."

The sounds of distant hooves filled the air. The creaking of the wagons and the whistling of the troops floated over my ears as the guard moved from the trees. They spilled across the ground and poured over the cemetery, finding places to tie their horses and dismount.

"Commander, Sergeant," Bullet said as he emerged from his swirling wind, standing before us. "Kye, are you well? You gave us quite a fright."

Kye nodded. "I'm surprised that you would ask... I thought you bore anger towards me from our earlier arguments."

"I do not hold on to such things for long," he said gently. "And I could never remain angry with you for more than a moment."

A shy smile spread across Kye's face.

Bullet sat with us beneath the tree. "Kye, do you know I had a daughter?"

She looked up and searched his face. "Nay."

"She is a lot like you... Or she was... Until she crossed over," he said. "You have the fire within you that she also possessed. I admire it greatly."

"Thank you," Kye said with a smile that faded quickly. She paused before continuing. "If you don't mind... how did she die?"

"A mining accident," Bullet said. "In our homeland, it happens more often than we wish. People are sometimes lost in cave-ins or wander off and are never found. My Rena had been exploring a particularly fruitful shaft and was separated from the rest of her crew. There was a minor quake... when they found her, she had been crushed by falling boulders."

"I am so sorry," Kye said.

"Her crossing led me to the castle, to become acquainted with her protector while she lives in the underworld," he said.

A somber silence hung in the air between us. There were no words Kye nor myself could offer Bullet. As much as I wished to grant him a minute to remember his daughter, time was passing rapidly.

"The sergeant has offered to rest with the general for a while... so the pair of us can situate camp and discuss next steps," I said.

"There's the alchemist garden," Bullet began. "It's in a small clearing over yonder, and it could pose a comfortable place to reconvene."

Lifting Kiyoko once again, I bore his weight with much effort as I draped him over my shoulder. Following Bullet and Kye to the east, we found a small garden of plants and flowers secluded with a border of high hedges. Thick, soft clover was surrounded by chrysanthemums and hydrangeas. A dry, stone fountain of a swan sat in the middle of the garden.

Sighing deeply, I watched as Kiyoko lay sleeping, praying with all I could to the Gods and Dreamweaver that he would remain resting. Turning then to Bullet, I informed him of Hazel's threats to Kiyoko, indicating her intensity in conveying he remain resting and out of her path.

"Real twat she's becomin'" Bullet said angrily, "tell me true, who hath poisoned her watering hole?"

"I cannot say," I said, deciding again to keep the knowledge of my seeing the shadows in her aura quietly to myself. "For if I knew, I certainly would not allow it again to be so."

"I reckon that's true," Bullet said, shaking his head in anger and disgust. "I reckon 'tis even worse knowing we are to associate with her as if she hasn't slighted us, until we can converse with Knomucca about the events of the day since her departure."

"Aye," I thought, deciding to test the strength of Bullet's bindings and release Kiyoko from my grasp.

Kiyoko nestled deeply into the grass, his breathing long and rhythmic as if he were entranced in deep meditation. The serenity of his face conveyed that he had been deeply asleep, brought to the realm of unconsciousness by my hand, for which I bore anger toward my being. The sight of him shackled nearly brought tears to my eyes, my head suddenly jerking him from my sight as I turned to watch the fountained swan.

Silent tears suddenly spilled down my cheeks as the weight of the passing days settled against me. Distant crickets filled the night, their sounds masking the sobs that threatened to consume me.

"Oi, Everett... Look there!" Bullet said, his far too chipper tone shocking me from my stupor.

Across the silver of the nearly full moon, a large shadow began to take shape. Large wings moved through the wind and began to barrel towards us.

"It's Thornin," Bullet said in excitement.

The dragon sped towards the ground, landing in the clearing with a hard crunch upon the grass. I took in the sight of his empty saddle, my heart plummeting with sadness as I noticed Knomucca's absence.

"Thornin," I said, stepping closer to him. "Thornin, where is Knomucca?"

XIII

KNOMUCCA

The hawk vanished from my line of sight, disappearing behind distant trees that had materialized on the horizon. A lush green island sprouted from the expanse of the sea, signaling the prospect of my survival. Seagulls flocked overhead, migrating westwards towards Belleview, carrying my sadness with them. With renewed strength and vigor, I paddled through the waves, feeling the waters begin to shallow beneath my makeshift raft as I pulled my body forward. Waves crashed against the large boulders surrounding the shoreline, spraying white mist through the air.

I lingered briefly, nervous about what awaited on the island. I sighed heavily and pried myself from the water, pulling my body off my bedroll. I gripped the stone tightly and began climbing, fighting my exhaustion. I heaved my body up the rocks despite feeling my legs weighing me down as I pulled myself from the water. I could feel the sting of the warm tropical air, my skin exposed painfully after too much sun and salt water.

"Up like a daisy now, Knomucca," I soothed to myself, focusing on my steps as I woozily wobbled across the rocks. "Aye, find your rhythm..."

Centering my energy, I released a series of breaths, taking time to reacquaint myself with my body and its inflictions from my night in the tides. The residual salt from the water grated harshly against my dry, raw skin. The need for freshwater was so intense it nearly made me weep, providing me the motivation I required to fumble forward. Stepping across the stones, I watched as the shoreline gradually began to smooth.

"Slowly now... easy does it," I said aloud, gently coaxing myself to move despite my sore and throbbing muscles.

The sunbaked stones were hot against my bare feet, burning my skin. While removing my excess clothing had been necessary in the water, I now feared it would prove to be problematic on land. My eyes burned from the salt water and throbbed in agitation, my skin scorching painfully from the day in the sun.

I wish I had a change of dress... I thought tiredly as I picked at my tunic. My thoughts drifted to the dress I was meant to wear for The Ascension, sitting in the supply wagon with the troop's dress armor.

Pausing amongst the stones, I searched my pouch, finding a single green tunic nestled at the bottom. I pulled it hastily from the enchanted leather, catching it against loose herbs and parchments only to send them flying into the treacherous space between the rocks. Groaning in annoyance, I recollected what I could and shoved it back into the pouch. I peeled off my drenched tunic and replaced it with the dry one, sliding it over my head and letting it drape loosely against my body. The light silk felt cool against my radiating skin, the fabric providing protection from the sun.

"Oi, Gods... it is warm..." I said aloud, focusing on my words as I climbed the rocky shoreline. I shall be in need of water soon... Without proper hydration, I fear I shall certainly find myself on a journey to Heimaaila with no body in this realm to return to...

Placing my feet against the wet and slick stone, I fumbled across the large and jagged rocks, seeing a smoothed beach of white sand in the distance. I stumbled onwards slowly, allowing myself to swear intensely as I moved towards the beach. Far off cicadas forbode the remaining day's heat, their crepitations accompanying the intense sun as it radiated across my face.

The sun's blaze here is hotter than the Seven Rings... Musing dramatically to myself, I released a laugh to cleanse and brighten my spirits. My legs were sore and shaking as I cleared my final path across the stones. The moon and the night's chill shall be much welcomed... I wish not to spend another moment beneath the sun for as long as I can help it...

A refreshing breeze swept across my back, blowing my hair into my face. Absently, I began to run my fingers through the knots, detangling my thick blonde hair as I lifted it from the nape of my neck. The wind across my newly exposed skin brought a blissful relief from the heat. Twisting my fingers through my hair, I tied it in a loose braid. My stomach lurched in horror as I discovered the absence of my mother's broach, my eyes threatening to brim with tears as a feeling of panic washed through me.

Turning abruptly, I searched in vain through the surrounding rocks, my panic shifting to rage when I found them revealing nothing. My thoughts drifted towards Syler, fixating on the pain and sadness she would hold in her eyes when I disclosed to her the pin's absence. Her cries rippled through me as they had done through the waves; her soft green eyes flooded with pain and betrayal as they pleaded for help and screamed with pain.

Why must I have lost my mother's broach? I thought with frustration, my eyes too dry to release their tears, though the urge to cry welled within me.

Momentarily, I allowed myself to grieve, disappointed about losing the broach, yet another piece of her I had had to hold on to. A hollowed sadness speared through my heart, spidering outwards in a web of grief and sorrow. I had yearned to find comfort by holding my mother's broach in hand, for I feared I was far from home and knew not how to find it again.

"Her sword is all that remains of her now," I said heavily, absently squeezing the blade beneath my tunic and feeling relief in discovering it against me.

I released another sigh and continued my climb across the rocks. The nearing white pebbled sands promised the prospect of rejuvenating my spirits.

I shall set camp once I arrive on the beach, I thought to myself, jumping across a rock gap as the sand drew closer. I need shelter from the sun... and a new source of drinking water... and once I have recovered, I can seek out a better vantage point.

Crossing the final stones was long and tedious, my feet surprisingly steady as I alighted upon the white pebbled sands. Large, leafed plants punctuated the island's shoreline, casting long shadows across the scorching hot sand. Palm trees swept tall beside blossoming shrubs and were bordered with bright blooming bromeliads. The sight of coconuts nearly brought tears to my eyes, for the promise of the refreshing water they held within would certainly help satiate my thirst.

I came to a rest at the base of a palm tree. Reaching upwards from the cylindrical trunk, I found a low-hanging coconut; pulling it from the branch as I forced the sword from my spine. The outer green husk was warm and leathered, the shell not yet hard with age. Pressing the tip of my sword into the coconut, I was surprised when the blade punctured the flesh. My removal of the steal was slow and precise as I fought to keep the liquid from spilling.

I held the coconut aloft, giving thanks for my fair fortune in finding such refuge and escaping from the salted seas. Pressing the coconut to my lips, I inhaled the water within the husk, relishing the thick and sweet liquid as I attempted to satiate my thirst. The taste was so refreshing I allowed myself to moan with delight, finding immense pleasure in the firmness of the mild and nutty flesh.

"Gods, that was divine," I said aloud, placing the emptied husk of the coconut into my pouch and setting to consume another.

The second coconut was equally magnificent as the first, bringing with it a blissful nirvana as I consumed it beneath my tree. I rested with my back upon the trunk and watched the waves crash against the rocks, noticing the mist spray as it scattered against the late summer sky.

If only I could capture the mist somehow, I thought, fantasizing for the waters I so desperately wished could quench me. Though I may find my thirst temporarily tamed, I fear I shall have issues if I overindulge in coconuts...

Polishing clean the second coconut, I placed the empty husk in my pouch along with the first, then quickly indulged in a third. Reaching upwards a hand, I collected seven coconuts, pulling them from the branches of the tree and slipping them into the enchanted leather to consume as needed. I collapsed in the shade of the tree as my exhaustion overtook me. I hit the ground painfully, my body yearning for a moment's rest as I fought to rejuvenate my energies.

Inhaling deeply, I drifted into meditation, my spirits swirling as my balance shifted with my relaxation. Exhaling a tense breath, I cleared my mind, focusing my aura inwards as I began rejuvenating the energy within myself. Relaxing into my breathing, I allowed my spirits to realign, my vital energies and body disentangling blissfully after my time in Heimaaila and my night in the tides.

My breathing deepened, the ground melting away beneath me as I concentrated on the movement of my diaphragm. The far-off sounds of a soft rain filled my ears, the drops containing a metallic tone as they clinked in a soothing rhythm. The droplets turned into the tiny tinkling of bells, their shining silver spheres cascading from the moon as they shed streams of salted tears.

"Amoris et Lucis," a familiar voice whispered through me, my heart fluttering as the smell of hibiscus and sandalwood floated through the rain.

Senaya's silver eyes flashed brightly before me, cutting through the sunlight with the intensity of a steel blade. Her long hair was woven in thick braids down her spine, her enchanted silver hair sticks poking elegantly through the interlocking knots. The silk of her white dress draped across my skin; the cooled fabric felt quite exhilarating after the lengthy day in the heat.

"Senaya," I opened my mouth to speak her name, yet no sound escaped my lips. "Hark, Senaya... can you hear me?"

"Knomucca..."

Senaya... I am here with you, Senaya...

"Come to me, Knomucca," Senaya whispered. The gentle lull of her voice was welcome in the silence of the island. "In the meadow of fragrant flowers... that is where you may find me."

How am I to come to you? I thought desperately, I have not the strength...

"Complete the cycle," Senaya soothed, her voice soft as a reem of velvet. "You must transcend to ascend... from water grows mist, only to rain again..."

Senaya... I beseech thee, be frank and clear... I fear I doth not possess the wits to comprehend such a riddle with my head so dry and my spirits so numb.

Raindrops fell into flower-shaped puddles, the ripples forming the folds of roses and daisies. The daisies shifted into the bitter scent of mugwort, perfuming the wind with the sad sounds of a reed flute. The distant hooves of a running horse sent a jolt of unexpected sadness through me, the sadness overtaken with curiosity when a steel blue wolf charged forcefully across the horizon. A veil of plum purple trailed the wolf's paws, reflecting in the iron that sculpted the wolf's teeth and claws. Clusters of cherry blossoms bloomed beneath the wolf as it ran across the sky, silhouetted with the distant bliss of Kiyoko's joyous laughter.

"KIYOKO!!" I screamed in desperation as I called for him, my stomach dropping in alarm as he materialized across the distant planes.

Hot, searing gold sliced across the meadow, the shade akin to the glinting sunlight that shone in his eyes. His face met mine in an unpleasant sneer before turning angrily away as I reached out a hand. Forcefully, I began to run towards him, my feet heavy in the waist-high grasses. My voice cracked helplessly as I shouted across the wind, realizing with pain and rage that he was ignoring my pleas.

"Kiyoko... stop... please... why must you turn from me!?"

With every step I took towards him, he drew further from my sight, disappearing through the stems of lavish purple flowers. The scent of mugwort burned bitter and painful through my senses, sending my head reeling.

"Kiyoko... Return to me... Gods, please... Kiyoko!"

Sadness and anger disrupted my breathing, the hurt flooding through me. My body tensed, jarring me forcefully from a field of tall, fragrant flowers. My energy failed to realign as I baked in the heat of the sun, my exhaustion finding me once more. The songs of herons and hawks guided me back to the present, and my body began to feel heavy and sore as I found my way back within myself.

With lethargic movements, I peeled away from the palm tree, unsticking my tunic from the fibrous trunk. Though my body had rested, I felt little in the way of being refreshed. My energies and muscles throbbed and weighed heavy as I began to contemplate my course of action. A subtle breeze floated gently across my skin, rustling my tunic pleasantly as I yearned to consume countless tankards of water and ale.

There must be a source of water somewhere near, I theorized. How else can such abundance of plant and game frequent a land surrounded in salt...

The breeze shifted its direction, carrying the calming scent of sandalwood through my awareness once more. The sounds of metallic raindrops tinkled lightly like soft bells all around me as I suddenly stopped my movements.

Sounds as though raindrops are collecting in a bucket, I mused, mildly unnerved by the metallic tinkling that plagued my ears despite being free of my meditations. What I would not give for a long and cleansing rain... would not only be good for my spirits, but I could capture the rain and drink it.

Glancing upwards, I searched the late-day sky, growing dismayed when I found it to hold no sign of coming rain.

"Flophenne, please... share with me your wisdom... shall it rain this upcoming night? May I expect relief from the waves of dreaded heat and intense humid air?"

The sun shone maliciously through the sky, radiating relentlessly over the rocks and sea.

"How unjust," I scoffed, rolling my eyes despite myself. This night passed a storm worthy of the Underworld itself tossed me from course, yet now the sky shines clear and blue...

Sighing heavily, I thought of how I was to procure my own rain, leaning my shoulders against the palm tree to help me keep my focus. Watching the waves, I envied their droplets flashing across the late-day sky, noticing the molecules spread through the golden rays of the sun. Lazily, the water droplets fanned across the surface of the sea, rippling outwards in spectacular rings that fanned large and stretched endlessly.

Steeling my strength, I rose to a stand, forcing fresh coconuts into my pouch before retrieving my emptied husks. The late-day sun warmed the sand beneath my feet, forcing me to dash across it as I found refuge beneath another coconut tree. Reckon I shall need shoes before I am to proceed, I sighed heavily, grateful to find an extra pair of dragon scale gloves at my belt and only the left boot from a set made of black leather. I shall have to fashion something...or else my feet are likely to burn...

"This shall have to suffice," I said, examining the boot carefully. "I cannot risk the dragonscales."

I returned the gloves to my pouch and removed my sword from its sheath. I sliced the boot horizontally, separating the shaft and sliding the now ankle-high boot over my left foot. Using my blade, I cut small holes into the remaining leather and used loosed strands from my tunic to sew it into a slipper. Once crafted, I slid it upon my right foot, testing the weight to ensure it would not slide away.

"This will have to do," I said, musing at the hilarity of my unmatched shoes but thankful my feet would not burn.

Finding renewed courage, I moved into the open sands, beginning to dig a hole with my fingers. My metal gauntlets tore into my skin as the padding beneath them slid and contracted with water. Moisture was trapped painfully against my wrinkled palms, the backs of my hands cracking from the salt. After I had finished my digging, I retrieved more coconuts from the tree to harvest the nectar within. Using the pulp, I transformed the base of the hole into mud, foraging for more fruits and dumping their flesh in the sands to make a paste. Using my blade to prick my fingers, I smeared my blood through the ground, enchanting the sand in the sunlight to harden it into clay. The hole became impervious to water, and the adobe cooled and carved from my hand in preparation for my water collection. I looked upon my work with pride as I set to preparing another three holes.

"Now to fill this with water," I said, marveling at how far the salted sea had seemed across the heated stones. "Flophenne, I implore you, you and Piscaro, God of the Sea to give me strength."

Returning across my path traveled, I filled my emptied coconut husks with salted sea water. Filling all four sand traps using only the husks to carry the water took several moments. Once that task was complete, I placed the hollowed husks to float in the center as an open goblet.

Searching the beach, I found a gathering of giant rhubarb plants. Admiring their large leaves, I pulled them into my hands. Trailing across the sand, I brought the leaves to my holes, laying them across the tops. I piled sand around the edges to hold them in place and trap them in the heat before placing a small amount of sand in the center to make it concave.

Growing pleased with my work, I returned to a stand, though saddened that obtaining fresh water would still take several hours. Begrudgingly, I indulged in another coconut, satiating my thirst with the thick and mild nectar as I continued to set my camp. Not far from my water traps, I began to dig a pit for a fire, finding dried driftwood and branches of trees to use for kindling when the sun would set. Preparing a fire during the night could prove to be dangerous as it would draw my location outwards from the privacy of the shadows, yet without a fire, I feared I could not cook the game I had hoped to catch once I had settled for the evening.

Once my firepit was set, I found my path along the shore and returned towards my palm tree, producing my dagger to use the blade to mark the trunk. I drove my tip into the palm tree trunk and began to etch my lines, carving the crest of my mother's coven into the fibrous wood. Regarding the sun's position, I marked the time with a hastily drawn sundial, indicating that in several hours, the moon would be beginning to rise. With a compass, I drew an arrow towards the northwest, indicating my path of travel as conditioned by my Commander. At the same time, I began to explore my surroundings.

I sighed heavily and stepped away from the tree, leaving the palm at my back as I walked across the shore. Following the curve of the coast, I moved northwest, admiring the abundance of flowers adorning the edge of the water. Beautiful orange bromeliads clung to weather-worn rocks and were being swarmed hungrily by fluttering hummingbirds as they explored the plants for nectar. Tall pink orchids wove between hibiscus and stocky reeds, the delicate petals wafting a sweet, musky scent that allowed me to feel at ease despite my anxiety.

Veering leftwards, my trajectory turned westward, the shore curving in an expanse towards the horizon as it arched around the island. The jagged coast was deceptive in providing clear direction, jutting outwards in large boulders that had suffered from the relentless tides. The clarity from the sun and sky allowed my eye to search nearly a league, discovering no docking piers or signs of naval life upon the island's shoreline.

How strange, I mused. How do those who dwell here expect to prosper with no boats or trading ports...

Placing my feet delicately, I prudently moved through the sand, disliking how the gritty white pebbles were gradually replaced by larger stones. Exploring the coastline, I searched for any indicators that would allow me to identify this island's location. I grew dismayed as the landscape merely blossomed in beautiful blooming flowers atop the rocks and crags. There was no lighthouse or fisher's shed and no hanging lanterns to provide light when the moon ascended.

Unless... nobody doth dwell here, I thought. And thus have no need for such luxuries...

Nearly a league fell beneath my sore and wrinkled feet, my body protesting the heat as I moved over rocks and stepped through the shrubbery. The rocks grew taller and clustered thickly, the impassable rockfaces looming upwards with moss and thorn-covered vines.

It appears I lack the proper footwear to climb such bramble, I thought with a sigh, disliking how I could not see around the rocks and plants to know what lay beyond them. I fear I must venture inland unless I wish to return to my camp...

I collected my composure with a long and deep breath, deciding to continue south along the sand whilst I became oriented with the local wildlife. Ferns and flowers grew beneath lumbering banana trees, the trunks lined with holes from birds drilling through the wood. Swooping branches, shaded shrubs, and wild roots, the pungent odors of mushrooms and other fungi ripe in the moistened soil. Long, wisping trees housed red, lantern-shaped fruits, the berries eerily hypnotic as I crossed the shore and examined them.

"How beautiful," I mused, regarding the berries with a curious eye.

A sweet, fruity scent wafted from the leaves of the trees, rustling lazily in the late-day breeze. The fruits were quite large, attached to the branches of the trees by thick, stocky stems. The husk of the fruit folded over itself, creating layers upon layers in a way that reminded me of the lanterns released during the Festival of Lights, the sabbat occurring between the winter solstice and spring equinox. During this sabbat, the people celebrate light and spring as they return to the Realms. They release ornately carved, enchanted lanterns into the night sky to carry fair fortune into the upcoming spring.

Thinking of this sabbat made me smile, as it reminded me of Kiyoko, given that this Festess was his favorite. Though he had fancied celebrating this sabbat with his late wife, Paedie, he still enjoyed reveling in its luxury. The lanterns he chose to carve and enchant each season took him months to finalize and perfect.

Oi... Kiyoko, I thought, remembering the sneer he held on his face during my meditations in the meadow. "Right foul arse... ignoring my calling him and turning away."

I sighed again, speaking softly to myself as I continued examining the fruits. "I do not blame him... the moment hath finally presented itself to exact revenge for the grief and anger he possesses towards me for Paedie's death...

"Although Kiyoko is knowledgeable of the natural flow of time and energy, he fails to grasp that despite my echelon or love for him, there is nothing I can do when it is a person's time to die... he blames me and holds hate in his heart for this..."

Sadness and anger yanked at my spirits, weakening my psychic protections as I lingered in the presence of the mysterious berries. The sun warmed my skin and coaxed a memory to the surface, the castle library again filling my mind's eye.

---//---

I found myself in one of the library's secret study rooms, the scent of a cherry log burning brightly in the fireplace. The sweetened wood was a ritual passed down from my mother and her coven to aid as an anchor when traveling the astral plane. The alcove was ordained with hooks for our cloaks, many of our favorite pillows and blankets, and my prized altar.

Mother had been sitting at the circular, wooden table beside me, and my sister was resting her finger against the parchment of a book she held in her hands. A long green dress flowed beneath the table; the sleeves rolled back delicately above her wrists, which had begun to look thinner than usual. Her hair, once red as the coals in the smithing forge but now greying, fell in waist-length waves beneath a silk shawl draped around her.

"It is then at this time you add the lavender," Mother instructed amid her lecture on brewing an advanced protection potion, her voice catching on the wind. "It will begin to boil shortly after, and that is well; doing your best to combine the elements thoroughly so as to not allow any to coagulate or adhere to the bottom is going to prove best for it in the long term-"

"Oi... can we take a moment's rest please, Mama?" Syler whined, her parchment half abandoned with the words she had been instructed to inscribe. "We've been at it all day now, Mama... and I haven't been allowed to draw anything for my own pleasure-"

"There will be time for fun and frivolity later on, Syler," Mother said, narrowing her eyes with a stern expression. "Now, I need you to be a good lass and focus on your work..."

Shifting her gaze, Mother watched my lettering as I scrawled across the parchment, my younger hand of only seven years not yet housed in an iron prison. "Aye, excellent work, Knomucca... your writing has really improved from your dedication and practice-"

"Of course, Knomucca has the dedication," Syler said as Mother ran her hand through my hair where the broach had been. Her eyes flashed sadly as she continued. "She gets to become Goddess of Death... she'll never die, and she'll always have the time to learn all this and everything else she might fancy-"

"Syler," Mother scorned. "You could not be further from the mark... what is to come for you both will be far from a leisurely stroll through the peach grove."

"I am right though, aren't I?" Syler hissed from nearby on my left. "She'll never have to worry about what is going to happen to her in this life or the next, or what becomes of anybody else she might love-"

"It is not so glamorous," Mother said, dropping her voice to a whisper. Absently, she began to draw markings upon her parchment, the lines forming a protective sigil before she began to speak. "As a Goddess of Love and Goddess of Death, there will be many people who form resentments towards you both because of situations they shall hold you responsible for. Failed relationships or continued rejections... death of spouses or loved ones leaving those left behind feeling empty... Having an abundance of power, will, and resources has its advantages, of course. However, the pain and heartache you shall witness during your time as Goddesses shall certainly keep you humble."

"Why do we have to be Goddesses, Mama?" Syler asked, using her pencil to connect my lines and form a portrait of a spider from my runes. The ink bled a deep plum purple, the smell of mugwort filling the parchment where I had not remembered any previously. "I don't want to be a Goddess, Mama, I want to leave the castle and be free with the trees in the meadow of fragrant flowers..."

"I wish nothing more than to be able to grant you such a request, Pumpkin," Mother said, running her hand affectionately through Syler's curly hair.

"Then can't we leave, Mama?" Syler asked, my heart pounding with anticipation as I hoped my mother would agree. "We could take our cloaks and flee before the coming supper, like we did before."

"We mustn't, Dearest," Mother said, pressing her pencil hard into the lines of her parchment. "The Creator will find us wherever we run to, and He shall bring you back here regardless if you wish to do so compliantly or with your hands and energies bound."

"Do you know this for certain, Mama?" Syler adjusted her pencil, beginning to add shading to the spider and a web between its pincers. "We're strong, Knomucca and me... we can run quite fast and far..."

"I doth not doubt such an ability, Pumpkin," Mother's voice was serious yet gentle. "You may not remember, though we spent the first years of your life fleeing sanctuary after sanctuary as The Creator hunted for us."

"Why does he want us, Mama?" Syler asked, her words sending a nervous jolt down my spine into my slippers. "Couldn't he find somebody else to be Goddesses instead of us, Mama?"

---//---

Mother paused, her eyes narrowing as she drilled her pencil into the parchment. The mild, earthy scent of daisies wafted in a soft white whisp from the tip of her stylus, perfuming the air protectively from the dark flash through her energy.

'The Creator is corrupted,' Mother whispered through me, her words carried across the salted winds of my tropical confinement. 'He sought you for your lineage, the timing of your birth, your innate gifts, beauty, and strength... and the power He sees that is great within you. You were both brought here for selfish reasons,' Mother said through us gently. 'From those who only wish to wreak havoc on the worlds they help create and thrive in the ruins of what is left behind. The Creator Ascends Gods only to ensure they help Him destroy Crossfire and never allow it to prosper... He could have found alternative means to recruit assistance in governing His world, yet He hunts for those He believes He can corrupt and use their power as His will to keep Crossfire in a dark, imbalanced place. Nary hath a God of Death ever Ascended upon this place for The Creator shall not allow it so. Not after Anteyus was entrapped for displaying the knowledge that possessing power with a true heart, love, and gentleness is what is most important...'

Mother's words and memory floated through me, flowing like the waves that crashed against the distant shore.

---//---

"I am still going to die one day, Mama," Syler said angrily, sharing an expression with my Mother I could not understand.

"You were born of power and contain it within you..." Mother's words rang. "Though you both are promised immortality upon your Ascension, it comes with the respect of knowing not to use it for malicious gains or ill intents... you must always be humbled, do what you can for others, and fight for balance. Nature is to take its course here and the realms are to be gifted with prosperity."

---//---

A sudden cool breeze brought me back to the present, the beginning of the descending sun promised on the refreshed winds. Distant crickets began to chirp, their songs promising a humid night. The lantern shaped berries thrummed and reverberated in the nearing sunset, a soft hint of burned cherry logs perfuming from their tight and wrinkled husks.

"Mother was right," I said aloud, my words grounding me in the present moment of the island. "Regardless of the good I do, I am rarely forgiven for deeds I am forced to fulfill."

A deep sigh escaped me, the lantern-shaped fruits bobbing heavily in the changing winds. The branches swooped low and brushed across my face, the fruits sending a familiar, glittering warmth down my spine and through my energy. Kiyoko's laugh whispered through me, his mirth ending abruptly as the fruit returned to hang above my head.

"How curious," I said, regarding the berries heavily whilst they swayed in the wind. "It is strange I should be hearing Kiyoko's laugh..."

The wind blew the berries downwards once more, brushing them again across my left shoulder. Broken whispers of Kiyoko's voice wove around me, the scent of mugwort overrunning the sweet scent of cherries, which had begun to fade in the air. The metallic tinkling of chiming bells murmured through the rustling leaves, the bells fading as the branches fell still and silent. A heavy, uneasy feeling shifted in the shadows around me, my stomach churning in a sharp jolt as Kiyoko's distant singing filled my ears.

With my words I beseech to thee,

Come to me through the roots and trees,
To the meadow of daisies and sweet peonies,
Beyond where harm and threat can find thee,
The in between is where in lies your safety.

Kiyoko's voice sang across the wind, his melody vibrating through the fruits as they hung firmly on the branches. Purple tinted the trees for the faintest of moments, my energy warming in anticipation of his healing touch. A bitter cold chilled my bones where his warmth had been, and the icicle formed from his energy, which was most unwelcome despite the day's heat.

"Kiyoko?" I said instinctively, reacting to the rhythm of his words as my heart began to race. "Kiyoko, are you there?"

"Knomucca..." he replied, his voice so faint through the rustling of the leaves I thought I had imagined it. "Knomucca... Knomucca..."

I seized the lantern-shaped fruits in my hand, focusing on them with my breathing as I fought to summon Kiyoko. Widening my stance, I dug my feet into the soil, centering my spirits with several lengthy inhalations. I pushed my energy outwards, seeing blurred images of Kiyoko's plum-purple kimono through my mind's eye. The connection fizzled painfully with a jolt down my side, accompanied by a sudden gnarled voice that cascaded in a horrid shudder.

"Help," it screamed, the thick, curdling agony bleeding through the irises of Kiyoko's distant glittering eyes.

His energy pushed firmly against me, my sternum throbbing in pain as the feeling of a phantom hand pressed me backward.

"Damn it," I swore, suddenly overly aware of my body. I released my breath in a frustrated sigh, feeling the lingering chill of the shadowed fingers where the hand had been.

Our connection popped and suddenly sizzled, forcing us apart with a pained push. Sharply, my breath was ripped from my lungs, the air returning in chilled gulps that sent me reeling. Nausea overtook me, and I collapsed to my knees as the aftershocks quaked through my spirits. Fragments of screaming and purple light shattered through me, the urge to vomit nearly consuming me as I shoved my hands into the soil.

Slowly, the dizziness left me. The connection to the physical plane helped to ground my spirits. The excess energy bombarded from Kiyoko faded away as I pushed it into the earth. My breathing lengthened as I regained my composure. I sat against the tree to smoke a much-deserved spliff from the few I had saved from my smoking sack.

There must be trouble, I thought with a sigh, my knees wobbling as I attempted to stand.

Shifting to a seat, I sought shelter in a nearby palm tree, observing the curious lantern-shaped fruits as I collected myself once more. My chest rose and fell heavily as I slumped against the trunk, my ears ringing with the distant, disturbed tones of Kiyoko's singing. I shook my head hard to clear it. I retrieved another coconut from the branches, leaning firmly against the trunk as I set to consuming the nectar between deep pulls of my spliff.

"What a journey I shall have ahead of me," I said with a sigh, feeling my shoulders droop with failure and defeat. I pushed aside the feelings, rose to a stand, and walked on wobbly legs.

I wove through the branches of low-hanging trees, embarking north as I followed the curvature of the landscape. Thorns and bramble snagged across my slippers, forcing me to finish my smoking before drawing my sword from its sheath. Swinging wildly, I hacked through the underbrush, crawling through the space I created. I slid beneath the branches, falling upon a thicket of blossoms laced with ferns and vines. Bright blue leaves resembled perching parrots, the likeness nearly causing me guilt as I parted them from my path. The chirping of birds and bugs filled the twilight, the terrain ahead appearing as unkempt and wild as the land from whence I had come.

Through the trees, I climbed and stumbled, passing beneath ripened papaya, glowing yellow star fruit, and unfamiliar berries. Red, bleeding roses tugged at my tunic harshly, threatening to cut through the fabric and scratch me deeply. Growing with frustration, I shoved my body forward, losing track of the setting sun as it dipped in the trees' cover.

The sun! I thought in horror, disliking that I would fail in meeting Thornin, and he would be forced to find Everett.

And what of Lyle and his companions? I thought, slicing through the trees with the sword. The likelihood I shall find them is awfully grim indeed.

My swinging came to a sharp halt as the landscape thinned and changed. The trees became tall and slender, their trunks a rich shade of brown. Long, knobby roots swirled perfectly into the solid soil beneath them, the wide, leathery leaves jutting with runic-shaped veins from which the roots claimed their origins.

How strange, I mused, remembering a fire-red crest upon the wall of the Southern Watchtower of Morriraen and the oil painting near the servant's annex.

"Ozwal's crest," I said in amazement as the significance of the landscape became clear to me, regarding the trees in awe as I knelt to examine the roots. "So fascinating that they should be growing here..."

These must be the Eastern Islands that Ozwal spoke of in the legends... I gasped, elation sparking a surge of adrenaline through me. It must be true, then... he must have discovered the Islands in his search for Pinta Berries. Though... why would the belief of these islands be discouraged if Ozwal had found them to exist?

My excitement dimmed as anxiety began to brew like a storm within me.

If the Eastern Islands exist... And the Creator did not wish for me to know it... There must be other secrets He is hiding.

aimlessly over the far eastern sea, glowing with an emerald energy that tingled through my fingers. The stone gleamed softly and dropped from my hand, landing on the parchment with a firm thud. A ripple of green bled through the parchment, the twine landing in a neat curl around it as it quieted against the paper.

"Oi... the Baulhtunac Ocean," I said in shock. "This would imply she is far passed the reefs..."

"Aye..." Bullet said.

A silence fell amongst us, interrupted by Thornin's heavy breathing.

"What do you propose we do now?" Bullet asked.

"The solution is simple," I said heavily, feeling as Thornin playfully nipped my fingers. "I shall have to go in search for her..."

"That is far from simple," Bullet sighed.

"Thornin can travel at a mighty fast pace," I said while glancing about the map. "The pair of us can venture eastwards and search for her beyond the reefs."

"Your arguments are sound," Bullet nodded slowly in agreement. "I shall do all I can to ensure that everything here continues smoothly with the troops."

"With my being gone...and the General unreachable... command of the troops will fall to Lieutenant Tyfis..."

"Such is the way of the law," Bullet said. "Though... I shall admit I don't much like the idea of your leaving Kiyoko to fate and its whims..."

"His entire fate shall not be left to chance," I said, meeting Bullet's eyes. "I am leaving Kiyoko in your care, and I trust that you will do all to keep him safe."

"I'll do what I can, certainly," Bullet said gently.

"You shall manage fine," I said in confidence. "You shall have to for the sake of the realms. Should you require aid in any way for any reason, Kyreese is plenty capable of assisting... and I would like a close eye kept on her anyhow due to her interactions with the Spider Vines."

"I strongly dislike you traveling alone," Bullet said.

"I recognize my traveling alone is risky," I said, releasing a silent prayer to Anteyus. "Unfortunately, it is a gamble that must be taken. Hazel can no longer be trusted... Kyreese needs to be here alongside you should any ill will befall you."

"What if ill will should come to find you?" Bullet said sternly.

"I shall weather the storm," I said, firmly grasping the head of my hammer for comfort.

"What am I to do if you doth not return?" Bullet said, his pitch elevating in worry. I raised my hand to quiet him, watching as Kiyoko shifted slightly in his sleep.

"You must find a way to sober Kiyoko," I said, releasing a breath as I continued watching him. His breathing remained soft and rhythmical, his disheveled hair brushing messily across his face.

"I s'ppose I can try," Bullet said.

"It is imperative that the Priestess and the General do not cross paths," I said.

"Understood," Bullet said. "I give you my word I shall do everything I can."

"Should anyone find Truff, they are to leave him here as well," I said, pointing to a sturdy stone fence where his reigns could be tied. "I hope I shall see him, along with Kiyoko awake and well upon my return."

"So shall be the hope," Bullet said. "Will there be anything else you require in your absence?"

"Aye... reckon there is," I said, unfastening my smoking sacks and obtaining the tonic I had stolen from Samarin. "Do what you can to determine what can be learned from this... but for the love of all that is divine and good, do not allow the Priestess possession of the vial."

"Understood," Bullet said, plucking the shining blue tonic from my hands and placing it in his pocket for safekeeping.

"I believe we have discussed the essentials then," I said, checking that I had full water skins and all my weapons hanging from my belt. "If the pair of us have finished, I reckon I ought to be setting on my way."

"I suppose so," Bullet said. "Safest travels, Commander."

"Stay wise," I said. "And thank you for looking after Kiyoko..."

"It's my pleasure," Bullet said, sitting on the grass beside Kyreese and Kiyoko as to move from Thornin's path. "Love and light, Everett... may the Gods gift you with fortune and strength."

May they, indeed, I thought with a sigh.

Turning towards the dragon, I continued to pat his snout, running my thumb between his eyes in a way I knew he liked. His long, roughened tongue swiped at my fingers, his continued search for sweets oddly endearing and amusing despite its distraction.

"How are you fairing from all this, Thornin?" I asked him, finding his contentedness unsettling, considering Knomucca's absence.

Thornin huffed through a cloud of smoke, wafting a faint scent of nettles and sweet grass across my skin. The heavy, iron smell of blood filled my nose, blending terribly with a stinging salt that burned my senses.

Silently, I pushed my energy towards him, trying to speak through his senses as I would with Kiyoko. A heaviness slammed my chest, and I fought to breathe, my eyes widening in panic as I searched Thornin's face. I struggled to keep my breath so as not to frighten Bullet as I centered my spirits.

Oi... what are you on about, Thornin... I thought, wishing I had Kiyoko's wisdom.

Sliding along Thornin's right, I began to lightly pat his scales, speaking to him softly as I did not wish to startle him.

"Aye, reckon I'm going to climb into the stirrups now," I soothed, tugging on the saddle before placing my foot into it.

Thornin made no objections, the dragon scale saddle accepting my weight as I swung my leg across the dragon's back. The purpled scales were carved perfectly for Knomucca's body, the seat snug against the wool of my leggings. Checking once more that I had all I required, I glanced over my shoulder towards Kiyoko, my heart plummeting painfully into my stomach as I prepared to leave him.

"I love you," I whispered through him, hoping wherever his energy was, his spirits would hear me.

Reaching out a hand, I grasped tightly onto the spikes protruding from Thornin's spine, finding comfort in the way they aided my balance.

I whistled a command to Thornin to find Knomucca, feeling elated when he took flight.

Lurching forward, Thornin leaped from the grass, carrying us upwards from the tranquil courtyard. The night air was as thick and dark as ink, the cold winds whipping furiously, threatening to tear my clothing. Shadows of the landscape were a darkened blur beneath me. The moon shone brightly across the horizon, its radiance a comfortable beacon as we traveled eastwards.

Whistling loudly, I commanded our direction veer leftwards, carving a curve to the northeast through the clouds. Moonlight sparkled across the Snake River, the water glowing as the moon neared full. The silvered waters vanished quickly from my sight, bleeding into the abyssal darkness that stretched endlessly. Upon reflex, I tightened my grip against Thornin, admiring Knomucca's courage in constantly choosing to fly when such form of transport made me terrified.

Fighting through the wind, we flew onwards, the seaside city of Belleview coming fast into focus. Torches, fires, and enchanted lights lit up the port, the shape of the settlement resembling the spiraled shell of a mollusk. To my surprise, Thornin flew towards the city, edging past the coast of the Luna Sea, soaring over crumbling cliffs and caves.

Let us investigate the docks, I thought, guiding Thornin toward the piers with a series of commands and whistles.

The docks were lit with enchanted turnip lanterns surrounding the ships, bobbing gently in the light waves of the sea. Catamarans, caravels, and a familiar oak boat floated against the docks, the one-man vessel reminding me of the boats from the Snake River trading port.

Strange, I mused, as I recalled seeing Lyle leave down the Snake River in a similar fishing vessel this day past.

A small guard shack rested at the end of the piers, its doorway illuminated with intricately carved turnip lanterns. Pine-scented smoke wafted upwards from the chimney, the fresh fragrance filling the damp night sky. A white pebbled beach stretched towards the road into the city, the distant sand dunes decorated with lights for the Festess.

"Move on down," I signaled to Thornin with a whistle, ordering him to begin his descent.

Guiding Thornin lower, we hovered above the spruce planks before he gently settled us on the pier. Leaping from the saddle, I began to search my surroundings, finding nothing out of the ordinary.

Damn this darkness, I thought.

Moving down the port, I began to investigate, examining the unoccupied spaces along the docks where several boats were missing. The sudden shimmer of a silvered medallion caught my eye, the familiar translucent blue illuminating the crest of Morriraen.

Oi, that's Captain Southwell's broach... my thoughts raced, confused to find it hanging from such a post when it should be tied to his front. That must be his boat, then... why should he be here in Belleview instead of at the Trading Port?

Cautiously, I ran my thumb across the metal, the silver wet and chilled from its time spent upon the post. Lifting the medallion, I held it in my hand, feeling a sharp chill through my gloves. A heavy dark energy moved through the medallion, the subtle scent of cypress seeping from the metal. Turning the medallion over in my hand, I noticed the silver had been tinted to a dark black, the etchings of Captain Southwell and his station smearing like ink placed on wet parchment.

I wonder how this has come to be... I thought as I ran a finger over the smudged etchings on the rear. I think I shall take this for further investigation.

I removed the medallion from the post by untangling the heavy iron chain. Sliding the pendant into my smoking sack, I guarded it closely. I listened as the metal glided softly against the leather.

I ought to investigate the guard shack, I thought, whistling a command for Thornin to wait for me where he stood.

Moving across the docks, I approached the small, thatched hut and regarded the lanterns that bordered the doorframe. The leftmost turnip proudly displayed etchings supporting The First Warrior. The artistic expression made me smile proudly. His axe, runic symbol, lover's knot, and name were cut deeply into the hollowed white shell, the soft smell of a fresh cinnamon candle wafting delightfully from within the husk.

Anteyus, I prayed silently, I beseech thee... grant me the strength, wisdom, and means to find Knomucca and bring her home...

The lantern flickered, and an emerald green energy pulsed from the candles within the turnips. Sighing, I hoped Anteyus had heard my pleas, releasing a breath before I continued forward. Stepping from the swaying docks, I gently pushed the door open as I entered the guard shack.

The tiny hut was clean and orderly, with a slim woolen bed nestled tightly in the corner. A slender cabinet was perfumed with the scent of smoking herbs, the door slightly ajar as if recently opened. A small iron brazier was lit with a burning pine log, funneling smoke upwards and out through the chimney. Iron hooks for hanging clothes were currently occupied with a heavy grey cloak, the upright, rounded scarlet petals of an oleander embroidered into the wool. A leather black tricorne hung beside the grey fabric, the hide adorned with shards of sparkling moonstones.

A desk too large for the space took up the back wall, standing beside a whicker cabinet and padded leather chair. Candlesticks were lit in each corner, the delicious smells of cloves and oranges mingling with the pine. A book lay open, the neatly looped letters of a journal catching my eye as I leaned over the desk to read.

"It was absolutely blissful," the written words flashed through my mind's eye, my voice whispering the secrets of the text as I read quietly. "The warmth was exquisite, mounting to such unbelievable nirvana I had become temporarily blinded. I could have died from such pleasure... allowed it to consume me thoroughly and completely until my essence, my very being, craved nothing but such sweet euphoria worthy of my eternity..."

"Oi, what happened to your horse?"

A sudden voice made me jump, turning instantly over my shoulder. The barkeep, Bashrol, stood in the doorway of the guard shack, his plain dark tunic and tan leggings illuminated by the light. His soft blue eyes were hidden beneath windswept hair. His tunic was torn, the missing fabric used as a makeshift bandage to wrap around his palm.

"Reckon I would consider telling you, if you disclosed what happened to your hand..." I said, gesturing towards him.

"'Tis not important," Bashrol said as he waved away my curiosity. "I merely wish a needle and thread dwelled within that desk as I desire to mend my tunic..."

"Aye... reckon that would indeed be useful," I said.

"Indeed-"

"Oi, I am through exchanging pleasantries... how do you find yourself here so quickly?" I asked, raising an eyebrow quizzically. "Did I not see you this night past at The Ironsides Inn?"

"You did indeed," Bashrol said.

"The only boat here on the docks from the Trading Port belongs to Captain Southwell," I said. "And unless you somehow convinced him to allow you to join him, I see not how you managed to travel such distance when Belleview is at least two days' ride from the castle in good conditions..."

"I'm unable to reveal my secrets," Bashrol said. "At least, concerning these matters..."

"Then what is it you should wish to reveal to me aside from your presence?" I asked, noticing as Bashrol stepped between the lanterns framing the threshold.

"Insight," Bashrol said, turning over the pine log in the brazier. "Though Knomucca's presence would be appreciated... for I need to speak with her."

"I could relay the information to her for you," I said, absently laying a hand on the hilt of my hammer beneath my cloak.

"I'm unable to have a messenger," Bashrol said, sliding the book from the desk and closing it in his hands.

Bashrol unfastened a pouch at his waist, slipping the book into the leather. An energetic sigil remained on the desk beneath where the book had rested, flashing briefly before it faded into the wood. The bright green energy had shimmered in a triangle, vines fluttering through the edges with small and intricate flowers. I looked towards Bashrol's pouch, but no trace of the energy lingered.

"Perhaps there is something I can use to persuade you," I said.

"I'm afraid not," Bashrol said. "When you find Knomucca, and the pair of you are ready to converse again, you may call for me in the field of fragrant flowers."

"Explain yourself," I demanded, watching as Bashrol procured his cloak and slid his cap from the hook.

"I've said all that I can," Bashrol said gently, draping his cloak around his shoulders and placing his cap atop his head in a fluid motion.

"You have said nothing," I declared, drawing my hammer and moving angrily towards him. "You will explain yourself."

A silent thrum stopped me suddenly, his aura flashing briefly in a sky-blue. The screams of a hawk played through my ears, the gentle crashing of foaming waves echoing amidst their tyranny. Tall, dark trees lined a clear sky, the leaves laced with veins and roots, their shadows rippling against the sand. The tightening of a boom and winch fragmented in a broken hiss, the shadowed mists of a phantom ship filling my vision in a bright oiled painting.

"I shall do what I can to heed your riddles," I said to him, the fresh scent of coconuts lingering in the air.

"Very good," Bashrol said, nodding as he returned to the door. "Stay wise, Sir."

"Love and light," I said, watching as Bashrol vanished from the threshold.

Sighing in confusion, I allowed him to leave my sight, noticing a green energy flashing quickly between the lanterns from behind him. The energy collected between the pumpkins and floated away through Bashrol, the clear, strong green failing to force its way through the lanterns.

Gods, grant me wisdom, I thought in frustration, resisting the need to rifle through my smoking herbs.

Sighing, I turned on my heel and ventured from the guard shack. I gently pushed myself through the door, stepping between the lanterns and into the night. Turning to the sky, I regarded the moon's position, surprised to find that the witching hour had come and gone. The flight from the Rose Lily to Belleview had taken longer than expected, forcing a wave of anxiety to surge painfully through my stomach.

I approached him and gently slid into the saddle, whistling a command for Thornin to take to the skies. The dragon leaped from the docks, unfurling his immense purple wings as he propelled us forward. Guiding him with another whistle, I urged us eastward, watching as the lights of Belleview blinked into darkness.

"Where are you, Knomucca?" I whispered, using a set of whistles to keep Thornin close to the water.

The silver moonlight shone brightly off the sea, the waves rippling and sparkling through its radiance. Fish leaped from the waters, catching bugs to fill their bellies. The waves churned beneath us, slamming against floating driftwood and other debris blown seaward from the storms.

"Blasted dark," I cursed.

Whistling, I attempted to slow Thornin's speed. His wings flapped through the wind, propelling us quickly across the water. The mist sprayed upward in freezing droplets, soaking the leather of my boots as the waters became more treacherous.

"Aye, slow your speed," I commanded with a whistle, disliking the unpredictable waves.

We are almost to the reefs, I thought, noticing the water's reflection as it changed in depth against sudden shoals.

The moon shifted into the predawn hours, the sky teasing a tint of cerulean across the horizon. The air began to warm, the scent of salt strong and welcomed as the morning fell upon me. The Luna Sea Barrier Reefs began to sparkle in the moonlight, the pink and yellow hues of the coral marking the drop from the shallowed sea into the vast, expansive waters of the Baulhtunac Ocean.

"Aye, halt!" I commanded Thornin, feeling the air shift as he slowed.

I began to search the waters, commanding Thornin to hover with a whistle. A raft of ducks moved across the water, suddenly taking flight in panic as they fled from the reefs. I quickly froze with fear, noticing a volt of vultures circling nearby. Squinting through the dim light, I spotted three corpses floating face-down in the water. Blood spread across the sea, attracting predators from the depths and the sky. Dorsal fins circled the floating bodies, indicating that the sharks had also detected the potential feeding ground.

"Thornin, slow approach," I said as we neared the deceased.

A hawk flew from the east, circling thrice counterclockwise before landing atop the driftwood. The bird regarded the vultures almost apologetically, its eyes sad and sorrowful instead of consuming the bodies alongside the others. Fanning its wings, the hawk flapped intensely, screeching loudly in a piercing tone that scattered the vultures into the sky.

"Feisty little devil," I said, watching the hawk settle against the driftwood.

I had expected the hawk to take to the corpses, preying now upon the dead as there was no carrion to contend with. The hawk merely stayed upon its perch, glaring into the water as though it would strike any of the sharks who dared to surface. Their dorsal fins continued to circle the fallen, the hawk never breaking concentration as it guarded them from atop its log.

Gently, I nudged the dragon forward and slowly approached. Three bodies floated amongst the shoals, their cloaks rippling with the waves around them. I fought to recognize those who had met their fate, praying that Knomucca would not be one of them.

"Gods..." Panic flowed through me as I drifted closer, my heart pounding so quickly it threatened to blur my vision.

A gentleman with hair as blond as the sun floated face down in the water. Long, blue hair from his female companion was tangled in the clasp of his cloak, pulling her towards him. Beside them, the third body captured my gaze. A harpoon I recognized from my years as commander lay snagged across driftwood, keeping the familiar, waterlogged face from being dragged beneath the surface.

"Lyle," I whispered in horror, my eyes brimming with tears.

The rope of his harpoon lay across the large blonde gentleman, his black cloak torn from the predators who thought the fabric an inconvenience. His face was unrecognizable, his skin stained from the sun and salt of the sea. The blonde gentleman's hand reached across to the blue-haired lass, her garments dark from their time soaking in the water.

The hemp of the heavy rope from Lyle's harpoon was pecked through and torn to tatters. The corpses had been there several hours, their eyes plucked clean from their sockets by the vultures that fought atop them. Water created deep wrinkles in their darkened skin, their bodies bloated and putrefying amongst the sandbars and coral. Large pieces of their flesh had been consumed by the carrion, revealing exposed bone in the fading silver of the moon.

"I am sorry Lyle, and to the friends at your side," I prayed, hoping he could hear my words somehow through my sadness. "I wish you an ever-peaceful rest. I am sorry I lack the strength and ability to care for you. May the Gods protect your soul."

Whistling to Thornin, we turned to the east, continuing to scour the reefs as we moved across the sky.

"Knomucca!" I called at the top of my voice, frantically searching the water.

I strained my ears as I listened for a reply, continuing to scan the surface in all directions.

"I doth not see her," I said to Thornin.

I failed to see Knomucca or any sign of unordinary movements anywhere through the waves. Panic and anxiety fought to burst forth, a heavy bile rising from my throat as I swallowed it down.

"Anteyus... what am I to do?" I whispered in desperation, trying in vain to sense Knomucca's energy.

My breathing raced, my thoughts failing to quiet as I attempted to center my energies. The scent of coconuts bombarded my senses, mingling with the overwhelming fragrances of rosemary and field flowers. The wind snapped in a painful echo through my ears, carrying away my visions of Knomucca in a horde of swirling mosquitos. Exhaling, I grasped onto the spikes of Thornin's neck, wedging the points into my palms in order to keep myself grounded.

"It was hopeless to think I should reach her," I said, wishing I could behold her glowing hair and emerald eyes. Perhaps I ought to be strategizing an alternative...

Clearing my mind, I began to think of how I could make this moment useful, hoping that my time spent here was not in vain.

"I will search for an Angelfish," I said, refusing to acknowledge the fear that Knomucca may have found herself with the same fate as Lyle. "Even if she has managed to obtain one, it could be useful to have a spare."

Whistling once more, I guided Thornin eastwards, wishing to provide plenty of distance between myself and the fallen. I slid my cloak over my head, untying the heavy ropes that fastened it and knotting them around Thornin's saddle. My boots were next to follow, tied together with the laces, as I did not wish to wear wet shoes. I untied my smoking sack and placed it inside the cantle of Thornin's saddle alongside several bottles of Tora berry wine that Knomucca had stored. I kept a small dagger at my waist and secured my hammer to my back.

I whistled a command for Thornin to wait as the ascending sun began to fill the sky. I swung my right leg across his back, glancing into the looming waves. I released a breath and closed my eyes, praying one final time for strength before steeling my preparedness. Leaping from the saddle, I splashed into the water, hitting the surface with immense force. Water filled my ears, my weight creating a large splash to greet the hovering dragon.

My sights blurred as I cautiously opened my eyes, the salt stinging my irises as my vision adjusted. I began turning over shells and stones, searching beneath them for Angelfish who enjoy hiding in dark places. My chest tightened with the need for air, and I forced myself upwards, cresting the surface and beginning to tread water as I filled my lungs once more.

Diving down again, I began to swim through the reefs, the water sparkling in the early morning sun. Schools of clownfish and clusters of crabs swirled through the sea anemone, swerving past lazing starfish that clung to coral and rocks. Clams, kelp, and moon guppies wove among the reefs, decorating the sand barges elegantly in a palette of infinite colors.

Seeing no Angelfish, I again crested the surface into the crisp morning air, feeling the chilled wind on my face as a cough escaped me. Treading water proved tiresome, and I nearly whistled for Thornin, my exhaustion brewing as I repeatedly dove and searched. My arms grew weighted and sore as I pushed through the water, my building frustration threatening to impact my breathing.

I returned to the surface for a fresh breath. The thick, heavy scent of burning coal began to fill my senses, a deep and curling smoke tinting the morning sky. A shadow moved across the horizon, the liquid fire through the sails catching the beauty of the ascending sun. The ores of the galleon dipped lazily into the water, accompanying the distant sounds of a haunted flute, keeping the cadence of its sculling. No fires burned in the brazier, and no hands tended the ores or rigged the sails, which flapped chaotically in the breeze.

The galleon was slender and long, its shallow drafts providing shelter from the growing waves. A red, slim crest of a tree with runic symbols in the leaves flashed across the hull, vanishing quickly amongst the waves as it bobbed beneath the surf. The ship traveled from the east, sailing smoothly across the ocean as it disappeared in the distance.

"Gods," I said aloud. "Is that Ozwal's galleon?"

The waves jerked suddenly, disturbed by the passing vessel. Propelling my arms, I fought to stay afloat, tightening my hammer across my back as its weight rippled the waves. Thornin hovered overhead, his ears flattening against the distant chiming of a large copper bell.

"The sea is maddening," I said, taking another immense breath to collect myself.

I held my breath, turned, and pushed beneath the surface once more. Searching the reefs, I found a patch of thick, dark kelp, seeing a school of fish swim towards it far off from my right. Following behind them, I reached my hand outwards, grateful for my gloves as no thorns or stingers disturbed me. Rifling through the foliage, I was pleased to discover an Angelfish, seeing one lingering beneath a stone within the plant life.

I am sorry, little fellow, I thought, capturing the Angelfish in my hands and beginning to swim upwards.

Suddenly, bone-riddled hands shot through the sea anemone, locking around my neck in a fierce grip. I fought to keep the air in my lungs, my vision blurring as the water threatened to consume me. A glittering, gleaming tail cut across my awareness, and the distant humming of a somber song snagged uncomfortably against my ears.

Darkness dwells in deepest seas,
Where drowned souls drift, never free.
Betwixt worlds, you stand alone,
Frozen heart, flesh turned to stone.
Chosen Creatures guard His throne,
Blood corrupts, yet He atones.
Creation's treasures, honor bound,
Lost souls trapped, forever crowned.
In His realm of endless night,
Failed breaths echo, out of sight.
Gods have blessed this sacred space,
Where time and death have no place.
Damned and chosen side by side,
In twilight depths they now reside.
Eternal servants to His will,
Bound by power, deathly still.
His essence, a poisoned well,
Corrupts the gods who once rebelled.
Divine beings now bend the knee,
To darkness vast as starless sea.

A glimpse of long, tangled hair whirled quickly to my right, misleading me to think it was beautifully flowered plants. The hands tightened their grip against my throat, water beginning to fill my nose as I fought to keep my mouth closed. Reluctantly, I released the Angelfish from my hands, watching as it bolted away and escaped through the reefs. I quickly dropped my right hand, securing my dagger as my hammer was unreachable.

Dislodging my dagger, I flipped it into my hand, using my final burst of strength to ram the blade forward. The tip made contact and dug roughly into the flesh of my attacker, unleashing a piercing scream across the waves. Blood spread in a mass of salt and iron, the water tinting in a horrid rust as I fought not to swallow it. The taste of iron filled my mouth and lungs, the salt stinging painfully as I pushed myself free.

A dead Naiad drifted amongst the reefs, my hand reaching outwards instinctively as I clutched her forearm in my fist. I stared as the blood pooled around her, rippling outwards in the underwater currents. Thoughts of sharks and other predators that would be attracted to the blood floated through my mind. I released the Naiad and swam quickly away, cresting the surface for a breath. I dove one final time into the reefs, searching for yet another Angelfish. My exhaustion pulled against me as I dug once more through the coral, grateful when I procured another. I clutched it in my fist and forced myself to the surface, feeling the fish quiet in my hands as the life left its body.

Breaking through the surface, I began to cough intensely. Thornin had drifted several yards away, though returned at the sounds of my ruckus, circling overhead before he settled in his hovering. I whistled for him to drop lower and watched as he alighted upon the water, his claws splashing softly as he floated atop the waves. I adjusted the Angelfish and hoisted myself upwards, grabbing onto Thornin's saddle and flinging myself into it.

Thankfully, the rising sun warmed the humid tropical air as I pulled my cloak around my shoulders. I dried my face as water clung to my skin, dabbing my eyes gently. I took a moment to dry my hammer, refusing to risk it rusting before I returned it to my back. I lifted the compartment of the cantle and placed the Angelfish within it, angry I had no proper means to transport it or keep it preserved.

"Gods, keep it safe," I said, taking a moment to regard the fish before closing the saddle compartment.

The Angelfish was fairly long, sporting silvered scales with dark vertical markings. Its face was yellowed with large black eyes, its lifeless stare was quite unsettling, as I had not properly prepared for her demise. The tail was striped with flecks of blue, and the specimen was quite beautiful even in death.

"How I wish to be rid of this place," I said, stealing my strength to continue onward.

With the fish secured, I began to reassemble my appearance. I fastened on my boots and retied my smoking sack before adjusting myself in the saddle. I was grateful for the warmth provided by the cloak draped across my shoulders as the rising sun dried my pants.

Resuming my search for Knomucca, I squinted through the horizon. I cupped my hands over my mouth and shouted at the top of my voice, hoping my words would be carried across the wind.

"Knomucca! Can you hear me?"

The morning hours spilled around me. To the east, the hawk rested upon its driftwood, the circling sharks having decided to abandon their patience and venture elsewhere. The hawk met my eyes and took off from its log, dashing eastwards and flying fast across the horizon.

"Thank you kindly," I whispered after him, guiding Thornin in a cursory circle to search the reefs by the light of day.

Flying once more over Lyle, I did not allow myself to divert my gaze; instead, I forced myself to look downwards to see him floating in the water. I prayed once more for their resting before realigning my sights eastwards, gawking in curiosity as the hawk circled in the east. It leveled its gaze and stretched its wings, fluttering a moment's soft purple energy as the breeze carried the scent of mugwort. Thornin flattened his ears and released a low grumble, his scales prickling painfully through the wet lining of my leggings.

"Aye, easy there, laddie," I said to him, feeling Thornin's growls beginning to grow like a roaring thunder.

The hawk screeched, refusing to lower its eyes against Thornin and pounding his wings mightily. Thornin paused suspiciously before raising his ears, watching as the hawk circled rightwards and darted east once more. Thornin flapped his wings and lurched forward, leaving the wreckage of the reefs behind.

XV

KNOMUCCA

The sun had finally shed its light, the thick forest of the island beginning to dim as dusk curled around me. Songs of crickets filled my ears, accompanying the wind that had chilled in the setting sun. A bright silver radiance had begun to paint the leaves, promising a bright night under the magnificence of a nearly full moon.

Cautiously, I continued examining the Banyan trees, trying to sort through the thoughts that whirled inside me. Ozwal had known these trees contained great power and secrets, for he endorsed their symbolism on the crest of his ship. He had searched for the Eastern Islands in an attempt to find a rare Pinta berry as a sacrifice to the Creator at his Ascension. His reputation had been subject to rumors and slander, mocked through folklore and legends to be depicted as weak for failing to complete his Ascension. A sinking feeling flooded through me, and I knew the Creator was not to have the fruits. Nausea rose like bile in my throat as I envisioned Him holding them in His heron-clawed hands.

Despite my nerves, I was drawn to the trees, indulging in my urge to touch them. Gently, I ran a finger over the roots that filled the leathery leaves, feeling the prominent veins that carved their symbols. Three runes wove through the roots, the first depicting endurance, healing, and courage. The next shone of ancestry, breath, and the passing of power through lineage and knowledge. The third described brute force as protection, signaling that change and understanding was soon to rumble across the realms through clouds of lightning and thunder. This rune resembled a hammer, its triangular top extended with a straightened line that bled into the other runes amongst the leaves.

I scanned the leaves, tracing the three runes beneath my hand. Their life force whispered through my fingers, their energies illuminating their veins in a soft purple. A familiar voice floated through my awareness, the bitter smell of mugwort a comfortable clash against the syrupy, sweet scent of figs.

"Uruz, Ansuz, Thurisaz..."

Kiyoko's voice flooded through me, the soft scent of cherry blossoms floating warmly in the air. Briefly, I searched over my shoulders and saw I was alone, dropping my voice instinctively as I began to whisper.

"Kiyoko?"

I held my breath as I waited for him to reply, straining my ears as I fought to listen for his voice. The banyan trees rustled against the continuously chirping crickets; their noise carried clearly on the cool night breeze. Frogs croaked on the beaches, and distant waves crashed against the shores. Owls screeched in the surrounding trees, their hoots and screams overrun by the clicking of colonies of bats that had risen for the evening.

I sighed, growing disappointed that I had not heard him reply. I resumed inspecting the banyans, smiling as an idea fell upon me. Slowly, I pulled open my enchanted pouch, adjusting it at my front as I began to speak aloud.

"If it is well with you, I shall be harvesting some of your spoils," I said to the tree, placing my hand against the trunk and procuring my dagger.

The Banyan gave no sign of protest, its leaves rustling in the oncoming night. I steadied my hand and pressed the blade against the bark, sliding the iron downwards along the grain of the wood. I shaved off the jagged bark that remained from my blade, knowing the tree would need a flat wound if it wished to callus and prevent the risk of infection. I accidentally removed more bark from around the branch than was needed, disappointed that the tree should have a larger area to heal.

The bark was warm from its time in the sun, the thick, smooth wood sliding easily into my pouch. I then turned my attention to the fruits hanging from the branches. Gently twisting, I plucked a number of fuzzy, red-seeded fruits resembling small figs or pomegranates. Their weight was comfortable in my palm as I harvested them for later examination.

"Thank you, kindly," I said.

The bark upon the Banyan rapidly began to heal, producing smooth, fresh leaves over the holes where the bark had been taken. The scales were large and glossy, a green leathery ellipse which covered the marks of my blade. The new leaves began to harden, the fresh cicatrix blending flawlessly into the trunk.

"How impressive you are," I said, running my hand along the Banyan.

My gauntlets thrummed gently. A soothing vibration like that of a cat's purr moved through my fingers, my palm warming as the Banyan nuzzled against me. I watched as the Banyan continued its healing, baffled by its ability to regenerate instead of compartmentalizing the wound in accordance with typical tree biology. A red tint flashed through the new bark that melded into the wood as knots formed in the tree. I searched the trunk for the callouses that typically form. Still, I was surprised not to find any markings.

Impressive indeed, I thought, grateful to have samples of the bark in my pouch to investigate further.

"I shall be going," I said, giving my farewell to the tree. I pressed on through the foliage, moving deeper toward the center of the island as the witching hour fell.

The sounds of bugs and crickets rang through my ears. The high whine of insects buzzed painfully as they bit against my skin. My steps quickened as I moved through the trees, and my gait became clumsier as I dodged the insects.

"Oi these bugs are maddening," I swore as my focus was threatened by feelings of anger.

I thrashed my arms wildly, swatting bugs and branches from my path as I fought to keep my footing. The grove thickened around me, making it nearly impossible to see, as the moon's light could not permeate the branches. My thin leather shoes caught on ferns and roots that wove beneath the trees, and my balance was hard to find while fending away insects.

Darkness filled my eyes, the absence of the moon's light rendering me blind. The scratches of branches and biting mosquitos had torn my skin unkindly. The urge to scream was overwhelming as the scratches along my face deepened, with four lines spreading down my cheek. Blood poured down my face, smearing across my tunic and down my collarbone.

A low growl, resembling a saw grinding against wood, sounded at my front, sending a spike of fear through me. Bright, golden eyes materialized from the shadows, and the image of dark orange fur with small black spots entered my awareness. The spots were shaped like roses, accentuating short, muscular legs and a gaping maw. The front claws of the large cat's immense paws extended outwards in another attempt to swipe at me.

"Easy there, big fella," I said as I began to slowly back away, grateful it had not chosen to pounce upon me from the shadows.

The cat stepped forward, its growling echoing as it continued to pursue me. My slippers snagged clumsily as I moved backward through the banyans, the relentless bugs soon forgotten as I fought to maintain my balance. A sharp pain met my temples as I backed into the trunk of a tree. I freed myself from its grasp and hastened my retreat. The cat swiped once more and snagged the silk of my tunic, ripping it loudly to expose my bare torso.

"Woah there..." I pleaded, reaching my left hand across my back and quickly drawing my sword.

Stepping leftwards, I dodged the cat's advances, seeing its glowing eyes dip lower as it began to crouch. Fearing it should pounce, I quickly swung my sword, angry when the closely knit branches restricted my movements. My sword snagged on the branches, the Banyan ripping it cruelly from my hands. The wind rustled the leaves maliciously, mocking me as the sword vanished in the darkness.

"Fuck," I swore aloud, watching as the cat leaped towards me.

The weight of the large cat pushed me to the ground as sharp claws dug into my collarbone. The wind was knocked clear from my lungs, stealing the sound from my screams. I raised my head upwards and smashed it into the jaguar, hearing it hiss as its large paws pinned me down. Squirming viciously, I fought to free my arms; twisting my left hand, I pulled it from its gauntlet, feeling as it painfully transitioned. I swore as blood ran down my body, luring hoards of stinging mosquitos to feast alongside the jaguar.

I raised my hand and shoved it forward, feeling the warmth of fur and flesh as my fingers passed through the cat's chest and into its ribs. Bones crunched loudly as they fragmented around my fist, my fingers opening instinctively as I searched for its heart. The organ pulsed and thrummed beneath my palm, quivering slightly as I seized it in my hand. I pulled my arm forcefully and wrenched the heart from the jaguar, feeling the hot splash of blood spray through the night. The eyes of the jaguar flashed as life left them, its body rapidly decaying from the touch of phantom hands. The decayed corpse pressed against my legs, its lifeless body pinning me to the ground. I allowed myself a moment for a sigh of relief.

Suddenly, the sound of a low growl began to permeate the air around me. I looked up to see a hollow light filling the jaguar's eyes. It lurched towards my left hand, snatching its heart from between my fingers and swallowing it whole. My eyes widened as a new surge of adrenaline coursed through me. I swiped my hand in an attempt to wound the feline, scratching it deeply against its front right shoulder. The cat did not waver or falter its movements, only climbing up my torso, inching closer to my face with slow, deliberate steps.

Gods, save me, I thought with a panic, fighting the urge not to close my eyes.

A sudden thudding slammed my ears, the rhythmic pounding recognizable as the hooves of a trotting horse. My heart skipped a beat, and I yearned to see Truff and Everett, for I craved to be saved by the iron of Everett's hammer. My eyes burned in surprise as a radiant light filled the banyan grove. A shining green horn sitting atop a dazzling mane barreled from the right. I blinked rapidly, watching it dart through the trees towards the snarling jaguar.

The unicorn lowered its head, ramming its horn through the jaguar's eye. The feline screamed as the unicorn lifted it high, arching the jaguar through the air and hurling it into the trees. The unicorn reared and whinnied fiercely, turning on its back haunches as it spun triumphantly. A dark spot adorned the horse's sternum, the black fur resembling the shape of a crescent moon. The unicorn's radiance was warm and soothing, its glittering silver light illuminating the heavy woven branches of the banyans.

"I owe you much gratitude," I said.

The unicorn settled its footing, bobbing its head as it watched me speak. Slowly, I rose to a sit, using my right hand to inspect my injuries. Blood stained my hands and ran down my body, the pain intense and nauseating. Glancing about, I noticed the glint of my mother's sword and my gauntlet, forcing myself to stumble to a crawl and fetch them. My movement was awkward as I fumbled on my knees and right hand, not wishing to risk touching the banyans with my phantomic fingers.

The unicorn whinnied gently, lowering its nose and nudging my gauntlet towards me. A silver-white glow rushed through the metal, thrumming lightly with a soft song. I failed to recognize the melody, though I was enchanted by the lullaby and yearned to hear it again.

"Thank you kindly," I said, retrieving my gauntlet from the unicorn as it met my eyes.

I sheathed my hand within the metal, finding the iron oddly soothing against my skin. The feeling was light and relaxed, akin to when I touched Thornin or partook in Tora berries. The gauntlet flashed suddenly and extended an aura of radiance briefly across me, the scratches and wounds from the jaguar quickly fading away. Fresh skin formed, and my body felt rejuvenated. However, the torments from the sun and my previous dehydration had only temporarily subsided.

"Your kindness knows no bounds," I said, reaching my hands upwards and patting the unicorn.

Its face was soft, its breath hot against my hands. The unicorn nuzzled my palm, biting playfully against the tips of my fingers in a way that reminded me of Thornin. My heart sank as I thought of him, and I wished he had been with me at that moment to guide me through the islands and behold such a radiant wonder.

"Thank you again..." I said slowly, pulling my hands away after a moment had passed. "I shall leave you be."

I rose to my feet and retrieved my mother's sword, sliding it beneath my tunic and along my spine. After adjusting it to be comfortable, I briefly saluted the unicorn. I stepped cautiously around it to continue exploring the banyans. Its big blue eyes regarded me curiously before it moved across my front, blocking me as I tried to pass.

"Is all well?" I asked, confused by the unicorn's bold spirits.

The unicorn whinnied, turning to face east. It searched my eyes and then began to walk slowly forward, pausing as it flicked its tail impatiently.

"Oi... are you wanting me to follow you?" I asked, wishing for Everett's innate ability to bond and speak with animals.

The unicorn whinnied once more, flashing a subtle purple energy.

"Very well," I said, trying my best to hide my confusion.

We moved to the east, gracefully parting the branches of the banyans. We walked towards the island's center, the unicorn's radiance casting light across the forest. Shadows of branches, ferns, and flowers spread across the floor, the mosquitos buzzing into the light and thankfully leaving me be.

I pushed forward, finding it increasingly difficult to move through the trees. A large hill began to form underfoot, slowing my steps as I followed behind the unicorn. The sudden scent of rosemary, eucalyptus, and lavender began to fill my nose, the big bushes of herbs and flowers protruding from beneath the branches. So fragrant was the air that the insects did not pass their barrier, buzzing away in an angry hoard. The unicorn sneezed unexpectedly and shook out its mane, its hair tinkling in a storm of soft bells.

"May your wish be granted," I said politely, courteous as it was to say the phrase after someone sneezes.

The unicorn cocked its head, turning briefly over its right shoulder before pressing forwards. Brambling rose bushes, thistles, and hawthorn came into view, and my footing faltered as I realized I did not have the protective means to traverse such thorns. The unicorn slowed, sensing my hesitation, and turned to face me.

"I cannot continue our trek through such dangerous plumage," I told the unicorn. "I am sorry to say I fear we must part ways."

The unicorn stepped forward, crushing a path through the thorns with its hooves. It did not flinch or whiny in pain, merely turning once again to search my eyes as I watched it curiously.

"I did not notice you bore horseshoes," I said, searching its hooves for iron yet failing to discover its presence. "I reckon I shall cross then."

I was surprised when the thorns failed to pierce my slippers, yet I was grateful to have them all the same. I quickened my pace and soon met a bank of tall grass, sighing in relief as the threat of thorns subsided. Pushing forward, we continued to climb, our path slowed by the thickening of branches. I ducked through the banyans and crested the top of a large plateau, excitedly inhaling the crisp and salted night air.

A small clearing unfurled around me, overrun with an immense banyan tree that stretched into the sky. The branches cast long shadows across the forest floor, their leaves swooping downwards with hundreds of hanging fruits. Large, flat slabs of stone jutted from the ground near the Banyan's trunk, the cracks in the rock elegantly formed. Large mushrooms grew in a circle in the shade of the Banyan, their odor pungent in the still night.

A portly shadow perched on a low-hanging branch, a deep green cloak draped around its form. A bright carnation hairpin gleamed in the moonlight as it held the cloak's fabric closed. Red hair peeked out from beneath the hood, framing my mother's face. She gazed upwards towards the stars, her face gaunt from her years of sickness. Her skin was darkened and smoothed like my own, the olive tones illuminated in the soft moonlight.

"Mother?" I said hopefully.

Mother's red hair brightened like smithing coals in a forge. The brightness of the flames was blinding, forcing me to look away. The brightness grew still behind my eyelids until I was met with silver light. Curiously, I opened my eyes.

The silver light faded but did not dissipate as it dimmed to reveal Senaya, goddess of the moon. Her bright blonde hair was pulled atop her head, the silver sticks of her hairpins cleverly tucked within the curls. She wore a short silver tunic of tight, shining fabric fraying into small strings of beads. Her waist was encircled in a large iron belt, where a beaded pouch hung.

Deep black and purple ink marked the back of her right hand, the etching of a tree and flowers, which I failed to recognize, spreading across her fingers. A pair of shining silver boots stretched upwards to Senaya's knees, glittering softly in the moonlight. Bracelets of bells hung around her ankles over the boots, twinkling lightly with the matching pair at her wrists.

"Senaya... It's nice to see you," I said.

"I agree," Senaya sprung lightly from the tree. "Though, if I am honest... You look as though you have seen better days."

"Perhaps I have," I said, always appreciative of Senaya's blunt honesty.

Senaya stepped around me, walking over to stand before the unicorn. She clicked her mouth softly, and it stood still as Senaya ran a hand along the length of the unicorn's body.

"You look strong, fierce...," Senaya said to me with an unreadable expression. "As though you have been again to the Seven Rings yet risen from them like a phoenix."

"Your words are kind," I said, shifting my weight to hide my embarrassment. "Though I am afraid they are unjustified..."

"How do you mean?"

"I have failed the crew I took to sea and am now lost on this isle," I began. "I am far from the troops, and fear I may not reach Riverside in time for The Ascension-"

"There is still time and strength for that," Senaya said. "The Creator still wishes for you to take His blood, accept His essence, and ascend."

Relief washed through me. "I am glad to know I am still desired."

"Aye, Knomucca," Senaya absently ran a hand across her unicorn. "Though it is dishonest. He wishes for your strength, not to bring balance but to ruin the realms. It is not for your wit, and the years your mother helped shape you, but for the wisdom you possess to undo what has been done. He wishes to use your gifts, insights, and knowledge to continue leading Crossfire through the dark."

My heart thrummed in panic.

"He uses the Prospects that He Ascends to continue perpetuating his corrupt cycle. He chooses Prospects that He thinks shall become suitable soldiers."

"He is wishing to corrupt me..." I confirmed. "I have already hurt those I love in service to Him, and you believe that it will never end?"

"He will meet his undoing," Senaya said, holding my gaze, hiding the meaning behind her words. "You shall need to stay the course and create the Elixir—with some modifications, of course."

"I have not the ingredients I need to prepare it," I said.

"That is no matter," Senaya began. "Tell me, Knomucca... What is the purpose of creating this potion for Him?"

"It is to help him recruit more Prospects," I said.

"In a manner of speaking..." Senaya drew a breath. "The Elixir will weaken your magical defenses and make you more susceptible to his corruption."

Fear washed over me. "What am I to do?"

"Move swiftly. Choose your potion elements with as many protective intentions as possible."

I sighed heavily. "If I am to accept His blood... I fear it shall be difficult to deceive Him. And what of the elements here on the island? I know He is not to have the pinta berry... And I fear I shall give Him more that He is not to possess."

"The pinta berry is a metaphor," said Senaya slowly, the rising sun making her shine more brightly. "The pinta represents the unification of five elements; strength, earth, spirit, love, and harmony. The fruit symbolizes a noble heart, one born from seven of seven. This is what you are not to give. Other fruits and natural elements of the island... these can be used in your Elixir to open your energy yet shield you from His corruption. Am I gifting you clarity thus far?"

I nodded slowly.

"Excellent. I have a final warning. The full moon shall be upon us in a night's time," Senaya said. "Once your Ascension is complete, you will have a mere three days until the effects of that potion fade. The elements within the Elixir could still leave you vulnerable unless you can find other plants and botanicals resistant to His corruption."

"Very well," I said, dragging out the words as I gathered my thoughts. "And how am I to know which elements are needed?"

"Return to their histories and legends... Select elements that draw on the symbolism of the pinta."

My breath caught in my throat, my words lost as I listened to Senaya's wisdom.

"What troubles you further?" she asked softly.

"Where have we found ourselves?" I asked.

"You have found a nexus whereupon the realms collide."

Understanding washed through me. Such high concentrations of magic would create many manifestations, from the lantern-shaped fruits and unfriendly animals to the regenerating trees and vivid visions.

"What is the origin of this place?" I asked.

"This meadow was blessed by the powers of the ancestors of your mother's coven, through magics performed in seven series of seven days. The Banyan was grown from the elements of the elder tree, containing all of life's vital essences. From that consumption, the Banyan too would come to know all things, and become another omniscient anchor in the realms."

"Am I correct in assuming you were involved in the creation of this place? Were you not in the hallowed circle alongside my ancestors?"

"Your words hold truth," Senaya said. "I led you to this place when you were unconscious in Heimaaila... or if I am honest the moment you stepped upon the catamaran."

"Thank you kindly for my rescue," I said.

"I needed to bring you here... This clearing is a safe place to converse about the Creator as it is currently free of His corruption."

A silence fell between us, interrupted by the gentle swishing of the unicorn's tail as it fanned itself in the humid night.

"I have a few more matters to discuss with you before I depart," Senaya spoke urgently.

"Very well," I said. "Though I suppose I also have several more inquiries... if that is well with you."

"I pray you speak quickly."

"Your unicorn... She saved me from a Jaguar and healed me from the wounds it caused-"

"A jaguar! Where in the Seven Hells did you see a jaguar?"

"Here, on the island," I said, gesturing over my shoulder. "Down the hill, in the banyan grove."

"I am glad that you are well."

"Thank you, As am I."

Senaya's face fell. Her eyes grew serious, her mouth curling in a thin line to hide her expression. Her shoulders lowered with a heavy breath. Senaya absently ran a hand along the barrel of her unicorn's body, focusing on her affections before beginning to speak.

"The Creator had discovered these islands in the year of Ozwal. He fights fiercely and often to penetrate the enchantments around the Nexus, but He has yet to breach them."

"What would happen if he were successful?" I asked.

"Should He manage to do so? The forces that wish to overtake Him shall have to convene elsewhere..." Senaya gazed thoughtfully towards the Banyan. "The realms flow through all things and have many ways in which they connect... Another Nexus or hiding place would simply have to be secured with better enchantments."

I nodded in agreement.

"What other inquiries did you wish to express?" asked Senaya.

"What more can you tell me about the Banyan trees?"

"The Banyan is sacred. It too is capable of withstanding corruption." Senaya informed me. "Have you ever wondered why Ozwal the Great chose the Banyan as his symbol?"

"Of course, I have pondered such," I concurred. "There was never any indication in the legends, nor is there any sort of written explanation."

"Ozwal heard of the clearing from gossip and legends from those who were attempting to overthrow the Creator. He came searching for the islands and discovered the Banyan trees and their protective power. The grove was grown from magic of the elder tree and is eternally bound to it through the vital life energy of its enchanted roots. The Banyan is the tree of life... a tree that connects the realms... it is one with everything, and everything with one. It is wise beyond years, rooted in the deepest truths, and is watered with knowledge of the universe. Ozwal eventually found the trees and incorporated them into his crest, feeling compelled to harness their protective powers."

"It is logical that he should have been in need of such protections if he was planning a coup or attempting to overthrow the Creator... Our present conversation is enough to warrant my execution should anyone come to discover it."

"You truly are your mother's daughter. Exceedingly bright, indeed." Senaya nodded. "I wish to take you to his shipwreck. If you are ready, shall we set off?"

Glancing about my shoulder, I noticed the late morning sun. My anxiety grew greater as I realized my Ascension was within a day's time.

I began to follow Senaya, listening as her soft silver bells chimed through the crickets. The unicorn stepped forward, following alongside Senaya on her left. Distant croaking frogs accompanied the soft hooting of owls, their calls high in the branches of the Banyan.

The Banyan swept along my right, its branches glowing with playful clusters of fireflies. As we left the center of the clearing, the grass lengthened, growing long and snagging across my slippers. Bright orange lilies punctuated the foliage, entangling in the morning glories and vines that had spread from the back of the Banyan.

"I am sorry I cannot gift you a proper rest," Senaya said gently as she withdrew a waterskin from the belt at her hip. "Drink this as we are walking."

"I am grateful for your support," I said.

The water was refreshing as it passed my lips. As I drank, it lightened my spirits and left me feeling rejuvenated. The fabric of my tunic stretched and swelled as it repaired itself. My boots rose, properly covering my feet in order to shield me from the elements.

Feeling refreshed, we pressed forward, moving through the large plants and hedges surrounding the clearing. The banyans shifted into sweeping ferns and large shrubs, returning to the tropical fruits and plants of the island outside the clearing. The hill descended, and we marched through the forest, clambering in a slim single line through the branches and bramble. Small trails and tracks of animal prints began to appear across the ground.

"How much farther?" I asked, keeping my voice low as I did not wish to encounter any other unfriendly forest dwellers.

"We are nearly there," Senaya said, pushing aside the branches of a large banana tree. "It is just beyond these leaves..."

A white pebbled beach came into focus, glowing softly under the bright blue sky. Small pools of water were collecting along the shoreline, and the salt and impurities filtered through cracks in the stones. Several animals scattered into the tree line as we traversed the sand, skittering fearfully out of our sight.

"My apologies everyone," Senaya said gently.

We followed the shoreline and encroached on a large stone structure; the wall was cracked and covered with vines and thorns. I remembered this structure from my earlier explorations, recognizing the trees and roots that curled across the stones.

"Ozwal's ship crashed beyond these cliffs," Senaya said. "We shall need to climb the rocks to reach the wreck." Senaya turned towards the unicorn and pressed her palm against her face. "Delphine, it is always a joy and a gift to find your company... though I am afraid we must be parting ways."

Delphine huffed a hot breath.

"How I wish you could traverse the cliffside and immerse yourself in the water alongside us," Senaya began, scratching the side of Delphine's ears.

"How I wish I could spend more time beside you, though I fear I have none to give. I, too, shall have to make a hasty retreat though I strongly dislike doing so."

Delphine winked, biting Senaya playfully. Lifting her head, Delphine met my eyes, swishing her tail in delight and flicking her ears softly.

"It was a pleasure to make your acquaintance," I told her. "And I thank you again for saving me."

Delphine whinnied politely, turning suddenly and moving towards the trees. Her trot sped into a gentle canter, the sand flinging loosely beneath her hooves as she disappeared. An emptiness reverberated in the silence that followed her absence, the air warmer and unpleasant as her radiance no longer shielded us from the elements.

"Such a good lass," Senaya said, turning to place her hands atop the vines protruding from the rock.

With Delphine gone, I followed suit. I stepped onto the stone, hoisted my body upwards, and began the climb. I followed Senaya's path as she secured divots in the stone. As I climbed, I found my rhythm and moved with ease, overtaking Senaya.

I reached the top and flattened my body against the ledge, turning over my shoulder and dangling my arms downwards. Senaya was perched a few feet below me, her muscles rippling as she pulled her body upwards. Steadily, I lowered a hand, offering it to her in an attempt to aid her climbing. Senaya reached towards her front and clasped her hand around my wrist, tightening her grip against my arm. Her weight tugged at my arms and made me feel unstable, my feet digging into the stone behind me to keep my footing.

"Up like a daisy," I said, gently pulling against Senaya.

Senaya paused, her face contorting. A thick shadow moved across her, darkening her eyes like spilled ink. My fingers pulsed painfully in my gauntlets, pushing a heavy heat wave between us. The energy burned, jolting sharply through my arm up to my elbow. An involuntary groan escaped me as my fingers convulsed tightly around her. Senaya's breathing lengthened, her body recoiling with a shudder as she forcefully freed herself from my grasp.

"My apologies," I sputtered, shaking my hands in an attempt to soothe them. "I know not what affects me so."

Senaya's breaths were measured, her muscles rippling as she clung to the cliffside.

"Senaya, are you well?" I asked, growing frantic.

"Not quite," Senaya said as her face cleared. "I... I needed to resist the sudden desire to hurt you and drag you downwards from the rock... But I sincerely do not wish to, I assure you. You know my conversing with you this close to the Ascension is dangerous. Due to the darkness lingering inside me from the corruption of The Creator's blood, I am still susceptible to the calls."

My heart lurched, and my breathing quickened as worry washed through me. I pushed myself from my stomach and curled into a sit. I opened my mouth to speak but could not find the words to express myself.

"I apologize, though you need to know everything so as not to be forced into the darkness like myself and those before you," Senaya said as she pulled herself from the cliffside, coming to rest alongside me. "My connection to the moon, and the lunar magic I possess as goddess of it, helps keep me resistant to most of the calls from darkness inside myself."

My hands ached as I tightened the gauntlets, the pain making it hard to focus on the moon goddess's words.

"Allow me," Senaya said, reaching toward me.

I hesitated.

"I am sorry I made you worry," Senaya said. "I promise, though His blood and corruption swirl inside me I shall not hurt you."

Cautiously, I reached toward her, placing my hands in hers. Instantly, the pain relented, and relaxation flowed through my fingers and into my energy.

"Thank you, kindly," I said. "I apologize if the energy that flowed from me has hurt you."

"It has not," Senaya said, gently massaging my fingers. "It temps me towards dark deeds... though I was able to resist."

I held her in my gaze, studying her closely.

"I assure you, I am well now," she said again. "Though you must heed my warnings... if you cannot protect yourself from His corruption, you too may be tempted to hurt those you care for... and I wish only for you to help us shine light into the darkness, not indulge in it."

"I shall do everything I can," I said.

Senaya smiled as she released my fingers and slowly rose to a stand.

"Come along," she said, gingerly moving across the rocks. "We must continue."

We stepped across the large, smoothed stones that spilled along the coast. Sand was spread around shallow pools of water that echoed in the mouths of hollowed caves. Water sprayed from the waves, which were heavy with the tides, the mist coating our skin and clothes in more layers of salt.

We moved down the rock along the shoreline, seeing a large boulder beneath the water's surface. Thick green algae formed on the rocks and swayed into the waves. The seabed dropped suddenly beyond the boulder, creating a strong current along the shoreline. Looming shadows rippled through the currents, my stomach churning uneasily as I watched them move.

A water-sodden hull protruded from the surf, the planks wet and withered from the elements. The waves crashed against them and spilled inside the cabin, filling it with the sea. Driftwood floated around it, connected haphazardly with rusted screws. The rigging was hanging in the breeze, jingling loudly like Senaya's bells as the metal jostled in the wind.

"We are fortunate the currents dragged it so close to the shore," Senaya said.

"Is it safe to explore?" I asked.

"Aye, it has been searched before," Senaya said. "Please, lead the way..."

I stepped into the shallows, the cold sending a chill through me. Seaweed clung to my legs as I waded through the water and up to the galleon. The ship rose before me, its ghostly hull creaking ominously in the early morning tide. The sound of splashing behind me told me Senaya was following nearby.

"Over there," she said, pointing to a tattered ladder hanging down from the main deck.

Gathering my strength, I gave a firm tug to test its stability. When it held steady, I hoisted myself up, climbing slowly. Gingerly, I stepped onto the deck of the ship, grabbing cautiously onto the rigging. A flag once resembling living fire lay sopping wet and extinguished, the shreds of red cloth flapping pathetically. Symbols of spirit, fire, and cycles were carved into the elaborate masts, matching the runes woven amongst the leaves of the Banyans. The boat groaned beneath my weight, deeply nestled in the nook where it had run aground.

Senaya stepped onto the deck, placing her feet exactly where I had stepped. Together, we moved across the quarter-deck. The planks creaked loudly beneath our feet, the oak splitting from exposure to the salt. As I stepped, the wood snapped beneath my foot, my leg sinking below the deck, dragging me down to my knees.

"Knomucca!"

Senaya seized my shoulders and pulled me upright, standing behind me atop the deck. The boards shuddered and gave from our weight, dropping us into the captain's cabin below. Fractured light glowed between the planks, illuminating the exposed captain's quarters. The wooden slabs to the east were exposed from the persistent winds, the warped oak planks fracturing off into sharp spikes in all directions. The framework was rotted, sagging downwards into the dirt beneath the wreckage. Skeletons lay preserved amongst the wood, the empty orbits of their eyes pleading for help as they yearned to be laid to rest.

I moved freely about the cabin to thoroughly examine the remains. Ozwal's ship was no longer the mighty vessel it once was, slamming a surge of sadness through me. Holes sliced through the hull, gaping and pulsing as the wood withered away. I ran my fingers over the dark oak planks, feeling the coarse grain caused by the years of exposure.

I walked through the captain's quarters, noticing decrepit tables, cracked chess boards, and eroded barrels of wine littering the passageway. I moved carefully to the ship's starboard. I found an open hatch, deciding I was to twist through it to continue exploring.

"Senaya, keep guard if you would," I said.

"Oi, be mindful of your step," Senaya said.

I crawled through the hatch, finding myself in a darkened room. I blinked rapidly, though I could not see beyond my nose, prompting me to turn back.

"I cannot see," I said.

"Allow me to assist you," she responded.

Senaya rummaged through her pouch, producing a large moonstone. Holding it in her hands, she lifted it towards the sky, drawing in a deep breath. The stone began to glow with a soft silver light, illuminating the room around us.

"Impressive," I said.

Senaya pressed the stone firmly into my hands. I ducked through the hatch and then held the stone aloft. The large bed was rotted and sagging, and the blankets shriveled and absorbed into the mattress. The warped fireplace looked sad and lonely in the wreckage that surrounded it, the stone cracked and chipping jaggedly. A fractured iron cauldron sat abandoned in the brewing station that once stood strong along the back wall, the metal red with a thick coat of rust.

"Knomucca, how are you fairing?" Senaya asked from beyond the hatch.

"All is well," I said.

"Continue cautiously."

I moved gingerly across the cabin and approached the brewing station. A marble pestle and mortar had been used and now rested dormant beside an oxidized blade. Broken teeth and claws of many types filled a small jar, though the station was clear otherwise.

"I am going to disturb some of the artifacts," I called to Senaya, jumping with a horrible fright as she appeared behind me.

Senaya smiled, fighting the urge to laugh.

"Are you certain that is wise?" Senaya asked as she regained her composure. "The dead linger amongst the planks... it is their tomb..."

"I am aware of such risks," I said heavily, "though I fear we ought not discover anything of use if we do not allow for such action. I shall do all I can to lay their souls to rest... I can only pray they understand why I must disturb their peace."

"Very well," Senaya said. "May they have mercy on us ..."

I cautiously lifted the cauldron from the table, freeing it from its stand. Quickly, I also began to clear the jars but gasped and flinched backward as a rat scuttled across the table. I momentarily held my breath as I waited for a trap to trigger; when none came, I breathed a sigh of relief.

"Bloody hells," Senaya cursed.

Once more, I stepped closer to the brewing stand, squatting down beside it. I inspected a large wooden drawer centered on the table, noticing that it was slightly open. Outstretching a hand, I seized the loose iron handle and pulled it free, revealing a hollowed, empty hole within. Whatever had once occupied the space had long ago disintegrated.

"How unfortunate," I said, exploring the remaining drawers only to find the same.

I rose once more and moved about the cabin again, this time in search of Ozwal's altar. I paced around the outer wall, lightly running my fingertips over the wood. The cabin opened to the west, and I proceeded down the passageway. Using my moonstone for light, I followed the curve, finding Ozwal's altar tucked into a distant corner.

The altar rose from the shadows and ruins, the space nearly indistinguishable from the darkened wood around it. A smoothed obsidian hutch held gems, the remnants of parchments and bones. Painted ceramic chalices still remained intact across the far back wall, filled with rocks, nails, and coins. Soaked and torn books were bloated amongst the shelves, the leather bulging and torn from the salt. A thick, carved wooden wolf's head had decayed and split down the middle, revealing a sodden green candle. Three wide stone pillars protruded out towards the ceiling from the hutch, their centers hollowed and open to the air.

I placed the moonstone atop the altar and felt no ramifications, failing to trigger any trap or threat from my general touch. I lifted the goblets and peered behind them, seeing only the signs of weathered obsidian beneath.

Lowering a hand, I set it upon a large amethyst that sat amidst the pile of gems, wishing to avoid the altar's centerpiece until necessary. Three sharp needles shot up from the stone and pierced my palm, forcing a scream from my lips. Blood spilled out and spread across the altar. My vision quickly began to darken as I fought to keep my focus.

"Senaya! Help!" I cried out.

A sudden metallic click rang through the darkness, and a sequence of lights ignited. Flaming torches burst forth a bright cherry glow onto the altar, illuminating the air with a fierce whooshing. The needles retracted into the amethyst as the tabletop turned a full circle, cracking loudly as it split into quarters. A piece fell away, and a large glass bottle came into focus, the glass kept closed with a secured wooden cork.

"Knomucca, is all well?" Senaya asked as she regarded the altar.

A concealed bottle glowed beside the moonstone, reflecting silver in the light. I placed my hand on the bottle. Pain shot through my forehead, and I released a sharp breath and tried pulling away, feeling paralyzed where I stood. Sudden vines began to climb from the glass, clinging to my arm and squeezing like snakes.

Damn it, I thought, discovering I could move my right hand.

I brought my free hand to my left and released it from its gauntlet, unfastening the side of the iron. I allowed my hand to become spectral, relaxing into the pain and discomfort. The bottle broke free of the vines, releasing me from where I stood. Using my corporeal hand, I refastened my gauntlet. I then scooped the bottle in my grip as my body ached. I slipped the bottle into my pouch, not wishing to misplace it.

I looked at my surroundings as I caught my breath, noticing that Senaya was no longer in the room. Deciding it was better to leave the space rather than explore any further alone, I retraced my path through the ship, searching for her.

Eventually, I found myself on the top deck near the bow. Ozwal's crest shined brightly in the midday sun, the cherry red fire glowing intensely through the water. Absently, I ran a hand over the crest, feeling a magnetic thrumming wash over me.

"HELP!" A startling voice whispered through me, my heart pounding in my chest.

"Senaya!" I called through the stillness, stepping backward from the crest.

Silence echoed around me as I climbed back down the ladder into the sea.

"Senaya?" I called again, wading through the water and stepping away from the ship's bow.

The distant calls of pigeons and seagulls were the only reply. Anxiety flooded through me, my heart lurching in my chest.

"Senaya, where are you?" I said hurriedly.

Senaya had vanished, and the scent of sandalwood lingered as a reminder of her earlier company. I glanced around the shoreline and grew disheartened, fighting not to panic as I stood alone amidst the wreckage.

A flock of birds flew overhead, scattering wildly through the sky. I turned over my shoulder and peered to the west. A large shadow suddenly obscured the sun. Immense purple wings unfolded in the wind, soaring gracefully across the clouds.

XVI

EVERETT

The water stretched endlessly beneath me, glittering brightly in the sunlight. The wind bit around me, the air warming with the promise of the day's heat. Whistling loudly, I commanded Thornin to dip lower, scanning the tops of the waves thoroughly. No sign of Knomucca peeked through the waters, and my stomach wretched with a horrible anxiety. My despair willed me forward. Tiredness tore at my eyes, my muscles becoming sore and stiff from my time flying in the saddle.

Thornin sighed heavily, his wings fluttering slowly as exhaustion overwhelmed him. His wings flapped lazily, and his momentum dipped and slowed, dragging us through the clouds like molasses.

"Just a bit further, Laddie," I said to him. "If we have no sight of her by evening, we shall turn back towards camp and give you time to rest..."

Thornin pressed on, his wings spanning wide through the wind. I observed scattered, floating debris sprawled across the waves, bobbing gently in the water. Loose articles of clothing, apples, writing utensils, and alchemical supplies floated at the surface, lulling lazily in the water.

"Lower to the water," I urged Thornin through my whistles.

We came to rest above the piles of debris as Thornin hovered gently atop the water. The red, green, and purple silken tunics were unmistakably familiar, their fabric rippling softly amongst the waves.

Knomucca, what happened to your belongings? I wondered.

"Thornin, it is your time to submerge yourself," I said, commanding him to float in the water with a whistle.

Thornin landed with a heavy splash. Mist sprayed in a circle around us, showering my face. Reaching outwards with a hand, I patted Thornin's hide gratefully, appreciating his willingness to delve beneath the sea's surface.

"Aye, that is a good lad," I told him fondly.

I returned my hands to the center and began unfastening my belt, tying the heavy iron lower against my waist. The iron clasped securely against Thornin's saddle, allowing me a more flexible range of motion without toppling from his back. Leaning left, I stretched my fingers outwards, sweeping objects that floated atop the water's surface into my hands. Bundles of lavender and large feathered quills bobbed amongst the waves, slipping easily into my grasp as I pressed them into the compartment of Thornin's saddle.

I reached as far backward as I could, rescuing rogue apples and tinted glass bottles from the tides. The glass bottles were etched with various runes and symbols, some containing herbs, nuts, and fruits, while the rest remained empty. The apples were shining red in the light of the sun, their rouge an angelic halo around them. I plucked the apples gingerly, fitting one each in the palms of my hands. Several stretches passed before half a dozen apples had been placed in the saddle's secret compartment, the red bushels punctuated by crisp green and yellow.

I reached outwards again to retrieve one final floating apple, feeling it slip securely into my fingers. A wedge of cold metal pressed into my palm, settling against my skin. Cautiously, I turned the apple over in my hand, releasing a sharp gasp when an ornate hairpin pierced the apple's core. The silver carnation twinkled softly, appearing unharmed from the salt and its time in the sea.

"How strange!" I exclaimed, examining the pin closely.

The carnation glowed subtly, releasing a brightly-hued, fiery red through my awareness. A set of familiar, bright green eyes reflected into my own, the irises of an electric emerald I often saw in Knomucca. However, the eyes did not belong to her, for they appeared wiser in years and enlightened with the knowledge and passing of time. The kindness held within them was the same as my beloved. Yet, the energy floating through them felt instinctively maternal and protective.

"Cornalla?" I asked timidly.

The eyes vanished, showing only the runes and silver metal in their place.

"How odd," I mumbled to Thornin, taking the pin and placing it in my smoking sack for safekeeping.

Reaching around me once more, I collected the remaining debris, securing three spare tunics, an enchanted book, and a set of mismatched boots.

"Aye, Thornin... that shall do for the moment."

Thornin merely swam forward, finding it difficult to cast into the sky.

"Oi... come along there, fella," I said to him gently, patting him as he continued to swim. "These treasures we found belong to her... I reckon it cannot be much farther now..."

The dragon swam onwards, forcefully pushing his legs and claws through the water. The wind increased its speed, sending the waves cascading and spraying around us. As Thornin continued to the east, I gently nudged his ribs with my heels as if he were a horse in an attempt to communicate.

"We ought to leave the waters, Thornin," I prodded him in annoyance when he stubbornly failed to comply.

Thornin huffed, the waves rushing us forward. They slammed at our backs and sprayed cold water around us, my skin in desperate need of the warmth from the sun.

"Up, Thornin." I urged frustratedly.

Thornin craned over his shoulder and glared into my eyes, his irises turning a piercing cold blue, harsh as winter.

"Oi... very well then," I surrendered, not wishing to anger him any further.

The wind ruffled my garments, sending a chill down my spine. Through the wind, to the east, the horizon grew heavy. The air began to blur as if observed through soiled glass panes. The winds welled, and a bright purple mist shimmered through the sky, revealing a jagged shoreline of boulders and rocks. The gales roared, and the coast vanished. The stones disappeared as the mists covered them from sight.

I watched the horizon, noticing the rocks as they rippled and disappeared with the air currents. Palm trees reached into the skies beyond the shoreline, framing the outline of a white-pebbled beach.

"Stay true," I whistled to the dragon, communicating to continue our trek to the east.

The purple mist shimmered through the wind, growing brighter as we drew closer to the island, a familiar sense of protection coming over me. The winds slammed us violently, forcing my eyes to close as saltwater sprayed my face.

"Easy," I ordered Thornin.

Thornin paddled against the water, the waves pushing us away from the islands with the heavy slamming against our fronts. I guided Thornin eastward as best I could, fighting to keep him toward the islands as the purple mist flooded my eyes.

Thornin forced his way forward, the wind ripping the air from my breath as we pressed through the wall of purple mist. The air was heavy and smelt of mugwort, the bitter scent overwhelming and disorienting against the sea and the skies. My vision blurred, and a melodic singing filled my ears, accompanying the scent of charred coal and the creaking of a ship's rigging. The pounding of a drum slammed the wind, weaving through broken voices and the sounds of faint and distant crying.

"Everett," whispers rippled through me, sending waves of anxiety cascading down my spine. "Cursed you shall be to enter this place. Sacrificed. Suffocated. Trapped between Time and Space..."

"Show yourself! I do not fear your threats!" I called.

Broken, jarring laughter rang through me, sending searing pain through my forehead; I took a breath to center myself, attempting to close my energies against the noise and voices. The wind bit through my chest, wrenching my speech from my throat. The fierce gales whipped through my ears, the lulls transforming into piercing screams and sobs. I shut my eyes against the pain, stealing my strength as I pushed through the veil of mist.

"Only emptiness lies beyond... lifeless suffering... abyssal gloom. Death, torture... Turn around, plan your retreat with the treacherous moon."

A tenebrous veiled face materialized, stretching outwards a set of heron-clawed hands. The thick scent of salt shifted into the heavy smell of iron, the metallic aroma morphing into the pungent odor of blood. A curdling laugh prickled through me, lingering in a piercing, sharp shiver. A horrendous pain spidered through my chest, the agony so intense I had to fight to breathe.

"To the Hells with you," I said, drawing my hammer from my waist.

Swinging it viciously, I was half-surprised when the iron struck solid, blurring the vision quickly away from my awareness. A distant scream flooded my ears, blaring uncomfortably through my head. The wind quieted as I smashed my hammer through it, feeling the thick and heavy air begin to disperse. The purple mist shattered and thinned, the energy falling away and cascading into the water in neat ripples. The air suddenly calmed as the sun crested the horizon.

"Aye... away with you, you blood-curdling fiend!" I said, returning my hammer to my waist.

Thornin pressed forward, standing to attention following my attack and our visitor. Gradually, we continued through the water, feeling the air suddenly warm as the winds began to settle. Small smatterings of rocks began to punctuate the shallows, jutting jaggedly from the waters around us. Large flocks of birds were traveling from the west, moving in the air currents that coaxed them over the islands.

I combed the shoreline, summoning my full voice as I began to call for my beloved.

"KNOMUCCA!" I shouted, hearing only seagulls as a reply.

My heart gave a sudden lurch. A floating bedroll smashed against distant rocks, glowing brightly in the sun as it bobbed gently in the waves. Weaving Thornin through the boulders, we obtained the bedroll; I scooped it firmly onto my lap before examining it. There were no identifying features, nothing that indicated how the bed roll had come to land beside the rocks.

I did my best to dry the bedroll against my cloak and secure it tightly, placing it under my legs to fasten it within the stirrups. I pressed my foot into the roll to keep it steady, ensuring it would not fall again and return to the waters.

Interesting discovery, I mused to myself. I wonder how this came to float amongst the stones.

We continued scouring the rocks, our path becoming difficult to maneuver as the boulders pushed closer together.

"Thornin, we need to seek a better vantage point from the sky," I told him sincerely. "Come now, Thornin... up!"

Thornin lurched forward, deciding he would finally respond. The dragon unfurled his wings and pressed against the rocks, lifting us high into the air. As the sun climbed the sky, we followed its pursuit, remaining low over the ground to continue our search. Sweeping palm trees and banana groves came into focus, with cliffs of rock and bramble along the shoreline. Curving around the coastline, we discovered a secluded white pebbled beach. We noticed four large banana leaves placed in a symmetrical line through the sand.

"Thornin, touch down," I commanded through my whistles, feeling the wind whip as Thornin sped towards the ground.

We flew towards the beach with the neatly placed leaves, Thornin landing in the rocks with a heavy thud. I hopped from the saddle and moved through the pebbles, gingerly approaching the banana leaves on the ground. I squatted down beside them and cautiously lifted the fibrous material, noticing a coconut half-filled with water floating in a small hole.

"Such ingenuity," I said, impressed. "A water collection system..."

I replaced the leaf and stepped away from the traps, not wishing to disturb them any further. I rose to my feet and moved across the sand, thoroughly examining the trees bordering the beach. My heart thrummed and slammed through my chest as a tall palm tree along the coast displayed the crest of Knomucca's mother's coven. A compass had been drawn, and the arrow pointed North-West, indicating that Knomucca had taken a trip to explore the coastline.

"Let us follow her path," I said to Thornin, sliding once more into the saddle.

Thornin spread his wings, and we flew into the sky, moving behind a scattering flock of hawks and seagulls. We swooped low and edged along the tree line, winding along the beaches with the sea to our left. We combed the sand slowly and thoroughly, my heart racing with every passing moment. A tall figure stood beside the shoreline, my heart lurching into my throat as I discovered Knomucca on the beach.

Her hair was disheveled, glowing magnificently in the midday sun. Her hands were dirty, though her gauntlets bore no signs of use, sparkling mischievously. Her trousers and the bottom of her tunic were drenched as though she had recently been in the water. Large scratches trailed down her face, her skin wrinkled and aggravated from too much salt and sunlight.

Despite her obvious signs of struggle, she remained beautiful. Her scratches and wounds shrouded her with an aura of strength, painting a shining silver radiance through her energy. Knomucca's eyes brightened as they met my own, her face breaking into a smile I would cherish for eternity.

I whistled for Thornin to land, feeling him alight softly upon the sands. Knomucca regarded us curiously as she waited for us to settle. I swung my leg across the saddle and leaped from Thornin's back.

"Knomucca," I said with a trembling breath, reaching a hand towards her and lowering it out of embarrassment. "I feared you were dead..."

"Everett," she said, her voice hoarse and tired, "I am merely lost... though well all the same."

"It is the finest fortune I should find you safe," I said, smiling despite myself as she took another step towards me. "Right smart dragon Thornin is... he found us at the Rose Lily and helped lead me to you."

"The Rose Lily," Knomucca said, puzzlement painting her expression. "The troops ought to have come to Ostarie by now... why has your course been so horribly altered?"

"It is my unfortunate doing, if I am honest," I said guiltily. "Kiyoko and I wished to investigate the apothecary in hopes of obtaining new elements for the Elixir of Life... yet we ran into some trouble with the Priestess and our endeavors proved useless..."

"That is incredibly kind of you both," she said with a soft smile. "Though I must ask you to explain further."

Knomucca listened as I regaled her of the incidents that occurred within the Rose Lily, her face composed in an unreadable expression.

"He absorbed!?" she questioned in shock.

I gave her my water skin and watched her drink it dry before unburdening my heart. "I feel quite guilty for leaving him."

"And what came of the Rose Lily after the fire?" Knomucca asked.

"We have sent for the people and resources to rebuild it," I said. "Though the Priestess hides inside, and we could not extract her."

"Riverside is not in the cards," she sighed heavily. "Though, I suppose it never was. We are to find our own elements and forge our own way for The Ascension, as was told to me by her Radiance, Senaya."

"Those are complex tidings," I said, my guilt for leaving Kiyoko and the troops behind at the Rose Lily deepening. "Knomucca... per chance did you ask Captain Southwell to escort you to the reefs?"

"Aye," Knomucca said eagerly. "Have you heard news of him and his companions?"

Slowly, I opened my smoking sacks, produced his medallion, and handed it to Knomucca. She turned it in her hands, studying it gently.

"Unfortunately, it appears they did not survive the storm," I said heavily, watching her eyes widen in horror. "I found them floating in the reefs."

Knomucca's shoulders tightened, her face contorting as pain flashed through her eyes. Tears threatened to spill down her cheeks, though dehydration and tiredness would not allow her to properly cry.

"I feel terrible," she said. "How can they be dead... how could I have been so reckless and selfish..."

"Please, do not burden yourself with blame," I said gently as I wished to take her in my arms. "You are pursuing noble means on behalf of the Creator... you cannot allow yourself to harbor such negativity when you are doing what is demanded of you..."

"Your words are kind," Knomucca said. "Though they shall not alter the sadness I feel."

"You shall have to search for him in the Underworld when a spare moment permits you," I encouraged, "to be certain he is well."

"I shall do so indeed," she said.

A silence fell between us, interrupted by the waves crashing against the coast.

"I found this as well," I said, producing the carnation pin from my smoking sack and pressing it into her hand.

Knomucca's eyes brightened, a smile flashing across her face.

"Everett, thank you," she said. "Wherever did you find it?"

"It was piercing the core of a floating apple," I said nonchalantly. "Why did you part with it?"

"Our ship sank from the storm when we were near the reefs and barges," Knomucca began. "When I woke after what seemed to be an entire night floating in the tides, I was in a right lot of trouble. Lyle and his guard were nowhere to be found. I had long passed the reefs and I did all I could to stay afloat; When I opened my pouch to retrieve anything I had that may have been useful, I spilled my belongings. I do not know when my mother's pin fell from my hair, though I suppose during my unconsciousness it fell into the water along with all else I had brought along. I am very happy to see it again."

"I..." I hesitated briefly, taking an immense breath before sharing my confession. "I saw her, Cornalla... her eyes appeared in the leaves, and... I simply knew it was your mother."

Knomucca regarded me curiously. "That is rather peculiar," she said, sliding the pin again into her hair. "I thought I saw her too... though it was someone else."

Another silence fell between us, accompanied by the distant calls of hawks and seagulls.

"What do you reckon should be our first course of action?" Knomucca asked.

"I suppose Thornin shall need a rest before we are to return on our path," I said, noticing as he lay to bathe in the sun. "And once he has recovered, I fear we shall be pressed for time in returning to the troops."

"It will not be possible to return in time," Knomucca said. "We will have to make the potion here, on the island. However, for now we ought to make camp. I fear I shall not have the strength to Ascend at all if I am not fed a proper meal and imbibe sufficient water."

"I can assist in providing you nourishment," I said.

"That is kind of you to offer," Knomucca said with a smile. "Everett...words cannot express how happy I am to see you."

I took a deep breath, stealing my strength and bravery.

"Knomucca... I promised myself I would never dishonor my station as commander or be the one to contribute to your Fall from Grace... though the thought of never seeing you again was unbearable. I too lack the proper words to express my devotion, so I must allow my actions to do so."

My lips found hers eagerly, my arms tightening against her with excitement. I ran my hands through her hair, detangling it gingerly with my fingers as our bodies pressed together. A soft moan escaped me as my fingers tightened in the roots of her hair. Her breath was hot, and she tasted of coconuts; her tongue was sweet and salted like the air around us. Brushing a hand along her jawline, I marveled at the shape of her face, my heart lurching as I inhaled the taste of her. I swept my hands across her muscular shoulders, caressing the back of her neck with a gentle touch. The tattoo I had drawn for her thrummed beneath my fingers; the prospect of inking a dragon against her smoothed silk thighs stirred my manhood excitedly.

"Everett," she said as our lips parted. "Everett... I must pause and catch my breath."

"I love you, Knomucca," I said, failing to fully grasp her previous words.

A sudden burst of adrenalin floated through me, my heart leaping as Knomucca slowly pulled away. I took a breath and held her in my arms, watching as her eyes drank me in.

"And I, you," she said, a smile filling her face.

I took a step backward and released her from my arms, not wishing to trap her against me.

"Everything is unfolding quite rapidly, and I simply need a moment to collect myself."

"Come along then," I said.

Knomucca squeezed my hand and smiled wryly, stepping around me along my right. Her gait was unstable from overexertion, and her footing tired as she moved through the sand. Knomucca paused and knelt beside Thornin, his eyes opening suddenly as she obscured his sunlight.

"Thank you for coming to find me," she said to him, kissing his nose lovingly. "It is mighty nice to see you... I hate to disturb your resting, though I reckon you ought to follow us to camp."

Thornin blinked and huffed a cloud of smoke, then pulled himself to his feet. Knomucca rose to a stand and clasped my hand once more, tugging me forward as I gave a passing salute to Thornin. We moved along the island's coast, watching the waves crash against the rocks and spray water into the sky. A comfortable silence fell between us, Knomucca's hand warm in my own as we walked across the pebbled sands.

We returned to the secluded beach, the banana leaves lying across the holes of filtered water. A small cluster of trees formed where Knomucca had carved her mother's crest, their trunks a perfect equidistance for constructing a tent or shelter.

"Are these receptacles your design?" I asked in awe.

"Aye... I crafted them myself," she said proudly, guiding Thornin and me into her camp. Turning towards the dragon, she added, "You are free to explore and hunt on foot, though I ask you not to separate yourself from us for too long."

Thornin nipped her playfully in reply, releasing another cloud of smoke in her face before promptly laying in the shade.

"You ought to check them," I said, freeing her hand though I had not wished to do so. "You have a fair bit of water collected already, and it would do you well after your time in the sun."

"Aye, it is rather warm here," Knomucca said, lifting the first of the four banana leaves. "Am I to assume you stumbled upon these on your search?"

"Aye, that we did," I said fondly. "Along with a few other treasures."

I approached Thornin and opened the saddle, producing the bedroll, apples, alchemical supplies, and boots in a pile beside him.

"My, the Gods were good to you," Knomucca said gratefully.

"There were a few other oddities," I said, "though I can trouble you with them after you have eaten, and we have proper shelter from the sun."

"That would be appreciated," Knomucca said, a hopeful spark flashing through her eyes.

I obtained the mismatched leather boots and unstrung the laces, tucking the leather back into Thornin's saddle. As Knomucca drained and refilled her receptacles, I obtained several large banana leaves, stringing the laces through them to weave a large but rudimentary shelter. I bent the branches of the trees and made a thick patch of shade, sliding her still-damp bedroll underneath it to allow her comfortable rest. After the tent was constructed, I moved through the woods to find kindling, obtaining fallen sticks and brush to begin building a fire. Outside the tent, I began to stoke the flame, using a match from my smoking sack to spark the kindling. Bright orange flames ignited with a woosh, producing a wave of heat that did not complement the rising humidity of the day.

As I finished constructing the fire, I looked at Knomucca, who was assembling a spit out of large sticks. Minutes later, several large fish were spinning over the fire, the scent of them cooking filling the air deliciously.

"You obtained fish rather quickly," I said, impressed, watching as she gingerly tended to the fire.

A long moment passed, and Knomucca did not speak, her gaze lingering upon the flames as they danced and sang. A darkness floated through the fire, my hand tightening against my hammer as the shadow quickly disappeared.

"It was easy once I carved a spear," Knomucca said, leaning her sharpened stick near the tent.

"I am in awe of you," I said sincerely.

"And I of you," she said, wrenching her eyes from the fire and meeting my own.

We held each other's gaze for a long moment, the fire crackling softly beside us.

"Would you care to sit?" She asked.

My heart lurched, my breath catching as I nearly stumbled forward.

"I would love to," I said, joining her beside the fire.

"Thank you again for searching for me," she said, her voice catching for the faintest of moments. "I... was fearful... and worried I was to perform the Ascension by my lonesome."

"I am glad to be with you." I said, gently placing my hand against her leg. "Once you Ascend, all shall be well, you will see."

Knomucca stared into the fire, growing quiet.

"What troubles you, beloved?" I asked, smoothing my hand across her skin.

"How I wish I could easily find the words to explain," she said forlornly.

"You can trust me with anything," I said.

"I know, dearest. The moment I am comfortable disclosing it to you, I shall shed the weight."

I reached my hand towards her, cupping her face in my palm and turning her towards me. "How did you get this scar beneath your eye?"

"I..." She paused for a long moment. "I was visited during recent reminiscence, and it would appear I was attacked."

"Whose company did you have the displeasure of entertaining?"

"He for whom I am to Ascend..."

My heart raced. Anger flooded through me. "The Creator attacked you? Why?"

"I cannot discuss the matter in its entirety at present... Not without proper protections..." she said as she turned to look at me. "Can you see the marks he left me?"

"Aye." I said, tracing the curved, gnarled scar beneath my thumb.

"Her Radiance said nothing of them when I saw her."

"Perhaps she could not see them." I offered.

"How is it you find yourself able to do so then?"

I took a measured breath. "I... I can see energies and auras..."

"Is that so?" She asked. "That is a useful gift, and one you have hidden well."

Guilt washed through me.

"Tell me, from where do you draw your talents?" She asked.

"A winter solstice night 3 years prior... After Kiyoko absorbed my energy, it seemed... he bestowed upon me some of his gifts."

Knomucca nodded, eyeing me slowly.

"I know I should have told you," I said heavily. "Though we tread water around Kiyoko when we first learned to shield ourselves from him, I did not wish to cause any discomfort. I wished to keep it to myself... I can see that my doing so resulted in an invasion of privacy to your energy. I do apologize."

"I would have liked to know," she said. "Does Kiyoko?"

"Nay."

"May I ask why?"

"I thought it would go away after a while if I am honest," I said.

"Aye, it is rare to naturally possess such a talent," she began. "I myself was taught to interpret and manifest energy through breath, herbs, and the knowledge I have learned through the books I have studied. To be able to perceive it naturally like Kiyoko can... is certainly coveted."

I nodded slowly.

"Once he has righted, you shall have to disclose this to him," she said. "All of this... everything, not just about your abilities but also what has happened between us."

I sighed heavily. "Reckon I shall..."

"Thank you, Everett... for telling me," she said.

"I should have long ago," I said, defeated.

"We all have our yoke to bear," she said. "I know ill intent did not hide behind your actions."

"That is a relief," I said. "I thought they would disappear in time... And my opportunity to tell you both never felt right."

"What other gifts were you given from the General?" She asked.

"Allow me to show you." I tried to whisper through her, though my energy rebounded. I took a cleansing breath. "Allow me to show-"

"Everett?" she asked, searching my face. "Is all well?"

"I can project my words into Kiyoko's mind," I said. "I had hoped I could do it with anyone... though it does not appear to be so."

"I too, can project my words into his mind... Though the General had to teach me how to do so... If you are able to project your words into him... Without him having shown you... then I am certain he is somewhat aware of your newfound talents..."

"Gods..." I exhaled heavily. "How foolish of me to think otherwise."

"Your ignorance is endearing." She said with a wink. "Though your secrecy... That is another matter."

"Aye..."

"If you have been able to read my energy so clearly all this time, then certainly, you must have known I carried a deep devotion for you. You must have had insight into many of the intimacies of my inner world."

I lowered my gaze shamefully. "I suppose I did, however I felt our reality forced me to deny this truth."

Knomucca kissed me gently. "You never used your gifts to pry, better yourself, or take advantage of anyone. You may have collected secrets, but you carried them admirably. I love you just as much now as I did before you told me. Maybe even... a little bit more."

I exhaled with an elated breath and pressed her against me, my lips hungrily meeting her once more. Our hands tore excitedly at each other, our breaths hot and mingling as our lips parted. Knomucca ran her hands down my arms, tugging my soaked tunic free.

Following the movement of her fingers, she tore my undershirt from my chest, draping the thick fabric across the sand. Knomucca slid her hands across my abdomen, sending a thrum wildly down my spine. Her fingertips glided upwards, trailing the line of bruises along my neck. Her hands continued upwards softly on my face, her thumb gently caressing the contours.

"You are beautiful," she whispered through our kissing.

A moan escaped my lips, my grip tightening her body against mine. Knomucca purred in satisfaction.

A playful laugh escaped me, Knomucca inhaling it blissfully as her lips met mine. I cupped my hands low beneath the small of her back, delighting in the way her curves felt in my hands. I held her tightly as I lifted her and moved away from the fire, lowering us neatly into the shelter.

I pressed Knomucca into the bedroll, feeling the damp hempen fabric eagerly accept our weight. I slid my hands beneath her tunic and slipped it from her skin, guiding it easily over her head. A heavy, eager breath burst forth as I admired her beauty, relishing in the way her breasts invited my touch excitedly. I scanned my eyes along her rich olive skin, my view lingering along the trail of her collarbone.

Large scars and scratches that resembled a feline's claws were etched along her skin, the marks heavy and dark against her.

What a monster he is... I thought, running my thumb along the scratches.

Our lips met again hungrily, jolting me from my momentary distraction. My manhood spilled from my leggings as Knomucca pulled them down my hips, working my body free with her hand. I kicked my boots towards the tent's entrance and slid Knomucca's leggings free, placing her boots in a pile beside my own.

"Gods, how I wish I could stop time and live only in this moment," I said, running my lips along her navel.

"Aye, I would like nothing more," Knomucca said, exhaling in delight.

My heart raced, fueling the blush that painted my cheeks. I buried my face against her neck, taking an immense breath as I inhaled her deeply. An earthy musk scented her hair and skin, the faint tones of vanilla entangling in her energy deliciously. I ran my tough, callused hands across her, feeling her back arch as a soft moan escaped her lips.

I scanned my thumb across the owl sprawled in ink along her rib cage.

"I should like to go exploring," I whispered, my breath hot against her ear. "If that is well with-"

She bit my lip in reply, preventing the rest of my words from brimming and spilling over. Our kisses grew deeper, the bedroll creaking beneath us in eager anticipation. I tore my mouth away, lowering myself against her breasts. My breath caught in my throat, bursting forth in a growl as I caressed them. My tongue spread across her nipples, my teeth closing around it as I pulled it in hard.

Knomucca cried out, shuddering in my jaws.

"Exquisite," she whimpered.

Enjoying her opposite breast, I took it inside my mouth, biting with such force I nearly broke the skin. She cried out once more, grabbing forcefully into my hair and wrenching a laugh from my lips. I kissed a trail along her body, descending lower with every touch against her. She sighed blissfully, her body relaxing beneath my caress as I moved slowly toward her center.

Parting her legs open, I began to kiss along her inner thighs. She moaned, her body opening to me as I slid a finger inside her. I began to move it quickly, matching the intensity of the rhythm of my hand and my tongue. Her taste was luxurious, her legs shaking slightly from the warmth and pleasure building within her.

Knomucca panted heavily and arched her back, securing her legs tightly around my shoulders. Her hands wove through my hair as I bit down gently and took her across my tongue.

"Everett," she moaned.

My lips sped faster as her breathing lengthened.

"Knomucca," I said with a primal growl.

Reaching with a free hand, I returned to her breasts, feeling her nipples harden beneath my touch. The climax that took her was sudden and hard, forcing her body to convulse madly. Knomucca clawed her nails into my skin, leaving small half-moon crescents engraved in my flesh. I moaned and devoured her, taking every fold and inch of her enthusiastically into my mouth.

"You taste divine," I said, licking the fingers I had removed from inside her.

"I am pleased you have discovered so," she said, leaning forward to kiss me.

She pulled away after a short moment, her hands sliding down my arms and chest. I exhaled an elated breath, feeling as Knomucca trailed her lips down my jawline. She continued her exploration lower, coming to rest her mouth hotly against the bruises on my neck.

"Are these still hurting you?" she asked sincerely.

"I have forgotten them at present," I said, savoring the way her voice vibrated against me.

Knomucca reached downwards, grasping my long and slender shaft. I shivered in her hands, feeling her lift my face to gaze into my eyes.

With certain hands, she squeezed me playfully, a pulse of pain and pleasure flooding through me. Knomucca kissed me deeper, securing her legs tightly around me. Guiding her body against my own, I found her entrance and slid inside. She cried out as I moved deeper, pushing through the fold of her to caress her center within. She was tight around me, the angle of my entry warm and satisfying. The bedroll shifted beneath us as we moved together, our breathing quickening as we found our rhythm. Knomucca moaned deliciously, sending a spike of tingling pleasure down my spine. She bit my shoulder, plunging her teeth into me as I moved within her. Our tempo quickened, our bodies slamming together as she squeezed her legs around me.

I clambered to my knees, kissing Knomucca fiercely. She shifted her weight, her body becoming easier to hold in my arms. I flexed inside her, jerking her up my shaft in short, sharp shakes. She moved atop me, enjoying the swell of me from this more intense position. Screaming her pleasure, Knomucca bounced her breasts and body as I wriggled and writhed against her. She yanked my hair once more, and we increased our speed, the warmth of her orgasm tightening her body around me. I felt her moisten and smile seductively, her heat flowing forth and spilling from her. I shuddered, tensing my lower body as I continued my rhythm. She shook unexpectedly, her mirth feeding my body in a fresh wave of hunger. My body convulsed within her, a climax fast approaching.

"Do not stop," she commanded.

I shifted our weight and slammed her against the bedroll, ravishing handfuls of her breasts as I pinned her down. Another orgasm burst through her, her energy filling with vibrant colors. The scent of raspberries wafted across her skin, her eyes flashing in a deep green as the hardships from the elements left her.

"Everett...do...not...stop," she said again.

We climbed faster and faster, sliding from atop the bedroll as we moved. I lifted Knomucca into my arms, thrusting as hard and deeply into her as I could. She screamed between orgasms, begging for me to push myself further inside her.

"Knomucca, I am close," I warned breathlessly, bliss and satisfaction coloring my eyes.

I moved with long, hard thrusts, spilling inside her. I cried out, growling with a might and strength that rivaled the bellows of monsters and dragons. Releasing myself into her once more, I screamed with pleasure, my legs twitching beneath me as I collapsed onto her.

"Aye... glorious, Everett," she purred.

We fell apart in blissful helplessness, my body feeling warm and elated. Knomucca's energies were full and bursting, the evidence of her sun-burnt skin and salt exposure quickly washing away. The scars remained against her collarbone, darkening maliciously as her pleasure spread and healed her body.

Meeting her eyes, I tried to conceal my judgment, leveling my voice so as to keep it from sounding accusatory.

"It is true then," I said, "your way with energy... I mean..."

"Unfortunately," she said, lowering her face in shame. I pressed my thumb beneath her chin, guiding her face upward to stare into my own.

"Do not think yourself a monster," I said comfortingly.

"I feel as though I am one," she said, interlocking her fingers with mine.

"How did you come upon your abilities?" I asked curiously.

Knomucca loosed a heavy breath. "When Mother brought us here, she took the responsibilities of the Underworld I was meant to endure... She..."

Knomucca paused to gather her thoughts. "She would bury the dead, and guide their souls to Heimaalia... She witnessed sickness wreak havoc. She saw war destroy families. And she would damn the unworthy souls to eternity in the Seven Rings."

"She is a kind and devoted mother, to want to protect you from such things," I said.

Knomucca nodded. "Though her devotion to me had a price... She was never meant to bear such weight and she grew ill."

"That is terrible," I said softly.

"She drank tonics from the Priestess, though they only seemed to cause her more pain. She sought books to read and learn of her disease, though none held the answer. Do you wish to know what still drives me mad to this day?"

I nodded cautiously.

"The guilt I carry for casting Rejj to the Seven Rings for killing her... When what he accomplished was freeing her of a pain I now understand. How wronged I feel in knowing even if I am to Ascend, I can never gift her the afterlife she deserves... Because I have never found her in Heimaalia, even after all this time."

"Gods." My voice was a pained whisper.

"At first, I was glad to fully accept the privileges that my mother had possessed, in the hope I would see her again, a prayer I still whisper to the stars. Though... when I accepted them... my energy pathways began to be impacted."

"How do you mean?" I asked carefully.

"He had given my mother power He claimed I was to need, saying it would help me preserve and manipulate the dead. Though from her protections, only my hands began to change in appearance at first, and He was never able to give me everything He had forced upon her. The Gods know He will still damn me to that fate, it is why I must make and consume the Elixir during the ascension."

"So, how did you come upon the rest?" I asked.

Knomucca swallowed hard.

"Senaya was hosting her winter solstice gathering..." She hesitated before continuing. "I had attended and found myself lost in my cups. It was the first time I had done so since Mother crossed over, and... I allowed myself to overindulge."

I comfortingly rested a hand against her knee and patiently waited for her confession.

"As the night progressed, I found myself craving the warmth of another and I sought the company of a stable hand. Whilst we were intimate, I noticed the pulse in his neck... The way his heart beat rapidly in his chest and the need to possess it overtook me. I needed it like I need air and before I fully realized what I had done, I had torn it clean from his chest."

I nodded slowly as she pressed on. "I... It kept happening... As my energy changed and the Creator's voice grew louder, I continued to bury my burdens in others, while I buried my hands in their hearts. I grew disgusted with myself.

"The power it... It causes me anguish unless I submit to its demands. I try to ignore it. Even now... I am selective in those I choose to bed as I wish not to claim anyone else before it is their time. In recent months, I have confessed my plights to Kiyoko. He has been teaching me how to control it, and how to transmute the unwanted energy into healing my body." Her eyes began to gleam with unshed tears.

"Tell me more about your transformation," I said gently.

"Some of this shall come from memory whilst others shall come from Mother's tellings."

I nodded encouragingly.

"When Syler and I were born, the Creator began to pursue us. He had known my mother, and He coveted her strength and wisdom," Knomucca said. "When Mother birthed twins on the autumnal equinox, the Creator wanted us to receive His essence. Mother always told Him she did not wish for us to endure the Trials. She said that she would teach us how to be strong and give us the knowledge and reverence we needed to learn the wisdom and magic of the realms."

"I am certain that the Creator did not take kindly to her defiance," I said, caressing her shoulder.

"Aye, this did anger Him. For the first five years of our lives, we never stayed in one place for long. When He finally managed to take us to the castle, Mother struck a deal with Him," Knomucca sighed. "She said she was to assume His essence until we came of age. Though this pact was often dishonored."

"How so?"

"During my fifth year, terrible dreams began to fill my consciousness... He would show me disturbed phantoms, dark shadows, and the Seven Circles of Hell. He would force me to travel with Him during my sleep and show me those who He tortured for punishment. He always said He was showing me what I would have to do when I ascended," she said, pulling away from my touch.

"Bastard..."

"During my tenth year, an unbearable pain began in my hands. The Creator said He would make the pain stop. All that was needed was for me to begin accepting His essence... and succumb to whatever dark urges might be brewing inside me. At first, I ignored it, but the pain only intensified," Knomucca hesitated before continuing. "Soon, we were travelling together during my sleep once more, and I would indulge in the torturing of those He captured. He would praise me for what I inflicted on those He damned, and the pain would subside for a while. When I did what He asked, He would leave me be for a short time."

My heart welled with sadness at the thought of what she had endured for so many years.

"But then, as I came of age and Mother died... I assumed the burdens she had been carrying for me. My hands began to change, transforming into the phantoms they are now," she said, staring at her outstretched hands encased in the gauntlets. "The Creator said it was to assist in my ability to prepare the dead. But soon after their transformation, the Priestess gifted me with my gauntlets. Then the hunger, the craving for hearts, and the ability to heal from the intimacy of others all began to haunt me. And now, with the consumption of the Elixir, my psychic defenses will be weakened, and He will be able to corrupt me with His vital life energy."

"It is true then as well that you killed the servants," I said heavily.

Knomucca nodded sadly. "Aye, though I had not wished to... His influence is hard to ignore."

I brushed the hair behind her ear and gifted her a soft kiss.

"I feel so saddened you have had to endure such hardships," I told her, holding her tightly in my arms. "That we all have... that you have been forced to end life and carry blood when you deserve only kindness and a vast library of books-"

"You are kind in saying so... though I fear you are misled," she said somberly. "I could have fought with more strength and vigor, once my childhood innocence had left me. Still could if I am honest-"

"You cannot hope to quash Him by your lonesome," I said gently, lowering my voice protectively. "You must allow yourself to become strong and entrusted so that we may wrench His corrupted tree upwards by the roots- and return Anteyus to rule amongst his people-"

"Everett," Knomucca pushed herself onto her elbows, her hair draping over her shoulders, "I do not wish to burden you with my insecurities, though I fear my Trials from the Creator have made me perform tasks that do not deserve my pride. I cannot risk abandoning those who have been lost to the chance of someone new, nor can I fight the growing darkness that wells within myself."

"Aye, I believe you can," I said seriously. "You are strong and determined—if you discipline yourself and discover there is another way."

"Not when the Creator forces my hand," she said heavily.

"You will learn to circumvent Him," I stated. "Knomucca, everything is going to be well. Your mother will not have died in vain, and neither shall anybody else who has been lost. You make them comfortable, and the Underworld a brighter place. Do not allow these fears to rattle your roots or tug intrusively at your branches. You have studied all your life, forged your body and mind into your greatest weapons, and they shall be the arsenal that cripples Him."

"Your words are kind, and I love you all the more for them," Knomucca said.

"And I you," I said, kissing her softly. "And I know you are going to honor the realms."

Our tired, ensnared bodies tangled together against the bedroll, the soft fabric inviting us for a well-deserved sleep. Knomucca nuzzled her face in my chest, sighing deeply as her breathing slowed. Her eyelashes flickered against my skin, her breath hot as she sought shelter in my arms.

"Close your eyes," I said, brushing my fingers through her thick, wavy hair. "You shall never be alone again, and you shall always have my hands to fight alongside you should you wish for them."

"I do wish for them," she said softly, her voice muffled against my skin.

"Then yours I am. Yours I shall always be," I said, holding her closely as she drifted into sleep.

XVII

KNOMUCCA

My breathing lengthened as I fell into a deep sleep. Everett's voice unfurled like deep velvet, his body floating away from me. I reached out in an attempt to hold onto him, feeling my fingers clutching the air as the scent of him faded. My hands were skeletal and free from their gauntlets, shedding blood and decaying flesh in a strong, pungent smell. Pain seared across my palms, forcing my fingers to tingle harshly.

Swirls of color painted beyond my eyelids, smattering my sights in dark, shadowed hues. The distant lapping waves blurred away, carrying with them the lullabies of the island birds and the warm tropical winds.

A dark, twisted corridor materialized through my awareness. The smooth stone path beneath my boots echoed with my steps, my breathing heavy and loud in the silence. Tall, iron doors punctuated the hallway, the handles inscribed with symbols and runes I failed to recognize. Soft voices emanated from beyond them, the discourse muffled by the protective enchantments of the metal. Fire and music blinked under the thresholds, tempting me to test their openness despite my hesitation.

Flickering torches began to appear along the sheer and slick walls, their fires crackling against the rock. Petrified stone statues glowed in the firelight, their eyes pleading as I moved past them. Horror painted their faces, their mouths open with screams of pain and fear as their spirits crossed over. Some wielded weapons in their hands, the tips of swords and axes shining in the light of the flames.

I moved through the passage, avoiding the stares of the statues as their eyes followed my movements. Chains rustled and clanked in the distance, the thought of them weighing heavily on me. The creaking of their iron churned my stomach nervously, sending a spike of anxiety surging through my racing heart. My pace quickened, my boots running faster to carry me through an endless hallway of stone and doors.

A figure appeared further down the passage, their body hunched, tired, and sickly. A deep green hooded cloak dragged across the floor, the ghostly fabric whispering against the stone. Vibrant red hair poked from under the hood, framing the exposed bones of a skeleton that had begun rising from beneath the skin.

"Mother?" I called after her, hastening my pace.

Despite my steps forward, her apparition drew further away, her body shrinking as I sped towards her.

"Mother, please... wait..."

She hesitated, her image rippling as she fought to stand her ground. I pushed closer, my heart palpitating with every pounding footstep.

"Mother," I called more urgently, feeling a sudden cold breeze behind my ear.

An arrow whizzed from beyond my shoulder, hurling down the corridor with great speed. The obsidian tip pierced my mother through the chest, spraying blood across the stone floor. A silent scream escaped her lips, her mouth falling open soundlessly. Her hollow eyes flashed with a vibrant green once more before fading, her body shaking uncontrollably with pain.

"MOTHER!"

I sprinted forward, watching as she dropped onto her knees. The night of my Blood Solstice rushed brokenly through my sights, the memory of my mother's assassination spilling through me. I began to sob as I rushed myself forward, fighting through the moment when my mother had died in my arms. I wiped the tears from my eyes as my mother fell to the floor, her knees giving way beneath her.

"Mum," I said, swearing breathlessly as I pushed on, finding the hallway cooperative beneath my steps.

Mother lay crumpled on the floor, her body cold and frail as I approached her. Gingerly, I took her into my arms, crying into her receding hair in horrible, racking sobs. Remembering my Blood Solstice, I recalled how she lay upon the floor of Valvang, her breathing rasped and hollow as the arrow had pierced her lungs. I remembered how Rejj's first arrow had missed, grazing my ear before the second shot struck true. Shallow, horrid exhalations began to flow from her, slicing a fresh wave of grief through me.

"Mother..." I cried. "Mother... I am here, I am here..."

Pressing her against me, I felt her body stir, her hands moving upwards to clasp my own. On that night, she had taken my hand, her palm against my skin, the final touch I would know without gauntlets. Her pulse leaped from her fingers, her hands warmed and calloused from the lengths she had gone to survive.

"Stay strong," her parting words from my Blood Solstice floated through my memory, though her lips did not move with them. "Until we meet again..."

Pain erupted through my fingers, my mother pushing power and energy into my palms. I screamed through the burning, trying in vain to release her from my grip. My forehead throbbed, my awareness blurring as I escaped her grasp. Reaching up for her shoulders, I held her at arm's length and gasped with sudden surprise, seeing her rotten corpse and exposed bones decaying in my hands.

Earwigs swarmed from her eyes, and the intense scent of lilies threatened to suffocate me. Her body shattered and transitioned to ashes, her remains coming to rest in a scatter across the floor. Her blood coalesced with the ashes, leaving a rusted silhouette where she had laid.

"Mother," I sobbed. "Not again."

My tears consumed me, my crying becoming painful as my grieving tore me raw. I hugged the place where my mother had been, my tears soaking her ashes in warm spouting drops. My body shook in sadness, my desire to hold her and seek comfort from Syler unbearable. I took a breath and released a well-deserved scream, channeling my rage and frustration into the pain liberated from my lungs.

"I am so sorry," I cried. "Mother, I am so very -"

Suddenly, familiar footsteps interrupted my grief. Over my shoulder, I saw Rejj moving towards me, his appearance wrenching a horrid gasp from my lungs. His eyes were glowing a vibrant yellow, his pupils holding all the cunning of a feline. His head drooped and hung low, sweeping disturbingly across the floor.

"You cannot save her," he rasped.

The bow in his hands was dripping with blood, smattering across the smoothed stone as he walked forward. His feet shuffled beneath him, his skin a pale grey and lifeless.

"You should have left me to rot in the Seven Rings," he continued in a terrible whisper. "Where you sent me to die."

He lulled towards me, opening deranged and foaming jaws. I rose instinctively and began to move backward, allowing myself to succumb to the urge to escape him. He swiped with the bow, and I dodged left, hearing him grunt with anger as his fist slammed into the wall.

"Your treacherous mother deserved what she got," Rejj rasped, swinging his bow across my face.

Blood clung to my skin, the scent of iron piercing through the darkness.

"You cannot save her," he rasped. "You cannot save anyone."

Turning my back to him, I allowed myself to run, pushing free from the stone walls of the hallway and retreating in the opposite direction. My boots slammed in a frightened drumming, my breathing hard and labored as I forged distance between us. The torches along the wall brightened my path, illuminating cobwebs which housed hanging spiders. The sounds of dripping water echoed around me, failing to be masked by the slamming of my shoes.

The hallway shifted and suddenly split in two. Just before the fork lay an empty window that shone into darkness, an abyssal chasm contained behind glass. To the left lay an endless corridor lit intermittently with torches. The righthand passage split into a small alcove containing a cauldron and a sparsely stocked brewing station. Large cacti protected the corners of the alcove, their needles the length of a small knife.

Curiously, I approached the brewery, peering into the cauldron. The metal was rusted with viscous blood, containing floating fingers, bones, and chunks of corroding silver. Broken knives surrounded the brewing station, hanging beside large tongs, skewers, and clamps. A book bound from human skin rested along the back wall, the ink marking the title and cover a dull and dried red.

Shuffling footsteps dragged distantly through the corridor, the desire to remain unseen by them compelling my movements. I threw myself forcefully from the brewing stand. I fled across to the lefthand passage, moving as fast and silently as I could. The hallway warped beneath my steps, expanding to a circular chamber that cut suddenly into the far wall. Large pumpkin lanterns rested against the threshold, the husks carved with malicious faces and deeply demented eyes.

I pushed through the doorway, my breath escaping me in a wave of heavy panting. An ornately decorated atrium consumed the twisted corridor, vanishing it swiftly from my awareness. The ceiling was high and arched, the supports whittled from bones, skulls, and thick metal piping. Ethereal harp music played softly from the right; the strings plucked gently by a purple-cloaked figure with a hidden face.

An immense fountain lined the center of the entrance hall, the rock spouting and collecting glimmering blood in its large basin. Small orange orbs illuminated the water feature, providing the room's only light source as there were no windows or sun. A large stone Naiad sat atop the fountain in its center, her eyes unsettling and malevolent with deep blue irises. A human skull was held in her hands, her fingers jabbing unsettlingly through its eyes.

I moved deeper into the chamber, hearing my boots muffled against the floor. Along the left rested a small wooden table tucked neatly out of sight in a corner. Cautiously, I approached, discovering an open book lying against the oak. Names in unreadable handwriting blurred down the parchment, my eyes failing to decipher any runes or letters. A carved bone quill rested beside a vial of blood, the deep red ink dampening the pages darkly as it dripped across them. The symbol of Kiyoko's coven blossomed from the blood, rippling and spreading over the book the longer I held it in my sight.

I shook my head to clear it, then followed the lefthand wall. Tall, shadowed figures moved alongside the fountain, carrying brightly lit torches in their hands. Their faces were covered in ornate masks, their hoods pulled high and pointed atop their heads. Voices broke into panicked muttering, my heart leaping anxiously in my chest with their sudden noise. The figures turned their masked eyes toward me, rendering me paralyzed by the intensity of their gaze. One of the red-beaded cloaks swept across the room to where I stood, breaking free of the shadows around her.

"Your Worship."

Hazel's face peered from behind the hood, her voice venomous and menacing. A dark shadow filled her eyes, shrouding her face contemptuously. Her neck thrummed with her pulse, vibrating her skin excitedly.

"Everett is not the only person capable of locating you," she said in a thick whisper.

Fear slammed at my heart, and I clenched my fists, though I did not offer a spoken reply.

"It disgusts me to discover how far you have ventured from the course," she said, rolling her eyes. "Obedience should be a skill already learned when requesting to Ascend... The Creator may come to find you... unreliable."

"My apologies," I said slowly, though my voice felt lofted and distant. "I meant no offense."

Hazel's charcoal eyes burrowed through me, her glare a stinging hot fire. The rounded scarlet petals of an oleander flower were pinned to her lapel. The tall, pointed hat atop her head cast shadows across her face, obscuring her features from my sight.

"If you are done wasting time," she said, gesturing towards the wall opposite the center fountain. "Everyone is awaiting eagerly to see you."

Hazel turned, moving quickly through the hooded figures inside the atrium. I regained my footing and followed behind her, joining her at her shoulder as we walked through an embellished bronze doorway. Disturbed voices and fragmented cackling echoed through the large ballroom, amplifying the hysteria off the smooth stone walls. The harp music began to shift, the chorus lifting into a dinner feast's twisted, jubilant rousting.

The ballroom was grand, though sparsely decorated. Large golden candelabras were firmly on each table. Spider Vines looped across the ceiling, sputtering soft purple energy as they clung above us. A small quartet played music atop a circular stage, the instruments held individually by the same purple-cloaked figure.

A long table materialized on my left, brimming excitedly with occupants. A game of Shepard's Claw had been spread across the oak, the cards blurry as I tried to read them. Bright blue hair glowed from the surrounding lights, blending flawlessly into a heavy woolen cloak. Ilesa sat in a chair dealing cards, her infectious laugh and bouts of swearing cutting through my awareness.

Ilesa met my eyes with a twisted smile, fanning her cards outwards in an arc before she spoke.

"Care to join us for a hand?" she winked.

I stopped walking abruptly, watching Ilesa as she held her cards outwards.

"Ilesa..." I began frantically. "Ilesa... I am glad to see you, I owe you my deepest regrets for your untimely crossing-"

"You are shrouded in clouds," Ilesa continued as though she had not heard my words. "You appear as though you could use some clarity,"

I stood rooted in place, watching as Ilesa pulled a card from her hand. Atop the river of cards flooding the table, Ilesa placed the first, depositing a card with two reversed swords.

"Choices, choices," Ilesa shuffled the cards through her hands as she continued speaking. Her eyes glossed over, the deep blue irises glowing in a layer of frost. "When trust is scarce, you will need to invest yourself wisely."

A second card fell from her fist, showcasing a large sun rising peacefully over a tranquil forest.

"Not all is lost," Ilesa adjusted the river of cards flowing across the table. "Your secrets are not as well kept as you may have hoped... though not all find your discretion's problematic... all the same... those who do have become unfortunate enemies."

Ilesa rifled the cards through her fingers, their glossy blue backs glowing in the candlelight. She released a tense sigh, her skin wrinkling suddenly as the scent of salt filled my nose.

"How peculiar," she said, dropping a final card onto the table.

A lavish and handsome knight was surrounded by cascading coins, his hands tough and callused from a life of intense labor.

"He carries the light with him," Ilesa said, shuffling her cards back into her hands. "The darkness will toughen his spirits, time will prove its use."

I paused for a brief moment, regarding Ilesa, as she wove her cards across her palms. I searched her face, waiting for a moment before I spoke.

"My apologies for failing you," I said sincerely. Ilesa's eyes hollowed.

"You cannot save me," she said, jolting me horribly and wrenching me away from the table. "You cannot save any of us now."

"Tut, tut, what in the Hells is keeping you?" An annoyed voice cut from the right.

"This is no time to delay," Hazel reappeared at my front. "Enough with the games... it is rather unbecoming..."

I swiveled away from Ilesa, hearing her return to Shepard's Claw as Hazel led me away.

"Allow me to show you to your seat, as you cannot seem to find it yourself," she said as the ballroom filled with guests.

We began to walk forward, leaving Ilesa as she blurred into the crowd. The guests in attendance turned to glare as we moved through the ballroom. We came to rest at the high table in the front beside the stage. Briefly, I turned towards the quartet, noticing a bamboo flute, iron strings, a set of bagpipes, and a drum stretched from human skin. The purple-cloaked figure met my eyes, reflecting glimmers of golden sunlight beneath his hood.

"Your chair, m'lady," Hazel said with a curt nod.

I took the high-backed chair, pulling it free from the table.

"Sit," Hazel advised, "Drink some wine and indulge... your guests shall be with you in a brief moment."

Hazel departed, disappearing swiftly through a small door beyond the tables. A long instant passed with disjointed music, the laughter and chatter from the tables warping to screams and terrified groans. Impatience began to swell within me. I pulled away from the table, rising quickly to stand before releasing an audible gasp. Everett had come to sit across from me, his chest exposed to the light of the golden candelabras. His heart had been torn clean from his body, his muscles and skin hanging loosely as he dripped blood across the cutlery.

"Greetings, my beloved," he said, his lips soft against my own.

The scent of leather and horses filled me, the taste of coltsfoot and smoking herbs stirring my pulse. I pulled away quickly, feeling as blood dripped from Everett's chest and spilled across my skin. My hands thrummed painfully, sending a searing sharpness from my fingertips into my shoulder. Bile rose into my throat as the urge to scream nearly overtook me.

"Everett!" Adrenaline rushed through me and enabled me to speak. "Everett...who did this to you?"

"I have been fantasizing over your Ascension feast for quite some time now," Everett said as if the words were intended with jubilance. However, his voice felt void of emotion. "How I hoped you would wear a dress... one made of a lavish green to complement your brilliant eyes..."

"Everett... please..."

"The venue is quite pleasing to the eyes," he went on, glancing about the table for a glass of wine. "I shall admit, I am interested in discovering what courses you have chosen to serve for the dead... a fine hostess such as yourself ought to have planned something rather magnificent."

"Everett.... How did you come to get these wounds?"

Everett found a chalice of wine beside his left hand and grasped it eagerly.

"To Anteyus," Everett said, "rightful and true, Bringer of Balance prevails, swift rescue."

He lifted the wine to his lips and drank it deeply, causing my blood to run cold. Wine spilled from his chest and fell to stain the table, splashing loudly as he drank.

"Here, here," I said uncertainly.

"Oi," Everett lowered his glass and gestured to the right. "Here comes Chatza now with this evening's affairs."

Chatza swept from the door, moving through the room with trays in her hands. She approached the table and placed two covered dishes atop it, pushing one each toward Everett and me.

"I do hope you enjoy what I have prepared, Your Worship," Chatza said, beaming brightly. "When you feel ready, you may proceed. We have already said the blessing, during which your tardiness and absence were certainly noticed."

"My deepest pardons," I said again.

"Do not delay a moment more," Chatza chided. "Take and eat."

Hesitating, I pulled the cover from my dish and gasped in horror. A plump human heart was floating in a soup of blood accompanied by various herbs and spices. A pungent, earthy aroma floated from the dish, bringing forth the need to consume it deep within me.

"Chatza, what happened to the dish I requested?" I asked, surprised by the ease of my words.

"How ever do you mean?" Chatza asked. "You wished to prepare meat for the dead... I simply decided to oblige."

I tore my eyes from my plate and stared across at Everett as he lifted the heart firmly from his dish. Opening his mouth, he ravished the heart from his cutlery, swallowing it in one breath. I screamed and smacked his hand from his face, though he had been too quick.

"I would pay him no mind," Chatza said encouragingly. "He has already been marked and shall gift you the ultimate sacrifice to express his devotion to you."

'I shall always fight to keep you safe,' Everett whispered through me.

Horror and guilt slammed my heart.

"Everett," I said seriously, "we need to leave here... Now!"

"You cannot save him," Chatza sighed heavily.

I pushed away from the table and stood abruptly. Edging around it, I sped towards Everett, fighting to maintain my footing as the ballroom stretched beneath me. He lurched from my reach, his woolen cloak tearing away through my fingers. I leaped forward and seized his shoulder, turning him away from the table to face me.

"Release me, disgusting woman," he hissed.

His eyes were emptiness; vast voids filled them where his once blue irises had been.

"Everett... it is I..."

Everett's hammer materialized in his hands, the head warped with twisted iron. I released his shoulders and moved backward, wedging myself against a table as he shambled within reach. His chest heaved as he swung, my reaction nearly causing a fatal moment as I ducked beneath him.

"You cannot save me," he said as he lumbered forward. "You cannot save anyone..."

"Everett, I love you..."

"Keep your devotion," he hissed. "Your gifts have turned you monstrous... unworthy. Never again shall you be allowed to feed from myself or anyone!"

"Everett, those were accidents..."

"Perhaps in the beginning," Everett accused. "Though you continue even after you have learned control... and you have killed innocent people."

The guests around the ballroom rose from their places, lurching towards me with long outstretched hands. Their eyes were yellow and glowed like a feline, their mouths opening in blurring screams as they shambled towards me. The music warped and twisted, disappearing into broken melodic fragments as the purple-cloaked figure vanished through the crowd. The scent of mugwort filled the air, and a brief feeling of warmth and strength floated across my skin.

I fought to keep grounded, scrambling to find a weapon from atop the table to defend myself from Everett and the crowd.

"You are damned," Everett said as they surrounded me. Groaning and screams overcame me, sending a searing pain through my head and hands. "Disgusting, and damned-"

"Knomucca!"

Chatza reappeared suddenly at my side, holding a pewter mug. The tea steamed into the air, the scent of cinnamon fragrant beneath the rim.

"Knomucca, it is not safe here," she said as the guests drew closer. "You will want to follow me."

Chatza dropped her boiling mug of tea from her hands, throwing it downwards to shatter on the floor. The guests slowed in their steps, the room falling silent from the broken screams and music. Strong smells of cinnamon and apples flooded the ballroom, their aroma disorienting whilst it blinded my senses. Glancing towards Everett, I noticed his body slacken, his eyes vacant and hollow, though failing to glow like the others.

"Aye, this way Lassie," Chatza said, tugging my hand despite its gauntlets and yanking me harshly away from him.

Chatza rushed me through the ballroom, gripping tightly to my hand. The guests broke free from their lethargy, charging forward as we began to move. Their yellowed eyes and clawed fingers stretched outwards, swiping at our clothes and hair as we wove amongst them. The ground shuddered beneath us, the stone rebelling against our escape.

Dragging chairs from the tables, I attempted to slow our assailants, shoving the oak wood seats hard into them. Guests fell though more clambered over them to fill their place, their eyes darkening maliciously as they pressed forwards.

"Focus on our escape," Chatza pleaded as she dragged me forward, hoisting me from the reach of a man with sprouted horns. "Continue to flee, get us out."

Chatza lunged forward, shoving me fiercely through the small door on the opposite wall of the ballroom. I stumbled through and continued running, sprinting through a deep and cold tunnel. The scent of rosemary filled me comfortingly, the familiar feeling of the tunnels of Morriraen entering my awareness.

My running slowed, and my exhaustion and hammering pulse overtook me. I forced my feet to continue forward, stepping across a roughened stone passageway. My footfalls were alone in the silence, echoing off the walls as

I continued along my path. I turned about my shoulders and searched for Chatza, sad to discover she was no longer by my side.

"Chatza?" I called, hearing only my voice reverberate from off the rocks. "Chatza! Where have you gone?"

I sighed heavily and pushed onwards. A wide and smooth cavern unfolded at my front, the entrance materializing through the stone. Water was dripping in the distance, forming large puddles across the floor. Silver radiance loomed from the water, rippling and ringing like a piercing bell as I trudged through the puddles.

The light grew with my walking, shining brightly with every step. I pressed my foot through the water and felt a hand suddenly shoot from the puddle. The fingers seized my ankle, tightening their grip around my shoe painfully.

"Away with you," I said, grasping my mother's sword, panicking upon discovering its absence.

Senaya pulled herself from the puddle, her chest streaking with hot blood. Her eyes were red and warm from her screaming, and her mouth still slackened with pain and terror.

"Save me, Knomucca," she said, releasing my ankle as she clambered from the water. "Do not let him kill me. Please... save me."

Footsteps began further down the passageway, shuffling from beyond the entrance of the cavern.

"She cannot save you... she cannot save anyone!" a venomous voice hissed through my awareness.

The image of a laced black veil flooded beyond my eyes; the sweeping shadowed cloak and heron-clawed hands lurched fear through me. The vision faded as the distant footsteps drew closer, my speeding heart encouraging their pace.

"You must not let them see you," Senaya said, blood pooling from her chest. "You must run Knomucca... RUN!"

I broke free from Senaya's gaze, turning on my heel and lurching down the cavern. Emerging through another doorway, I pressed into the tunnels, feeling them growing narrow and dark around me. I ran as fast and long as I could, my breath catching as I panted from exhaustion.

Distant crying echoed through the air, tugging at my heart painfully. I turned a sudden left and curved onward, finding a large, exposed stone room. Small lanterns hung from the ceiling, casting a soft orange light from their iron. A woman with curled blond hair knelt in the corner, her shoulders racking silently with sobs. A tattoo of a flower bouquet on her leg poked from beneath her elegant pink skirt. I rushed forward as my twin continued crying, hearing her sobs only growing louder as I approached her.

"Syler, what troubles you?"

My words were wrenched from my throat. Syler leaned forward as she knelt crying, curling over the mirroring image of her corpse across the floor. Marks of torture and damage from Spider Vines were etched into her skin, and her eyes and cheeks were drained of life and color. Her elegant dress was stained and rusted with blood; the bodice was torn to reveal bruises beneath.

"Syler," I said again, kneeling down beside her.

Her sobs only increased, her wailing deafening through the vast tunnels.

"Syler, come with me," I said, grabbing my sister's shoulder and tugging her.

Syler's skin was cold. Dark patches had formed where pockets of her blood were collecting, the skin turning purple from her loss of pulse. Her body was bruised with my touch, her grip only tightening against her fallen body as I tried to pry her from it.

"Up like a daisy."

"You cannot save her," Frek had appeared from the shadows, growling low. His eyes flashed from the wolf within, his spine growing rigid as he searched my face.

"Frek, I only wish to help." I pleaded.

"You cannot help anyone!"

His body began to transform, his shoulders widening as the wolf took him. Large paws formed from his fingers, his figure dropping downwards as he swept onto all fours. Dark, black fur blended into the walls of the caves, his form illuminated by the deep yellow eyes that were not his own. A sleek tail curled upwards angrily, thrashing as another growl escaped him.

"Frek, this is not your true form," I said with reason, stepping slowly to my right. "Your tail and eyes resemble a feline though you are of man and wolf."

Frek growled, moving closer as his jaws opened.

"Frek, please," I said, regretfully placing Syler at my back.

"Run, Knomucca," Syler said in a cold, rasping whisper. "I do not love you more than Frek, and I never shall."

"Syler-"

"RUN!"

The sudden need to leave them overtook me, fueling my movements forward. I pressed myself against the wall and stepped around Frek, narrowly dodging the snapping of his maw. I urged myself to a sprint and curved down the corridor, hearing the scratching of claws as Frek lunged forward.

My breathing sped as Frek fled in my pursuit, his teeth scraping my heels with every step forward. I pumped my arms and wove down the passageway, jumping behind rocks and corners in an attempt to shake him from my trail. I pushed beyond exhaustion and ran across a large stone grotto, feeling the distant tropical winds against my face.

I turned over my shoulder and saw Frek had retreated. The tunnels shifted and suddenly split in two, leading to the left and right. An empty stone window revealed darkness, an abyssal chasm contained behind glass.

"Gods... why have I returned here," I said.

The righthand passage split into a small alcove containing the same cauldron and sparsely stocked brewing station. The large cactus plants protected the corners of the alcove, dripping blood from their menacing needles.

I turned away from the brewery, not wishing to reencounter the tome bound from human skin. I spun on my heel and made for the left, pausing abruptly when the brewery appeared at my front. I swore loudly and moved again leftwards, hearing the rusted cauldron begin to bubble as it blocked my path again.

"Persistent pissant," I cursed.

Sighing, I approached the brewing stand, noticing the book no longer lay across the wood. A small podium had been constructed beside the cauldron, showcasing a flattened piece of yellowed parchment. The writing was blurred yet somehow legible, revealing only partially what had been written on the page.

Cinnamon had been scrawled in clear looping letters.

I ran my eyes down the parchment, noticing the roses and daisies pressed into the paper. The ink blurred as I read downwards, registering cloves and mugwort amongst the fading lines. I read to the very last line, my breath catching as the ink swirled into blood.

The words a heart blessed, seven of seven, were etched in thick and rusted red.

The letters burned into my eyes, vibrating with a note of finality I found disconcerting. A heavy cloud of fear and anxiety washed through me, the cauldron bubbling and hissing as it boiled absently.

I flung my body to the left, running as fast as I could away from the cauldron and cacti. My boots pounded with my breathing, failing to mask the distant shuffling footsteps that had returned to my awareness.

The passageway widened, and the air chilled as I moved further into the tunnels. Stalagmites and stalactites sprung from the floors and ceiling, dampening the air into a cold and dark cave. More stone statues filled the cavern, some appearing with venomous faces as they swung their swords. Snakeskin littered the dust-covered floor beside bones, broken statues, and long-forgotten corpses.

Distant music began filling my ears, the melody and instruments foreign in their sounds. The notes were choppy and lacked confidence, stumbling and squeaking as though played by an inexperienced hand. My boots echoed painfully against the lullaby, every step fracturing through my consciousness. The notes grew louder and ricocheted from the walls, ringing painfully through my head and threatening to burst my ears. The harmonies ran and slurred together, blurring into a cascading cacophony that shot pain from behind my eyes.

Strained voices groaned through the air, their pained words indistinguishable against the pounding of my heart. The clanking of chains filled my ears, cutting through the distant sounds of rolling servants' carts. Figures in long white smocks moved through the corridor, carrying tinctures, herbs, or pouches of crystals in their hands. Their faces were blurred, and their conversations muffled, the vivid large oleander flowers embroidered upon their lapels the only thing that was distinct amongst their hazy persons.

A small, concealed doorway appeared towards the left, blending flawlessly into the wall. A carved sign rested against the iron, showcasing the words "authorized personnel only." Fire spilled from beneath its threshold, illuminating the darkness beyond. The temptation to explore overtook me, and I seized the handle. I was surprised to find the door unlocked.

Silently, I crept through the threshold, wishing my mother's sword was hidden down my spine. A wide, smoothed cell unfolded around me, a small fire glowing in the corner. No other light source brightened the room, and the walls were scarce aside from a hanging rack of tools and weapons. Clamps, scalpels, and branding irons all gleamed maliciously, their metal heavy and eerie as my gaze fell upon them. Large chains hung from the center of the ceiling; their point of connection was raised to allow their captive inability to touch the ground.

At the end of the chains, Kiyoko swung by his wrists, his body nude and exposed to the fire. Large burns covered his abdomen, forming the shape of an oleander flower in the blisters. His skin peeled and flaked as he began to heal, the scar tissue red and raw as it was repeatedly forced open. Lacerations sliced across his forearms, trickling blood softly down his body.

His eyes were closed, and his face slack. His breathing was shallow and slow as he had fallen asleep from the pain.

"Kiyoko," I whispered to him, wishing I could cover his vulnerability with a cloak or blanket. "It is Knomucca... can you hear me?"

His breathing hesitated, his body stirring against my words.

"Kiyoko, awaken," I pleaded. "I must make certain you are well... Kiyoko..."

His eyes flashed open. The normal sunlit flecks that painted his irises burnt my skin like fire. Anger clenched his fists and muscles, rattling the chains that contained him. An irritated sigh escaped his bleeding mouth, his nostrils flaring indignantly with his exhalation.

"Aye, Knomucca... it is you..." He said in disgust.

"Kiyoko," I stepped closer to him. "Kiyoko... I wish to free you from your chains..."

"Do not be daft," he snorted, his muscles rippling with his laughter. "The iron is enchanted against you... and all the same, I would be able to break free from them myself if they were not charmed."

"I wish to help," I pleaded, reaching my hands upwards to grasp his shackles.

A shocking blue energy bit through my fingers, jolting me from him. Kiyoko's eyes flashed purple, his mouth slackening as he absorbed the pain. The taste of cherries filled me, my tongue turning bitter as Kiyoko's aura brightened. He blinked a shining gold and blinded my eyes, my forehead searing intensely between my ears.

"Delicious," Kiyoko crooned, "I had begun feeling quite ravenous..."

I sighed heavily. Though it had been evident he had endured much while hanging from the iron, he was fighting to stay sober, keeping his breathing level and his aura clear.

"I must admit," he went on, "your mistrust of my word cuts me deeper than any torture I have so far endured."

"Nothing here is how it should be," I said, holding his gaze.

"Everything here is how it shall be," he said seriously.

"Everett sent me to find you," I admitted, watching as the light flashed through his eyes.

"Impressive magics he possesses," Kiyoko said with a smile he allowed to escape. "He is worthy of chosen blood."

"He fears for you," I said, drawing closer to Kiyoko again. "And so do I..."

"Did you fear for me whilst you were fucking him?" Kiyoko asked, the fire burning within his eyes. "You feared for no one, and no consequence when you let him spill himself inside you. You fed from him, relished in the taste that sculpts him, and you fear not in how doing so should affect him."

I took a breath, hearing as Kiyoko tugged against his chains.

"Would that I was not restrained," he said, a heavy shadow flashing through him. "Perhaps then you should have something to fear."

"Please, do not be angry," I pleaded gently.

A brief silence fell, interrupted by the crackling fire.

"In truth, I believe it rather selfish of you to pursue anyone given the precariousness of your situation. Much turbulence swirls around your station, and I do not wish for him to be dragged down alongside you as you fall from Grace. Everett does not deserve such a disservice."

My breathing sped, my heart lurching into my throat with Kiyoko's words.

"Do you sincerely believe those thoughts have not plagued me?" I countered indignantly, watching as he shifted his weight in the chains. "They drive me mad..."

"I can give him stability, my undivided devotion, and my mortality, none of which you can gift him."

Distant footsteps shuffled through my awareness, my anxiety driving my pulse in a panic.

"They are coming," Kiyoko said, his attention breaking from his antagonizing.

"Who is coming? Where do we find ourselves?" I interrupted. "How did you come to procure these quite ... artistic wounds?"

"Burn in the Seven Rings," he retorted, darkness flashing again through his eyes. "Take your lust and your thirst for blood and burn yourself alive."

My anger seized hold of me. I flung out a fist, punching Kiyoko squarely across the face. His body lurched, and his chains rattled, his momentum forcing him to dangle and swing like a tortured pendulum.

"You anger me," I spat through gritted teeth.

"It is but a dream."

"This is a nightmare," I said plainly, "and it shall continue if we cannot control ourselves."

The distant shuffling footsteps drew closer, the scraping leather loud against my ears.

"They are coming for you now," Kiyoko said, his laughter rattling his shackles. "It will not be long before their ranks grow in number, and you find yourself outmatched."

"Kiyoko... your cruelty hurts me..."

"We like to see you hurting," voices rasped suddenly from my right.

Through the doorway, Lyle's bloated corpse led an angered entourage, their footsteps shuffling beneath them as they had little strength to walk. Ilesa and Jorden flanked him on his left, nearly distracting me from Everett, who was lumbering behind them. Syler clasped hands with our mother's enchanted skeleton, dragging her frail, fragile bones across the floor.

"Your spirits hath not yet deserted you," Everett's voice broke from the throng.

He moved forward past Lyle, pushing himself towards the front of their ranks. He lulled across the room and stood at Kiyoko's front, lifting him from the chains and placing him in his arms.

"Thank the Heavens and Gods, I have found you," he said to Kiyoko, wrapping his body around him.

Everett leaned forward, kissing Kiyoko intensely. Their lips hungrily found each other, their arms securing one another in a passionate embrace. My heart thundered as I watched them express their devotion.

"To what are you eyeing?" Everett broke away from Kiyoko and snapped at me fiercely, his words cutting through me like a harsh whip. "Our affections are not to be enjoyed for your liking..."

"I thought we-" my words were snatched from my mouth.

"He shall never choose your hand over mine. He shall never want to part from my company." Kiyoko said bitterly, running his hands down Everett's chest.

"Your fall from Grace shall damn us all," Everett said, grazing his hands across Kiyoko's inner thighs, "and I do not wish to fight for you."

"Everett..."

"You ruin the lives of those you are near," Everett hissed, coaxing Lyle and the others farther into the room. "You have lost your way, and you cannot save us..."

"You cannot save anybody anymore," Kiyoko confirmed, turning his body away from me and pulling Everett in to kiss him.

Lyle moved from the shadows, ragged groaning escaping him. Ilesa fanned her divination cards from her hands, the edges sharpened into slim square knives. Syler screamed horridly, her dress tearing at the seams as blood painted her thighs. Pain rang through my head and eyes, my body going rigid as Lyle locked his fingers around me.

"You cannot save us," the voices said in tandem.

Broken images of Everett and Kiyoko's kissing flashed behind my eyes, their obliviousness to my suffering apparent through their moaning. I opened my mouth and released a scream, feeling my voice ripped from my throat as Lyle began to squeeze. My windpipe pained, my eyes watering as I fought for my breath.

"You cannot save us... you cannot save anybody anymore.

"You shall fail Knomucca."

"Knomucca...."

"Knomucca-"

XVIII

EVERETT

Knomucca's breathing lengthened, her eyes drifting closed as sleep consumed her. A dark, red energy flashed around her, diffusing the stench of iron in the wind. Instinctively, I held her against me, wrapping my arms securely around her waist. I watched as her chest rose and fell with her breathing, reveling in the way her hair spilled across her face.

"May the Gods grant you peaceful dreams and rest, beloved," I whispered, kissing the corner of her mouth. "Safest travels."

For a long, tender moment, I watched her sleep. Her hands gently cupped my arms, and her gauntlets left an indent in my skin. Timidly, I pulled her hand from beneath me, examining the ornate metal that imprisoned her.

A subtle glow thrummed from the gauntlets, the current thick and heavy against my touch. The blood pulsed beneath Knomucca's hands, twitching her fingers painfully every few moments. Large blisters were forming beneath the metal, her body rebelling from their constant imprisonment.

"You bear impressive strength," I whispered admiringly.

Gingerly, I examined the clasps, visualizing a pair of enchanted, fingerless gloves that would suit her nicely.

"Perhaps I ought to broach the subject," I said to her softly, tracing the gauntlets absently with my thumb. "You are always tinkering with these metal entrapments and leather would prove more comfortable."

Bringing her fingers to my lips, I kissed them furtively, hating how much pain and discomfort she had to endure in order to please the Creator. Vividly, I remembered the decaying of her hands, disliking how purple and phantomic they had turned after her mother's passing.

Anger flashed through me, and I fought to swallow it down, not wishing for my emotions to negatively impact Knomucca's dreaming. I leveled my breathing and placed a hand on Knomucca's hair, feeling it slightly damp and snarled.

She will have time to tend to it, I thought, not wishing to wake her with my worries. The Creator shall not like her appearance out of sorts, though I cannot remember a moment with more beauty than this.

Knomucca stirred and inhaled sharply. The scars along her collarbone pulsed, throbbing in a deep red. Her eyelids fluttered, and the scent of apples filled me. It was so fragrant that I wondered if there were any nearby.

She must be dreaming, I concluded, watching as her breath rose and fell. The thought of sleep and dreams suddenly felt alluring, the exhaustion from the days of travel and battle finally setting in.

My breathing began to lengthen, my body sluggish and heavy. As my head drifted down into sleep, a large crack from the fire jarred me awake. The scent of charred fish filled the air, the aroma darkening as it continued cooking.

Oi... reckon there is work to be done, I sighed, regretting that I would have to untangle myself from her and deprive myself once more of the rest I so desired.

Knomucca shifted as I slid my arms from around her body. Her breathing became short and ragged, her body tightening as she fought to remain asleep. Reaching downwards, I collected her tunic and draped the fabric across her. My gaze lingered on her sleeping against the bedroll, disliking the lingering scent of iron that clung to her aura.

"I shall always fight to keep you safe," I whispered softly into her ear before kissing it gently. "You shall never again be alone in your travels."

Rising to a stand, I began to move from the shelter, stopping to don my garb and boots. My leggings had been tangled around Knomucca's, thrown haphazardly into a pile. The stiff fabric of our garments was still stuffed into our boots. Grasping the wool, I yanked it from my footwear, feeling it snag against Knomucca's. The leggings tore free and knocked over her pouch, shaking loose a slim corked bottle that had been concealed inside.

I loosed an exasperated sigh.

The bottle glimmered and glinted, sparkling despite the shade our sleeping structure provided. The glass was immaculate and flawless, appearing exceptionally clean. Simple gold embellishments wove around the bottle's stem, blending into the design of Ozwal's crest. The rim was tipped with gold around the cork, and the glass of the bottle was thin and transparent.

The cork was wide and flat, displaying the symbol of my lineage. A tightly rolled cylinder of paper was encapsulated within the confines of the glass. Soft singing emanated from the bottle, accompanied by the distant strings of an ethereal harp. The voices grew clearer as I studied the bottle, the chanting slowly beginning to repeat my surname.

"Rosewood... Rosewood... Rosewood..."

Compulsion overtook me, and I seized the bottle, firmly grasping it. I hastily found a dagger to pry loose the seal. The cork released with a soft pop, and the scent of roses wafted from the bottle. I placed the cork into my smoking sack and turned the bottle over in my hands, feeling a soft scroll fall against my palm. I shook the parchment free and began to unroll it, noticing the pages were still held together with fragments of a book binding.

The paper curled and was hard to keep flattened, its time within the glass forcing its shape.

A sprawling hymnal was inked clear and dark across the pages. Musical staves lined the parchments, the notes written chaotically in the spaces. My inability to master the talent of reading music left me unable to recognize the composition. Though the music was indecipherable, the accompanying words were written beneath the staves, and the syllables spread amongst many lines.

Ancient rosewood, timeless tree,
Roots deep in eternity.
Seven sons of seven born,
Lineage by fate adorned.
Divine soul from hallowed fruit,
Chose mortal love's bittersweet pursuit.
Cast from grace for mortal's sake,
A choice that made the heavens quake.
Iron hammer rends the night,
Piercing darkness, shattering light.
In void's embrace, he waits alone,
Love destroyed, fate's cornerstone.
Prophecy whispers through time,
Of one to come, of paradigm:
Seventh son of seventh born,
To mend what centuries have torn.
From depths of void, divinely sparked,
A child of rosewood, fate-marked.
Bearer of balance, love's true heir,
To lift the world from its despair.
Anteyus rises, saved at last,
As present breaks free from past.
Divine and mortal blood combined,

Power that leaves the dark behind.
The hammer falls, night retreats,
As destiny itself completes.
Corruption fades before the dawn,
A new world order being drawn.
Rescuer of souls long lost,
Bridging realms at untold cost.
Forging future from the old,
A tale in starlit sky foretold.
Balance restored, the cycle ends,
As heaven to earth once more descends.
Through sacrifice and timeless wait,
Rosewood's child fulfills their fate.

I reread the hymn several times, my heart thundering in my throat. I glanced towards my hammer and observed its iron head. It thrummed softly as I slung it comfortingly across my shoulders.

"This has to be written for another," I said, wishing I could justify the calling of my surname and the references to my family tree. "I am seventh born of seven sons... though I possess a younger sister and that must certainly muddle the dynamics..."

I stood for a long moment and read the parchment again, listening to Knomucca turn over as her breathing shifted uncomfortably. A pained moan escaped her, and I lowered the parchment, returning to her side. Her sleep became more restless as the scent of iron turned to blood.

"It is but a dream..." I whispered to her. "I have you here with me."

I rubbed her shoulders gently, coaxing her to remain peaceful while she continued sleeping. Sitting beside her, I read the parchment again, ignoring the scent of cooking fish once more.

What was Knomucca doing with this parchment? I wondered, resting the bottle beside her shoes as I tucked it into my belt. Does she know what its implications are? There must be an explanation as to why she thought it prudent to guard this hymnal from me. And where is the rest of the book? I am certainly in need of some answers...

Knomucca's sleep quieted, her eyes softening as she breathed deeply. I crept from the tent and rifled through the woods, finding a large, flat stone to serve as a workspace. I heaved it from the ground and placed it between the tent and fire, concealing it partially beneath the shade of a coconut tree. Reaching a hand upwards, I grasped a coconut from the branches, piercing the husk with my dagger and drinking it dry.

"It is warm indeed," I said, wishing I could remove my tunic, though unwilling to risk sun damage.

Glancing about the camp, I noticed Thornin lying sleeping, his eyes heavy and intoxicated from the sun's warmth. I gave him a soft smile and ventured towards our supplies, fetching apples to hang on the spit. I approached the fire, shaking loose the fish from the spit onto the surrounding stones. Grasping the spit, I pierced the apples onto it, watching as they began to cook and spin.

A sudden scream jolted my heart, turning to see Knomucca thrashing wildly in her sleep. Her hands were clasped around her neck, the scars along her collarbone pulsing red and dripping blood.

"Knomucca!" I said, lurching towards her.

I pulled her hands from her neck, hearing her breathing rasp.

"Knomucca," I said again, shaking her urgently.

She woke with a start, her eyes flashing open. Panic filled her emerald irises. She inhaled a sharp breath and coughed suddenly, trying to push herself to a seat. She was strong and bucked against me, shoving me forcefully from her shoulders.

"Oi, it is Everett," I said. "Knomucca... is all well? Your sleep was rather restless... and I woke you just now by thwarting your attempts at self-strangulation."

"I believe you know the answer already," she said heavily.

"Do you wish to discuss it?" I asked comfortingly, taking her hand in my own.

She flinched and pulled away suddenly. Pain washed through me, my eyes widening with my worry.

"Knomucca... please do not construct a bulwark against me." I said, lowering my voice gently. "I love you and am deeply devoted... I do not wish for you to suffer in silence any longer."

A long pause fell between us.

"You must have seen me in your nightmares," I concluded from her silence.

Knomucca met my eyes.

"I did dream of you," she said slowly, "and the reminder that if I pursue you that I risk Falling From Grace and gambling your soul."

"You already know of my fondness for such sport," I said lightheartedly, grateful when she began to laugh. "You would not be alone in having those fears... the Gods know I have had them. Though it is also known I have carried a great pain for many years because I have kept my emotions quiet. I shall not contain them, and if fighting means there is risk, then I see this as no other war."

Her eyes brightened, her shoulders relaxing as I kissed her.

"In the same river," I continued after a moment's indulgence, "I have battles that overlap with your cause, and I believe our union shall prove quite beneficial."

"How do you mean?" Knomucca asked, watching as I unrolled the parchment from my belt.

"I must know why you have kept this from me," I said; my voice was gentle and level so as not to seem agitated.

I extended a hand and held the parchment out to her. Our fingers brushed together as she took it from me, beginning to read it. Her eyes widened, her brow furrowing in concentration as she took in the words.

"Where did you find this?" she asked.

"It fell from your pouch when I retrieved my garments," I said.

"I did not wish to imply I had been guarding anything from you," she said sincerely, meeting my eyes. "I only found the bottle in an altar upon Ozwal's forgotten shipwreck moments before you and Thornin found me." Knomucca held my eyes as she continued. "My thoughts have been elsewhere since we have been reunited."

"I believe you," I said, touching my thumb affectionately against the corner of her mouth.

She smiled and caressed my arm.

"I should like to see the shipwreck," I nodded. "If that is well with you."

"Certainly," Knomucca said softly. "Gift me another moment's concentration if you would... I wish to read it once more."

I nodded, watching her face as she reread the parchment twice through.

"Curious inquiry," Knomucca said, lifting her eyes to meet my face. "How were you able to read this? It is written in Decastitci... I was not aware you had an affinity for endangered languages, and we shared such an exciting pastime."

I blushed before speaking.

"The writing appeared to be in the common tongue," I said. "It held no ancient text in my eyes."

"Fascinating," she said."Reckon you were meant to find it then."

Another moment fell between us, Knomucca's gaze quickly returning as she finished reading for a third time.

"This must be what Kiyoko meant," she said, her lips moving softly as she introduced the melody.

"How do you mean?"

"He said you were worthy of chosen blood," Knomucca said with a level voice.

"Do you understand what this scroll implies?" I asked seriously, searching her face.

"Aye... that you are descendant of Anteyus," she said with a nod. "That the First Warrior is right to be worshipped and shall be rescued by your hand."

I opened my mouth to speak but fell silent.

"You have concerns in voicing the implication that you are to Ascend," she said, her words barely above a whisper. "I fear those anxieties are sound of mind. Uttering such is grounds for your execution should anyone untrustworthy come to hear them spoken aloud."

"What can this mean for the Creator?" I asked, matching her bravery with my own. "What does it mean for you?"

"There are secrets being kept," Knomucca said, her face hardening. "The truth in why Anteyus was cast away has been called into question with recent events, and one wonders for the true motives."

"When did Kiyoko disclose this to you?" I asked, my heart hammering in my chest.

"During my dreams," she began, folding her legs beneath her, "he was... in a poor state if I am honest."

My face fell.

"It is rather worrisome," she said, gently clasping my arm.

"Tell me of what else you dreamt," I coaxed, brushing her hair from her face.

"I dreamt of The Ascension Banquet," she began. Knomucca hesitated, and her face shifted, "I can only hope we have regained a semblance of normalcy before then and that all planned is easily executed."

"I have been fantasizing over your Ascension feast for quite some time now," I said excitedly. I leaned in close to her. "How I hoped you would wear a dress..." I continued, tracing a finger along her inner thigh. "One made of a lavish green to enhance your brilliant eyes."

"We best not allow ourselves to indulge in any further distractions," Knomucca said, pulling away abruptly, "or I fear I shall be fruitless with our remaining hours."

"I can agree with such sentiments," I said with a smile, even if slightly disappointed.

Slowly, I removed myself from her side, saddened to leave her warmth. Tiredness flooded me, and the image of a thick, dark veil with heron-clawed hands slammed through me, sending a surge of fear and uneasiness down my spine.

The fire crackled, jarring me back to reality. The scent of roasting apples was fresh across the wind, their aroma sweet and inviting.

"Everett?" Knomucca asked as I twitched unexpectedly. "Are you well?"

"I am simply tired," I admitted disappointedly. "Though worry not, I can carry on.

"It saddens me to know you shall go another night without sleep," Knomucca said.

"Aye... However, there is work to be done," I said, rising to a stand.

"It is cruel if I am honest," Knomucca said gently. "The moment your insomnia lightens, and you wish to sleep you are unable to do so."

"Aye... it does bear such irony."

Knomucca began to assemble herself. Her scars vanished from sight, the dark red lines disappearing beneath the fabric. She secured a set of dark leggings and slid into her boots, ready to face the sun.

Knomucca reattached her pouch and belt before sliding a carnelian sword down her spine, tucking the hilt beneath her snarled hair. Squatting downwards, Knomucca fetched the torn hymnal from the ground, handing it to me cautiously.

"I reckon you had best keep this safe," she said. "Though I must remind you to share it with no one aside from Kiyoko."

The sun beat down across our camp, forcing Thornin to take refuge in the forming shade around the border. His tail was lazily coiled beneath his head, keeping his face aloft. The coconut trees swayed in the wind, the breeze cooling us from the scorching air. Long shadows draped across the sand, indicating that the evening hours would soon fall upon us.

Glancing about, I assessed the status of our camp, thankful to see the fish we had procured still resting atop the stone. The fire flashed and cracked loudly, drawing my attention to it. The apples were soft and browning, spinning gently atop the glowing flames.

Turning away from Knomucca, I approached the fire, grasping the spit and shirking the apples free. They landed softly upon the stones surrounding the fire, gifting me the chance to pierce them with my dagger and move them near the fish.

"Oi, you were hard at work while I slept," Knomucca said, sitting beside the fire.

She was tending to her hair, draping it across her shoulder and combing the salty knots out of it. As she combed it, she rinsed it with a coconut filled with water.

"Indeed," I said, regarding her longingly. I blushed as she turned her attention to me, busying myself with a coconut to hide my expression.

I secured a spliff and cleared the large, flattened stone, gathering the fish, apples, and coconuts. Clasping them tightly, I returned to the fire, approaching Knomucca again on the right and sitting beside her.

"May I offer you some nourishment?" I asked. "It is wise to replenish after the expenditure of energy, and to refill while the night remains so full of work."

"Indeed..." Knomucca said, her fingers lingering as she procured the food from my hands. "I thank you for your thoughtfulness."

"I am honored to be of service," I said with a wink as Knomucca chuckled.

Exhaling through my grin, I relaxed into a brief silence, pausing to say thanks before consuming my sustenance.

"How I wish we had found our own paradise, instead of this foreboding place," Knomucca said.

"I certainly agree," I answered. "Though once our meal has passed, I fear there is work to be done."

"Agreed," Knomucca said.

Knomucca lifted her apple in a gesture of thanks, then bit into it. A silence fell once more as we indulged in our feast, the coconuts pairing well with the cooked apples and salted fish. I watched the dancing flames and rested my leg beneath Knomucca's, feeling once she relinquished her weight against me.

"You are comfortable to sit against," I admitted to her. "And the flames are enjoyable to observe."

"Once more I find no pause for disagreement," she said. "And the fire is exhibiting quite a lovely glow. Perfect for a reading, I might add, were we at home."

"What do you see if you peer into it on my behalf?"

Knomucca studied the flames for a long moment. They danced and darted together, spreading an orange glow across the early evening sky.

"Strength," she said, "loyalty. Honor and bravery... an old, gnarled tree, the glint of your hammer," she paused, releasing a breath. "Truff is searching for you. He scours, saddened, beyond the woodlands of Woodroe. He knows where not to find you- his smell of you lost in the trees."

"Truffles," I whispered softly.

A hot and silent tear rolled down my face. Knomucca reached out her hand and brushed it gently with her thumb, holding my gaze. Her eyes grew serious as they began to dart between my face and torso.

"We shall find him," she said. "Fear not, Beloved. While this tiding of him is troublesome, it yields hope; he is alive and well."

"Wise words," I said as more silent tears escaped me. "Thank you kindly for the comfort."

"He is a cunning creature," Knomucca said. "I see no reason why he should struggle to find you once we return."

"I hope your words ring true," I said, taking a moment to compose myself.

Knomucca kissed me softly, running a hand across my shoulders, the hand shaking with unease as she caressed me.

"Knomucca, is all well?" I asked cautiously.

"As well as can be expected," she said quietly.

"I have a suspicion you are withholding something from me," I said.

Knomucca grew still.

"I..." She paused and ran a shaking hand across my chest. "I simply fear for you... With all we have discovered this day and I wish never to be without you."

"Fear not; you shall always have me beside you," I soothed. I worry for you... and Kiyoko and Truff... though as long as we fight side by side, we will keep everyone safe."

Knomucca hesitated before she spoke.

"Let us pray it is so."

A silence fell between us, and I released a breath.

"I suppose we ought to be setting off towards the shipwreck," I suggested. "It would be best to explore it again before the sun should set. We can begin to prepare the elixir once we have returned... and we can partake in our smoke whilst we walk."

"That is well with me," Knomucca said. "I am in need of a space to boil my ingredients, perhaps we can find something suitable on the ship."

Knomucca snuffed out the fire, pouring sand from the surrounding beach atop the flames. The air was heavy with the scent of fading smoke. I found it difficult to pull myself away from the comforts offered by the camp. I exhaled heavily and pulled myself to my feet, sweeping sand from my leggings and adjusting my belt.

"May I borrow your water skin," Knomucca asked suddenly, squatting beside her water receptacle.

"Aye," I said, unfastening it from my belt and holding it outward to her.

Knomucca slid it from my fingers and began to fill it with the water she had collected. The water tipped from her coconut slowly, pouring into its leather with a rush.

"That ought to hold us until we return," she said, tightening the cork securely.

Knomucca turned over her shoulder and whistled suddenly to Thornin.

"Oi, we are set for exploring," she said to him, gesturing up the coastline. "Come along if you would - follow on foot."

Thornin lifted his immense body and lurched lazily from the sand, swiping his tail lazily. A long groan escaped him, his eyes sparkling roguishly as he spewed smoke towards us.

"Cheeky little devil," Knomucca mused, waiting for Thornin to appear at her side before setting up the coastline.

We headed along the pebbled beach, the water lapping against the shore. The tide had shifted and moved drastically inwards, depositing debris dramatically as it demolished the sand. Mist sprayed upwards, fracturing clear tiny rainbows in the late-day sun. Orange had begun painting the horizon, the threat of nightfall encouraging our pace to quicken. The breeze was eerily still and calm, failing to match the violent waves that slammed across the sand.

"It is strange the waters should choose to be so aggressive, when previously they had been calm," Knomucca observed, allowing me to walk along her right.

"Perhaps the moon and its cycles behave differently here," I suggested, lighting the spliff I had prepared for us. "The island was surrounded by a tangible barrier when I stumbled upon it. Perhaps my breaking through it with my hammer in order to find you has damaged some of the enchantments."

"I wonder how it possessed the ability to tear through such a weave," she said after a silence fell between us. "It pleases me to know you are well after such an obstacle from the Creator."

My heart plummeted with the revelation, my hand fumbling for the spliff as Knomucca returned it to my fingers.

"I dislike that He conceals His face," I said, uneasily touching my hammer to ground myself. "It is cowardly."

Knomucca said nothing, composing her face to hide her emotions. Her footing never wavered, and her gaze failed to falter, yet her fingers clenched with a sudden aggravation. A silence fell across the beach as we walked. We passed the smoke between us, enjoying the herbs in the late afternoon sun. Thornin trampled behind us, knocking through ferns and banana leaves as he shoved through spaces far too small for his build.

"Hover or linger," she whistled, pressing her fingers between her lips.

Thornin rustled his wings, though he did not leave the sand, his neck arching playfully as he regarded the sky.

"Very good," Knomucca said, turning away from him and pulling herself onto the stone.

I waited for her to begin her ascent before following at her heel, grasping the vines and stone with my dragonscale gloves. I focused on my footing as I climbed the cliff face, remaining vigilant of her movements.

I heaved myself up and came to rest beside her, enjoying the view of the surrounding sparkling waters and the distantly setting sun.

"The wreck is just beyond these rocks in the shallows," Knomucca said, her gaze fixed upon the sea below.

"Why would Ozwal have come to search this place?" I asked curiously, wishing for a smoke to calm my raging nerves.

"He was in circle with my mother's coven and the forces conspiring against the Creator," Knomucca said, her voice dipping below a whisper.

I exhaled a breath I had not known I was holding, seeing His veiled image flash again behind my eyes.

"To restore Anteyus," I deduced with a nod.

Knomucca nodded in agreement.

"One begs the question... how did Ozwal come to know of the First Warrior... and become spiritually aligned with him. I would certainly appreciate learning about the First Warrior from you," Knomucca said, whistling to Thornin again, the option to hover or linger. "Should you ever wish to enlighten me..."

"There is no returning if I open that door with you," I said, watching as Knomucca began descending the rocks towards the water. "We have already tempted fate with our intimacy... to speak of a forbidden god... that is sure to enrage Him. Are you certain you wish to risk this on the day of your Ascension?"

Knomucca turned very seriously towards me.

"My concern for risks became redundant the moment I confessed my feelings for you. Tell me of your family in greater detail than you ever wished. Tell me the stories of Anteyus and how he has shaped you. I wish to know you as fluidly as I know myself."

I blushed, allowing her a kind smile before turning my face to my boots.

"Father gifted me my hammer on my fifth Winter Solstice, and began to teach me of Anteyus and his teachings. Stories were told of the stars from which Creation found Crossfire, and though dark energies were born from the cosmos, so was the light. Anteyus is a being of true balance, of love and war. He, too, wielded a hammer, believing it to be a sacred tool toward enlightenment. The hammer too represents the forces of balance, forgiveness and revenge; destruction and creation; discordance and harmony. Possessing a hammer gives one the insight to know when to act, how to execute those actions, and how much force needs to be applied."

"Those stories fall in parallel to the legends spread of the Creator," Knomucca said. "His heron features the substitute for the hammer, of course. He was born of the stars to bring peace and prosperity to the realms."

"Then why would he shut someone away for wanting to build a home?" I asked a bit too harshly. I exhaled to clear my energy, "Anteyus found love and wished to work in tandem with his responsibilities... none should have to handle the burdens of life in their lonesome."

"I can agree," Knomucca said, our eyes locking again as she slid off the rocks and onto stable footing. "If his truest teachings empower balance, certainly he could have handled separating his time."

"I said the home and hearth are his highest values," coming to stand beside her and search her face. "Family... comfort... He did not often choose a violent hand in his myths, but when he did, he was a force to be reckoned with."

"Tell me one where he was gentle," Knomucca said as we began to wade through the water toward the wreck. "And one when he was unkind."

"Anteyus was born during the Winter Solstice." The warm salt water slammed against my boots as we continued to walk. "He loved to visit Crossfire and watch as everyone partook in the Festess. He loved the pastries, the lights, and the way everyone was kind to one another."

"Aye, it is a wonderful time," she agreed as the waves pushed against us.

"Well, one solstice he stumbled upon a poor farm town. They had been through hardship and did not have a bountiful harvest. Root rot had destroyed their crops and sickness was overtaking the people. Anteyus wished to help and wanted to gift everyone with time to rest and heal."

"So, what did he do?" She asked, splashing through the sea.

"He gifted them an abundant solstice... so he blessed their bread to always rise, their chickens to have an abundant roost, and their rivers to always flow heavy with salmon. He slipped into their homes while they slept and enchanted their food stores so there would be twice as many, leaving small silver whistles for the town's children.

"He sounds truly benevolent."

"Aye... His horse was gifted with traveling through the realms so he always came back every solstice to see how the town was fairing and leave gifts for the children. And in this small town is where he met his love, the squash farmer. Though I suppose that story is for a different time, if you wish to hear a myth in which he was unkind then that is not the story."

"Aye... Though I do wish to hear it another time." She said, the wreck drawing closer. "So, what sorts of acts drove him to anger?"

I fell silent for a moment, recalling the tales told to me by my father and many brothers.

"High in the western Mountains, a small village struggled to grow crops. A nobleman who oversaw the village would claim all the food and precious gemstones for himself and leave the people with nothing. One winter solstice when Anteyus was riding through the realms he stumbled on the village and grew displeased with the nobleman. He visited him in his home and told him if he did not start showing his subjects some generosity there would be consequences..."

I took a breath as we worked through the waves and then continued. "Of course the nobleman did not heed his warning, and when the mountain berries were ready for harvesting, he took them all for himself."

"Gods," Knomucca sighed.

"When Anteyus returned, he cursed the nobleman so everything he ate turned to ash... And told him if he could learn to be generous, he would set him right. But the nobleman only grew angrier. He began to enter the homes of the townsfolk and take more of their shares in an attempt to right his taste. Anteyus succumbed to ire, so he tore the noblemen's tongue clear from him. His blood ran over the fields, and his body fell to make fertile soil. And so, it was said, the town would become the most prosperous town in the mountains. And anyone who deceives the people who live there is doomed to have a cursed life."

"Thank you for telling me the stories that mean so much to you." She said, absently trailing a hand down my arm. "Anteyus sounds like a fair and noble person... The Creator does not wish for us to know it."

"My father preached that Anteyus was wrongfully cast to the Void for choosing love over the creator's power..." I said as we finally approached the wreck. "I too know it to be so and am glad we shall set him right."

We rounded towards the ladder, finding the frayed ropes hanging against the warped wood of the ship.

"I will climb first," Knomucca said. 'I have explored the deck already and know where it is safe to step."

"I shall follow your footfalls," I said, giving her a salute.

"There are traps, so be incredibly cautious..." She paused, then added, "I was struck with some sort of needle in my earlier explorations and had to be saved by Senaya... best if we can avoid such from happening again."

"Very well," I said, wishing to cradle her next to me. "I am glad you remain with me."

"Aye," she said, squeezing my hand firmly before hoisting herself up the ropes.

I tugged against the ladder, checking its stability before I began climbing. When the ropes held, I began my ascent, following behind Knomucca and cresting the bulwark swiftly.

I cautiously stepped onto the deck, testing the firmness of the wreckage before settling my weight. A flag once resembling living fire lay sopping wet and extinguished, the shreds of red cloth flapping pathetically in the gale. Familiar runes were carved into the elaborate masts, the symbols identical to those etched upon the mahogany handle of my hammer.

"Knomucca?"

"Aye?"

"Can you see these runes?" I asked, sliding my fingers across them. "Ansuz, Urus, Thurisaz?"

"Nay." She shook her head. "You are certain it is them?"

"Aye... Look."

I drew my hammer and presented it to her, moving my finger down the edged symbols across the handle. The runes flashed a bright purple, the scent of mugwort filling me furiously.

"Turn back," Kiyoko whispered through me. "Please, Everett! She is going to-"

Pain shot through my chest in a wave of hot fire. I gasped, reeling from the pain as his voice faded away.

"Kiyoko?" I said, fighting for breath and turning frantically to search for him. "Knomucca... Did you see that?"

"Nay," She said, growing frustrated. "I did not perceive anything out of the ordinary."

The scent of mugwort swirled away into the wind.

"What did he say?" She asked after a tense moment.

"That we ought to turn back." I said. "The rest was... unfinished."

"I certainly hope we can return to him soon." She said.

I fell silent and sad, gesturing for her to continue onward with the wave of my hand.

"I found the hymnal this way, in the captain's quarters," she said, beginning to step cautiously forward. "Follow me."

Together, we moved across the deck, my eyes following the path of her movements so as not to disturb any traps. The planks groaned loudly beneath our feet, the oak splitting from exposure to the salt. Further down the deck, the wood lay severely fractured, caving into a hole that led into the quarters below.

"I fell here, through the floor.... His altar is down there... I shall drop in first."

"Excellent, I shall be along behind you," I said, hearing as her boots hit the ground below.

I grabbed onto the slick wood planks and dangled my body through the hole. I lowered myself as far as I could, then released my fingers. I plummeted to the floor, landing heavily on the wood slabs. I rolled from the added momentum before finding my footing, coming to rest against a nearby wall.

Skeletons lay preserved amongst the wood, the orbits of their eyes deep empty voids. A veil of red viscous energy lingered around them, the scent of blood catching in my throat. A deep, deep cold began to set through my bones despite the heat of the tropical island air that swirled around us.

"Knomucca?" I spoke despite my teeth threatening to chatter. "Could you resurrect these skeletons? Perhaps they can share with us some insight about Ozwal."

"Nay, not until I Ascend... Cypress only allows for me to temporarily reanimate the vessel of a spirit that has recently crossed over."

"Damnit." I swore, giving into the cold and allowing my body to tremble.

"Everett? What plagues you?"

I opened my mouth to reply, though I could not through the chattering of my teeth.

Suddenly, the skulls began to whisper through me.

"You should have listened to that sneaky little worm and left, Everett." A familiar voice churned my stomach.

"Show yourself!" I shouted, both aloud and in my mind.

"Everett?" Knomucca's voice felt distant.

"Sharing her heart shall cost you yours," the Creator said, filling the quarters with the smell of blood.

I drew my hammer and slammed the head into the nearest skeleton, listening as the bones crunched solidly beneath it.

"Everett! What are you doing?" She shrieked. "You are disturbing their resting place!'

I smashed another skeleton.

"Stop!"

The remaining skeletons rose from the ground, their hands shifting into the sharp talons of a heron. The sound of iron cut through the air as

Knomucca drew her sword. She twisted and placed her back towards mine, protecting me against the skeletons encircling us from all sides.

I swung my hammer, cleaving through the onslaught. Skeletons' bones crunched into fine powder, disappearing into the salt and the wind. I swirled over my shoulder and slammed the iron head of my hammer into another wave of skeletons, then made swift work of the last rushing from the right.

I listened as Knomucca defended my back, her sword slicing easily through the skeleton's enchanted remains. Gradually, the skeletons disappeared from their tomb, removing the unpleasant smell of blood.

Knomucca's breath was heavy and labored.

"Their hands..." She shuddered in fear. "They were his talons."

"Knomucca, my deepest apologies for frightening you."

"What in the seven hells was all that about?" She asked.

"Knomucca, the Creator doesn't want us here, and told me to turn back." My words were threatening to grow frantic. "What's worse, he heard Kiyoko speaking through my awareness."

"Steel your mind. We cannot allow him inside our minds again." She said gravely. "Come. Let me show you to the captain's quarters."

She led me carefully to the ship's starboard and found a narrow hatch.

"His altar is just through here," she said.

We walked through the captain's quarters, noticing decrepit tables, chess boards, and cracked wine barrels littering the floor. I scoured through the broken remains of Oswal's life. I found a copper cooking pot still intact beneath several splintered table pieces.

"This ought to suffice for the Elixir," I said, hoisting the cauldron into my arms.

"Aye, indeed." She agreed.

"I shall carry it for you." I said, clutching it close.

"You are too kind," she said as she gestured across the room. "His altar is over there."

I started towards it, then halted as she whistled sharply.

"We ought to approach incredibly carefully... His altar is what delivered the unsuspected needle before I found the hymnal."

"Very well." I said, slowing my step.

I approached the altar, nervously grasping the copper pot to keep myself grounded. "Its aura fills me with the taste of rot," I noticed.

"Nothing appears out of place," Knomucca said.

I made to touch the altar, though my body held firm. My body shuttered, consumed once more by the cold that had filled me earlier. My spirits threatened to leave my body, yet I felt trapped in a place between this realm and the next. I was paralyzed by the cold, my blood slowing with my pulse to drip like molasses. My words were ripped from my lips by an iced vacuum of wind, making it feel impossible to catch my breath.

"Everett!" Knomucca's voice was far away.

The tourmaline in my pocket began to feel hot, bringing fire back to my bones. Kiyoko's gentle singing floated through my awareness, the melody and lyrics indistinguishable as if he were muffled beyond a wall of stone. The sudden rhythm of trotting hooves filled my mind.

"Everett." A voice I did not recognize began to whisper through me. "Everett, when all is nothingness and black, you must listen through stone... Following your heart is how you shall come back."

"Everett, Everett-"

I came to the floor of the captain's quarters, my back pressing firmly against the planks. Knomucca crouched over me, gently staring into my face.

"Thank the Gods," she said once I had opened my eyes. "Everett is all well? You gave me quite a fright."

I sat up slowly and soothed the scorching pain in my chest with a rub of my hand.

"What happened?" I asked, shaking my head to clear it.

"You fainted." She said. She handed me the water skin, urging me to drink. I took the water from her hand and drank it eagerly.

"How are you feeling?"

"Fine now," I said, feeling like a heavy fog had left my mind. "I am... uncertain what happened."

"Let me help you stand." she said, grabbing me beneath my arm.

She gently pulled me to my feet and retrieved the cauldron from the floor.

"Let's get out of here." She said, "and return to camp."

"Aye..." I said, retrieving the cauldron from her hands. "I have found my strength... Thank you for your help."

"I am glad you are well." She said, returning us back across the captain's quarters.

We left through the small hatch and returned on our path. Finding slots in the wood, we gingerly climbed the bulwark, passing the copper cauldron between us as we crested the top. We returned across the deck and found the waiting rope ladder, taking a final glance across the shipwreck as sunset fell.

"We should waste no more time," she said as we grasped the rope ladder and began our descent. "The time for the Ascension approaches."

XIX

KNOMUCCA

I stepped away from Everett, returning us up the cliff face. I listened as his boots started behind me, enjoying his movements across the stone. He fixated on his ascent, calculating where he placed his hands before he climbed behind me. Sadness and confusion shrouded his aura, his energy tightening with the emotional burden he now carried alongside the cauldron.

I fought to focus on the rock as I pulled my body upward. The wind whipped across me, smashing the growing waves against the steep cliffs. Water sprayed and misted, soaking the edges of my boots in an attempt to shirk me from the stone.

"Oi, mind your footing," I twisted as I called toward Everett.

"I appreciate the insight," Everett replied. "The waves shall only grow in strength as the moon begins to rise."

"Indeed," I said, pulling my body to the top of the cliffs and sitting gently.

I situated sideways, granting Everett space as he clambered onto the stone behind me. The sun dipped beneath the horizon, painting the sky radiant orange with swirling fuchsia. Everett's hair shone brightly in the setting sun, the tinting of reddening roses peeking through his lush auburn locks. My heart caught in my throat as my thoughts drifted toward my dream and the heart that had laid before me at that table.

Everett sat atop the ledge and found my gaze, his eyes studying me gently through the sunset. A silence fell between us as Everett held my gaze, my heart hammering with the enjoyment of his face.

"Let us return to camp," I said urgently. "We must start preparing The Elixir."

"That is well and good," Everett said, watching as I returned to the white-pebbled beach. "Though I ask that I may be allowed to assist with any and all preparations... I wish to make myself as helpful to you as needed."

"Your offer is kind," I said as my boots found contact with the shore. "And it shall not be forgotten."

I watched as Everett returned to the ground, coming to stand tall beside me. I stretched from our exertion and turned away from the cliffs, leaving Ozwal's wreck again behind me. Following the coastline, I gestured for Thornin, watching as he rose from the sand.

As we returned, all looked in order as we had left it, the fire smoldering softly in the rising moonlight. I stepped into the camp and set to rekindle the flames, pleased when matches from my smoking sack lit the logs promptly. The scent of smoke filled my nose comfortingly.

Quickly, I set to constructing a stand for the cauldron, building a frame from thick and heavy wood to rest far outside the bonfire. Unfastening chains from Thornin's saddle, I prepared a place to hang the cooking pot. I was glad to notice Everett had set it beside the bonfire. I secured his cooking pot to the chains and hoisted it from the fire, allowing the flames to crackle whilst I set about the camp.

As I approached on his left, Everett turned towards me, noticing the piles of possessions we still carried. He retrieved a spare tunic, which he promptly offered to me. "I know it is not your dress armour, however it will have to do," he stated before turning away to adjust the supplies in the saddle.

I took it with a thankful nod before swiftly exchanging tunics. "I pray The Creator will find my appearance acceptable."

"I wish not to pry... though I wonder if you can explain the mechanics of the Elixir?"

"What is it you wish to know?" I asked him gently.

"What exactly will happen once you brew the potion? All you have ever told me is that I shall be guarding your physical body after it has been crafted."

"In truth, I know merely that The Creator wishes I craft such a brew that will allow him to infuse me with his vital life energies."

"Is that wise? Allowing him past your psychic defenses?"

Hot pain pricked suddenly through my hands, my face contracting as I pushed it away. "It is the only way to possess the power I need to Ascend." I said.

"What are we using for this draught?" he asked. "You have lost most of your elements." "

"We shall find elements that suffice with what remains to us."

"Did he provide you any sort of instruction?"

"Aye, it remains pinned to the inner leather of my pouch," I said in a level voice. "Thankfully, I had the foresight to secure it."

"We ought to set to it, if no other hurdles presently befall us." Everett said, gesturing to the sky. The moon was bright and hanging above us, shining silver atop the sea. The waves pounded the shore, roaring loudly against the coast. Crickets and insects sang through the night, chirping through the tropical air.

"It is the hour of the Wolf," Everett said.

"I shall also need to check after Thornin before we begin... I will need a dragon scale."

"Excellent," Everett said, "I shall stoke the fire."

I saluted and stepped away from him. I found Thornin lying comfortably under a cluster of palm trees.

"I am sorry, sweetness, but I am in need of another of your scales, please," I forewarned, approaching him.

He huffed his displeasure in a puff of smoke, the tendrils rising to the darkened sky.

I squatted down beside him, running my gloved hand over his sharpened hide. Finding a loosened scale, I tugged sharply. Thornin growled resignedly.

"Thank you, old friend," I said, patting his shoulder. "Not just for the scale, but also for coming to find me."

Thornin nuzzled his snout into the nape of my neck affectionately.

"I appreciate your love and protection," I said with a salute before stepping away from him.

As I returned, the fire was crackling strong from Everett's tending. I dangled the cauldron above the flames, watching as the metal began to warm.

Reaching into my pouch, I unfastened my scrollwork on the Elixir, flattening it against a stone to make it easier to read. The Creator had written the recipe and request, his thick, dark handwriting unsettling against the page. I ran my eyes down the parchment and exhaled in mild frustration, angry that none of my previous elements were available.

A sad sigh escaped me, my pity ending abruptly as Everett resumed my side.

"Knomucca," Everett began to speak timidly, knowing how I dislike to be interrupted while reading. "I wondered... how I could assist."

"Immediately I find cause for alarm," I said, regarding the scroll. "I am to mix a base to begin this potion, and I do not have the sugar and wine I wished to form as my catalyst. I could craft such an alcohol from seeds, though I have not the time to ferment them."

"What of Tora Wine?" Everett asked. "Thornin has some bottles in his saddle."

"That sounds promising."

Everett retrieved a bottle from the saddle and passed it to me. Uncorking the bottle, I dumped the wine into the cooking pot, watching the thick blue liquid rise toward the brim.

"For my protection," I whispered softly.

Exhaling, I glanced around the camp, spotting coconuts hanging from the branches.

"Everett..." I said slowly. "Let us consider the coconut... animals and winds scatter them across the soil and produce future trees."

"Aye, the coconut produces life," Everett said, retreating towards the branches. "They satiated your spirits, preserved you, protected you and promoted your prosperity."

"So is my thinking."

Everett returned with an armful of coconuts. He sliced them through with a dagger, dumping the nectar into the wine. A delightful smell wafted through the air, the mild and sweet aroma making me crave such a treasure. I searched my firewood for a worthy stirring stick. I clutched it in my hand, mixing the liquid gently within the cauldron.

"I have a question that I fear may cause offense," Everett began slowly. "Though I wondered if I could read the parchment alongside you?"

"Certainly," I said with a nod.

Everett squatted beside the stone and began to read, his eyes flickering towards me whenever a spare moment beheld him. The cooking pot began to bubble, the elements warming as they danced atop the flames.

"Knomucca," Everett said slowly, using his finger to mark his reading place.

"Aye," I replied.

"These elements are quite dark," he said heavily. "Blood... no doubt your own. Sacrifice. Gnats and lice, babes of mice... Decayed teeth, foxes spines. All mixed with powdered dragon bones."

An uneasy silence fell between us.

"Aye... It is an unsettling limerick," I said, clenching my hands.

"You mean to tell me you had these elements prepared in Hazel's wagons?" Everett asked, rereading the scroll.

"Aye... most of them," I said. "Truthfully... I had not gathered owl or dragon bones and I planned on making substitutions."

"With what did you intend on exchanging them for?"

"Moon buds and the angelfish eye," I said gently.

Everett fell silent and reread the parchment, my chest hammering as he drew to the bottom. I knew terribly I was to add a myocardium to The Elixir. I grew nervous about Everett's discoveries once he connected the symbolism of sacrifice. His eyes never showed a sign of knowing, and his face never betrayed understanding. After a long moment studying, he rose to his feet, turning the parchment from his sight.

"I fear I am best used executing your spoken instruction," Everett said with a salute. "I worry I know not how else I may assist."

"Your sentiments are well and good," I drew away from the fire. I began to read the parchment again, my eyes flickering nervously. No such instruction or symbolism of Everett's words wove across the page, and there were no mentions of cats, owls, or their wisdom. Big, thick letters scrawled down the parchment, the words "The heart of Rosewood" bleeding in black ink. The paper fluttered harshly against the stone, rippling from the growing wind.

"Knomucca," Everett drew to his immense height and regarded me curiously.

I realized with a fright I had gone still, staring fixated at the parchment. Quickly, I fought to form rational thought, wishing to ignore the command that had strewn across the paper.

"I fear we are best disregarding this recipe altogether," I said, drawing up the parchment and tossing it into the fire. "The Creator is trying to break through my psychic defenses. We are going to stray from the scroll and attempt to protect ourselves."

I crumpled up the parchment and tossed it into the fire. The paper lay flat amongst the flames, the ink bleeding into a rose that thrummed like a heart. It beat against the paper, splattering ink as the pulse shook it. The paper failed to burn or blacken, resting wickedly in the fire beneath my cauldron.

"Cursed parchment," Everett said, oblivious to the spreading of the ink. Using the handle of his hammer, he buried the paper out of sight beneath the coals, stirring the fire intensely. "Pay it no mind..." he continued softly, "for all things yield to the tyrant of fire."

I took a breath to clear my mind, peering into the cooking pot. The liquid had bound and was boiling softly, popping in sweet, scented bubbles.

"I am in need of our next elements," I said as I dropped the dragon scale in.

"What do you have in mind?" He questioned.

I pondered for a moment. "If mother sent you her pin through an apple's core, then perhaps we should use one of those."

Everett retrieved an apple from our supplies before planting it firmly in my hand. I blessed the apple with a breath, held it in my hand, giving thanks for its knowledge, and dropped it into the cauldron. I was thankful for Mother's continual guidance despite never crossing her path in the Underworld.

"Everett," I said, noticing time had continued to pass quickly. "Please fetch what remains of our supplies."

He retreated across the camp with a salute, returning to our remaining belongings pile. I stirred as the elements melded, wondering what I was next to add. Rifling through the belongings attached to my person, I secured the herbs from my smoking sack and found the blend I had obtained with Lyle in Belleview.

"I shame myself for your loss," I told Lyle's spirit, hoping he heard my voice through the island's enchantments. "I only hope I can preserve the time you shall now spend with your mother."

I upturned the leather and poured the sachet into the cauldron, hearing the herbs plop into the solution. The scent of cloves wafted through the air; the temptation of such a delightful smoking blend warranted a true offering.

"That was beautiful," Everett said, returning with armfuls of supplies.

"You are kind," I said heavily. "And it was all for nothing. I lost Lyle and failed to secure an Angelfish... it is embarrassing, I failed his spirit."

Everett smiled unexpectedly, his face changing quickly when he regarded my confusion. He held a preserved angelfish wrapped in cloth in his arms, the scales glowing in the moonlight.

"Everett... how?"

"Thornin and I stopped to search the reefs and... I obtained one for you," he said.

I kissed him through my smile and hugged him hard before taking the fish from him.

"Thank you kindly," I said.

Everett blushed, watching as I prepared the Angelfish for the potion. I used my dagger to obtain the eye. I ritualistically burned the remains of the fish before adding it to the brew. The eye was large and floated in the mixture, popping with a sizzle before it dipped into the solution. The liquid flashed with the scent of chamomile, shimmering in the moon with the sudden green of Syler's eyes.

Syler.

In a panic, I recalled her pain when I swam the waves.

"Syler," I suddenly said aloud. "Syler! Syler... are you with us?"

Screams erupted from the cauldron, piercing my ears and eyes with a pained yellow light. Syler's voice was wrenched away harshly, her pleas ending abruptly. She vanished through her outcry, the cauldron bubbling acutely in her absence. Blood blisters popped in a horrid echo, perfuming the air with the earthy scent of iron.

"Syler," I called, aware Everett had approached the cauldron on my right.

"Knomucca, what did you see? Samarin taunted me with Syler's abduction. I did not think to mention it before, as I thought his words false."

My anger welled beyond my eyes, overtaking my temper.

"I see her torment," I lashed out, staring into the swirling liquid. "I wish you had mentioned this earlier."

"Is there nothing you can do to try to reconnect with her?" Everett asked fervently.

"I could attempt to access her vital life energy," I theorized. "But I cannot deviate from my task. You should have told me this before!"

"I realize now the severity of my error," Everett said tightly.

The cauldron bubbled, the liquid turning a plum purple, as Kiyoko's familiar voice emanated from its depth. "It's too late now to fix what cannot be undone."

"Something irreversible has happened to her," I said with a sudden knowing.

"We shall search for her before we return to the troops," Everett said. "When your potion is finished, we shall use the time before the Feast to find her."

"I fear she has joined our mother," I said, fighting the tightening of my chest.

"We need not give The Creator ammunition against you. We shall search west of the Rose Lily, comb the swamp lands and we will not rest until we have direction on her whereabouts. Fear not, Beloved... we shall learn what has come of her."

"You had best hope you are correct," I said heavily, watching the potion roar and boil.

"I can only hope," he said, his voice nearly lost in the chirping crickets. "Tell me... what shall we be adding into your brew next?"

Too enraged and anxious to trust my tongue, I searched angrily through my enchanted pouch. Surprisingly, the small sachet of moon buds lay crinkled and wet at the bottom. I centered my breathing once more and retrieved them. I added the buds into the potion with a soft pattering, watching them float among the bubbles.

All that remains is my blood, I thought, drawing a dagger.

"If you are in need of blood, you may use mine," Everett offered tentatively.

My stomach dropped in panic as I remembered my dream, a fleeting moment through my anger.

"That won't be necessary," I said, removing my gloves. With certainty, I drew my dagger across my palm, the burning sensation a welcome distraction from the fury.

My vital life energy trickled into the potion, turning it a hue of delectable sanguine raspberry. Midnight fell upon the islands as I worked, my Name Day beginning with the most unwelcome gifts.

"Blessed Name Day," Everett said with a brief salute.

"Thank you," I said shortly. Pain began to sear through my hands. I continued through gritted teeth, "And a Happy Festess to you."

"Aye, it is the Equinox," Everett said wistfully. Everett read my face and turned towards the cauldron, "What remaining elements do you require?"

I released an uncertain breath. "I believe we have added all of importance," I said, tapping my stirring stick against the cooking pot. The elements melted and dissolved, the potion deepening to a rich purple. I watched the fire as it boiled the potion, aware of the thick and churning liquid. The solution ruffled like feathers, turning the deep blue of a heron. The scent of blood filled the air, the potion sharpening as the bubbles popped across its surface.

I averted my eyes, gazing away from the uneasy feeling that overtook me. Beneath the flames, the parchment poked through viciously, splattering ink amongst the fire. The flames blackened, the ashes hardening against the parchment as they failed to consume it. I gazed into my cauldron once more, escaping the taunting of the paper that would not disintegrate.

Everett's face swam before me on the potion's surface, frozen in a pained scream.

"Knomucca... you look unwell," Everett said suddenly from my left, making me jump. "Pray tell, what do you see? How may I ease your discomfort?"

"There is naught that can be done," I said. "I simply must offer my Elixir to the Creator... and pray that He should accept."

The scent of cherries filled the air, and the potion suddenly sparkled with the moon's silver radiance. A long moment passed, and the wind rippled harshly through the flames. The dark blue of the potion flashed again, the Creator's face swimming in the tumultuous liquid.

"Knomucca..." Everett said more urgently.

"His energy has found my offering," I said in a level voice.

The cauldron boiled, the bubbles bursting into bright red eyes. They held my own with an intense heat, the flames rising dangerously high in the fire. "You know what I require in order to accept your offering."

"You cannot have it," I said aloud.

"Knomucca!" Everett exclaimed.

"Do you wish to withdraw?" His voice rasped against my mind.

"I wish for you to accept my draught... the elements are proper, and it shall function well."

"You know what I require in order to accept your draught," He said again.

"Knomucca... please... do not shut me out..." Everett cried.

"He requests a heart," I said, much too angrily. "A myocardium... that is the binding agent He wishes for me to obtain in order for him to accept the Elixir."

"We can procure one from game on the island," Everett said innocently.

"I am afraid his tastes are more refined," I said soullessly.

Everett's eyes met my own.

"You shall take mine then," he said, his face void of emotion.

"No," I said firmly.

"Knomucca," Everett stepped forward, taking my hands in his. "This transcends us. It encompasses the realms. If you withdraw, the realms shall be forced to endure more pain and suffering as another fails to take your place.

Everett held my gaze.

"What of the prophecy?" I asked.

"Perhaps this is how I am to return balance," he said, my fingers loosening from his. "By offering my vital life energy to you in a greater use... to complete your Ascension and help you prosper."

"Everett, I will not-"

"Knomucca, you must," he said urgently. "We need you ... When my father crossed you promised you would look after him... you gave me your word he would be in your care. And what of everyone else who has passed? We cannot abandon them."

"I will not give it to Him for His satisfaction," I exclaimed. "Stop tempting my ire."

"This is for the good of the realms," Everett said. "This is for Crossfire's future... Knomucca I forgive you and I love you."

"Everett..."

Everett kissed me intensely, wrenching my pleas from my lips. "I love you," he whispered again. "Know this to be true."

Our kiss lengthened; Everett drew me closer as he pulled against me. A pain throbbed through my hands, my arms pinned against me as Everett pressed his body forward. Distantly, I became aware my hands had transitioned, my phantomic fingers convulsing sharply. Everett held my body against his, guiding my hands upwards by the wrist.

He pressed my hand deeply into his chest, encircling my grip around his heart. The air left his lungs as he breathed into me, his life essence crossing over as my lips beheld him. His grip tightened instinctively, his eyes flashing with a brief moment's pain.

I broke free of our kiss and pulled away from him, severing his heart from his chest. He held my gauntlets in his hands, his grasp on them loosening as his body slackened. Everett crumpled into the sand and gazed emptily into the sky, the light of the moon of the Witching Hour falling across his face.

Anger washed through me once more as I held Everett's heart, the urge to withhold it from The Creator a great burn in my chest. Wishing not to disgrace Everett, I turned towards the cauldron, placing his heart into the potion. The solution brightened to a deep red rose, the scent of coltsfoot thick across the breeze.

Everett's heart dissolved, melting flawlessly. The cauldron suddenly ceased its boiling, coming to a complete stillness. The solution began to drain at an alarming rate, filling a clear-blue crystal flask. Herron-clawed hands reached through the liquid, snatching me around the wrists before I could return my gauntlets. Heat thrummed against my boots as my feet were rendered weightless, the distant echoing of Thornin's cries pounding against my ears. Darkness washed over me and swirled through my awareness. The chilled shadows welcomed against the fire beneath my feet. The echo of dripping water was maddening in the darkness, the steadying thrum painful against my ears.

My eyes fluttered open, and I became aware of the twisted stone room around me. The ceiling was high and supported with bones, and the smell of rot was pungent in the shadows. Shelves were etched into the walls, containing organs, tinctures, and limbs. Ancient weapons were mounted on hooks and wracks, their blades rusted with old and tarnished blood. Skeletons were strewn about the floor, their faces frozen with fear and screams.

From the shadows, The Creator materialized, his cloak swirling behind Him. In his taloned hand was a silver goblet. "Your draught has been accepted," He said darkly, "And I will thank you to dry your eyes. Such behavior is weak... and unbecoming of a god... Your intimacies were that of a slut and are best not repeated. Rosewood only served as a distraction, it is better He can no longer do so. Now drink the potion and cleanse yourself."

He held out the goblet towards me. I fought to steady my breathing, staring fixedly into the Creator's veiled face as I accepted the cup. Lifting it to my lips, I was engulfed with the taste and smell of burnt mugwort, a sharp bitterness stinging my eyes.

"Your draught was brewed well. Venturing from the scrollwork suited you and gifted me with the recipe I will need to recruit Prospects in the next Trials," he said in a tone I could not recognize. "I should find a God of War to be quite pleasing. And I reckon there shall be others."

My eyes blinked rapidly, the room swirling into a greater focus. An altar rested along the wall to my left, the jagged stone surface littered with ritual tools and elements. A book bound in human skin was positioned beside a cauldron, boiling high with bones, rats' brains, and thick red blood. An immense cactus rested beside the stand, its spikes long as pointed needles.

"You will forgive my ignorance," I began slowly, "I was meant to meet you in Morriraen alongside my sister... Though I recognize not this place and fear we are not in the Underworld..."

"Bright as the southern stars you are," he said. "We have ventured to more favorable waters."

"I fear we best migrate to the castle," I pushed, "my absence shall be noticed... and I must fetch my sister to offer her safe passage."

"We are perfect where we are," he said in a tone I disliked.

"What of my sister?" I asked.

"She finds herself tied up at the moment," The Creator said with a light laugh. "I do not foresee her accompanying you on this night, should I speak so plainly."

"Where is she?"

"She is not your concern at present," he said sharply. "And if you ask after her whereabouts again, I shall be forced not to respond in kind. You are to relish in knowing you are to Ascend... to elevate your blood and energy to my liking and prepare yourself to serve me."

I exhaled a breath.

"There is no reason not to be compliant," he said. "Should you wish to withdraw, I shall cast you away. Should you accept my blood you shall Ascend."

The memory of Everett's warmth flashed across my lips. His body crumpled as he rested in the sand.

"I wish to accept." I said, keeping my voice level.

"Excellent. You may wish to have a drink with me, or perhaps some herbs to dull the pain."

My stomach churned.

"I am fine as I am," I said.

The Creator glided towards the walls, procuring a rusted dagger from the shelf.

"Come. Sit," he commanded as my legs began to move automatically.

I approached a smoothed wooden table and sat, feeling a chill beneath me. The Creator filled a goblet with wine and placed it at my front, watching me curiously.

"You may take and drink," he said persistently.

I ignored the goblet, focusing intently on my hands. The memory of pulling Everett's heart through his chest thrummed inside me, the red of his blood reflecting the wine of my goblet. The Creator stood at my front and peeled back His long black sleeve. He drew the blade across the fur and scales that held Him, trailing a hot line of blood down His arm. He held my gaze as the blade moved, then offered the blade to me formally.

"Your left wrist shall do nicely," he said.

I reached forward and took the dagger, holding outward my arm. I slid the tip of the blade down my flesh, feeling it begin to spurt with blood. The Creator reached outward and seized my wrist, gushing His blood into my open wound. A horrid taste of iron flooded through me. I fought to keep my face clear, refraining from allowing it to twitch in disgust. His blood washed through my body and coalesced with my energy, my aura darkening in a heavy shadow. My skin shifted and darkened into ash, a heaviness swirling through my body.

My hands lurched and spasmed, twitching in a terrible sharpness. The rotten, decaying flesh of my hands spread up my arms, engulfing my elbows and shoulders.

The Creator tightened His grip, pushing His blood and energies into my body. I fought not to cry out, my eyes beginning to burn as my skeleton widened. Long, leathery wings began to unravel from my lower back, sprouting with them a tail that grew from the base of my spine.

Anger slammed through me, a rage so intense it burned through my rib cage. My eyes throbbed and burned, the urge to cry moving my lips in a silent plea for Him to release me.

"Relish in the pain," he encouraged. "My essence shall only make you stronger. You are a worthy vessel of my blood. My will is your will. My wants are your wants. Your blood is my blood. Bound are we as night and day. Ascended and whole. Goddess of Death, eternal."

Epilogue

KIYOKO

My eyes fluttered open, and the soft sounds of the night flooded through my ears. The taste of coltsfoot faded from my lips, and the feeling of Everett's arms wilted away in my dreams. I forced my eyes closed in an attempt to return to him, though I reeled awake with the sudden discomfort radiating through me. Heaviness and pain sagged over my body, my shoulders clenching tightly from the constraints that bound my arms.

Exhaling at length, I allowed my gaze to travel upwards, studying the sky. The sun had long set, the cloudless night smearing the moon's silver radiance across the treetops. Crickets and frogs began to fill the night, their lullabies eerie in the still air.

My cheek was pressed against the grass, and my arms wrenched uncomfortably behind me. Thorns dug into my ankles and wrists. My head pounded and throbbed from the contact of Everett's skull, which had rendered me unconscious. My muscles were solid and sore, my mouth dry with a horrid need of refreshment. My heart pounded through my chest, emphasizing a distant pain that throbbed across my sternum.

Where have I found myself? I thought through the pain between my ears.

I exhaled once more and reached my energy outward, sensing warmth from my left. Rolling slowly, I fought not to disturb my bindings, though I failed to keep the thorns from aggravating my skin. I shifted across my shoulders and lifted my head, my abdomen clenching to support my weight. Kyreese sat amongst the grass, braiding her hair in her hands. The strands glowed silver in the moonlight, her hair scented strongly of hyacinth and sandalwood.

Curling my lips, I whistled softly, trilling our signal for her on the wind. Kye flinched and turned abruptly, facing me with wide and alert eyes.

"Greetings, Kyreese," I said with a gentle smile. "I had not meant to give you a fright."

"Kiyoko," Kye rose to a stand, her hair only half braided. "Kiyoko... you're awake."

"Aye... and right as rain," I said as sincerely as I could muster. "I feel sobered, not a worry need be given to that."

A tense silence fell between us. Kye placed her fingers in her mouth and whistled sharply, summoning Bullet. Her summons vibrated across the wind, the tones painting thick blue lines through the air.

"Kyreese, are you well?"

"I was asked to alert Chief the moment you awoke," she said flatly, her eyes never leaving my face.

"You could have gifted me a moment's explanation," I said. "I sensed you during my dreams... your vital life energies through your hair secured my bindings and grounded me during my rest... you knew I meant you no harm."

"Aye... you've always behaved towards me like that of a protective brother... even during your last absorption... The events of that night now have clarity."

A horrible memory slammed my awareness, the cold winter solstice three years prior flashing painfully through my mind's eye.

"When I found you in the orchards you let me leave freely," she said, never lowering her eyes. "And because you hurt me not, I allowed you to walk free... you set to the mountains and made a ruin of them... I cannot allow myself to repeat the same mistakes."

"Kyreese..."

"I want to believe you've sobered," she said, "though there is no way to know for certain."

Shifting in my bindings, I began to pull myself to a sit, using my energy to protect my skin from the thorns.

"I'll ask you to remain still," Kye said, her tone spiking. "Receive my warning now Kiyoko, I shall be forced to respond violently if you begin to misbehave."

"Kyreese, I swear to you on all that is sacred I have sobered during my sleep."

A deep blue chill materialized from the right, the speeding silhouette charging into the courtyard. Bullet swirled towards us, running in a fast blur from the Rose Lily. His feet pounded across the earth, vibrating in a deep grey as he moved.

Bullet halted, coming to rest beside us.

"You have awakened," Bullet said with an exasperated sigh.

"Do not approach me with such outward hostility," I said, the red through his aura unbearable against my eyes.

Bullet chuckled paternally.

"My apologies. I shall attempt not to bleed my anger toward you... our night is in shambles," Bullet said. "I hold no blame against you for the Priestess and her actions... she's now being heavily monitored."

"That is well," I said, "Could you explain your meaning?"

"I would rather not reveal the feathers in my hat," he said in a level voice.

"That is well and good, though I should wish to assist in your observations," I declared.

"To express my honesty, however," Bullet said gently, "I cannot claim to trust your sobriety given past offenses."

"Where is Everett?" I asked hopefully. "Certainly, he should be able to test my clarity."

"Everett has gone in search of Knomucca," Bullet said heavily. "Thornin returned here and the pair of them left straight away. They have been gone near a days' time already and The Equinox is falling upon us."

My heart sank through to my toes. Gazing upwards, I again surveyed the sky, noticing the moon shifting into the midnight hours.

"Have you yet any indication if the pair of them reunited?" I asked, not wishing to recall the imagery I had had of them whilst sleeping.

"Not as of yet," Bullet said with a sigh.

"Why confess to me such information if you are fearing for my sobriety?" I asked pointedly.

"You're my General aren't you?" Bullet asked.

"I am."

Bullet nodded curtly. "That should be reason enough for you then."

It was then that I noticed his beard no longer covered his chest and face, his green tunic wrinkled from the journey.

"Whilst we are recognizing rank... I wish to be released from these bindings," I said, beginning again to shift into a seated position.

"I'll ask you to remain as you are," Bullet said in a level voice. "Recognizing rank, I may be, though I've already expressed my distrust of your stableness and wish to keep you bound until Everett should return."

"Bullet," I scoffed, tempted to use his birth name to emphasize my annoyance. "It is I, well and good, I mean no harm and shall give none."

"Kiyoko, I mean this with the most respect possible..." a long silence fell from him before he spoke again. "Ther's far more that needs tending to at present, and I cannot worry for the safety of the troops. The Rose Lily is being repaired, the Priestess is camped within the walls, and I need to resume my guard of her affairs. Everett is gone, and you've been compromised..."

"I am not compromised," I said, fighting to keep the annoyance from my tone.

"How am I to know such to be true?"

"Give me an examination," I said.

"To what effect," Bullet asked. "You can penetrate my mind... you can formulate any response to your liking with little to no struggle."

"Bullet, I promise you and all you hold dear, I am stable and solid of mind."

"I can't take such risk of your silver tongue whilst Everett's away," Bullet said in a tone reserved for scolding fathers. "I shall need to subdue you again, lest you decide to cause mischief in your boredom."

"Bullet, please," I said more heavily. "I do not need drowsing... I should like to be unbound and help you obtain the Priestess."

"This is not open to debate, unfortunately," Bullet said. "Your past holds marks against you... previous absorptions have created a need for protocol and as Everett is unable to vouch for you at present, I fear I'm to follow my instincts."

"Bullet!"

Bullet drew a dart from his pocket, throwing it swiftly through the air. A guided blue energy drove it towards me, the tip sinking heavily into my shoulder. Sticky, sweetened syrup began to course through my veins, my eyes threatening to draw closed.

"See you in a while, Kiyoko," Bullet said, his voice fading.

I allowed my eyes to drift closed, fighting against my energy to remain alert. Focusing on my breathing, I fought to stay grounded, feeling the thorns digging into my body as a means to remain anchored. I leaned into my discomfort, fighting to keep clear of my mind as I pushed awake.

Controlling my breathing, I feigned my slumber, listening as Bullet began to whisper to Kyreese.

"I shall need to return inside again," he said. "Should he reawaken, summon me once more with a whistle."

"Aye, Chief," she said, her energy flashing in a brief salute.

Bullet sped away to the Rose Lily, his deep blue swirling around him. The sounds of Kye's braiding resumed. The strands were illuminated in the energy of the radiant moonlight, the Equinox glowing a soft yellow. The light tinkling of metallic bells fell across my awareness.

Oi, I am at risk of dreaming, I thought in horror, jarring myself awake. With open eyes, I hallucinated the sight of silver hair sticks poking through Kyreese's braid. I shall need to act quickly.

Silently, I began to roll in my bindings, needing desperately to rid my body of the sedated and excess energy. Slowly, I wormed through the grass towards Kyreese, using my breathing and aura to camouflage my noise and movements. Sneaking behind her, I positioned my body, stretching outward towards her. Touching her gently, I released a deep breath, pushing the drowsiness and intoxication of Bullet's medicine into her energy.

Kye's hair glowed defensively, shining silver. Pain stung through my fingers, the urge to swear a growing need as her energy pricked across my skin. I fought through my breathing and pushed again past her aura, the pungent, earthy scent of alfalfa drowning my senses. Kye's hands fell silent, her body turning to see what had disturbed her energy.

My absence in the grass had failed to go unnoticed, the light of the high and full moon illuminating where I had once laid.

"Kiyoko..."

Her fingers flew towards her mouth in an attempt to summon Bullet again with her whistling. I rose sharply and bucked against her, crashing my pounding skull against the top of her head. A soft shriek escaped her, the noise quickly muffled as I redirected the energy of her complaints. Kye fell unconscious, her hair singeing my forehead in protest of my assault.

"Ay," I swore sharply in my native tongue, arching my face upwards and away from her.

Kye lay heaped in the grass, her chest rising and falling softly with sleep. I repositioned myself against her shoulder, beginning to breathe once more through the drowsiness that overwhelmed me. I pushed it outward with my exhalations, feeling it drift into Kyreese and her energy. My eyes lightened, and my breathing became less labored, rejuvenation wafting in an orange rush through my body.

Shifting my weight, I positioned my bindings against Kye's hair, using their protective energies to grasp onto the thorns. Heaving upwards, I slid my wrists from their knots, dropping my bindings softly in the grass. I procured a dagger from within my kimono and sliced through the knots at my feet.

Excellent, I thought proudly, rolling to a sit and briefly stretching my body.

"Sorry for my actions," I whispered in Kye's ear, tucking her gently into the grass and settling her in the flowers. "Enjoy your slumbering..."

Silently, I ducked through the courtyard, stooping amongst the foliage in an attempt to stay hidden. Turning from the flowers, I left Kye to her dreams, beginning to move toward the Rose Lily. Breathing steadily, I reached my energy outward, sensing my surroundings before plotting my path. Troops were moving through the grass and paddocks, oblivious to me as they set about their work.

Everett should be displeased in the lack of alertness, I thought, my chest throbbing with a sudden pain I fought to bear.

Inhaling deeply, I reinforced my shields and protective energies, feeling my aura tighten around me as I willed the pain from my sternum. My spirits realigned; my step lightened as I trod towards the apothecary.

Bullet's aerokinesis left a blurred blue line through the air, marking a path that thrummed in the night. The string of his energy swirled and shimmered, the molecules dense as heavy stone. Reaching upwards a hand,

I grasped onto Bullet's energy signature, pulling it firmly into my skin. It was cold and crisp as wind, pulsing thick through my veins. I scanned up the line as it disappeared into the Rose Lily, feeling it swirl as I stepped forward. Exhaling, I crept along the grass, moving silently in my slippered feet. I wove through the distracted troops, ducking behind debris and building materials to maintain my secrecy. I leaped through the shadows, moving as swiftly and silently as possible.

Approaching the apothecary, I paused, seeing the threshold occupied.

"You have struck stone in the search of Everett's horse?"

"Aye, Lieutenant..." Colonel Bailey said with a shake of her head, "We have scoured the area as complete as we can and have no sight of him."

"What of Syler?"

"Nay, we know not of her whereabouts either," Colonel Bailey said.

"You are to keep searching for her," Lieutenant Tyfis said, his voice growing frantic. "My Lady cannot have gone missing... I shall never forgive myself in deciding to venture south instead of to the north... I should have been with her and her trusted... this is disastrous, and I cannot bear the thought that something has happened to her."

"We have traveled west... we combed the swamp lands and exhausted what we can with the resources that remain to us... we shall not discover her without the proper means to search."

"What is it that you should need?" Tyfis asked, anxiety stretching across his aura. "I shall provide it so you can search for her."

"Rest is my priority," the Colonel said sincerely. "I have traveled here from Kyraulh in search of Everett's horse... then proceeded to search for Syler... I mean no disrespect, though I should fear for my safety if I re-embark so soon."

Tyfis exhaled deeply. His energy flashed angrily, and the scent of chamomile floated through him in a yellow-green.

"I understand," Tyfis said, though his aura hung with sadness. Tyfis glanced westward, his energy yearning and distracted as he attempted to sense her spirit.

"When I awaken, I should then again set to searching," Colonel Bailey said with a salute.

"We shall await Knomucca's return with the Commander and devise a strategy with their assistance," Tyfis said. "It shall be my best hope of finding her."

A silence passed between them. Tyfis sighed, his eyes filling with a deep sorrow.

"What of the General?" Colonel Bailey asked. "Could he not assist in searching for her?"

"The General is occupied at present," Tyfis said, my gratitude in his discretion released with a smile.

"That is well and good," Bailey said with a salute. "Reckon I should clear off towards camp... I shall come to find you once I awaken."

"Very good," Lieutenant Tyfis said.

Colonel Bailey saluted once more, then turned from the threshold. Tyfis sighed heavily and leaned against the outer wall of the apothecary, producing a smoke from his smoking sack. He struck a match and began to partake, blowing lavender and coltsfoot across the air. His hands trembled slightly, and his eyes remained sad, his shoulders stabilizing as he began to compose himself.

Stealing my strength, I released a breath, opening my mind and reaching outward my energy. Tugging against Tyfis and his aura, I penetrated his defenses, feeling his energies relax as I moved through their currents. His thoughts began to fill my ears, the scent of chamomile fragrant and suffocating.

"Syler, Beloved... I shall not rest until I hear of your safe return. The Gods bear witness... I should wish to hold you once more."

Tyfis continued his smoke in silence, ashing the remains into the lantern that depicted the symbolism of Anteyus.

"Anteyus, strong lover, fierce warrior... protect Syler. She has always expressed her devotion for you, vouched for your innocence, do not prove heartless and allow her to suffer."

Tyfis allowed a moment of meditative silence, staring longingly into the lantern with sad eyes. He surveyed the area and returned solemnly through the threshold, disappearing into the Rose Lily. I reinforced my energies and emerged from behind a pile of chopped wood, dashing forward. Running swiftly, I slid through the doorway behind him, gliding inside before the door swung closed. The heavy wood clicked behind me, the oak remade and reinforced from the fire.

The Rose Lily had been well tended during my absence, and the ashes and debris were restored and contained. Enchanted tools had allowed for rapid progress, recreating a functional structure with the help of hired hands and the troops. The ashes had been scrubbed from the walls and floor, though the miscellaneous herbs, crystals, tools, and cauldrons that had littered the isles were not yet returned to their hooks and shelves. The blood and remnants of our earlier fight had been cleansed from the stone floor, their absence trying in vain to wrench it from my memory. Anger flooded through me, and I shoved the feeling into the stone, watching the burnt red of the emotion disappear into the ground with my breath.

I inhaled deeply to center myself, refocusing with a clearer mind. Scanning my surroundings, I noticed Bullet's energy, finding the thick blue thrumming just above my eyes. Following his energy cord, I wove amongst the shelving and isles, ducking behind them to remain out of sight from passing troops.

Bullet's energy signature spread past the counter, turning through the threshold into the storage space beyond. Twisting among the shelves, I leaped atop the counter, bounding clearly from the aisles away from the patrolling troops to follow his path. The back rooms of the Rose Lily were quite complex, leading through a flurry of chambers that stemmed from a circular room. The floor was speckled in black and white and carved in geometric shapes, the lines running parallel upwards from the right to slope across the floor crisply. Torches of a red fire were burning brightly, flickering and glowing across the stone. Carved and chiseled pillars provided their support, towering to caress the vast and arched ceiling.

Footsteps echoed through the passages, shuttling thick, heavy shadows from the chamber to the left. Iron chains rattled against my ears, the taste of blood vibrant and sweet between my teeth. Crying punctuated the clanging of metal, bringing a woman and her suffering across my awareness. Her sobs morphed into terrorized screams, her pleas drilling madly into my eyes.

I shook my head to clear it, exhaling to regain my footing. Searching upwards, I spotted Bullet's energy thread, turning down a smooth, slim path to the right.

Sneaky bloke, I thought, following behind his energies.

The passage was lit with iron sconces, the walls cracked and splitting like the tunnels of the castle, Morriraen. A faint scent of rosemary perfumed the air, the subtle mint and pine fragrance a welcome comfort through the darkness. Barrels and crates lined the tunnel walls, wafting an array of floral, fruity, and earthy smells into the musty air. Casks, rolls of cloth and linens, and spare tools made the passages feel tight and disorganized, encouraging my footsteps to quicken. Large, dark cracks in the wall tunneled out of sight amongst the rubbish, the twisting passages omitting eerie shadows and thick black energies.

Weaving through the hallways, I followed Bullet's energy, confused when it suddenly disappeared into a smoothed stone wall. Sensing outward, I felt his aura harden, his blue shifting into the protective vibrations of stone. Controlling my breathing, I pushed beyond his energy as I drove through a concealed circular doorway, hidden flawlessly in the stone.

Stooping through the doorway, I entered a quaint living quarter, sliding the door closed again behind me. A comfortable cotton bed was dressed with green blankets tucked beside a wicker chair and a stone fireplace. An iron cauldron hung above the fire, boiling seasoned wild root soup. Whisps of steam wafted from the cauldron, the smell of peppers, chives, and bitter greens fragrant in the air. A wooden bookcase was resting beside the wall, decorated for the festess with a small carved pumpkin lantern. The lantern was glowing with soft candlelight, its energy shrouded in a deep rose red. The scent of coltsfoot teased my senses, the herb strong and sweet across my skin.

Bullet has certainly fought to be evaded, I thought, wondering why I should not find him if his energy had led me.

Inspecting the chamber, I rifled through the desk, finding a leather-bound book, parchment, and ink. Sachets of smoking herbs were tucked neatly into the wood alongside a compass and a spool of red thread. Empty space was beneath the bed, and the chair held nothing of substance, gifting me merely the magnificence of a moment's rest as I collected my thoughts.

I am to search for him, I thought with a sigh, beginning to relax.

Focusing on my breathing, I stretched my spirits outward, feeling the thick blue of Bullet's energy beyond the bookcase. The deep, rose light thrummed around the lantern, filling the carved husk with a vibrant red. Breathing deliberately, I pushed my energy into the lantern, hearing it click through my awareness. The lantern flashed, and the bookcase swung open, revealing a door that had been hidden beyond.

Excellent, I thought, feeling Bullet's energy reappear in the passageway.

Rising to a stand, I slid through the doorway, pulling the bookcase flush with the wall again. Darkness overwhelmed me, and I released a breath, stretching my aura outward to use as a guide. I pushed forward and felt along the passageway, moving to take a sudden left through the darkness.

The tunnels twisted forward, tugging me gently through the dark. Bullet's energy grew, illuminating the shadows with a deep blue. Gradually,

I wove through the tunnels, finding the soft glow of flames materializing from the end of the passage. The stone turned to a rusted red brick, the floor expanding into a wide, circular chamber. Drawers surrounded neat, empty stone tables lined with surgical instruments and crafting tools.

An uneasy feeling began to wash through me, my heart speeding in my chest. The distant crackling of a fire tugged at my ears, the smell of burning oak heavy in the air. Scanning my surroundings, I reached for Bullet in my awareness, finding his energy signature faintly across my eyes. The line grew frayed and frantic, shimmering painfully against my skin. His energy circled, and he felt disorientated, panicked, and fearful.

"Bullet," I whispered outward in an attempt to reach for him.

I sensed nothing by way of reply, failing to perceive his whereabouts from his energy. Sighing, I continued moving about the room, searching as diligently and silently as possible. A small doorway was tucked between a set of tall metal drawers, nearly blending flawlessly into the surroundings. Wishing to widen my search for Bullet, I pressed through the threshold, finding the source of the oak-scented flames. A fire roared in a great stone fireplace, crackling three immense oak logs. A cauldron was hanging within the fire, bubbling with a rusted red liquid. A smoothed stone table and a set of chains rested beside the fireplace, waiting eagerly to be used. The room thrummed uncomfortably, the urge to flee forming fast from over my shoulder.

Turning over my left, I made my way again towards the door, stopping abruptly in my step. The Priestess stood at the threshold, holding Bullet securely in bindings. His chest rose and fell peacefully, his body in a deep sleep.

"Hazel..." I said, fighting to keep my voice level, "I should offer you my thanks in ending my search for the Chief..."

"I found the leech spying beyond the doorway," The Priestess said, throwing Bullet at my feet. He hit the ground with a horrid thud, scraping painfully to a halt.

"His pockets were full of the most useful trinkets," she said, her face twisting with a dark shadow. "Clever little snake has been making fast use of the rubbish to fashion some interesting artifacts..."

Hazel produced a dart from her robes, throwing it through the air. Guiding blue energy was warped heavy with black, leading the assault toward me with a high-pitched hissing. I ducked instinctively, hearing the dart graze the metal of the cauldron behind me. Hazel produced another and threw it swiftly; the tip ricocheted off the wall as I dodged away from it.

"I shall enjoy making you dance," she said, throwing a third dart from her sleeve.

I bent from its reach, seizing it in my fingers as it passed in the air to my left. Changing its momentum, I returned Hazel's attacks, sending the dart on a path towards her. Hazel stepped to the side and moved from the dart and its reach, her body swerving gracefully.

"It shall be a pleasure to break you," Hazel said, aiming another dart toward my shoulder.

Hazel inhaled sharply, her aura blackening as she summoned an immense burst of strength. Her hand flew from her side, launching a dart silently towards me. The dart soared with a piercing whistle, puncturing my skin with a painful bite. A sweet, stickied syrup began to float through my veins, my body threatening to drag as it grew heavy.

"My complements to the chef," Hazel sniggered towards Bullet's sleep, "though I should warn you I did alter the recipe."

Fighting through the exhaustion, I burst forward, lurching towards her with a violent swing of my arms. My energies grew disoriented, my aim blurring as she stepped from my path. I charged towards her once more, my breathing growing heavier as I fought to remain rooted. My aura rushed and drained as a river, falling through my eyes and body as it tugged me to my knees. My bones crunched heavily against the floor, and my jaw wrenched painfully as I slammed downwards. Heaviness and sleep weighed on my energy, and my body collapsed and crumbled in a heap.

The scent of apples and coconuts flooded my awareness, and the sweet taste of vanilla painted across my lips. Pain erupted suddenly from my chest, wrenching my air and voice from my lungs. Emerald energy spidered across my sternum, striking me speechless from the discomfort. Phantomic fingers dug through my flesh, scratching me deeply. Weightlessness overtook me, my body falling away as my spirits left me.

The Priestess stood over me, her image rapidly warping with my disorientation. Her eyes were swirling in deep shadows, her pupils vast and empty voids. A long lace veil obscured her face, and her hands morphed into the long claws of a heron.

"Restless dreaming, Kiyoko," The Priestess hissed through my pain, her voice distant. "May you never wake again."

Pronunciation Guide

People:

Knomucca: gnome-uh-kuh

Syler: sigh-ler

Chatza: shot-suh

Everett: Eh-ver-eh-tt

Kiyoko: key-oh-koh

Kyreese: kye-ree-ss

Frek: fr-eh-k

Cornalla: corn-ah-lah

Senaya: sin-eye-ah

Samarin: sam-ar-in

Maliche: mal-i-k

Hazel: hay-zel

Bettylee: Betty-lee

Maliche: mall-ick

Marthen: mar-th-en

Thornin: Thor-nin

Anteyus: an-tay-yus

Ozwal: oz-wall

Flophennnne: flaw-fen

Bullet: bullet

Baldrumlin bharrum: ball-drum-lin bear-rum

Rejj: r-edge

Ilesa: il-lace-sah

Jorden: your-gen

Tahar: tah-har

Roice: roy-sssss

Captain Mirufin Nephaerri: mir-u-fin neh-fair-rij

Bashrol: bash-roll

Floyd: fl-oi-d

Shara: sh-ar-ra

Tyfis: tye-fis

Piscaro: piss-scar-oh

Places:

Morriraen: more-rear-rain

Kyraulh: kye-rawl

Belleview: bell-view

Heimaaila: hi-may-ee-lah

Morrireaea: more-rear-rear-a

diah: die-yah

Riverside: river-side

Ostarie: oh-star-ree

Valvang: val-vang

Woodroe: wood-row

About the Author

Erica P Christie has had many adventures, but only one dream: to tell a story that lets people escape their troubling times. As a blind author, she wishes to help people experience the magic of storytelling through our many senses. As a romantic, she hopes to spark heart racing warmth. Erica's book is heavily tied to her spirituality, her healing from abuse, and her desire to find balance in all aspects of her life.

Feel free to follow the fun online

🌿 Thank You For Your Thyme 🌿

⚠ Shop Site: Readings, Metaphysical Shop

THE SITE HAS A SCREEN READER, AS I AM VISUALLY
IMPAIRED. TURN DOWN THE VOLUME IF YOU DO NOT
WISH TO HEAR IT SCREAM AT YOU.

Bloopers!

Growing as a writer was... Well a journey... So enjoy some of the extra cringe worthy shit that was written along the way. Along with some commentary from friends.

"shoulder length hair down to my lower back."

"YOU ARE demented! I HATE YOU! I HATE YOU!"

The smells of laughter

Smoke billows, not goats

Rebecca! Set thine eyes upon her buttocks

Consecrate Everett's ham

We don't talk about Oz-Wal-Wal-Wal-Wal

Smiling inwardly towards myself

Stabbing through my skin to squirt blood in spurts

Though we cannot afford your keys to continue displaying their absence.

"My restlessness is in need of a task to accomplish"

Alternative trickery lurking beneath her robes

flinging her opulent hair in a surge of moisture

Find out what's her wearing

Knomucca had met Kioko on the Snake River, each traveling to Morriraen on a fairy they had boarded from different locations

I'm sorry Erica but "Fires alight with flames," has to go

Slipper pussy

We walked pasta forest

"Jeeze Erica I blacked out while reading this."

His green Alchemist robes appeared smooth and free of wrinkles, his energy bright and alert for someone whom obviously was not asleep.

"Where's Marmalad?" Hazel asked suddenly

Duke's eyes were wide in horror as he staired bewildered at his wife

fire that drives insanity through my instincts with desire fanning the flames.

Torcher

Hazel turned on her heal and whisked into the apothecary

"What's better do you wish to settle first?" Bullet asked bullet as we entered camp.

She sat in the grass looking pail

Footsteps began treading up the stairs to the sleeping quarters, the footballs growing louder with every step.

"What are you? Perceiving?" he asked

I gasped, my gays never leaving the table as hazel...

"Come, let us have tea whilst we wait," Hazel said, bleeding her apprentices through a far door on the opposite side of the chamber.

It slid in place from our crossing the threshold, shielding us from the horse that lay beyond.

I turned about my shoulders and searched for Chatza, failing to notice her standing at my side.
Erica I know what you are trying to say here, that Chatza sent there, but this reads as though Knomucca is blind and can't see her three feet away at her side

My pace quickened, my gate stretching into a run as I fled down the corridor

In recent months, I have confessed my plates to Kioko.
"Why universe?"
"It's not the universe it's Grammarly being a bitch."

"I don't think we need on the face... smiles don't have to come from anywhere else."

The name of our book club group chat according to the curse of autocorrect.

Uncle Brown's hooker bloob boob climbing cloth coupon clog three-foot blub club.

We hope you enjoyed the show